Ghoul of Sherwood

A ROBIN HOOD MYSTERY

Novels by Jay Ruud

THE MERLIN MYSTERIES:

Fatal Feast

The Knight's Riddle

Lost in the Quagmire

The Bleak and Empty Sea

The Knight of the Cart

To the Great Deep

THE ROBIN HOOD MYSTERIES:

Sleuth of Sherwood

Ghoul of Sherwood

Ghoul of Sherwood

A ROBIN HOOD MYSTERY

JAY RUUD

Encircle Publications
Farmington, Maine, U.S.A.

INTRODUCTION AND ACKNOWLEDGMENTS

When most of us think of the Robin Hood legend, we picture something like Errol Flynn swashbuckling through Sherwood Forest and fencing with Basil Rathbone's Guy of Gisbourne. In that version, Robin is a disinherited Saxon nobleman fighting Norman injustice while he steals from the rich and gives to the poor, until King Richard the Lion-Hearted returns from the Crusade and pardons him and his men. Some of that—the Norman vs. Saxon stuff—comes from Sir Walter Scott's 19th-century novel *Ivanhoe*. Some of it—the displaced nobleman part—comes from a tradition initiated by minor playwright Anthony Mundy around 1600 in his plays *The Downfall of Robert Earl of Huntingdon* and *The Death of Robert Earl of Huntingdon.*

But the Robin Hood legend had existed for hundreds of years before Mundy's time. Robin the outlaw of Sherwood, and his comrade in crime Little John, were popular at least since the later fourteenth century, when in *Piers Plowman* William Langland refers to the "rymes of Robyn Hode" well known among the lazy hangers on at the local tavern. This is where Robin's story came into the popular imagination, through widespread ballads that depicted him not as a fallen aristocrat but as a yeoman—that is a free commoner—associated with outlawry in the forest. And his companions are all peasants or lower class characters who join his *meinie* (i.e. his band of outlaws). That outlawry consisted chiefly in poaching the king's deer and robbing rich bishops and abbots and haughty noblemen. From the beginning, his role seems to be to tweak the noses of those in power, especially rich hypocrites in the Church hierarchy (though Robin's own simple devotion to the Virgin Mary is never in doubt).

Giving to the poor, however, is not necessarily one of Robin's original attributes. It's true that in the longest medieval text devoted to his adventures, the fifteenth-century *Gest of Robyn Hode*, Robin and his men help an impoverished knight, Sir Richard at the Lee, pay off an unjust debt with money they have taken from a rich bishop (a story that served as the kernel for the plot in *Sleuth of Sherwood*, the initial volume in this series). And it is true that the rough justice meted out in many Robin Hood ballads is balanced by a generous nature evinced by the hero. But truth to tell, Robin's giving to the poor is a rather idealized part of his lasting image. Still, I've made it a fundamental aspect of the outlaws' character in these stories.

Little John, Much the miller's son and Will Scarlet or Will Scathelock are part of Robin's band, and the Sheriff of Nottingham his chief nemesis, from the beginning of the tradition. Friar Tuck, Alan a Dale, Maid Marion, and Guy of Gisbourne are gradually introduced as the tradition grows. But it is important to remember that this popular medieval tradition, unlike the more aristocratic legend of King Arthur, never was given any kind of coherent and definitive shape, as Thomas Malory gave Arthurian legend. In 1795, Joseph Ritson gathered an exhaustive compilation of the Robin Hood ballads, including some written well into the seventeenth century, and included his own imagined "biography" of the bandit. In the later 19th century, Francis James Child published the definitive collection of Robin Hood ballads in the third volume of his *The English and Scottish Popular Ballads*. A more accessible version of these sources that you can read for yourself is Stephen Knight and Thomas Ohlgren's 1997 publication *Robin Hood and Other Outlaw Tales*.

One thing that is clear is that Robin Hood is a mythic, not a historical figure. The placement of him in the reign of Richard I is a modern contrivance. The earliest ballads place him somewhat later, in the thirteenth or early fourteenth century. In the *Gest of Robyn Hode* he lives during the reign of "the good King Edward," but whether Edward I, Edward II, or Edward III we do not know, so the time frame may be anywhere between 1271 and 1377. What I have done, therefore, is to depict Robin in a world that could roughly reflect an England of the thirteenth century, but one that reflects a kind of imagined peasant world paralleling the Neverland of Arthurian legend, without a clearly historical king reigning. In fact, I've set Robin's story in the world shortly after the fall of King Arthur. Several of the characters, in fact, are portrayed as refugees from the downfall of that world, and are drawn from my previous series of Merlin Mysteries. In this, I am making a radical departure from tradition, but have endeavored to keep the spirit of the original ballads depicting the yeoman outlaw and rebel against political authority.

The plot of *Ghoul of Sherwood* is mostly my own invention, but the kernel of the story of Meggie and Sweet Willie comes directly from the ballad tradition, from Child ballad 255, "Willie's Fatal Visit," an abridged and modernized version of which is sung by Alan a Dale in the last chapter of this book. Another Child ballad, "Robin Hood and the Curtal Friar" (Child ballad 123) appears, also in abbreviated and modernized form, in the book's first chapter. The story of the archery contest in Nottingham is first told in the Child ballad 152, "Robin Hood and the Golden Arrow," but has since been retold many times.

While I'm at it, I should acknowledge that the translation of the Latin text of the traditional requiem text *Dies Irae* comes from the Franciscan archive at https://www.franciscan-archive. org/de_celano/opera/diesirae.html. The names of Gill o' the Red Cap, Adam o' the Dell of Tamworth Town, and a few other characters appearing in the archery tournament come from Howard Pyle's chapter "The Shooting Match at Nottingham Town" in his *The Merry Adventures of Robin Hood* (1883), the first attempt to compile the disparate fragments of Robin's legend into a coherent whole. And yes, there really was a medieval Benedictine Priory at Wallingwells.

PROLOGUE

He moved cautiously through the woods. It was nowhere near dawn, he was thinking, so why had that rooster wakened them and scared him into thinking he'd waited too long to leave her bed? Now he'd left when it was still too dark to see in the forest that closed around him so that he couldn't even be sure whether he was still even on the path. The night was cloudy, so there was no moon to illuminate his way, and he was afraid he'd miss the tall birch that marked the fork in the path where he'd need to veer to the right to get home before he was seen.

He ran his hand through his close-cut sandy hair and peered ahead, straining his innocent-looking blue eyes to no avail. He could hear the forest creatures of the night scuttling in the underbrush at the side of the path, and heard the mellow, flute-like phrases of a nightingale in the tree—was it an oak?—above his head and his thick blond eyebrows relaxed the scowl that had been tensing his brow for the past quarter hour. The nightingale's song seemed to lighten the mood among the trees, and he even thought he heard a robin chirp in reply, he still wondered as he stole cautiously along his way why he heard no morning song of the lark. How early was it, after all?

A hundred steps more, another tiptoeing hundred, and he heard the long, low trilling he recognized as the song of a nightjar, on the low branch of a tree he was passing on his left—

was it an elm? It was too dark to make out. It must be getting on toward dawn, he reasoned. Wasn't that when the nightjars hunted for moths and the like? Or when they sought out goats to rob of their milk, as the old tale went?

Suddenly a huge bird swooped from a high perch directly past him, with a startling screech seizing some rodent in the grass to his left, then flinging off with a long wailing hoot. A tawny owl, he told himself, pausing for a few moments to allow his pulse to calm from the shock. Just an owl, he told himself. Nothing to fear. But just when he quietened his nerves and was about to move on, the bird made another pass above him crying out in a series of staccato *hu hu hu* sounds.

Hadn't he heard somewhere that an owl had been an omen of the death of Julius Caesar? Or was it that other Caesar, the one in the Bible? Or weren't witches supposed to be able to turn into owls, and suck the blood of babies?

Well, now his mind was just running away with him. Best he make haste and get home and out of these dark woods as quickly as he could. The trees here seemed to be thinning out. This must be that clearing that he knew so well. Now he squinted, looking for the white bark of the birch tree that must be somewhere on the other side of the clearing. But wait—wasn't there something light-colored there in front of him? But it was too close to be the birch tree. Damn these clouds, he thought, without the moon, there were not even shadows to help him make out the shape before him. Then with a shiver at the back of his neck, he realized the blotch of faded darkness before him was moving.

"Willie!" it moaned in a low, ominous female voice that found him out even in the smothering dark. "Willie, why are you out in the forest at night?"

"I… I… I'm on my way home," he faltered. Was this the witch who had been just now in the body of the owl? What did she want with him? Why was she stopping him here? "I have no wish to disturb your midnight ceremonies, I just want to hurry home as quickly as I can..."

"Willie, Willie," the portentous voice droned on. "It would have been far, far better for you to have stayed home tonight, and not been wandering where you had no business being."

Now he straightened up and, if one could have seen him, that worried scowl would have been visible again on his face. How could this apparition know who he was or what he may have been doing out of his home on this night of all nights? "How can my movements tonight possibly be of any interest to you? Please, whoever you are, just let me pass and I'll be out of here forever. I'll do nothing to offend you or interfere with you at all. Please, just..."

"You've been sinning this night, have you not, sweet Willie? Breaking God's laws and man's if the truth be told. Doing the devil's business, isn't it so?"

Vigorously shaking his head, he could only stammer, "N-n-n-no, never, not I..."

Now another sound rose to his ears. Very low, very hoarse, but becoming clearer as it continued. Willie shook his head, unsure whether he was hearing what he thought he heard. Was it laughter?

"Oh Willie, Willie, you've already interfered with me in ways that can never be forgiven. You've already offended me in the direst manner possible. You've already, sweet Willie, forfeited the vile existence you call life."

Now Willie's eyes grew wide and round and for a brief second—was he mistaken?—he thought that he recognized the voice. But no, it was not possible, that voice had been silenced long, long before. But whatever it was, the menace in the words was real, and all he could think to do was turn to his right and run through the clearing in the direction he believed was toward his home. All he could hear for several yards in his blind dash over the uneven forest floor was his own frantic panting and his pounding heart. Then, inevitably, he tripped over some protruding branch or stone under his feet and tumbled sprawling into the dirt. Twisting his panicked face upward and holding out his hands to ward off whatever evil thing was upon him, he saw the clouds part for an instant—part just long enough for a beam of moonlight to glint upon a shaft of metal above his head. Then he saw the axe come down.

CHAPTER ONE

"Confess!" the friar demanded, scowling down at him with piercing eyes. "You must confess for the good of your immortal soul!"

Will Stutely squinted up into the friar's piercing eyes and flashed his most innocent grin. Always acknowledged the most handsome of Robin's crew, young Stutely had a mischievous streak that surfaced regularly. Especially when gambling. Snatching up his dice, which had just registered a six—not coincidentally his chance—he reached out to collect his four silver marks from the center of the makeshift table they'd laid under the maple tree, to add to the growing pile in front of him. It was his third such win in as many tries, and Friar Tuck, as Groom-Porter in the game, was suspicious. His fleshy jowls quivered in anger, while the other players—Much the miller's son, Alan a Dale, and Skipper Haakon, the band's ex-Viking outlaw—were grumbling, amazed at Will's uncanny streak of good luck. Now the suspicious friar grabbed at Will's wrist and held on.

"I don't know what you're on about, you fat beggar. God's smiling on me is all. Don't you believe in God at all, ya great clerical heretic ya?"

"Lemme see those dice, Will," the friar ordered, peeling Will's fingers apart with his left hand as his right clutched the young man's wrist.

"Now, you're going to sprain my dicing wrist for me, Tuck! I'm still caster here," Will cried indignantly. The friar scoffed, beads of sweat appearing on the close-shaved tonsure at the crown of his head.

"You've nicked three times in a row," Much said, scratching his head and wrinkling his freckled nose. "Maybe the good friar's caught you out at something, eh?"

The dice had finally dropped from Will's fingers, and the friar snatched them up before Will could reclaim them, holding them up to get a close look at them. "I might have known," Tuck growled, his eyes narrowing angrily as he held the struggling Will at arm's length. "Take a look at these dice, gentlemen." With that he tossed them onto the table, from which Haakon immediately seized them, his yellow braid flying back from his head as he lunged forward.

"Well these are… they're not bloody normal is what they are," the Norseman said, just catching on.

"Each one of those dice has only a one, four, or five—two each on opposite faces of the die," the friar explained.

"So—no twos, no threes, no sixes," Alan continued, counting on his fingers.

"Right," the friar went on. "Twice as many chances to roll a five, a six, or a nine. No chance at all to roll a seven."

"But he kept calling seven as his main," Much said, scratching his head. "Why do that if he could never throw it?"

"Because in the game of Hazard," said Alan a Dale, catching on much faster than the others, "if he doesn't throw his main, the has to throw his chance on the next roll, and if he throws the main he loses. He also can't throw three, or an eleven, or twelve, any of which might throw him out. Plus, he's got twice as good odds to throw his chance if it's five, six, or nine, which it's likely to be!"

By now, Alan, Much, and Skipper had all stood up and were surrounding Will, who was squirming against the friar's grip on his collar. Stutely, with a trace of what may have been actual fear, looked past his menacing comrades to where Little John was making his way across the green to the cookfire. "John!" he called to his particular friend. "Help me! I'm being unfairly abused!"

The big man looked back over his shoulder and called back indifferently, "I told you to get rid of those crooked dice."

"Why Will Stutely, you're nothing but a thief!" Much said, his freckled face clouding.

Will shrugged. "We're all thieves, ya lunkhead. That's pretty much why we're outlaws."

"Will, Will, Will," the friar tutted. "Have you not heard that there is honor among thieves? Or at least, there is supposed to be. Now, what penance am I going to assign you for these transgressions?"

"On a Norse ship, we'd cut off his dicing hand," Haakon suggested.

"Turn him in to the sheriff at Nottingham," Alan a Dale teased. "They'll string him up there."

"Now, now," Friar Tuck soothed, "what's wanted here is a punishment that fits the crime. What we call in canon law the *lex taliones*: that is to say, one who inflicts an injury upon his neighbor is to suffer the same injury himself. How many silver pieces has he got there in front of him, boys?"

Much made a grab for the pile of coins before Will had a chance to snatch them himself and, tallying quickly, called out, "Twelve here, Tuck."

"So," the friar continued. "Three of those are his own wagers. Plus three each from the rest of you. Grab his purse, there, will you Much?" The miller's son snagged the purse from Will's belt as the young man, still flailing about as the friar held his collar, snatched in vain at his moneybag.

"They've got back more than what they lost," Will groused. "You call this fair?"

"I call it justice," Tuck said, opening the purse and tossing six more silver pieces onto the pile for Will's three victims to divide among themselves. "Penance, Will, must be painful to truly be cleansing."

And with that, he dropped the lad's collar and Will, knowing he'd got off lightly, rubbed the back of his neck and, holding out his hand, smirked insolently back at the friar. "Can I have my purse back now, father confessor?"

The friar tossed him the much lighter purse and, in a much sterner voice, commanded, "And say fifty Hail Marys as well, to atone for that saucy tone!"

"That'll be the day," Will replied, walking away.

"Then I don't absolve you!" Friar Tuck called after him. "And you'd better hope you're not caught and hanged before your next confession, or you'll die in a state of sin!"

"*Ave Maria, gratia plena, Dominus tecum...*" Stutely intoned as he walked away, doing his best impression of a cloistered monk, chanting in his abbey.

He was joined in this pursuit by Alan a Dale, who popped up, put his hand on Will's shoulder to show there were no hard feelings, and added his pleasant tenor to Will's monotone, chanting, "*Benedicta tu in mulieribus, et benedictus fructus ventris tui, Iesus.*"

It was not mockery, but only high spirits. May, after all, was the Virgin's own month, and this May Day of all days was a time to honor the Mother of God, who was especially dear to Robin himself, and consequently to all of his men. Alan and Will walked toward the cook fire at the center of the wide green that lay before Peveril Castle, seat of Lady Lydia Peveril, Countess of Chesterfield. On this great clearing among the budding trees of the surrounding wood, and at the countess's invitation, Robin and his meinie had been invited to help Lady Lydia and her household to usher in the gentle months of summer here on the northern edge of Sherwood.

Part of that celebration was to be an outdoor feast, and around the fire Little John, Alan a Dale's wife Ellen, and the gourmet knight, the Moor Sir Palomides, surrounded the countess's own chief cook, Oswald, as he turned a large wild boar on the spit.

"You must make certain that the meat is not overdone," the Moor was saying as Will and Alan drew up to the fire. "It should be brown on the outside, not black."

"But you must be sure it is done on the inside—nothing is more unhealthy than eating undercooked pork," Ellen was arguing, her hands on her hips and her bright blue eyes flashing. "Besides, you want to make sure the outside is plenty crispy. That's when the meat is most mouth-watering."

Alan, coming up behind his wife, took her untamed blonde hair in his hands and pulled her face toward him to plant a kiss on her rosy cheek. "I must take my wife's side in this controversy," he said. "She's never been wrong before."

"Except, perhaps, when I married you," Ellen shot back through grinning teeth.

The barb got the intended response from the men, though Palomides shook his head and shrugged. "It will be overdone," he said in a low voice. "I won't be responsible."

"And no one will hold you so," Oswald uttered through clenched teeth, throwing his own little barb at the Moor before shutting him down completely with the comment, "When it's brown, it's cookin', when it's black, it's done. That was me father's motto, and that's what I live by." With that, he gave Ellen a sly wink and bent his round, bald head forward to hide the smile that flitted across his pie face. Sir Palomides threw up his hands in mock horror and strode off toward the far side of the clearing, where several of the outlaws were engaging in an impromptu archery contest, entertaining the other women who were part of the outlaw camp—the dozen or so wives (common law or Church blessed) who shared tents or cave space with these men on the outer fringes of society.

Little John put his arm around Will Stutely and muttered in his low baritone, "Well, lad, I see they haven't marred that pretty face of yours. I'm thankful for that, at any rate. But if you don't stop getting yourself in scrapes with those bloody dice, one day you're going to come home to me without your head, and trust me, I'll never love you more."

John Naylor, all six feet six inches and twenty stone of him, looked down at Will for only a moment before his blue eyes lit up under his shock of blond hair and a handsome grin enlivened his neat-bearded jaw. "You had no interest in the games, then?" Stutely asked, nodding toward the noisy archery match.

"Oh no," John demurred. "I know my own strengths, and archery is *not* one of them. Now, if it were fighting with the quarterstaff, or even the sword, I might give them a run for their money. But my archery skills, well, I wouldn't bet my life on them. But *you*," he told Will, "or you, Alan, you might well have had a shot at the prize."

Alan a Dale, never shy of puffing himself up before Ellen, replied, "Oh, Robin himself knows that I'm the best archer in his band, and I should have had no trouble trouncing every one of those boys. But the trouble is, you see, that he's shooting in the contest himself, and it's never good form to show up the boss, is it? So I opted to have a go at Hazard with this famous cheat," at which he punched Stutely in the arm.

At that moment, a loud cheer rose from the archers and their supporters across the clearing, at which the rest of the band and their women, relaxing in the shade of the few scattered trees here, looked up, curious as to what feat of skill might have given rise to such an outburst. The cheering continued, and as it swelled to a crescendo Will Scarlet, Robin's nephew, his red cloak bright in the sunlight, came running toward the group at the fire.

"Little John! Palomides! The most fantastic feat of pure archery ever witnessed!" Scarlet was shouting as he approached the fire.

"And this from one not given to hyperbole," Friar Tuck murmured as he came toward the fire from the other direction.

Meanwhile, Ellen yawned and added, to no one in particular, "Boys and their games," and Alan a Dale couldn't hold back a snort of laughter.

"Scoff if you will," Scarlet continued. "But listen to what happened. So, Robin had a gold noble in his purse that he nailed to the trunk of a beech tree yonder." His arm swept vaguely in the direction of the shooting match, where it seemed that a whole group of cheering men were now lifting someone onto their shoulders.

Stutely, shading his eyes from the warm May sun, asked, "Say, is that Robin himself they are lifting up in victory?"

"None other," Will Scarlet answered. "So listen: Robin backs off a good sixty yards from the tree, and he says 'There's your target, boys! Whosever's shaft comes closest to the gold coin will win it as a May Day prize!'"

"Aha! So Robin must have shot closest, unless they're just lifting him up on their shoulders for his generosity in donating the gold noble for a prize?" Alan a Dale suggested.

"Let me finish the story!" Scarlet pressed on, annoyed at all the interruptions. "So there were ten other competitors for the prize, including myself and some other pretty sharp archers—Will Scathelock for one, and Arthur Brand, and even Alan of Winchester, who was everyone's favorite to win, But guess what?"

"He didn't?" Much the miller's son quipped, joining the group with a glint in his sharp brown eyes and a grin that displayed gums still bearing half of the teeth they'd once boasted.

"Will you let me finish this story?" Will Scarlet groused, as the crowd of archers and spectators began to make their way toward the fire with Robin bouncing on the shoulders of Alan of Winchester and young David of Doncaster. "Alan had put an arrow in the tree just six inches below the coin—an amazing shot, and everybody thought he'd win it for sure. And then Robin himself steps up!"

"And gets closer?" Little John teased, unable to resist joining in the fun of Scarlet-baiting.

"That's what I'm trying to tell you!" Scarlet sputtered in some frustration. "Robin takes his shot—and the arrow split the coin in two! He actually put it dead center, from sixty yards away if it was an inch!"

Now the kidding stopped, and most of the eyes around the fire grew large and round. There was no denying this was a powerful bit of shooting, the stuff perhaps of legend. Only Ellen seemed somewhat less impressed. "Hmmph," she opined. "Let him try to thread one of those tiny embroidery needles. Now *that* takes a truly talented aim."

"So that explains the hero's celebration he's getting, then," Will Stutely commented.

"No, that's not it," Scarlet added. "Robin declared that, since he'd broken the prize apart, and couldn't present it to himself anyway, he'd give a gold noble to every other competitor in the contest as a consolation prize! That's when they really started cheering and lifting him up to chair him through the green!"

Sir Palomides, come back to hear this last, laughed. "So, it is not an acclamation of their leader's archery skills, but a deeper appreciation for his generosity, that sparks this display. Why am I not surprised?"

At that point, the cheering mob reached the fire, and Robin, holding his handsome six-foot yew longbow over his head in triumph, was finally able to convince his bearers to set him down. Immediately he took his purse from his belt and tossed it to Scarlet. "Take your prize from there, cousin, and dole out a gold noble to every competitor in the contest, as I promised. And let me get my breath here."

He was panting a bit from the exertion and the rough ride he'd had, as Little John stepped to him to shake his hand. "An amazing shot, I hear, Robin! Congratulations are in order, it seems!"

"Absolute unconscious dumb luck," Robin whispered to his chief lieutenant as he accepted the extended hand, and then, raising his head and smiling, held his bow up in a last flourish of exultation, shouted, "There was never a doubt!"

Next to John, the outlaw chief looked small, but he was nearly as tall as his bow, well above the height of most of his men. He had long, wavy blond locks, which had given him his former surname, Kempe, when he was captain of the old king's castle guards before he'd taken to the woods after the fall of the kingdom. Now he was known throughout the north of England as Robin Hood, no doubt because of the hood he always wore over his Lincoln green forester's livery. His face was tanned, his eyes green as his tunic, and his lip and chin covered by a well-trimmed goatee. When he smiled, as he was beaming now, his joy was infectious.

But the group had little time to savor Robin's victory, for moments after his group had reached the fire, the assembly was hushed by the sound of a cart creaking out of the woods and into the clearing. It was pulled by an old chestnut mare, and driven by a dwarf who looked just as old, with a wizened face and a white beard, wearing a brown hood and clad in the Lincoln green livery of the Sherwood outlaws. It was Thorvald, one of Robin's band who had volunteered to guard the road while the others enjoyed their Maying. "I ain't much of a dancer," he had said, excusing himself. "And I'm not that keen on flowers, to tell ya the truth."

Behind him were two more of Robin's men, both mounted and each leading another horse behind him. The first was Jack Rolfe, the yeoman farmer who'd joined Robin's band when he'd lost his land. The other was Gilbert Whitehand, a former deputy of the Sheriff of Nottingham who, having met Will Stutely and Little John several times, had been persuaded by them to leave his unhappy life in the sheriff's employ and join the free men of the forest. As one of the best archers in the shire, he'd been a welcome addition to the group.

But what had really drawn the attention of the picnickers, and had shocked them into silence, was the sight of the two men who sat blindfolded, their hands and feet tied, within Thorvald's cart. One wore a chainmail corslet and a close-fitting steel skull cap or *cervelliere*. The other, more disturbingly, wore a purple cap covering his tonsured head, and a purple cape or mozetta over his shoulders that identified him undeniably as a bishop, one of the princes of the Church.

*　*　*

Robin had no difficulty recognizing the blindfolded prelate in the cart. It was Edward of Worcester, Lord Bishop of Hereford, one of the wealthiest and most powerful men in the kingdom.

And one of the most arrogant. He had been a dinner guest of Robin's band the previous year, much to his chagrin. For at the time the bishop had been carrying a chest containing 1,500 gold nobles, a thousand of which the Sherwood outlaws had relieved him of before bidding him adieu. It was a lightening of his load unappreciated by the good shepherd, who had complained loudly of his sheering when he arrived in Nottingham and set the sheriff on to redouble his efforts to catch and punish Robin and his men.

At that time, Bishop Edward had carped and blustered and threatened throughout his entire captivity. But oddly, this time around the prelate, bound and blindfolded, sat seemingly unperturbed in utter silence. Robin took Thorvald aside and whispered to him.

"That's the Bishop of Hereford," he told the dwarf unnecessarily.

"Oh aye, I recognized 'im right away with me own eyes, guvnor," Thorvald replied.

"Well, what have you done to him? Gotten him drunk? Knocked him unconscious so he's just coming around? Why's he so docile?"

"Docile as a little kitten 'e is, right? Been that way since we took 'im. I've no notion why, but if I was you I wouldn't trust 'im far as I could throw 'im."

Robin looked over the hefty bishop's bulk for a moment and calculated that he was unlikely to be able to throw him any farther than the ground beneath his feet. "No," he answered. "This looks suspicious. We need to tread carefully. Who is the guard with him? Anybody know?"

To that Gilbert Whitehand, who'd been listening to the conversation, volunteered. "I recognized him as soon as we took them. He was one of the Sheriff of Nottingham's deputies when I served that worthy. Name of Jankyn. From Hull. I never liked him much. Too much the sheriff's toady. You could never trust him to do anything except what would get him a leg up in the sheriff's graces. If you say you can't trust this fat bishop, well, you can trust this Jankyn even less. What do you want to do?"

"Divide and conquer, as Julius Caesar said," came a low murmur from Sir Palomides, who had moved in to be part of the conversation. "Let me sit next to the bishop when he dines, and engage him in conversation. I'll question him subtly, to see if I can make out what sort of scheme he may be hatching. Meanwhile Gilbert, why don't you sit next to your old friend the deputy, and pump him for information? He's likely to be less on his guard with you. How say you, Robin?"

"I like the plan," Robin returned. "If this proud peacock has some design on us, he's likely to be frustrated if he can't talk to me directly. But I'll treat him as just another dinner guest, until we're ready to release him."

"What do you think you're going to do with that bishop?" Oswald, the countess's cook demanded as he entered the swelling huddle of counsellors. "You know that my lady the countess cannot be part of the robbery of one of the great churchmen of the realm. She doesn't like you *that* much."

"Look, we have to do something with him now he's here," Robin told him. "Tell the countess to take all her household back into the woods to do more Maying. Or back to the castle. Or just congregate by themselves on the other side of the green away from our dealings with the bishop. We will make sure he and his deputy keep their blindfolds on so they have no idea where they are, exactly. All right?"

Oswald shrugged. "Let's see what she says. But be careful."

Now Robin returned to the cart and his surprisingly willing guests, while Oswald brought Robin's proposal to his mistress, who had just emerged with her entourage from the surrounding wood to lead the May Day festivities. Out of the corner of his eye, he could see that the countess was not amused, but led her entire household to the other end of the green where Alan a Dale took up his lute and sought to entertain the lady's courtiers with a few of his more courtly songs. Such background music, Robin knew, might have been expected at the outlaw camp, and the minstrel's voice might even seem familiar to the bishop, who had no doubt heard something of it during his previous visit among Robin's meinie.

"My lord bishop," Robin began, putting on his best courtly manners, and Bishop Edward's face seemed to perk up with the ghost of a smile visible below his blindfold. "I had not expected to have you as our guest again, and so soon! Why, it's less than a year, I'm sure, since you last dined with us. To what do we owe the pleasure of your company this time?"

The bishop shrugged, responding quite civilly, "Well, there are times one must take the Great North Road through Sherwood and so chance a meeting with the low scoundrels that inhabit it."

"Ah, my lord, to be named 'scoundrel' by your Grace is as great an honor to me as if you'd crowned me with the laurel. May I ask your Honor why you have found such a journey necessary at this time, and so far north in Sherwood?"

"You may ask what you like, Sir Impudence. Suffice it to say I had certain business on behalf of the Church. I was visiting the nuns at the Benedictine Priory at Wallingwells, and was on my way back to Nottingham after a disturbing discovery of a mutilated body near that place. But that is neither here nor there. The last I heard, the Sherwood bandits did not own the Great North Road. Besides, I had no thought of finding you and your band of outcasts this far north. I would have expected you closer to Nottingham, where I last encountered you."

There was some nervous stirring among Robin's men, and

after a moment their leader answered, "My lord, in our business it is advisable to move around. It would be far too easy for someone like yourself, let us say, to remember where we may have entertained him recently, and to lead back to that spot a group of far more disagreeable guests. Sheriff's deputies, shall we say. Which reminds me, my lord, to ask why you have come this far with but a single bodyguard—and one who is known to be one of the sheriff's men?"

The bishop gave an almost imperceptible start at that, but covered by simply shaking his head. "God protects His servants in this world, sirrah. I have no need to travel with a large entourage, like some proud secular lord. Master Jankyn is here to see to my needs and comforts on my journey."

"Of course, of course," Robin said, eager now to curtail the conversation, since the bishop was clearly not about to give anything away. "My lord, I must ask you and your faithful servant to dine with us, and, as you know, we will expect payment for our hospitality afterward."

"I would expect nothing less," the bishop replied, with a disconcerting air of nonchalance.

What was he up to? Robin wondered. He only said, "I must apologize, my lord, for insisting that you and your escort keep your blindfolds on through dinner, and until my men return you to the road. You can appreciate how uncomfortable it would make us, should you be able to find your way back here."

"I understand," the bishop said. "But I wonder if we might have our hands freed to dine? It will certainly be preferable to having one of your ruffians, or one of their doxies, feed me like some infant or helpless dotard. I will pledge on my honor not to remove the blindfold if you grant me this boon."

"And does your servant also pledge on his honor, such as it is?" Robin responded.

The blindfolded deputy, clearly annoyed—whether by being referred to as a servant, or by the suggestion that his honor was more doubtful than the bishop's, Robin could not tell—grumbled a barely intelligible "I swear" in answer.

"Then the boon is granted," Robin responded. "Thorvald, if you would, please, remove Bishop Edward's bonds, and those of his menial." At that, Jankyn gave an audible hiss of annoyance. "I will, however, have to give each of you a man to monitor your movements and see to your dinner needs, since you will not be able to see for yourselves. My lord bishop, in deference to your lofty social rank, I have asked our noblest comrade, Sir Palomides, to accompany you. As for you, Jankyn of Hull," at that, both master and man started briefly, surprised at Robin's knowledge of the deputy's identity. "Your former colleague Gilbert Whitehand has volunteered to escort you to table."

Jankyn's angry grimace relaxed at that, surprised and gratified as he was to have someone he knew, and of his own class, to spend the afternoon with. If it must be so, he reasoned, it could be far worse. The bishop, on the other hand, pursed his lips quizzically. "Sir Palomides? Tell me, is that that Blackamoor who spoke so disrespectfully to me about Muhammadanism when last I dined among your rabble?"

"The same," Palomides replied, taking the bishop's freed hand and helping to guide him down from the cart. "I suspect we shall have a fascinating conversation at dinner today, during which you will surely continue to school me about the faith that I grew up in. But come, I shall lead you to table and you shall enjoy our May Day repast."

As Sir Palomides led Bishop Edward to one of the tables, and Gilbert led Jankyn away to another, Robin winked at Thorvald and told him, "Check those horses to see where the good bishop's money may be today. I suspect he must not be carrying much, or he would not have taken his invitation to dinner quite so peacefully."

"I'll look through their baggage," Thorvald answered. "But I don't see any treasure chest, like 'e 'ad last time we saw 'im."

CHAPTER TWO

While Bishop Edward sat at table with Sir Palomides, and Gilbert hosted the deputy Jankyn at their own board, Robin strolled between them, eavesdropping on their conversations. Little John and Will Stutely acted the parts of servers to the new guests, bringing them bread trenchers heaping with slices of the company's roast pork, as well as the cheeses, fruits, and flagons of the countess's wine.

Palomides, of course, had the more difficult role here, since he had to stomach the condescension as well as the ignorant insults of the pontificating pontiff. But, the soul of patience, Palomides kept his temper as well as his tongue. For him, the bishop's overbearing egoism provided nothing more than an amusing character study.

"I see the quality of your wine is vastly improved since I dined with you last," the bishop commented after his first quaff, Palomides having placed the flagon in the blindfolded prelate's hand. "And what is that meat I smell? Still guilty of poaching the king's deer are you, fellow?"

Palomides rankled a bit at the unceremonious "fellow," a term he considered beneath his dignity, but he was all sweetness and light when he answered, "Not at all, my lord. The trencher I've placed in front of you is piled with roast wild boar."

The bishop pursed his lips, though Palomides could not,

of course, read any expression on his face, since his blindfold covered most of it. But Edward commented, "Hmmph, a very stalwart beast. Takes a brave man to bring down a boar." Was there a note of admiration in his voice?

"It was Little John who made the kill, your Grace. He and Will Stutely had tracked the beast, in the company of the dwarf Thorvald, your captor for the day."

"Ah yes. Odd little fellow, that. But as for the boar," and now the bishop took a large bite of the meat and, chewing, made his next point: "Leaving aside the courage it may take to bring down a boar, its capture in the royal forest is still an act of poaching. This John and Will and the dwarf should be put in irons for the offense. I'll definitely inform the sheriff of this when I pass again through Nottingham."

Sir Palomides paused, debating with himself the wisdom of continuing this conversation, knowing that nothing he said could have any effect on the bishop's absolute certainty of the rectitude of his opinions. Then, with a sigh, he decided he owed it to the truth to make his thoughts known, even though they fell on deaf ears.

"My lord," he began. "Has it never occurred to you that fully one-third of all England is designated as a royal forest? Most of the poorer part of the population would never eat meat at all if they did not do some poaching either in the king's domain or in that of some other noble lord."

Chewing another significant mouthful, Bishop Edward shrugged indifferently. "And what is that to me?" he asked. "Why should peasants eat meat? It would simply get their blood up, make them unruly, discontented with their God-given lot in life. Why, look at the rabble here around this Robin Hood character. Do they not have notions and perform acts inappropriate to their stations in life?"

Palomides, himself a knight formerly of the old king's retinue, did not know whether to point that particular fact out to the bishop, along with the information that most of Robin's meinie were free yeoman stock and not the villeins to whom the bishop referred, or to argue that Christian charity demanded that the poor be sustained by the wealthier in society. Ultimately, he decided against arguing either way, knowing that his protestations would be useless. But the thought of Christian charity did suggest to him another direction he might take the conversation.

"You know, my lord, that I myself have only recently discovered the joy of eating roasted pork. Under my former creed, it was anathema to eat the flesh of swine."

Now the bishop tilted his head and, Palomides imagined, must have looked puzzled under his blindfold. "But… I thought you were a Moor? A Muhammadan, is it not so?"

"Of course," Sir Palomides answered, not sure where the bishop was going with this. "Yes, I was born and raised in the Muslim faith, far in the east. I was baptized after I came to this country."

"Well then," the bishop went on with blind self-assurance. "You must be mistaken. It is the Hebrew heresy, not the Muhammadan, that forbids its followers to eat pork."

Palomides rolled his eyes and shook his head at the man's presumption, but decided he may as well let that go, and sought another direction to take the conversation. He still had no idea what the bishop's motive was in apparently deliberately allowing himself to be captured, so he returned to Bishop Edward's comment about returning from the convent in Wallingwells.

"So, my lord," he began cautiously. "You mentioned you have been visiting the sisters at Wallingwells Priory. Some emergency there, was it, or merely some routine visit?"

The bishop waved it off. "Routine business," he said indifferently. "A matter of some holdings of theirs that border on my own. I was quite glad to dispose of the business quickly, since I intend to travel through Nottingham again on my way back to my see in Hereford. There is some excitement there that it will be entertaining to witness."

"Excitement?" Palomides said, a bit warily. Excitement in Nottingham could very well mean trouble for the Sherwood outlaws. "What kind of excitement do you expect there?"

Their talk was interrupted at that point by a particularly loud and raucous tune from Alan a Dale on the other side of the green, who sang out cheerily *"Summer is icumen in, loude sing cuckoo!"* to the cheers and laughter of the countess's ladies, all of whom had gotten to their feet to dance a hearty welcome to the mild weather. Bishop Edward took the opportunity to finish off his cheese and his bread trencher, after which he remarked, "You seem to have far more women in your camp than when you last kidnapped me. Are those your own outlaw women, or are we near some village or castle where you may have enticed some of the young ladies to celebrate this May Day with you?"

Sir Palomides quickly demurred, silently wishing a pox on Alan a Dale for his showmanship in the presence of this particular guest. "No, no, just our own men's wives. Where would we find a group of ladies in the middle of the woods?" And he gave a nervous laugh that he feared would not fool anyone, and quickly renewed his questioning. "But what about this excitement in Nottingham you mentioned? Some Church gala at Newstead Abbey or Southwell Minster perhaps?"

"No, no," the bishop answered. "Nothing so tame as that. No, I'm speaking of an entertainment the sheriff is holding in the town itself. To mark the birthday of his wife, the sheriff, John of Oxenford, is hosting an archery tournament. His lady Maude will herself present the winner of the tournament with a golden arrow. All of Nottingham is buzzing with the news. I'm surprised you've not heard of it up here. Well, perhaps having moved so far north, you are less likely to hear the news of Nottingham."

Palomides shook his head—though, of course, the bishop had no way of seeing that. "No, we've heard not a whisper about that, I'm sorry to say. So, does the sheriff expect a large crowd for this event? A good number of competitors?"

"Oh yes," the bishop said with a chuckle as he drained his wine. "The merchants of Nottingham are rubbing their hands together with glee in anticipation of a great crowd from the countryside swelling the city and their coffers. The word has gone out to all the neighboring villages, and every hamlet's little local Apollo is itching for a chance to win that golden prize."

"No doubt. And when exactly did you say this tournament is to take place?"

"On Lady Maude Peveril's birthday next week, on the 8th of May. She'll wear a crown as the city's Queen of the May, and all contestants will do her honor as they take up their bows."

The mystery of Bishop Edward's nonchalant attitude toward his capture had suddenly clarified in Sir Palomides' mind. Here was no accidental meeting in the midst of Sherwood. This was a calculated and deliberate move in the sheriff's ongoing chess match with Robin Hood, in which the bishop, acting as the sheriff's willing catspaw, had been sent on through Sherwood— with but a single armed man as escort in order to appear the more vulnerable—for the sole purpose of being captured by the Sherwood outlaws in order to let slip, as if casually, news of this great archery tournament. He may as well have sent Robin Hood an engraved invitation to present himself in Nottingham on the eighth day of May just to be hanged at the sheriff's pleasure. Well, it was simply too transparent. It was too obvious. How gullible did they think Robin was, after all?

"Hmmph," came an unexpected sound over Palomides' right shoulder. When the knight glanced to his right, there was Robin's face. He'd obviously been listening to the end of their conversation, and by his bulging eyes and broad grin, his tense muscles barely containing his exultation, Palomides could see how thoroughly Robin had been reeled in by the bait. He sighed heavily.

"Your Grace!" Robin now exclaimed, all keenness and animation after the bishop's revelation. "I see you've finished your dinner. And our good minstrel has finished his entertainment!" And with that there was enthusiastic applause for Alan a Dale, looking pleased at this appreciation for his performance. "We do not wish to delay you any longer than absolutely necessary, and I'm sure you are anxious to be getting on your way, for you have a long way to go before you reach Nottingham, where I believe you said you meant to rest for a few days. So the time has come for us to bid you and your escort adieu, just as soon as you have provided us payment for your dinner. Thorvald!"

When his name was called, the dwarf stood up in his cart's driving seat and answered. "Right 'ere, guv!"

"Can you tell us what our wealthy prelate here had been transporting in his baggage there?"

"A change of clothes, foodstuffs, a few books, an' a bit o' paraphernalia for saying the Mass, is all we've been able to find on the horses, yer honor!"

"What then? No money at all?"

"Nary a farthing 'ere, on me mother's grave."

Robin frowned. This news was a surprise. And not a welcome one. "Will!" he addressed Will Scarlet, who stood directly behind the bishop where he sat. "Take a look in that purse, will you?"

In a single smooth move, Will snatched the small leather purse from the prelate's belt before he could object, and took a quick look inside as the blindfolded bishop groped vainly after it. But the startled Will only raised his eyebrows and turned the purse over into his hand. Three gold coins dropped out. "Three gold nobles, Robin. That's all he's got."

Robin's face clouded over and he crossed his arms in disgust. In the next moment, though, he had his hands on his hips and he was laughing heartily. "Well, my lord bishop," he said between guffaws. "The last time we met, you paid us a thousand nobles for your supper, and we made quite a large profit off you! This time, I see you have got the better of us! This amount won't even cover the cost of the feast! So you've bested us this time around, and we're even!"

"So we are!" the bishop said, laughing himself as he rose from the table. "And so the trickster is tricked, eh?"

"Indeed," Will Scarlet said. "So Robin, the usual tax, then?"

"Right," said Robin.

Will placed one of the gold coins in Robin's palm. "One-third for the outlaws of Sherwood!" he declared. Then, as Tuck held out his palm, Will placed another coin in the friar's hand, saying, "One-third for the poor!"

"I know of a family in Worksop to whom this coin will seem a fortune rather than a pittance," Tuck said. "I plan to visit them tomorrow."

The bishop, somewhat less ebullient after being stripped of two-thirds of his pittance, now frowned and held out his own hand. Will replaced the last coin in the purse, and placed it in the prelate's grip. "I suppose I should thank you for not taking it all," he muttered, then called to his escort. "Come, Jankyn, finish your holiday, and let's get back on the road. We still have some way to go!" Then, turning to where Robin's voice had come from, he asked, with some of his old bravado, "I assume you'll have some of your cutthroats convey us back to the road, where we can doff these ridiculous masks?"

"It will be my honor to lead you back, yer Grace," Thorvald answered him. "Let me 'elp ya up into the cart, me lord, and yer servant, too." Jankyn winced again at being referred to as the bishop's servant, but climbed as quickly as he could into the wagon. He was quite happy to be done here.

"Farewell, good bishop," Robin called as the cart pulled out, followed by Jack Rolfe on horseback, trailing the bishop's two horses behind him. "Have a pleasant journey! And we look forward to the pleasure of your company in the future, should you ever find yourself riding through Sherwood again!"

"Not without an army," the bishop griped as he, and the cart, disappeared into the surrounding woods.

*　*　*

Left to themselves, the little knot of Robin, Palomides, Little John, Friar Tuck, and the two Wills (Stutely and Scarlet), with Gilbert Whitehand coming quickly to join them after his picnic with Jankyn, immediately burst into animated conversation.

"Robin, tell me you are not seriously considering showing up in Nottingham to compete in that archery contest," Sir Palomides burst out. "Even you could not be that foolhardy!"

Robin puckered his features into a hurt look and asked in mock innocence. "Foolhardy? Me? You must have me confused with my good friend and sidekick Little John. I've never made a rash decision in my life!"

"Unless of course it involved tweaking the sheriff's nose," Will Scarlet suggested.

"And I've nothing in particular against that in theory," the

Moorish knight conceded. "But in this case, you'd simply be walking straight into a trap. It could be suicide."

A scowl had formed on Little John's face, and he scratched his blond, sun-bleached hair. "Wait. Who are you calling a sidekick?"

"Let it go, John, we're past it," Stutely told him in an aside.

"I think I must take up Sir Palomides' side in this," Friar Tuck said. "Suicide is, truly, a mortal sin, and to walk brazenly into the sheriff's deliberate trap, when you know it's a trap, is the moral equivalent of conscious self-destruction."

"Well," Robin returned, feeling the tide of opinion against him, "how do we know it's a trap?" Then, as Palomides and the friar scoffed audibly and Little John let out a derisive huff, he continued: "I mean, just to play devil's advocate: What evidence do we have that the sheriff has baited this trap for the sole purpose of capturing me?"

Sir Palomides began to count on his fingers. "First, the sheriff knows how vain you are about your archery skills, and knows you would do anything to show them off." At that, Robin shrugged in apparent concession of the point. "Second," the Moor continued, "we know that he hates you enough to spend an inordinate amount of money on just the kind of entertainment that would entice you to fall under his power." Again, nods around the ring of faces demonstrated the general acknowledgment of Palomides's analysis. "Third, he knows that you hate him enough that you'd never be able to resist the chance to beard him in his own lair, make a fool of him in his own domain, and so you'd love to come to Nottingham and best him there." Again, there was general assent.

"All right then," Palomides continued. "Now comes this puffed-up prelate into our woods, with but a single *sheriff's* deputy as his escort, like a fat chicken who just can't wait to be plucked. And he shows absolutely no displeasure about being trussed up and brought to our camp, sits down to a meal with us without hesitation, and turns out to have anticipated being robbed ahead of time so that he brings but three coins in his purse. As surely as the Holy Mother was a perpetual virgin, that bishop came here for the sole purpose of luring you into that trap." At this, Robin looked momentarily doubtful, and the exasperated Palomides added, "It's the only reason he was on the road! Why, I'd be willing to wager his entire trip to Wallingwells Priory was pure fabrication. I'll bet he never went there at all!"

"Well, there I'm afraid you've got it wrong, Sir Knight," Gilbert Whitehand interrupted. Everyone stared at Gilbert, surprised by the source of that new information. Gilbert shrugged. "I talked with Jankyn, the deputy, as you know, of course. He said they were there for a couple of days, staying not among the nuns, of course, but in a lodging house in Worksop, close by. And he says he got an earful of the local gossip from the serving maids there, too, especially when they found out he was one of the sheriff's deputies."

"Oh? And why was that?" asked Robin, his interest piqued, and not only because he was glad to have the conversation diverted, at least momentarily, from the foolishness of his taking the sheriff's bait.

"Because of the body they'd found in the woods a couple of nights ago. In a clearing somewhere halfway between the priory and the town. Blood all over, they said, and the bloke they found—well, the fact is they only found his torso. No legs. No arms. No head even. So no way to identify the remains, so to speak."

"What a horror!" Friar Tuck gasped. "The victim is a stranger, then? And no one knows who it is? Have they given the body a Christian burial, at least?"

"They placed the corpse in the priory's chapel, apparently, and word has gone out that whoever it belongs to should come and claim the body. But no one has come forward. There's a local magistrate in the village who's said that if nobody comes forward to say he's one of theirs, the body must go underground by tomorrow. But without knowing who it is, no priest will give it burial in holy ground. Now, Jankyn told me that the magistrate approached him, as a representative of the Reeve of Nottinghamshire, to see if he wouldn't want to investigate the murder. But nobody's claimed him, and the clothes he was wearing show he couldn't have been a man of any consequence, so there's no point wasting time on him. Must have been some vagrant tramping through the woods, they're saying."

"And so this foul murder goes unmarked and unavenged?" The friar seemed put out. "This is a soul as precious to God as you or I or the Bishop of Hereford. Is this the king's justice nowadays?"

"Well," Jankyn continued. "The word is that this kind of murder—the tearing of the bloke into pieces, if you will—isn't any normal killing. There's supernatural beings about in those woods—everybody in Worksop, and everybody in the priory, is saying so. This is the work of some demon, or some vengeful ghoul."

"Balderdash," was the friar's response.

"Well," Gilbert took on a defensive tone. "That's what they're saying, anyway. Or so Jankyn tells me."

"Well," Tuck replied, "I planned to travel over to Worksop myself tomorrow, to visit a poor family I know of there. I think I just might see if I can't find out anything more about this so-called vengeful ghost. Something about this unclaimed corpse doesn't sit right with me."

"And *I*," Robin concluded, "will begin to make plans for

my journey to Nottingham." He held up his hands to ward off exasperated cries from the others. "I will admit that everything Sir Palomides has said rings true. And I say, what better reason to take the sheriff up on his kind invitation? Can you imagine anything more exhilarating than winning the tournament and slipping from the sheriff's grasp at the same time? Could there be a better victory than beating the sheriff at his own game? I'm heading for Nottingham!"

"You're *what*?" came the voice of Maid Marion, who had just come up behind him. "What kind of bloody fool *are* you?"

*   *   *

Lady Mary of Winchester, known as "Maid Marion" to Robin and his men, was Countess Lydia's chief Lady-in-Waiting, and she and the rest of the countess's ladies had been quietly listening to Alan a Dale's ballads while Robin had entertained the bishop, but now a choir of tittering voices came bearing down upon the outlaw band and in a moment a score of girls and young women had burst amongst them laughing and singing, each of them garbed in a colorful samite or lighter silk bliaut belted at the waist. They wore no cloaks or hoods or surcoats—they were dressed all light for summer, and in lieu of head coverings, they wore flower garlands about their free-flowing hair, with their smoothly elegant blue, red, green, or white gowns embroidered with flowers as well.

Earlier, they'd been engaged in the custom of "bringing in the May." They'd been gathering flowers to make garlands for themselves, and some had been gathering woodbine and hawthorn to make wreaths to give to gentlemen they fancied. They had arisen at dawn, and come onto the castle green to wash their faces in the dew of the May morning—a ceremony said to do wonders for the complexion—and had set up a Maypole on the edge of the green closest to the castle moat, so that the entire ground had been prepared before Robin and his followers ever arrived for the celebration.

Now the ladies of the countess's court rushed into the yard in a kind of riotous celebration, and each of them grabbed a gentleman—some courtiers from Peveril Castle, some men of Robin's band—and pulled them along to the Maypole, for it was time for the traditional dance around that venerable icon. The countess herself grabbed onto Sir Palomides as she rushed past, and he, always the perfect courtier, bowed and led her toward the pole as to a courtly ball. Robin, however, was snubbed by Marion, as she grabbed hold of Will Scarlet's arm instead, to demonstrate her annoyance at Robin's foolish plan to go to Nottingham.

The pole, already decorated with long pink and green ribbons, now formed the center of the celebration. Alan a Dale, by previous arrangement, took up his lute and began to play a rollicking dance tune, and now a dozen women each took hold of one of the long pink ribbons and began to dance with a free, abandoned spirit clockwise about the pole, while each of the dozen men, holding a green ribbon, gamboled just as vigorously counterclockwise, capering to the rhythm of Alan's sprightly lute. At each revolution of the pole, Robin saw Maid Marion's azure blue eyes flash at him, and sighed with an emotion unconnected with the May Day dance.

When the dance had ended, and the twenty-four dancers all sat or lay exhausted on the green, the countess gave a nod to Oswald to summon the servers from the castle to begin setting up the boards for the feast—which Robin's men had already unceremoniously begun for the bishop and his bodyguard. As her kitchen maids and knaves bustled about the clearing, and several pages scurried back over the moat to fetch trenchers and fruits and cheese from the castle stores to lay before the May Day celebrants, and others to bring kegs of wine and ale to quench the thirst the dancers had worked up with their morning exertions, Countess Lydia stood in the center of the green before the fire. Certain from here she could be seen and heard by all the mixed audience of her courtiers and Robin's merry band, she clapped her hands until all eyes were on her.

With her long dark locks flowing free under the garland of flowers encircling her brow, and her dark brown eyes darting boldly from face to face, Lydia Peveril, Countess of Chesterfield, stood audaciously with her fists on the hips of her blue samite gown, in control of all she surveyed. With a confidence that belied her twenty-three years, the same confidence that had convinced her to rule in her own stead without consenting to marry any suitor who might stifle her fiery will, she addressed the assembled group.

"My friends, I can hardly express my joy at being here and having you join me for this first celebration of May Day in my new domain. Welcome to my courtiers who do me the honor to serve my will daily," and with that, she looked smiling into the faces of her closest ladies and squires. "And welcome, too, to my faithful friends, the lawfully appointed foresters of my domain, Robin of Sherwood and his loyal band." With that Robin nodded courteously at the lady as she smiled down upon him. This fiction of being the countess's foresters was simply her means of giving her friends some legal protection from local authorities like the Sheriff of Nottingham, or royal appointees like Guy of Gisbourne.

"And now," she continued, "before we eat and drink our feast to welcome in the first summer of my independent authority, I declare it time to choose our Queen of the May!" With that, a raucous cheer went up from all sides, and several of the gentlemen began to push their partners up to stand alongside the countess, to see if they might be selected. Lady Lydia waved to each of the girls or young ladies, beckoning them to her to stand before the judgment of the assembly to see who would win the greatest approval. "Come, come, don't be shy ladies," Lydia cried, encouraging her ladies-in-waiting to join her and embracing them all as they stepped up to her. When eight ladies had joined her, and all others held back out of modesty or bashfulness, the countess seized a short blonde girl of perhaps sixteen, with light brown hair and wearing a white gown, and called to the group, "Here is Lady Eloise of York! What say you, friends, shall she be your May Queen?" Polite applause mixed with a few enthusiastic cheers greeted Eloise's introduction, after which Lady Lydia reached toward an auburn-haired eighteen-year-old beauty in a green gown that matched her sultry eyes.

The countess went on in this manner, putting her ladies on display to the delight of her fervent audience, with a few of the ladies inspiring more and a few less ardent recaptions, until Lady Lydia reached the final contestant—who was, of course, Marion.

"Now finally, and fittingly the last and dearest of my household, Lady Mary. What about her, my friends? Shall it be Lady Mary who takes the May crown?"

Robin Hood and the best part of his troupe had been waiting for this introduction to make their loudest cheers and, since Marion was a favorite among the countess's household as well, there was no question as to the preference of the assembly for Queen of the May. When Countess Lydia declared, "The popular choice is crystal clear! Lady Mary of Winchester is undisputed Queen of the first May Day celebration at Peveril Castle under my auspices. Giles!" she called to the chief squire of her household, and a teenage boy called Giles of Huddersfield, stepped forward. He wore a red and gold tunic with gold hosen and a surcoat embroidered with flowers for May. In his hands, he carried a solid gold circlet, entwined with roses and lilies, and Lady Lydia took the crown from him and placed it on Marion's long golden locks.

At the touch of that crown on her brow, Marion could not keep tears from her azure blue eyes. "Sorry," she whispered to the countess. "The truth is, I've dreamed of being Queen of the May since I was a girl of thirteen. I never thought it would really happen!" She was surrounded by her peers at Lady Lydia's side, and the whole group of eight young ladies embraced one another in a large circle and jumped up and down in celebration.

After a moment of this, the countess clapped her hands. "And now, May Queen, it is your privilege to lead the group in a processional dance around the green, ending at the boards that are set up here to provide us our banquet. Choose your partner for the dance!" Marion's eyes perused the crowd, lighting momentarily on Robin but then passing playfully on from him until coming to rest on the gray-robed figure standing toward the back of the assembly.

"Good friar!" she called, to Tuck's great surprise. "Come up here and be my escort!"

Friar Tuck, with an initial show of modesty and blushing to the crown of his tonsured pate, at first seemed to demur. But as the group erupted into a joyous cheer at the choice, the friar stood erect, adopting the bearing of a noble courtier, and strode, in as stately a manner as was possible on his relatively short and stocky legs, to the front of the assembly and with a deferential bow to the May Queen, held out his right arm to escort her in the dance. Marion slid her left arm under the friar's offered elbow, placed her own right hand on his wrist, and the two of them began a stately procession, moving a step at a time and sliding the back foot forward to meet the striding foot, in perfect cadence with the dignified tune Alan a Dale began playing on his lute.

Two by two the other celebrants followed them in the traditional May Day procession. The countess, holding on to Sir Palomides, joined them first, followed by Robin, who had snatched Ellen to be his partner since Alan was busy providing the music. Little John grabbed hold of Will Stutely and the two of them sauntered behind Robin and Ellen, and Will Scarlet, his red hood brightly contrasting his Lincoln green livery, had grabbed the young Lady Catherine of Derby, while David of Doncaster, youngest of Robin's outlaw band, had shyly taken the hand of the petite Eloise of York, youngest of Lady Lydia's household.

When they'd made a wide circuit of the entire green lawn, Marion and the friar took their places at the head of the first table that had been set up on the green, to find that Oswald and his kitchen crew—too busy at their tasks to dance—had set the tables with trenchers piled high with slices of the well-cooked pork, small bowls of gravy, plates of fruit and cheese, and pitchers of wine and ale. It was as glorious a picnic as the Sherwood outlaws had ever tasted in the greenwood. And as was their custom, they began to call for a song to entertain them while feasting.

And so Sir Palomides, a troubadour who composed his own music and lyrics (some of which the minstrel Alan a Dale liked to borrow for his own repertoire), stepped out before the fire with his gittern and strummed a few times to command the attention of the diners. "My friends," the Moor began in his rich baritone. "We have had a glorious May Day, all thanks to the generosity and courtesy of our munificent hostess, Countess Lydia of Chesterfield!" And with that, the clearing echoed with joyous appreciation. "Let me crown the feast now with a composition of my own that honors one of the more surprising heroes of the day—our spiritual mentor and guide, the redoubtable Friar

Tuck!" There were more cheers until Palomides struck the strings of his lute again and began his witty ballad thus:

> *Robin Hood put on his harness good,*
> *And on his head a cap of steel,*
> *Broad sword and buckler by his side,*
> *And they became him well.*
>
> *And coming unto Fountains Dale,*
> *No further would he ride;*
> *There was he aware of a curtal friar,*
> *Walking by the water-side.*
>
> *The friar had on a harness good,*
> *And on his head a cap of steel,*
> *Broad sword and buckler by his side,*
> *And they became him well.*

At that, several of Robin's men gave a bit of a cheer. While Friar Tuck was essentially a man of peace and Christian charity, he was certainly no slouch when it came to swinging a sword himself in a pinch.

> *Robin Hood lighted off his horse,*
> *And tied him to a tree*
> *"Wilt bear me over this wild water,*
> *For sweet Saint Charity?"*
>
> *The friar took Robin Hood on his back,*
> *Deep water he did bestride*
> *And spoke neither good word nor bad,*
> *Till he came at the other side.*

When Robin leapt lightly off that friar's back
A long sword the friar drew
"Bear me back again, thou fine fellow,
Or this shall run thee through!"

"Woo-hoo!" Will Scarlet hooted, and there was raucous laughter throughout the listening assembly at the picture of the good friar forcing Robin Hood to carry his portly bulk over a running stream at swordpoint. The countess and her household, never having heard the story, were understandably a bit taken aback.

Robin Hood took the friar on his back,
Deep water he did bestride
And spoke neither good word nor bad,
Till he came at the other side.

Lightly leapt the friar off Robin's back;
Robin Hood said to him again,
"Carry me over again, thou curtal friar,
Or it shall cause thee pain."

The friar took Robin on his back again,
And waded to the knee;
Till he came to the middle stream,
Neither good nor bad spoke he.

And coming to the middle stream,
There he threw Robin in
"And choose thee, choose thee, fine fellow,
Whether thou wilt sink or swim."

Robin's entire band had been waiting for this particular detail, and exploded in rowdy cheers and laughter, for they knew the account of the friar's meeting with the head of their troupe, and loved the picture of Robin dumped unceremoniously into the middle of the water.

> *Robin Hood swam to a bush of broom*
> *The friar to a wicker wand*
> *Bold Robin Hood is gone to the shore,*
> *And took his sword in hand.*
>
> *They took their swords and steel bucklers,*
> *With might and main they fought;*
> *From terce to none fought all that day,*
> *Till Robin respite sought.*
>
> *"A boon, a boon, thou curtal friar,*
> *I beg it on my knee;*
> *Give me leave to set my horn to my mouth,*
> *And to blow blasts three."*
>
> *"That will I do," said the curtal friar,*
> *"Of thy blasts I have no doubt*
> *I hope thou blowest so passing well*
> *That both thine eyes fall out."*
>
> *Robin Hood set his horn to his mouth,*
> *He blew but blasts three;*
> *Half a hundred yeomen, with bows bent,*
> *Came hasting over the lee.*
>
> *"What is thy will?" the friar said.*

"Have done and tell it me."
"If thou will go to the merry greenwood,
A noble shall be thy fee.

"And every holy day throughout the year,
Changed shall thy garment be,
If thou wilt some to fair Sherwood
And there remain with me."

There was a wild surge of cheers from Robin's men at that, and from the countess's household, applause and laughter. Sir Palomides bowed modestly, pleased that he had been able to entertain the courtiers as well as the yeomen with his effort. Friar Tuck stood up at the head of the table and raised his hands for silence. When things had quieted enough, he raised his voice and called to Robin, who was seated at another table on the other side of the fire: "And where's that new robe I was promised? This one is getting threadbare, and I haven't had a new one in at least a year now!"

Amid the resulting merriment, Robin returned, "You eat so much, good friar, that I can't afford to pay for your new garments, I'm too busy paying for your dinners!"

And at that, the party began to wind down, and Tuck, left to his own thoughts, mused upon the mutilated body found in the woods near Wallingwells. He would go there tomorrow, as planned. And he vowed to himself that he would seek justice for the unknown victim.

CHAPTER THREE

By the next morning, Robin and his band had determined to move from the Peak district, where they had their winter quarters, back to the southern part of Sherwood, at the great oak closer to Nottingham. They had planned to make this move at some point anyway, but the need to do it sooner was forced by the Bishop's visit on May Day. For if he now knew that the band's headquarters were farther north, it would make it easier for the sheriff or Sir Guy of Gisbourne, commander of the royal guard at Nottingham Castle, to track them down. Ironically, it seemed they would be safer the closer they moved toward Nottingham, since that was the last place the sheriff would be looking.

Friar Tuck, however, had a call he wanted to make near Worksop, which lay due east of the duchess's castle, and would be as long a journey as the rest of the band would be making to the south. Thus, though Tuck generally walked on his charitable visits among the poor of his neighborhood, to walk this far was out of the question. Therefore, Tuck prevailed upon the dwarf Thorvald—who he knew had a heart of gold beneath his crusty outer shell—to accompany him on the road to Worksop, and to drive him there in his cart.

So it was that the morning after May Day, Tuck and Thorvald rose at dawn, and after a hasty breakfast of bread and cheese and a mug of small beer, they hitched Thorvald's old mare, Millie, to the cart and began to roll out of the outlaws' temporary camp. A few of the women were already up and beginning to ready such portable household items as they had for transport to the summer base camp. Thorvald and Tuck had packed their meager possessions—a change of clothes and a tent and sleeping pallet for each—in the cart, and as they drove out of camp they waved to Ellen and Gilbert Whitehand's wife Kitty, then halted the horse for a moment as Little John stepped toward the cart.

"We'll look for you in three days or so," he told the pair. "We'll be settled in our old camp by then, and see that you get back there, all right? I don't like to see members of the group so far off, ever since what happened to Will last year."

Will Stutely had been captured the previous year, arrested by a group of Gisbourne's guards while he traveled alone on the Great North Road, and held and tortured in the sheriff's dungeon before being led to the scaffold to hang. It was only with the greatest pluck and good fortune that John, Robin, and the rest of the band rescued him and saved his life. The band certainly did not need another such challenge at this point.

"Don't worry about us," Tuck told him. "Nobody's going to accost a poor friar on a mission of charity. Even one riding in the cart of some itinerant clown or juggler."

Little John chuckled at the stereotyped view so many strangers took when they saw the bearded dwarf driving his cart. Thorvald was less amused. "Yeah, I'll juggle *you* in a minute," he told Tuck. "Keep it up and you'll be walkin' to Worksop, and all you'll see o' this cart is me 'orse's backside."

"Now, don't be so testy Thorvald, you know I don't mean it. But John, it might take more than a couple of days in Worksop. You know I want to look into that poor mutilated corpse and his burial before I leave that place. If we don't join you in a week, you might think about sending a search party after us."

"Search party or a rescue party?" John asked, only half joking.

"Well now, we're not likely to need rescuing. But I'll tell you what I do know: You need to work on Robin while I'm gone and see if you can squelch that notion he's got of crashing the sheriff's archery contest. If anybody's going to need rescuing, it's him, if he goes through with that crazy whim."

"Two great minds with but a single thought," Little John responded. "I'll do what I can. But you know what he's like when he gets a notion in his head."

"My 'orse 'as got a notion right now," Thorvald said. "It's that we shouldn't 'ave got 'er up so early if we was just gonna sit 'ere gabbin' all morning. Say yer farewells and let's get on the road, Friar!"

"Yes, yes, we do have a long way to go today," the friar conceded and, as the cart began to roll away, he called back to Little John, "We'll see you in a few days, John! Keep things in order while we're gone, will you?"

"Always," John answered, waving his hand as the wagon drew away, and as the cart picked up a little speed, Tuck glanced back and saw Will Stutely step up next to Little John, as the big man put his arm around him.

* * *

In the early morning sun of a warm spring day, they drove down the narrow road on the northern edge of Sherwood Forest. New leaves were growing green on the oak branches and the birches along the road, and migrant birds like the chiffchaffs, warblers, and even the cuckoos could be heard on the fresh morning air. Along the road and in amongst the trees a rainbow of yellow St. John's wort flowers, purple foxglove bells, and red campions carpeted the forest floor, and Tuck and Thorvald found it pleasant to listen and to look about them as they rode along the first few miles of their journey. Eventually, inspired by the sound of a lark he heard among the trees, Thorvald began to whistle in imitation of the song. After a few moments of this, Tuck, not to be outdone, began to whistle his own version of the chiffchaff's notes. To which Thorvald replied with a whistling version of a tune he'd heard the previous day from Alan a Dale. Tuck caught him up and whistled a lower-pitched burden to harmonize with the dwarf's melody, and once set on that path, they traded tunes for several miles until Tuck could no longer contain himself and began to sing. And soon enough Thorvald joined him and they rolled along merrily singing, "*Sumer is ycumin in. lude sing cuckoo,*" mile after mile, until the birds of Sherwood, feeling outdone, stopped their singing to listen to them.

Eventually, they fell to talking, reliving some of the more memorable moments of the May Day celebration the previous day, then talking about the grim report they'd had from Gilbert Whitehand about the gruesome corpse that had been found near Worksop, and finally, Thorvald asked Tuck the question he'd been wanting to ask him since they had left Robin's campsite that morning.

"What I don't understand at all, brother friar, is why you've got to go all the way across Sherwood to visit some needy family what needs our charity, when there must be dozens of families just as poor within a mile or two of Peveril castle. What is there that's so special about these people we're drivin' all this way to see?"

Tuck pressed his lips together and looked to the side, deciding how exactly to explain his relationship with the women he was taking Thorvald to meet. Finally with a sigh he began. "I knew these two women years ago when I was a boy. I grew up, you see, in the neighborhood of Worksop. First learned grammar under a certain Father Walter, one of the Augustinian Canons in the priory there. My father, well, he was a yeoman who worked as a blacksmith on the estate that belonged to the priory, and they let me attend classes with the richer boys at no charge to my father. I was the oldest in the family, and my mother especially wanted me to go into the Church if I could. She had two daughters after me, and the older woman we're going to meet, you see, she was a midwife… among other things."

"Other things, ya say," Thorvald echoed thoughtfully. "Ya mean she was a witch."

Friar Tuck rolled his eyes. "Thorvald, that's just ignorance talking. Alison—this woman I'm speaking of, and her daughter Malyne too—grow herbs and know all their properties. There's no doctor in or around Worksop, except for the infirmarian at the Augustinian Priory or with the nuns at the Benedictine convent. They aren't readily available for the common folk. So they go to the women I'm speaking of to cure their ills as well as have their bairns. Or sometimes, not to have their bairns, if you understand."

"Oh, I understand," Thorvald said. "When I was still 'iring out my cart ta transfer prisoners, I brought quite of few of them kind of women to the dock for whippin' or, more'n once, for 'angin', for just such practices as them you mention, Friar."

"Pure ignorance, I say, Thorvald. Let me tell you my experience with this Alison. She is actually my godmother. When I was eleven years old, my mother fell pregnant again, even though she'd had a terrible time with my sister Jane and very nearly died, though Alison pulled her through it. She was sick as she could be with this new pregnancy, though, and she told me to run and fetch Alison and tell her what was happening. Well Alison, she grabbed a basket where she kept her medicines and whatnot, and followed me home straight away. One look at my mum and she knew what to do. Alison gave her something for the pain, and gave her something too that ended that pregnancy."

"And so you think this witch saved your mother's life."

"I *know* this healer saved my mother's life. Twice."

Thorvald was silent for a while. Then he shrugged. "So you say. So you think. Couldn't 'a gone over too well at the priory, if they'd 'a known. But then, women are losin' babes all the time, I know, so it ain't suspicious if one gets 'elped along. That is, unless there's talk."

Tuck gave a low groan. "We had a neighbor at the time, a beak-nosed carping gossip name of Sarah. She'd seen Alison going in to see my mother and she knew the kinds of help Alison gave. And she started spreading the rumor around the village."

"So the word got out, then," Thorvald prompted.

"Not so much as to Alison's role in it, but the word going about was that it wasn't God's doing that ended that pregnancy. Not that my mother cared for what people thought about it, but when my father heard about it, he went mad with rage. I mean, I'd seen him beat her before, usually just a blow or two, and she'd end up with bruised ribs, or a black eye, or her arm trussed up in a sling. But this time he kept hitting her. I ran like all the devils of hell were after me, into the priory to find Father Walter, to come and help."

Thorvald pursed his lips. He muttered, "I think I know what you'd 'a got from a priest, but why don't ya tell me any'ow?"

"Looked me in the eye and told me, with a long pious face, that it would be a sin to interfere with a man lawfully chastising his wife. Said that to my face. Told an eleven-year-old boy that his father was perfectly right to be beating his mother to death. Because I think you can probably tell that's what happened. When I got back home, she lay there a bloody mess on the floor of our house on those priory grounds. And he was back out at his forge like nothing had happened."

Thorvald's head was hanging. "And what did them canons say

about that? 'Cause even the priests don't allow a man to go that far."

"Truth is, I don't know," Tuck answered. "That was the last I saw of my father as well as my mother. I shoved in a sack what few clothes I had, my little knife, and a copy of Donatus's *Ars grammatica* I'd borrowed from Father Walter—I figured he didn't deserve to get it back—and I left that town. I never wanted to see my father or that priory ever again."

"Well, ya ended up a friar anyway, so I guess ya didn't leave the Church completely be'ind."

"Like I said, my mum wanted me to enter the Church, and I did after a while. But that's another story. When I left I went to Alison's cottage there outside of town and told her what happened. She let me stay there with her and her little daughter Malyne, who was maybe five or six at the time. She fed me and hid me from my father, though he didn't look for me long. Just as glad to be rid of me, I suppose. No reminder of my mother, or what he did to her. And one less mouth to feed. But anyway, like I say, I didn't stay around long enough to know what happened to him. After a day or so at Alison's, I lit out for the south and didn't look back."

"So you ain't been back there in what—decades? 'Ow do ya know this Alison is still there? Or even still alive?"

"It's twenty-five years since I left, yes," Friar Tuck conceded. "But I never said I didn't go back. I've been back to Worksop three times since. Once when my father died under mysterious circumstances. I can't say I mourned his passing, but I wanted to see what Alison would say about it. Alison had taken in my two sisters. I'm afraid neither one of them survived to adulthood. But that's not a story for today. Let's just say I passed that way a few more times in my mendicant days, and always stopped to see how Alison and her daughter were getting on. I do hear from her once in a while—she writes me every year or so. I had a letter from her a few months ago, in fact, and she told me then she wasn't so busy as she had been. Some new infirmarian at the Augustinian priory apparently railing against her and Malyne and their cures. Says they are foolish women probably in league with the devil, and that the only cure God sanctions is bleeding. Alison tells me there's been a pronounced upturn in deaths at the priory since their Father Michael's been treating the canons."

"And so we're going to give the old witch money, then, because folks 'ave stopped comin' to 'er for their med'cines?" Thorvald pursued.

"That. And because she's all I've got left of my mother, you see." And the friar cleared his throat. "I've sent her the odd farthing here and there over the years, but I wanted to see her this time. And besides," he added in a cheerier tone. "She's intimate with every gossip in the town, and I want to hear all the gossip about this body they found. Feel like I've got a personal interest in it, since both my parents were killed there."

"Well, I'm with ya there," Thorvald agreed. "It's some awful doings, and I for one'd like to see the culprit found. You an' I both know it ain't no ghost what done that to a man."

"Do we?" Tuck answered, with a lot less assurance than his friend.

* * *

"That's the most gruesome story we've had around here since I can remember. And I can remember more than sixty years since I was a wee one." Alison, or as Thorvald was beginning to think of her, Granny Alison, wanted to talk about nothing other than the murder. She did look a lot like a witch, Thorvald had decided upon meeting her. Long white hair, flowing unkempt. A wrinkled and weathered face with both nose and chin pushing forward in sharp points. Dark clothing little better than rags, and a rasping voice that erupted often into what could only be called a cackle. Yes, she did fit the witch's image in his mind's eye. There was probably a black cat around here somewhere as well. But despite the ramshackle house she and her daughter lived in, not much more than a hovel really, Alison was a good-humored sort, and wouldn't hear of her two visitors failing to sit down and have a meal with her, light as the fare might be.

Of course, she'd been delighted to see Friar Tuck, when they'd arrived there after some seven hours' journey from Peveril. And so had her daughter: Malyne was a thick, stocky woman with a round face, thick lips, and a pug nose. She had one brown eye and one green one, and that green one always seemed to be looking in another direction rather than straight at you. Thorvald could well understand why villagers hereabout might suspect the younger as well as the older woman of being a witch, or somehow fay. And both women had been overjoyed when the friar produced the Bishop's gold noble, and then added two more from his own store as gifts for them. Thorvald could easily deduce that, given the scarcity of their means otherwise, these three coins might keep the wolf from their door for a good six months or so.

But it was the recent gruesome murder that Granny Alison really wanted to talk about. The thought of it brought a flush to her withered cheeks and a ghoulish smile to her face. "They say that the body was wearing a brown woolen tunic and a fine leather girdle that looked new. And a purse hung from it with a few pence inside."

"So seems unlikely that it was a robbery gone wrong," Thorvald ventured.

"And what would a ghost want with a new girdle and

sixpence?" Malyne answered, her ghoulish smile matching her mother's, and her wandering eye staring off into the ether, where it may be she had some specter on view.

"Aye, we've heard the rumor of a supernatural murderer," Tuck said. "But that seems simply a good excuse for the local authorities to ignore the murder and shirk their own responsibility. I mean, seriously, what would suggest a vengeful ghost in this case?"

"Torn limb from limb, he was," Alison said. "Both arms gone. Both legs gone. And of course, the head gone. Who but some bloodthirsty fiend would kill a man that way? Visiting the torments of hell on the corpse, it was."

Tuck shrugged. "Seems to me the fellow's soul might be suffering those torments even now, particularly if he was attacked suddenly, with no opportunity to repent his earthly sins. But the body, once dead, would be unaware of being dismembered. Seems more a crime of passion. The murderer hated the victim enough to abuse his corpse in this way, as if just killing the fellow was not nearly vengeance enough to sate the killer's hatred. Still sounds like a human killer to me."

"Are not fiends the embodiments of hatred, my good friar? And what about ghosts? Why do they come back to haunt the living except to take revenge for past wrongs? Mark my words," Granny Alison concluded, "whoever this corpse was, he harmed some poor dead ghost abominably in life. Some poor dead woman's ghost, I'll be bound."

Thorvald scratched his head, picking up a crust of bread to feed his hunger. "A woman's ghost?" he questioned. "Why should it be a woman's ghost?"

"Because our experience has been," Malyne spoke for her mother, "that only a woman can be harmed so vilely by a man to make her hate him to that extent."

Friar Tuck's head shot up and he looked at Alison, who, knowing his thoughts, refused to look at him. Could Tuck's mother have hated his father so much? Could she have come back from the dead and killed him?

No, Tuck shook his head, this was silly superstition, unworthy of an educated friar in these enlightened times. But this was getting them away from the subject at hand, which, for him, was the identity of this victim.

"So his head was gone, and his clothes were the kind of everyday things that anybody might wear. But surely, if he was a local man, his absence must have been noted. Is there no one in the village or the near countryside who has reported anybody missing? Even if he was not living with his family or in some house where he served or rented a room, would he not have been working somewhere that, if he hadn't shown up for work for a week, they might have noticed he was missing? So in that case do we need to assume he was a stranger, somebody passing through town on his way someplace else? But why would anyone travel alone without protection in these times? And why travel in the middle of the night, which is apparently when this murder took place?"

Thorvald scratched his beard and, pursing his lips, put on his thoughtful face. "There's other possibilities, ya know," he said. "Suppose our man's not a villain at all but some yeoman farmer what's got 'is own free 'alf-acre of land up in 'ere? Lives alone, works 'is own field, self-sufficient like. Wouldn't nobody notice 'e was missin' for days. Weeks even."

"Don't know as there's anybody like that in the neighborhood roundabout," Malyne said. "No, he's likely to be some escaped felon, or maybe a runaway serf, traveling at night to avoid detection. Somebody who had done some horrible deed back in his own home, but couldn't escape the ghosts of his victims pursuing him through the night!" Her face lit up with a kind of glee at the prospect, while she imagined the terrible crimes this unknown man must have been guilty of to have been pursued and punished to this extent.

"You might imagine all you want," Tuck replied. "But the only crime we are certain of here is the one that took this poor man's life. And even if your imaginings prove to be true, haven't ye heard that it's written, 'Vengeance is mine, I will repay, sayeth the Lord?' Whoever it was who took it upon himself, or herself, or if it's some supernatural specter, *Itself*, to take this wicked vengeance on this man, then that person, or demon, is the guilty one here."

"Well, maybe," Malyne said, though she sounded unconvinced.

"And in any case, I'm concerned that the man's body receive a decent Christian burial. I heard yesterday, from the deputy sheriff we entertained in Sherwood, that nothing has been done yet toward that end."

"But the body can't be identified.," Alison objected. "How can it be given Christian burial? And how do we know it is even a Christian?"

Friar Tuck closed his eyes. He expected this kind of opposition from intransigent theologians, but not from someone like Alison, living on the edge of Christian society herself. "If he were a Moor or a Jew," Tuck sighed, "or even a pagan from foreign lands, his clothing would set him apart. You told me he was dressed like any local commoner. As for his name, God knows it even if we do not, and there is a committal ceremony I can perform without knowing the name. Where is the body now?"

"Well," Alison said, "the *torso* is actually at the nunnery. That's where it was brought after the magistrate and the deputy had examined it. It was the closest house of religion to the murder. From what I've heard, the nuns had a few of their villeins nail it into a makeshift coffin and bury it."

"Without ceremony?" Tuck asked.

"Quite without any," Alison answered.

"Well," the friar said thoughtfully, "tonight is Saturday. I assume they have a mass tomorrow morning in the chapel at this Wallingwells Benedictine Priory. Is it open to folk from the neighborhood? Might we attend?"

"Most local folk belong to the parish in Worksop, but the nuns' priest does a mass at terce on Sunday mornings that the priory's lay servants attend, and some of their families. You and your man there would probably be welcome to attend, since you're a man of the cloth yourself and out of your own parish."

Tuck smiled grimly. "All of Sherwood is my parish now. But I'm not sure that Thorvald approves of being called *my* man. Everyone in Sherwood is his *own* man."

"That's what makes us outlaws," Thorvald agreed, matter-of-factly. "But I don't mind the label none. I' been called a lot worse."

"So," said Tuck, his eyes ranging around the hovel's one simple room. Like most peasants, Alison lived in a cruck house—a wooden frame plastered with wattle-and-daub (basically mud, straw, and manure), with a thatched roof. The floor was simply lined with straw, and though it had a good wooden door, its windows were simply holes high in the walls. There seemed little chance that the women would feel there was enough room for the two visitors to sleep there tonight.

"We'll need to stay somewhere tonight. Is there, perhaps, an inn in Worksop that might put us up? I know the Benedictines are famous for their hospitality, but I hate to impose on the nuns at this hour."

"And I know you have our own reasons for not asking lodging among the Augustinian Canons..."

The friar nodded solemnly at Alison's surmise. "Father

Walter, I'm sure, is long gone," he said. "But I vowed I'd never return there, and I never shall."

"Ye're welcome to stay here with us," Malyne said. "It's no palace, and truth is, we've no beds for you, but we don't mind making a little space for the two of you."

"You'd have to sleep on the floor, it's true," Alison agreed. "But we've got an old blanket somewhere we can let you have."

"Livin' in the forest, we've both slept out under the stars many a time," Thorvald said. "This'll be fine, s'far as I'm concerned, ma'am. And we 'ave our own sleepin' pallets in the cart, so we'll be as comfortable as most nights."

"You have our thanks," Friar Tuck added. "And we'll be out of your hair in the morning, and off to the nunnery's chapel before breakfast." He did not want to impose on the pair further, and could see they had little food to spare. He would have to return again soon, he told himself, with a larger gift. His old friend—his savior, as he thought of her—was deeper in poverty than he had suspected.

* * *

The next morning well before terce, Thorvald drew his cart within the gates of the Benedictine Priory at Wallingwells, a quick two-mile drive from Alison's hovel. Thorvald, with the help of the convent's porter, a lively young man called Peter Beale, stowed the cart and tethered his old mare Millie. Meanwhile, Friar Tuck sought out the nuns' chaplain, finding him as he was donning his vestments for the mass in the chapel's sacristy, an annex behind the main altar. Father Bernard was as short and stocky as Tuck himself, with a florid countenance and smiling brown eyes, and was more than happy to welcome him and his companion to attend mass. But when Tuck mentioned the dismembered body that had been foisted on the priory, the priest frowned and shook his head vehemently, giving his jowls a good shaking.

"Bad business that," Father Bernard said. "A bad, bad business. Nobody could identify the body—that is, what was left of it. And nobody seemed to want to take responsibility for it, either. The nuns here had little say in whether to take charge of the corpse, but the magistrate seemed only to want to wash his hands of it. The Bishop of Hereford happened to be here when it arrived, along with a deputy sheriff of the shire, and it was the bishop who advised our prioress—that's Madame Veronica— to commit the body without ceremony outside the sisters' own burial ground. No one knew anything about him, you see, and it seemed indecent just to leave him unburied for long."

"Yes, I do see," Tuck sympathized. "But I may want to talk with you after the mass. I have no superior that I need to worry about displeasing, and may have some ideas myself about something that might be done for the dead man's soul."

By now the two clerics were leaving the sacristy for the chapel proper, and the sisters were filing into the choir. As three black-robed nuns approached him, Father Bernard quickly introduced Friar Tuck. "My good friar, here is our prioress now. Madame Veronica, this is Brother Tuck. Tuck, our prioress, her cellarer Sister Esther, and the convent's infirmarian, Sister Mary Barbara."

Tuck thought the prioress had an open, friendly face and manner. What he could see of her wimpled face was broad and sanguine, with high cheekbones, a small nose, and mouth, but large merry green eyes that sparkled at him as she greeted him. She was not a small woman, and her companions were slight by comparison. The cellarer Esther was younger than her superior, and had a wide mouth and dark, scowling eyes, while Sister

Mary Barbara, Tuck noticed, had a beauty her habit could not hide, with deep blue eyes and long lashes, a pert nose, and lush lips.

The latter two women gave brief curtseys and hurried to their places in the choir, which was filling with the two dozen nuns residing in the priory. Tuck thought, as he always did, that a choirful of nuns might make a joyful noise unto the Lord, but was much like a flock of larks singing in a tree: it was impossible to single anyone out as an individual, as they all looked and often sounded alike. He glanced around the choir and tried to single out different faces. There was one with a beaked nose like a large, black-and-white bird. There was one with a very pale complexion, sitting next to one with a sprinkle of reddish freckles across her nose. Closer to him was an older woman with wrinkles that turned her mouth into a pursed red circle like the bull's eye on an archery target. There was one with dark pools for eyes and thick, dark eyebrows that joined each other over her nose. But to note these distinguishing features was to miss the forest for the trees. Tuck knew that the strength of the convent was in the unity of its sisters in obedience to God's law and to the rule of Saint Benedict, and in the love and devotion to the service of God. And that service began with their singing of the offices, just now of terce, consisting mainly of psalms.

Taking his mumbled farewell of Father Bernard, Tuck exited the choir to find a place to stand somewhere near the back of the chapel. Just as he did so, the porter Beale opened the chapel's double front doors to let in the nunnery's lay personnel who formed the congregation here on Sunday mornings and feast days. The brilliant sunlight that flooded into the dark nave blinded Tuck for an instant, and he turned away, shielding his eyes. And just as he did so, he heard a collective gasp and a woman's blood-curdling cry. He looked back toward the door and saw Thorvald standing as if rooted to the spot, staring with a look of horror toward the rear corner of the nave.

There, hanging on a thin rope from the rafters of the chapel, looming over anyone who might plan on standing there for the service, was a bloody severed head.

CHAPTER FOUR

"You want me to climb up there an' get it down?" Thorvald asked after several moments of stunned silence in the chapel. He'd had some experience in his old life of taking bodies down from scaffolds and such. But his offer was rebuffed by the priest.

"Best leave it be for now," Father Bernard replied hoarsely in a voice barely above a whisper. "The local magistrate will need to have a look at it. Geoffrey!" A young page in a white surplice, perhaps thirteen years old, quickly appeared at the priest's side. "We will forego the mass today, Geoffrey. I need you to saddle old Bayard and ride to the Worksop manor house as quickly as you can. Bring back George Crisp." As Geoffrey doffed his white surplice, handing it to the priest, Father Bernard turned to Tuck and explained, "He's sergeant of the manor since the time of the old king, who appointed him keeper of the peace here. Not that he's worth a sparrow's fart at it," he spoke confidentially to the friar. "But he's the official representative of the king's law here."

Madame Veronica had by now come down from the choir and pushed her way through a small crowd of parishioners surrounding Bernard, Tuck, and Thorvald who stood directly beneath the gruesome head. "Father Bernard," she demanded. "My sisters are all quite unsettled by this business. I want to evacuate them from this chamber and try to settle them down."

"Of course, of course, Prioress, do what you must," Father Bernard answered absently, waving the white surplice dazedly. "Clearly we cannot say mass here this morning. Perhaps you can engage the sisters in some other way until we can cleanse this temple."

Sister Veronica's eyes lit up for an instant, as an idea had just come to her. "Rather than abandon the office of terce," she suggested, "I think it might be a calming diversion for the sisters to sing the office while promenading around the cloister!"

"Fine, fine," the priest answered, still not taking his eyes from the dangling head. "Excellent… piety." Though by the time he'd spoken the last word the prioress had started back up the aisle and was waving her charges out of the choir.

"So, does anybody recognize 'im?" Thorvald asked, gazing into what still looked to be the terrified face on the hanging object.

"Willie," came the answer from the parishioner pressing closest to the dwarf. He was the best dressed of the knot of worshippers, wearing an expensive-looking blue linen surcoat and hood and fine leather boots turned over at the calf and tied up the inside. And striped hosen, in the latest fashion, which Thorvald could not help staring at. Blue and brown stripes, he thought. What will they think of next?

"Willie?" Friar Tuck repeated. "And who is, or was, this Willie?"

"Just Willie of Worksop, is how people around here knew him," said the priest. "Local tinker. Not the best at his trade, it has to be said. Always seemed a bit hard up for two pence to rub together. Most people figured it was because he was too lazy to put much into it."

"All that's true so far as it goes," said the man in the blue surcoat. "But Willie did do a monthly circuit among the nearby towns, and that's probably why nobody missed him."

"Missed him?" Tuck asked.

"I mean, it's why no one was able to identify the body found in the woods," the man continued. "Nobody seemed to be missing locally, so we thought—or at least, the magistrate thought—it must have been somebody passing through, a stranger. But nobody would have missed Willie. He lived by himself and was often gone on his circuit."

"This, by the way, is the priory's bailiff, John Bryce," Father Bernard made the belated introduction.

"Friar Tuck," Tuck said. "And this is my companion, Thorvald. So we are assuming, then, that this head belongs to the dismembered body found here last week. Can you tell me, sir bailiff, how well did you know this Willie?"

Bryce scowled down at the dwarf as if he were watching a carnival performer, then continued to address himself to Tuck. "Willie rented a small hovel on the priory's grounds, and I collected his rent each month. It was but two pence a month, but there were times he was hard put to come up with that much. Lazy, as Father Bernard said. And a notorious womanizer."

"Now, now, John," Father Bernard felt the need to step in. "You know he'd had some sorrow in his life. He'd lost his wife before he moved here, what, some ten years ago. Always said he loved the woman and would never get over her."

Now one of the women, a middle-aged buxom brunette dressed in a much simpler gray tunic, spoke up. "Never stopped him from flirtin' an' worse with anybody'd give him the time o' day, though, did it?"

One of the younger women, an attractive redhead with bright green eyes, who was turning a bright shade of crimson to match her hair, balked at that, and blurted out, "How do you know *that*, Elizabeth? He pestered you, then, did he?"

"Pestered you call it, Meggie? Aye, that he did. But I didn't encourage him, that's the difference."

"What are you saying!" a large, burly man, with a bald pate and rough wool tunic in brown that Tuck noticed smelled vaguely of grease. "Elizabeth Liptrot, watch your tongue, or it'll be tomorrow's breakfast."

Tuck and Thorvald instinctively backed away from what seemed to be a long-running local enmity, and Father Bernard stepped in to attempt to throw oil on the waters.

"Peace! Peace in God's house!" the priest cautioned. "I know we're all tense and irritable because of this monstrous crime that's been brought so literally to our doorstep. But there is no call to be turning on each other!"

John Bryce took the opportunity to take over the conversation once again. "Yes, we've heard the story of how his wife was drowned in the River Ryton whilst he was living in some other town in the area, and how that drove him to drink and all. But that's just what we know from *him*. He was likely an idle drunk before that and just used it as an excuse. You all know my own dear wife Barbara died half a dozen years ago, but you don't see me falling apart over it."

"Yes, well, you do have her namesake left to remind you of her, at least," the priest said. "That must be some comfort, more than Willie had, I'm afraid."

"Such comfort as I can get from that quarter," Bryce shrugged. "Now that she's joined the nunnery here, I seldom see her."

Father Bernard let that pass, and in the pause Friar Tuck posed another question. "Why do you think the killer would have hung the head here, specifically in this corner of the chapel? Is it meant as a message? If so to whom? The nuns themselves? The parishioners? To you, perhaps, Father Bernard?"

While the priest frowned and shook his head, Bryce looked

about to speak again, when a smaller man who'd been standing nearby spoke up. "Well the folks who congregate here in this corner pretty much every Sunday are the ones congregating here right now," he said, his short cropped brown hair sticking up like bristles on his narrow head. He was a man probably in his mid-thirties, with a face like a sword blade, ending in a sharp nose flanked by scowling grey eyes. A woman an inch or two taller than he was stood meekly at his elbow, her hair covered with a linen wimple and her broad, bovine face staring dully up at the gory sight above them. "There's me and Hulga…"

Father Bernard whispered to Tuck, "That's the priory's baker Oswald and his wife."

The baker continued, "And then there's Master Bryce there, and Elizabeth…"

"The laundress, Elizabeth Liptrot, you've already heard from," Bernard whispered to Tuck.

"And Cook there with his wife and son and of course the daughter…"

"That's Ralph the cook, and you've heard from Meggie the girl, and the son there John and wife Margaret," came the priest's whisper.

"And who else is there?" Oswald the baker looked around at some of the rest of the crowd still pushing in to see what could be seen.

"Well," Bryce put in, seizing back his chance, "there's the old Widow Day, but she's been laid up with a fever all week, so she's not here today."

"And Kate from Worksop," said an older woman from farther back in the crowd. "She comes to mass here because she doesn't like the Vicar at the Canons…"

"She comes here because she works for the nuns and has a room here outside the nuns' lodgings," Father Bernard corrected her. Then looking at Tuck added, "Kate is the dairy-woman. Young unmarried miss, her parents keep dairy cows for the canon's priory in town."

"She's already gone," said Margaret, the cook's wife, who was trying to fan her daughter, who had come near to fainting and was seated on the floor with her head in her hands while her brother, his arms folded in disgust, stood over her scowling. "That Kate took one look at that thing hanging there are screamed and ran out of here like she'd seen a ghost. She might be all the way back to Worksop by now."

"Any reason to believe that this head here was meant to be some kind of warning to any of you?" Tuck asked again.

"None," came the gruff and decided answer from the burly cook Ralph. No one else in the crowd bothered—or dared—to contradict him.

"Besides," added the baker Oswald, "what business is it of yours, friar? Who put you in charge here? Why don't you keep your nose where it belongs, anyway?"

Tuck held up his hands in surrender. It was true that he had no real business here except his own burning curiosity about this murder, but he recognized he was being far too inquisitive for a stranger in town. Father Bernard put a hand on Tuck's shoulder and tried to ease the tension. "Now, now," he purred. "No call to be uncivil. Our new friend here is just trying to make sense out of this bizarre scene he's stepped into."

"Aren't we all?" asked Bryce again. "I certainly had no liking for Willie, but I never thought or expected to see his head hanging there so raw and ghastly."

"Seems like this Willie was not well-liked by anybody 'ereabouts," Thorvald said, letting his own curiosity loose now that Tuck's had been shut down.

"Bloody right he wasn't," Ralph the cook stated bluntly. "I

don't reckon any man here knew him all that well, and them as knew him at all didn't care much for what they *did* know."

At that, Thorvald noticed Bryce, Oswald, and young John all nodding their heads. Though there was an ironic sort of smirk on Elizabeth Liptrot's face that made Thorvald wonder whether the women of the parish felt the same way.

"Oh, now, *de mortuis nil nisi bonum decendum est*, as they say in Rome," Father Bernard coaxed. "Say nothing but good of the dead. Poor Willie isn't here to defend himself, and can certainly do no one any more harm, so let us leave it at that."

There was a bit of grumbling at that, but there were no more grumblings about the victim's character, at least for that morning. And since the girl Meggie seemed to have regained her stamina and was now standing, leaning on her brother, Father Bernard thought it a fitting time to dismiss what was left of his congregation. Tucking the surplice he was still holding under his arm to better gesture with his hands, he began, raising his voice to soar above the buzzing of the crowd that still pushed in the chapel's door, "Now you can see, we cannot possibly perform mass today in this chapel. The head must hang until the magistrate arrives to see the situation, but then it will be cut down immediately. We expect to return to strict canonical hours certainly by this afternoon. For now, go home and pray for the soul of this poor victim, whom we knew as Willie of Worksop. Go now…"

And as he spoke those words, the priest shooed his parishioners from the chapel like so many chickens. As the last of them slowly ambled out the chapel door, he raised his eyes to Friar Tuck and said in a low voice, "And once George Crisp has seen this outrage, we will have the head cut down and reunite it with poor Willie's body. And we will give him true Christian burial together, my good friar, you and I."

* * *

"Right. Willie it is. Cut him down, then," George Crisp, the local magistrate, waved a hand listlessly and sighed. "I suppose this case is solved, then."

He was a corpulent man who moved as if it were an effort for him to breathe. His hair was dark and brown and long, and his moist brown eyes drooped like a bloodhound's, as, for that matter, did his jowls. He apparently was a man of some substance, Tuck decided, since his olive green surcoat appeared to be made of pure samite, and it was girdled by a fine leather belt studded with brass, from which hung a heavy-looking purse. The friar couldn't help but consider what a boon it would be if the bandits of Sherwood might catch this fellow coming down the Great North Road sometime. But he quickly chastised himself for such a thought, and determined to give himself some penance later on.

But he couldn't quite be sure he heard the magistrate correctly. "I beg your pardon, Master Magistrate, I thought I heard you say something about the case being closed?"

"Of course it is," Crisp said, rubbing his red nose with his sleeve as he watched Thorvald climb a rope he had thrown over the chapel's rafters to reach poor Willie's suspended head and stretch toward it with a knife to cut the rope from which it hung. "Now we know whose headless corpse we found in the woods. Mystery solved." He shrugged, then added, "Quite an acrobat, your little dwarf there. You wouldn't consider selling him, would you?"

Sidetracked from his questions by the magistrate's tactless rudeness, Tuck was unable to close his mouth for a few moments, until the diplomatic priest stepped in. "Thorvald is of free yeoman stock, Master Crisp. He is the friar's companion, not his servant."

The magistrate's eyebrows shot up in surprise, and he murmured, "That so? My, my, what won't people think of next. Well, my work here is complete. I suppose you can bury the fellow now, Father." He waved his flaccid hand at the young page Geoffrey to have him go outside to bring the magistrate's horse over to the door so he would not have to walk far to climb on his back. Then he sighed again. "I suppose I'll have to send some sort of report to Nottingham. Let the sheriff and that fellow, what's his name, Grisbone? Let them know what's happened here. Well, I can just tell my clerk what to write."

"Gisbourne," Friar Tuck spoke through gritted teeth.

"I beg your pardon?" Crisp drawled.

"Sir Guy of Gisbourne you mean. He is currently the Crown's representative in Nottingham."

"Yes of course, now I recall," sad Crisp, stifling a yawn.

"Watch yer 'eads!" Thorvald shouted from the rafters, and a second later Willie of Worksop's severed head thudded to the floor of the chapel. The magistrate, shrinking in disgust as the object fell at his feet, gave it a slight kick to roll it toward the wall.

"But Master Crisp, surely you cannot simply leave this matter as it is," Friar Tuck cajoled. "You know who the dead body is now, of course. But you don't know who it is that killed him or mutilated his body! Surely that is the task the Crown expects you to devote some effort to!"

The magistrate blinked and looked at the friar with genuine surprise. "What, you mean find out who killed him? I? And how am I supposed to do that, Master Friar? I mean, nobody saw it happen, did they? Nobody missed him, and nobody came forth since his killing to claim the body or say who they think might have done such a deed. Ergo, passing travelers killed him, no doubt, long gone out of this part of the country by now, you can be sure. Unless, of course, it's as folks are saying, and it was some avenging ghost or demon that did this. And I don't want any part of *that*, I can tell you."

"Am I to understand, then, that you've no interest in bringing the perpetrator of this heinous crime to justice?"

"My good friar, I am not a seer. When a culprit is known, I punish him. When I have no means of knowing who the culprit is, I depend on God to make his justice manifest. Doesn't your Saint Job say, 'Doth God pervert judgment?' or 'doth the Almighty pervert justice?'" And with that, Master Crisp began his slow amble to the chapel door, hearing his horse stamping outside.

"I'm familiar with the scripture," Tuck answered drily. "But I note that God often needs to use people to bring his will about in the world. Master Magistrate!" Now Tuck raised his voice and stepped toward the door, to try to catch the fellow before he rode off. "Have you any objection to my asking questions around the village and environs? See if I can find out something for you that might reveal the murderer? I have some experience in this sort of thing!"

"Do as you like, Master Friar," the magistrate sighed before riding off. "It'll be fruitless, I'm sure, but if you fancy it, go right ahead."

Tuck, Thorvald, and Father Bernard stood speechless, staring after the retreating back of the magistrate, until the lad Geoffrey asked, "Shall I put Bayard back in the stable, then, Father? You'll not be needing him again?"

"Ah, quite right, my boy, quite right," said Father Bernard, startled out of his reverie and, as an afterthought, handing the boy his surplice again. "Return the old fellow to his home stall and give him a rest."

As Geoffrey took the horse away, Thorvald let out a low whistle and said, "Now that fella's one I think yer John Brice 'ld probably call 'idle,' wouldn't ya say, Father?"

Bernard gave an amused snort and nodded his head, while Tuck burst out, "Well if that's what passes here for a representative of the Crown, I'd be surprised if justice were ever done in this part of Nottinghamshire!"

Father Bernard slowly nodded his agreement to that comment as well. "I told you he was no great lord, but merely the old king's appointed sergeant. He's granted the Manor of Worksop, the largest estate in the area, on condition that he perform this service. He can't serve as a knight, and has no title, but he has some wealth by virtue of having the assignation of land, and in exchange, as sergeant, has this duty to act as 'keeper of the peace' in this district. You've just seen how well he does it."

"It never ceases to amaze me," Friar Tuck mused, "how great a portion of God's earth is given into the charge of those least likely to keep it well."

"Another way o' saying' the rich ain't worth the firewood it'd take to send their ashes to 'ell?" Thorvald suggested.

"Perhaps somewhat more colorful than the way I'd have put it, Thorvald," Tuck said. "But our Lord once said that it was easier for a camel to go through the eye of a needle than for a rich man to enter Heaven. That might be a way of saying the same thing."

Thorvald asked, "What's a camel?"

"What I want to know," Father Bernard said, looking at his two guests quizzically, "is what exactly you meant when you told Crisp that you had some experience in the way of tracking down perpetrators of crimes. Is this true? Do you have any ideas on how to track this one down?"

Friar Tuck colored a little at this characterization. "Well, I didn't mean to dress myself in borrowed robes," he said modestly. "But it is true that last year I... that is, *we*," and here Tuck gestured toward Thorvald, not to diminish *his* role in the matter, "we, uh, were involved in the events that brought to light the abduction of the countess of Chesterfield, finding where she was hidden and finding, as well, the murderer of her uncle, Lord Peveril."

Thorvald scoffed at the friar's boast, and rolled his eyes, demonstrating just how much he thought Tuck was stretching the point. The priest, however, looked impressed, then thoughtful. "Some rumor of those events did find its way even into this forgotten corner of the world," he said. But then added, "But I thought I had heard that those marvels had been brought about by Rob… uh, that is, by a certain band of outcasts of Sherwood Forest. Perhaps they would not appreciate their reputation diminished by the claims of a wandering curtal friar?" The priest gave Tuck a hint of a smile. In truth, he didn't know just what to make of the friar's pretension, but if he really *was* a part of Robin Hood's band, the priest wanted to assure him that he'd not betray the secret.

"Right," Thorvald said. "An' we want no squabbles with them folk, so let's just say we 'elped where we could and leave it at that."

"Quite, quite," said the priest, more than ready to drop the subject. "But tell me, good Friar, what did you mean about asking questions hereabout? Do you have some sort of plan as to how to go about finding this 'culprit,' as the good Master Crisp calls him? What kinds of questions do you think to ask? And where will you start with your asking?"

Tuck wrinkled his brow and sighed. He hated to think it, but at the moment he was wishing Robin Hood and some of his cleverer lads, like Will Stutely and Alan a Dale, were with him now, with their quick wits to complement what he knew to be his own plodding competence. He had a feeling they would be brimming over with ideas. But for now, it was just him and Thorvald—a pair of plodders, he thought—to look at this mystery. And where to begin?

"I'd say start wi' the women," Thorvald volunteered. And Tuck saw immediately where his friend was going.

"Right!" he exclaimed. "The men were doing most of the talking in that group around the bloody head. And they were essentially dismissive. They didn't like this Willie, and seemed pretty convinced they weren't going to miss him. The women were less eager to condemn him."

"Except that laundress wench, what's 'er name again?"

"Elizabeth," the priest helped. "Elizabeth Liptrot. Yes, she's the biggest gossip in the neighborhood. She's certainly worth talking to."

"And there was the wife of the baker and the wife of the cook," Tuck recalled.

"Hulga, and Margaret," the priest clarified. "And of course Meggie, the cook's daughter."

Tuck squinted, trying to remember everyone. "And there was also the Widow Day, and the other young woman, Kate the dairy maid, who screamed and left when she saw the hanging head. I think we definitely ought to talk to her. If the head was hung there for the express purpose of scaring the bloody life out of somebody in that group that gathers at that spot for mass, then somebody there knows the reason."

"But," Thorvald added. "You said yerself, Tuck, that it might just as well 'a been hung there to appall them nuns. In fact *they're* the ones that *'ad* to be there to see it, ain't they?"

"Absolutely right," Tuck said, rubbing his tonsured head anxiously. "I suppose we are going to need to talk to the nuns as well."

"And there are only a couple dozen of them," Father Bernard added, tongue in cheek.

"So, I'm beginnin' to understand why our good friend Master Crisp was so ready an' willin' to throw up 'is 'ands an' move on,"

Thorvald said. "More trouble than it's worth, some might say."

"The cause of justice is always worth pursuing," Friar Tuck said, a little too righteous for Thorvald's taste. Then he added, "As the Psalmist said, 'I know that the Lord will maintain the cause of the afflicted, and justice for the poor.' Well, this Willie looks to have been as poor as anybody here, and I want to see justice done."

"Willie was poor indeed," Father Bernard agreed. "But he was also thought to be something of a scoundrel around here. And what if what you find is that justice was done in the killing of him?"

Tuck shook his head. "Whatever he had done, as long as he lived there was a chance for him to atone for those things. To kill him is to take away any chance of that. To kill him this way was to kill his soul. That is not justice." Tuck paused, his face set in thought. "Well, Thorvald," he continued. "Perhaps I shouldn't have been so definite with John when we left, about being back within the week. It looks as if we may be staying here for a while yet."

The dwarf scowled. But he was glad, at least, that Tuck had not said "Little" John. It enabled the priest to continue to pretend he did not know they were a part of Robin's outlaw band.

CHAPTER FIVE

In the great red and white striped pavilion, which stood on one end of the spacious lawn before the city gates of Nottingham, Robin stood scratching beneath his faded red hood. The black henbane he had used to dye his naturally fair hair an ebony black was irritating his scalp and he longed to give his head a good wash after he'd thrashed all these other pretenders crowding the pavilion for the upcoming archery tournament. He also longed to remove the full black horsehair beard he was wearing, having shaved off his normal blonde Van Dyke to allow it to adhere better to his face, because it kept flying up into his eyes and nose and made him feel he needed to sneeze.

Nor were the bands of padding, which Ellen and Kitty and the rest of the outlaw band's women had wrapped around his midsection to make him look pot-bellied, designed to make him feel comfortable. He'd initially thought it would be enough to doff his Lincoln green garb and wear this old threadbare gray wool tunic and brown hosen, and come hooded to the tournament. Who would be looking for a Robin Hood dressed in such a manner? But the women insisted that if the sheriff had planned this whole contest for the sole purpose of trapping Robin, then every eye in Nottingham would be focused on every contestant, especially on the ones who were doing well in the shooting. And so the hair and beard must be as un-Robin like as possible. And as if that weren't enough, Will Stutely had talked him into the eyepatch. An archer blind in one eye was unlikely to compete well in such a tournament, and so he would be little scrutinized until and unless he actually began to draw away from the other contestants. But Robin made sure that the eyepatch went over his left eye, since the unimpaired vision of his right eye along the shaft of his arrows was absolutely necessary for his aim. Truth be told, he was likely to close his left eye anyway when competing, the better to focus his right.

For despite the irritation of his hair and beard, the discomfort of his padded torso, and the annoyance of his eye-patch, Robin was fairly certain he was the best archer in all of England, and expected to prove it today.

To his annoyance, however, there were several other blowhards in that competitors' refreshment tent who seemed to feel the same way about themselves. How could he suffer such egotistical fools to bray on about themselves, without putting them in their place? But no, humility, too, must be part of Robin's disguise, so he merely listened as he drank a cup of the complimentary ale the sheriff had provided in this pavilion for all the contestants—and there were now, by Robin's quick mount, something approaching forty.

The loudest, and vainest, of these self-aggrandizers was one Gill o' the Red Cap, the chief archer of Guy of Gisbourne's company from Nottingham Castle. He was stocky and muscular of build, broad of face, with nut-brown hair and, as you might expect, a red cap on his round pate. He was sauntering back and forth across the pavilion, sipping his ale and sizing up his competition. "Just wondering who I should bet on to come in second in this here tourney," he brayed loudly as he looked his competitors up and down. "You," he called out, stopping in front of a tall man with a quiver of arrows nearly a yard long, which had the narrow, armor-piercing heads meant for warfare rather than hunting. "You look like a soldier. Can you make those monster arrows hit anything?"

"Anything I aim them at," the tall fellow answered. He was dressed in a rather expensive-looking surcoat of green velvet worn over a fine tunic and hose. And he carried his nose quite high as he deigned to answer the guardsman. "So I'd stay in my good graces, if I were you!"

"Ho ho!" Gill o' the Red Cap cried, rubbing his hands together in glee. "Now here's a rival I can feel is worth beating! And what might they call you, soldier, when you're at home?"

"They might call me anything they like, but I'll only answer to Walter of Weybridge," came the tall fellow's reply.

"Well then, Walter of Weybridge, come drink with me if you're a man, and we'll exchange views of how badly I'm going to beat you in this here tournament!" Gill invited, good-humoredly.

But before Walter could answer, a gruff young fellow with Nordic-looking blond hair and bulging biceps protruding from a sleeveless blue-dyed tunic growled, "You may beat *him*, as badly as you want, but nobody here is likely to come close to me in dis competition. Hall of da Mill dey call me. I don't reckon dere's anybody in dis tent as hasn't heard of da arrows I rained down on dem Scots who tried to sack the priory at Lindisfarne last year. Yah, dat was me. And any of you really think you're going to beat me?"

"Well I ain't heard of ya," spoke up another. "I musta been too busy knockin' the eyes outta sparrows at fifty paces, practicin' for my more serious job o' shooting fleas off dogs at a hundred yards."

"Damn, you must kill a lot of dogs that way," Gill answered him, to which the new speaker doffed his green silk cap and bowed low letting his long red locks scraped the tent floor.

"Adam o' the Dell of Tamworth Town," the redheaded man introduced himself as he rose from his deep obeisance to his full five feet six inches. "At your service. Can't say I expect a great deal of competition from any o' you boys. Except maybe Hall there. If he can rain arrows down single-handed, he must be a really fast bowman. But he never said if he ever hit anythin'."

"I be hitting you pretty soon by damn, if you keep up dat talk, yah," the Norseman answered.

"Now, boys, let's keep this civil, shall we?" tall Walter of Weybridge intervened. "Let's all go over to the fresh barrel they've just brought in, and have us another cup of ale, shall we? And lift it to pledge 'may the best man win.' Eh?" This suggestion was met with enthusiasm by a good number of the archers, and Robin made his way over unobtrusively to the fresh barrel and joined in the salute.

"May the best man win!" they cried in unison, after which not a few of them cried out, "and that's me!"

The drinking went on for some time, and many a man left the tent briefly to relieve his ballooning bladder, though Robin only sipped slowly at his cup. He didn't see how his aim might be improved any by an abundance of ale and reasoned rather that, if things went on this way for long, he may have no competition at all for the Golden Arrow prize. Indeed, some of these would-be champions might be hard put even to send an arrow in the right direction toward the target.

The contest was to begin promptly at sext, or so went the crying about the town the last day or so. There were minstrels entertaining the large crowd that had gathered around the green, and Robin knew that before the contest could begin, the sheriff would take the opportunity to say a few words of welcome and introduce his wife who was to present the golden prize. And at that point, the heralds would blow a fanfare on trumpets, and the actual competition would begin. But the minstrels were still entertaining. So he knew there was plenty of time. He stretched himself out on the tent floor to relax and watch his rivals.

By now, as might be expected after the lubrication of vocal cords by the application of ale, the men had passed from comparing the length of their arrows to speculating what the length of a man's arrow might say about the dimensions of various parts of his anatomy.

"You there, soldier," Gill cried, baiting Walter of Weybridge. "I'm wondering what the great size of your arrows is saying about you? Are ye compensating for particular shortcomings in other areas then?"

After the roar of laughter that greeted that pious sentiment, Walter smiled and answered, "There's many a former maid of Weybridge town can set you right on that score. That is, once they can walk straight again." Another explosion at that word. Walter continued, "But I'm wondering about all those arrows our friend Hall looses—is that because he's hoping just *one* of them finds his lady's proper target?"

"No worries dere, by damn!" Hall answered. "She can tell you how many times a night I can hit it, too!"

A number of ironic "Ooohs" and "Ahhs" met this declaration, until red-haired Adam pushed the mock abuse back to Gill again. "Now I can name the prettiest flower in all of Tamworth Town, and she's been mine a lyin' in the dell. Hair gold as the sun. Breasts fair as the mists of spring and lips like roses sweet with the mornin' dew. No names, but her father is keeper of the barbican at Tamworth Castle. Truth now, ya ever had any wench can compare?"

The conversation having taken a semi-serious turn, Gill o' the Red Cap stroked his chin, but his half-smile suggested he knew precisely how he would answer. "Hair russet as a wild fox, and a face so fair it rivaled the glow of her hair when she blushed. Turned-up nose with a sprinkle of freckles like glitter scattered by the sun. Sweet mouth fresh as apples in the autumn. I had her, yes I did!" that last to put down a few unromantic scoffers. "I had her not two months ago, up north on the other edge of Sherwood. She had summat to do with the Benedictine Priory up there at Wallingwells."

"What? A nun you're sayin'?" Adam now scoffed.

"I'm not saying a nun," Gill answered. "Maybe she worked for the nuns. Or her parents did, or something. *Coulda* been a nun, though, I reckon, out of her habit. Poverty, chastity, and obedience, eh boys?" he shouted now, and the others guffawed. "Well, there's at least one of those vows she didn't keep!"

Robin had only been half-listening to all of this, but he did catch the reference to Wallingwells, and was about to ask what had brought Sir Guy's head bowman into that territory at that point in time, when his outlaw band was wintering in the neighborhood, when three loud blasts of a dozen trumpets sounded, announcing the beginning of the tournament.

On the meadow that lay outside the city walls, bright green with spring and dotted here and there with wildflowers, a great space was roped off. On Robin's left were three rows of benches stretching from the large pavilion along the wall some two hundred yards, on which were seated the petty nobility and the richer merchants of Nottingham town and its environs, dressed in their finest clothes, the better to see and be seen. On Robin's right, behind the rope that framed the shooting range, were the poorer artisans, peddlers, and laborers of the city, the free yeoman and the villeins of the countryside, dressed in the simple, everyday tunics, hoods, and hose that in many cases were their only suits of clothes. It was a holiday in Nottingham, and the town was hopping with the booths of traveling merchants, acrobats, jugglers, and minstrels.

Robin scanned the front row of commoners on his right, and glimpsed a gray-hooded Little John, holding his quarterstaff before him on the grass, and not far behind him, standing and leaning on a staff of his own as if it were a walking stick, was Will Scarlet, dressed in a red hood that matched his name. Neither outlaw wore the Lincoln green known to be the livery of Robin's meinie, and both kept their faces well shadowed by their hoods. Robin knew that farther off, on the other side of the city gates and a furlong or two into the woods, Much the miller's son waited with four horses, in case it turned out that the outlaws would need to bid a hasty adieu to Nottingham town before, during, or after the tournament. Robin had brought only those three men with him. Stutely had begged to come, but Little John wouldn't hear of it. Having been a guest in Sir Guy's dungeons, he was sure to be recognized by somebody, and John had no desire to risk his neck again to save Stutely's. Robin would not hear of a large entourage: It would be much easier to slip in and out of Nottingham with just a few cohorts than with a whole gang, any one of whom might be arrested. The fewer he brought with him, the fewer he would need to keep track of.

Of course, there was some deep consternation at the outlaw camp, with Sir Palomides, in particular, expressing concerns that to have Robin and his men off on a dangerous lark in one direction while they still had heard nothing from Tuck and Thorvald in the other direction was spreading their resources too thin. And others had agreed. Robin had mollified them somewhat by promising that as soon as he returned from the archery contest—from which he promised to return in a single day, and to bring with him the arrow of pure beaten gold—he would himself lead a group north to the edge of Sherwood to seek friar and dwarf in Worksop.

But he knew winning that arrow would be much more difficult if he let his mind dwell on anxieties like the whereabouts of

Friar Tuck and his companion. The allusion by Gisbourne's man Gill o' the Red Cap to having been in Wallingwells within the past two months had lit that nagging fire he felt in the back of his neck when he knew there was something to worry about somewhere. He tried to loosen his muscles, letting his arms sag and moving his weight from foot to foot. He moved his head in a circle to ease the tension in his neck. Looking once more far up the shooting range, he thought it curious that he could not see any butts or straw targets for the archers to aim at and wondered where the targets were. He also noticed that a good hundred and fifty yards distant on the left side, a raised dais stood on which sat John of Oxford, High Sheriff of Nottingham City, dressed ostentatiously (and well above his station) in a purple samite jerkin, while at his right sat his wife, Lady Maude Peveril, cousin of the Duchess of Chesterfield and his one-time lover, in a tasteful gown of blue silk, smiling gaily and clearly enjoying her birthday celebration. On the sheriff's other hand, Robin recognized Sir Guy of Gisbourne, wearing armor to remind the spectators of his position as captain of the king's guard at Nottingham Castle. Over the armor was a surcoat bearing the Gisbourne coat of arms: on a field *or*—that is, gold—a sable lion rampant. Not that Robin could actually make the device out at this distance, but he knew the crest without having to see it. And once again his mind drifted to Thorvald and Friar Tuck and the possible danger they might be in.

But a loud voice was interfering with his thoughts just now, a voice calling, "Hodden? Hodden of Barnesdale? Is there a Hodden here? Speak up, Hodden of Barnesdale, or be disqualified!"

With a jolt Robin remembered that *he* was Hodden of Barnesdale—at least, that was the name he had given the heralds when he had entered the contest. He'd been so lost in his thoughts that he hadn't realized what was going on around him.

"Hodden? Here, yes, Hodden of Barnesdale, that's me," he called out to the herald, trying to speak in a hoarse and rasping voice, the better to disguise his own.

"Group Four!" the herald barked, then handed Robin a wooden disc with the number "34" burned into it. The disc hung from a leather thong. "Wear that," the herald commanded, then ordered, "Give me one arrow from your quiver." Robin did as he was told, and the herald, all business, drove the point of the arrow through a scrap of parchment that also bore the number "34." A second herald, carrying a thin bound manuscript, scratched a "34" next to the name "Hodden of Barnesdale" where they had written it in the book when he'd registered.

"It's so's they can tell which arrows belong to which shooters when they check the target," a voice said behind Robin's left shoulder, so close it nearly made him jump.

Recovering quickly, Robin turned to see a stoop-shouldered yeoman in a clean but worn gray tunic and green hose. He was studying Robin with kindly hazel eyes set in a clean-shaven face that was also worn, by at least sixty winters, Robin judged. "You're Hodden of Barnesdale," he said. "I'm called Jock o' Barlborough. I saw your mind was elsewhere—first time in the big city? The pomp and circumstance of the great ones, and the pageantry of the fairs in these towns, can be a bit bedazzling if you're seeing 'em for the first time."

"Yes—Jock was it?—dazzling's the word for it," Robin replied in his affected rasp. He also began to slouch a bit, taking his cue from the old fellow. It would do his disguise no harm if he also seemed to be shorter in stature than that notorious woodsman, Robin Hood. Then he added, "Group four the herald said? What's that? I guess I wasn't paying attention."

"No," Jock said. "You were in your daze. Look now, they've divided all the contestants into four groups, with ten archers in each group. You can see, I'm '33,' I'm in the same group as you," and he held out his own wooden disc hanging from his neck. "They must be having all ten of each group shoot at once, and so they need to be able to tell whose arrow is whose."

"I can see where that makes sense," Robin said. "But what are we shooting *at*? Where are the targets?"

"Ah, you must not've heard the heralds that were crying the news about the town the last two days."

"Heralds?" Robin said, a bit bewildered. "Crying? No, I just got to Nottingham this morning, I haven't heard any news."

"This here is to be a clout tournament," Jock told him. "See that short stake a-comin' out of the ground out yonder, right across from the dais where the sheriff and his lady are sittin'? That's the center of the clout." Robin squinted down the lawn, and saw a red stake about an inch in diameter, protruding above the grass about two feet.

Clout shooting. Robin groaned inwardly. He had heard of this newfangled fashion by which military archers were training nowadays—training to "rain down arrows" on an enemy force, as the Norseman Hall of the Mill had put it. The clout was a white cloth target perhaps a yard in diameter, with a black center maybe a foot wide. It was placed level on the ground and held in place by small stakes on four corners, and this large red stake in the very center of the black—which gave the archers something to aim at. A white circle was painted on the grass around the clout, which formed the outside border of the target. The entire target area was thus perhaps three yards in diameter, with the white of the clout a yard wide in the center, and the black a foot wide in the center of that.

Robin knew he was the best archer in England when it came to straight shooting at a target. If you didn't believe it, all you had to do was ask him. He had little knowledge of clout shooting, though, and no experience of it at all. He knew that military archers like Gisbourne's Gill and the Viking Hall of the Mill, and the green-coated soldier Walter of Weybridge, would have the advantage in a tournament such as this, and perhaps Gisbourne had even prevailed upon the sheriff to set up the tournament this way to give his man Gill a leg up. Hmmph, Robin thought, Sir Guy probably has a good sum of money wagered on his man. Well, he'd see if he couldn't disappoint the Captain of the Castle. But if things were arranged to ensure Robin's defeat here, then what of the sheriff's plan to catch the outlaw prince of Sherwood? In such a tournament, he might actually be among the anonymous company of also-rans, among whom the sheriff could not possibly know which he was.

Robin shook off those thoughts and concentrated on listening to the chief herald, who was now standing atop a wooden platform that stood before the door of the great tent, and addressing the assembly in a booming voice.

"Let all those who mean to compete in this tournament step forward and hear the rules that shall govern these games," the fellow boomed, and Robin and the other archers pressed close to the platform to be sure not to miss a syllable. "In the first round, archers shall shoot in groups of ten. All must shoot from behind the white line here before the pavilion. The clout is staked precisely one hundred and fifty yards from that line." Robin hadn't noticed it before but now saw that a thin white line had been painted on the lawn, from the benches on the left to the rope that barred the commoners from the field on his right. "Each man in each group of ten shall shoot a single arrow on my command. On that single shot will depend your advancement to the next round! When all four groups of ten have taken their shot, then the ten whose arrows landed closest to the center of the clout shall advance to the next round!"

This felt like a blow to Robin's chances. Since he was not used to aiming at a clout, he would have liked a few practice shots before risking all on a single chance. From the grumbling all around him, he was fairly certain that most of the other archers felt the same way about this particular rule. Only Gill, Walter, Hall, and a few other military men seemed pleased by the announcement. In his ear, old Jock whispered, "Well, that's a blow to some of you. As a veteran of a war or two myself, I've probably got an advantage here. You?"

"Well," Robin admitted. "I've been to battle with the old king years ago. But that was shooting at an armed camp full of the enemy, not at a single target a yard wide. Nor've I practiced at all with the clout."

"Aye, you're definitely at some disadvantage then," Jock said. Then, more cheerily, "but not so much as if you'd never been in battle! Perk up, boy. I'll give you what help I can."

"Much appreciated," Robin answered, though what he was really thinking was, "Great. I'm going to be advised by this old penniless veteran who's probably got to beg his meals." But the herald had continued:

"In the second round, the ten archers who came closest to the mark with their first shot will each take two shots at the target. The three archers whose best shot comes closest to the mark will survive into the final round!" Robin felt somewhat better at this. He could get the feel of things with two shots. If he could get past that first round, then he would feel that he truly had a chance to win.

"The three finalists competing in the championship round," the chief herald called forth, "will each have three shots at the mark. These will be loosed one at a time, alternating among the three archers. The archer who puts his closest shot nearest the mark shall be named champion of the tournament, and will receive the golden arrow from the hands of the sheriff's lady herself!" And with that pronouncement, Robin saw Lady Maude stand and hold aloft what looked to be a solid gold arrow—though at this distance one could hardly be sure.

"Group number one, prepare yourselves and step up to the mark!" said the herald. And at that word, thirty of the archers backed up toward the tent door, while the designated first ten strung their bows and stepped forward, eyeing the distant red stake that marked the center of the target, testing the wind, planting their feet to ensure sound footing, and by eye and feel gauging the precise angle at which the arrow must be fired in order to come down exactly one hundred and fifty yards from the spot on which they stood. Those that had not already done so were fastening bracers on the inside forearm of the hand with which they would grip the bow. Such armguards protected the bow arm from painful bruising by released bowstrings. Robin took the opportunity to strap on his own leather bracer, noting as he did so that Gill o' the Red Cap, who would be shooting in the first group, wore an expensive armguard made of horn, carved with what looked, from his vantage point, like the rampant lion of the Gisbourne coat of arms. A gift from Sir Guy to his champion archer? Robin had no doubt.

"It's our luck to be shooting last," old Jock said quietly. "We can observe how the weather conditions will be affecting the flight of the arrows, you see. Watch, when they fire, what happens aloft!" Robin probably would have realized himself how significant the wind was with such shooting, though it hadn't immediately occurred to him. He was used to shooting straight and true at a nearer target, and when an arrow whistled like that at closer range only a strong gale would affect its flight. But here, when the arrow must fly in an arc over a space of four hundred and fifty feet, even a slight breeze might alter its course by several degrees.

"Right…" Robin said, drawing the word out thoughtfully, as the first group stepped up to the line. He found Gill o' the Red Cap in the group and resolved to watch him, and his single arrow, to show him how to set up his own first shot.

Gill tested the direction of the wind by holding up his right finger, then kicked his right foot against the earth to ensure his footing was solid.

"Group one at your mark!" called the herald. All ten men toed the line with their front foot. "On my call! Now, nock!" Each of the bowmen notched an arrow in his bowstring.

"Mark!" called the herald, and each bowman held out his bow arm and, looking down the shaft of his arrow, took aim at the red stake.

"Draw!" At that word, the bowmen drew back their bowstrings while holding their aim, and then each bent backward in order to elevate the bow to achieve the proper arc. Robin studied closely the angle at which Gill raised his bow and tried to make a mental note of the bow's position, the better to duplicate it when his own turn came.

"Loose!" cried the chief herald, and ten arrows flew upwards toward the clout. Robin watched the arrows closely, keeping his eye particularly on Gill's, and noted that there was enough of a breeze coming from the left to force all of the arrows a few degrees to the right. At one hundred and fifty yards, those few degrees would make a considerable difference.

There was a kind of beauty to the arc made by those arrows, and their collective plunge as they dipped toward the target. Some applause at the other end of the shooting range made it clear there had been some excellent results from the shooting, and immediately the two heralds who had been assigning numbers to the contestants and collecting sample arrows from them rushed out from the sidelines to see which arrows had come closest to the center of the clout. After several minutes, they ran back to the chief herald to report their findings. He announced, "Results of the first group: two archers hit the black—those would be Gill o' the Red Cap and Thomas of Southwell, each four fingers from the stake. Two others hit the white—Jack of Newark and Roger Rolle. Jem of Scarborough Castle, William White, and John o' the Glen landed within the outer circle. Three others missed altogether and are therefore out of consideration for the next round. Group two, ready yourselves!"

There were a few grins and a few more groans of disappointment as ten new competitors moved into position to try their skills. A grinning Gill raised his red cap to the other competitors and to the cheering spectators, and gloated to Walter of Weybridge, who was stepping up to the line as part of the new group, "See that, soldier boy? Match it if you can! I told you I was the one to beat here!"

The green-coated archer paid little attention to Gill's boasts, so focused was he upon the task at hand. His face was stone cold as he strung his bow and glared ahead at the distant red stake. Once more the chief herald called "Nock! Mark! Draw! Loose!" and ten new arrows made their graceful arc from bow to sky and down to clout. And once again the two judges gathered the arrows and examined their placement. Walter of Weybridge had been the only one of the ten who had hit the black, "three fingers from the stake," the chief herald declared—at which Walter looked back to where Gill stood and gave him a withering look. Five other contestants had hit the white and the other four had all been within the outer circle of the target. But it appeared that realistically, Walter was the only one of the ten likely to move into the next round. Robin felt a bit more confident now—he had studied both Gill and Walter's angle of trajectory, as well as how they had adjusted for the wind, and felt he had a sound idea of how to take his shot.

Adam o' the Dell of Tamworth Town and Hall of the Mill were both part of group three, and when that group had shot, they had done the best yet: Three of their number—Adam and Hall as well as a young boy of fifteen or so called Matt Straw—all hit the black, five others hit the white, and the last two had shot within the target's outer circle. "They've all been doing what you've been doing," Jock o' Barlborough spoke quietly in Robin's ear. "Studying what the first two groups did right—and did wrong. We've got an advantage going last. But that means everybody in this final group is going to be harder to beat than the folks in that earlier group."

"Thanks for building up my confidence," Robin said, with just a tinge of sarcasm. He took a sturdy hemp string and strung his six-foot yew bow. Slouching as he had been, the bow stood a few inches taller than him, even bent as it was now, but he would of course have to stand to his full height to aim and shoot, and hoped his stance would not give him away. He pulled out one of his light ash wood arrows, pointed with barbed steel arrowheads and fletched with three Lincoln-green-dyed goose feathers held in place by wax, and he waited for the herald's first cry to nock arrows.

When that first cry came he toed the line and notched his arrow, stealing glances at Jock out of the corner of his uncovered eye. When the command "Mark!" came, Robin looked down his arrow shaft with his right eye and pointed it straight at the red stake he could just see in the distance.

"Draw!" came the command, and Robin pulled back his string and elevated his bow at about a sixty-degree angle, as he'd seen Gill and Walter do. Then, glimpsing Jock on his right making a very slight adjustment to the left to account for the breeze, Robin did the same, then let the arrow fly when the herald called "Loose!"

Robin held his breath as he watched his arrow soar, winced slightly as he feared he may have overcompensated for the wind as the arrow appeared to be veering too far to the left, then sighed with relief when it curved back to the right as it reached the top of its flight and plunged downward toward the target. There was a great cry of delight from the crowd when the arrows struck home. And now Robin waited, his hand clenched around his bow and his breath coming in quick puffs, to hear the results of the round. He had done what he could to study those he knew were more familiar with this kind of target than he, but there was certainly an element of luck involved as well—his luck depending on whether the wind picked up or shifted; depending on whether the particular arrow he had shot was fletched and pointed well and perfectly; depending, indeed, on how well the other nine archers had shot, and how they measured up to the thirty who had shot previously. Finally, the field judges brought their results to the chief herald, who looked at them and nodded, then called out:

"Results of the final group of the first round are as follows: Three archers hit the black. They are Jock o' Barlborough—" at that, Robin's neighbor gave a triumphant but restrained "Yes!" and Robin smiled at him, happy for the old fellow's fortune. The herald continued, "Stephen Longshanks, and Rupert of the Vale." Robin's stomach dropped several feet. He had nearly forgotten what false name he had given, but he knew it was not one of those. With quick mental arithmetic, he counted nine contestants who had hit the black of the clout on this first shot. The tenth contestant in the second round would have had to be closer to the black than all other archers who had hit the white part of the clout. And that would take a wagonload of luck.

"Four other contestants hit the white—they are Arthur Wells, Andrew son of Bran, Hubert the Black, and Hodden of

Barnesdale." That was the name, Robin remembered. Well, at least he hadn't been completely humiliated. While the herald gave the names of the last three contestants, all of whom had shot within the outer circle of the target, Robin tried to add up all the archers who had hit the white of the clout. Seventeen, he told himself. Might as well be a thousand, he thought bitterly. There was just too much competition for him there. He was the best bowman in England, he remained sure, in shooting straight at a target, but this competition was too much to master, even for him, in a single shot. Still, he had done reasonably well. Now the chief herald was naming those ten archers who officially would move on to the second round:

"Gill o' the Red Cap, Thomas of Southwell. Walter of Weybridge, Adam o' the Dell of Tamworth Town, Hall of the Mill, Matt Straw, Jock o' Barlborough, Stephen Longshanks, and Rupert of the Vale," the herald pronounced, "all of whom hit the black. And the tenth archer to move on the round two is—" he carefully consulted the written text he'd been handed by the field judges, "Hodden of Barnesdale, whose shot to the white missed the black by only a single finger's width. Congratulations to you all, and we will have a brief pause before that second round begins for us all to refresh ourselves."

Robin could barely believe his luck, and his new friend Jock was pounding his back with joy as he looked, dazedly, into the crowd behind the rope barrier, to see Little John standing and cheering. "All right!" Robin said to himself. "Luck was certainly with me there. After that first round I can feel the range; let them try to catch me now!"

* * *

Well along the sideline on the left side of the archery field, upon the raised dais that overlooked the clout itself, Lady Maude Peveril squinted as she watched the distant contestants celebrating their good fortune at surviving the first round of this heady competition. They were too far away for her to recognize Robin Hood, but she suspected that he may not even be one of this exclusive set of archers. She knew he was not well practiced in this particular form of target, which was why she had suggested it to her husband in the first place. John of Oxenford had no particular interest in archery, and there was only one conceivable reason why he should suddenly be enthusiastic about holding a tournament in Nottingham: He wanted to set a trap for Robin Hood.

Oh how transparent was her husband. And how unimaginative. She guessed from the first that this was an idea Sir Guy of Gisbourne had put into his head, and consequently it was up to her, she figured, to make sure it went awry. Robin didn't have many friends among the better classes of Nottingham, but he did have her.

Though a married woman, Maude wore her luxuriant auburn hair free and unbound today: Under the conceit that she was, for her birthday, "Queen of the May," she was wearing a silver tiara studded with gems, which the sheriff had presented her with that morning. She knew it was not the sort of thing she could ever wear except on some very rare occasion like this, since under normal circumstances she should be wearing a fillet and barbette or something equally modest. But the sheriff was fond of showing off his wife as if she were some rich woven tapestry he'd just purchased to hang on his wall—something beautiful to show off his wealth. And so the tiara was really for him, not for her. And she knew it. And he knew she knew it. And as long as she let herself be brought out and put on display thus, he was content to let her lead her own life as freely as she dared. In the past, at least, Robin had been an occasional part of that.

So intent was Maude upon studying the group of archers that she nearly forgot the others with her on the dais. It was Guy of Gisbourne whose voice pierced her reverie. "No one can beat my own man, Gill o' the Red Cap. He is the best I've ever seen at clout shooting. But I suppose your Robin Hood may be among the others in this smaller group. Of course, I'm sure the stories of the outlaw's prowess with the bow are exaggerated, so he's not likely to join Gill among the final three. But what of these ten? Can you see your outlaw among them, sheriff?"

"How can I say?" the burley John of Oxenford, a head shorter than his friend, growled back into Gisbourne's pinched-looking face with its perpetual twisted sneer. "At this distance? Besides, he's certain to be wearing some kind of disguise."

"Of course he is," Maude muttered, annoyed at the inane conversation. "All we can say for certain is, Gill o' the Red Cap is not Robin Hood. And I think we can probably rule out the slender young lad, Matt Straw. It would take two of him to make a Robin."

"So what of the other eight?" the sheriff wondered. "Can we rule out the old gentleman, that Jock o' Barlborough?"

"That may be premature," Gisbourne shook his own long dark locks. "It would be a simple thing to whiten his hair and walk with a stoop. No, I'd say that an old man is just the kind of disguise it would be easy for the outlaw to assume. I would not rule the old fellow out."

It was precisely Maude's own reasoning. But Maude did have an advantage over her fellow spectators. She alone among them had actually seen Robin Hood shoot a bow. And change his face and physical appearance all he might, she did not think he could disguise his posture and the form of his shooting. She would watch very carefully the postures of these ten in the second round and, if she recognized Robin among them, would do her best to steer Sir Guy and the sheriff onto another candidate.

The ten surviving archers now lined up, toes to the mark, and looked again toward the clout. They had two shots apiece in this round, and would loose the arrows on the call of the herald, just as in the first round. Maude studied the physiques of each of the competitors. She knew Robin's well. Intimately, it must be admitted. And none of the archers remaining reminded her in any way of Robin's sleek, muscled torso. Perhaps that Walter of Weybridge in the green garb? But no. He was definitely taller than Robin, and one thing Robin could not have done to disguise himself was add inches to his height. Besides, Robin would not have made the mistake of coming dressed in his signature green. Hmm. That red-headed fellow, Adam o' the Dell of Tamworth Town, had something of Robin's bearing. And it might be easy to color his hair red for the day. But Adam looked too short to be Robin, and he was not slouching or slumping to make himself *appear* to be shorter. He really was that short. What about the last fellow in line, that Hodden of Barnesdale? He might be about the right height, though he had a deep slouch which, Maude reasoned could be deliberate in order to conceal his real size. And hair could be dyed. And a beard faked. But that paunch? No, this Hodden bloke was just too fat to be Robin Hood.

"Nock!" called the herald, and all ten archers notched their arrows. "Mark!" and they aimed at the target. "Draw!" now they drew back their bowstrings and elevated their bows. And Maude studied the posture of each man. When her eyes rested on Hodden of Barnesdale, she gave a slight gasp. "Loose!" the arrows flew. And Maude had a strong suspicion.

Before waiting for the field judges to examine the first set of arrows, the chief herald called for the archers to toe the line once again. There was no need to make any kind of determination until all the second arrows were loosed. Then the only thing for the field judges to do would be to collect the three arrows closest to the center of the black, and those would be the three finalists.

The ten archers stepped to the line, followed the herald's commands to "Nock! Mark! Draw!" And when Maude watched the posture and bearing of Hodden of Barnesdale a second time, she gave a thin smile of recognition and knew with absolute certainty that it was Robin Hood. And then she watched the last set of arrows fly.

* * *

When the judges had cleared the field, they collected three arrows, which had all been within four fingers of the center of the black circle on the clout. They belonged to Jock o' Barlborough, Gill o' the Red Cap, and the ever-more confident Hodden of Barnesdale. There was some disappointment among the spectators whose favorites did not advance to the final round—especially Walter of Weybridge, who had won over a great many admirers with his tall, handsome green figure, and red-haired Adam o' the Dell of Tamworth Town, who seemed to have brought all of Tamworth along to cheer him on. Gill o' the Red Cap was not a favorite, even though he was a local talent, Gisbourne's hirelings being tolerated but not especially trusted and certainly not loved by the local community. But Jock o' Barlborough had won over a lot of the crowd, especially those who wanted it well known that the older citizens of the shire were valued members of the community. As for Hodden of Barnesdale, he was a complete unknown before the tournament, and a surprise last-second addition to the second round, but those who liked to see the underdog triumph were definitely on his side. And if Jock was the hero of the old folks in the crowd, Hodden, with his all-too-visible paunch, was the hero of the rounder-bellied folks.

While Jock and Hodden were warmly congratulating one another, each delighted with his new friend's good fortune, the field judges approached them and had the three finalists draw lots to determine the order in which they would shoot in the final round. Then the chief herald made his final announcement:

"The championship round shall proceed this way: Each contestant will shoot three arrows. They will take these shots one at a time, and will do so in the following order, just established by lot: Jock o' Barlborough will shoot first; Gill o' the Red Cap second; and Hodden of Barnesdale third. Each will shoot at his own pace when I call his name. There will be three rounds in this last contest. One of the field judges will call out the positions of all three archers at the end of each round. When all shots have been taken, the man whose arrow is closest to the center of the clout will be declared the winner. Ready?"

All three archers answered in the affirmative, and when the herald called "Jock o' Barlborough!" Jock stepped to the line. He notched his arrow, aimed, raised his bow, and fired. Gill did the same when his name was called. Then Robin stepped up to the line as Hodden, and went through the same series of steps. But just as he loosed his first arrow, he felt the wind die down suddenly, and knew that he'd adjusted his aim too radically toward the left. At the end of the first round, the field judge called out to the assembled crowd, "Gill in the black, four fingers from the center. Jock also in the black, just on the edge. Hodden—in the outer circle."

There were audible groans from the crowd, not only from those pulling for Hodden, but from everyone who resented Sir Guy's bullying guards in Nottingham. Lady Maude Peveril smiled to herself. Hodden was out of danger, at least so far. If he was smart, he would lose at this point, and count himself victorious in having made the final round and still having avoided the sheriff's trap. Already the sheriff and Sir Guy were talking: Gill was obviously not Robin Hood. Could he be one of the other two contestants? Or was he one of the others from the second round who had not quite made it this far?

But the competition was not over yet. The herald called for the archers to stand for their second shots. Jock loosed his arrow, and seemed satisfied with the result. Gill loosed his, and when it came down there were stunned gasps from those close enough to see where it landed, and visible excitement among the field judges. Robin tried to ignore these reactions and concentrate on his own shot, and when he made it, he felt much better.

But when the field judge called out the positions of the shooters, it was clear things had taken an unfortunate turn. "All three archers landed in the black!" called the judge. "Jock o' Barlborough's arrow is five fingers from the center." A cheer went up. "Hodden of Barnesdale's is four fingers from the center!" Another small cheer rose from the crowd, but Robin knew this was not going to win—it only tied Gill's first shot. "And Gill o' the Red Cap…less than one finger from the center of the black." A roar went up from much of the crowd, though a chorus of groans formed an undertone to that cheer. It was an epic shot, the stuff of legend. But it had come from Gisbourne's man, and that caused a good number of spectators, especially among the lower classes seated at the right of the field, to get up and begin exiting the area. Why wait for a third shot? The competition was over.

That certainly was the attitude of Gill himself, who strutted about the whole area in front of the pavilion like a rooster among his hens waving to women in the audience and preening like the cock of the walk. On the dais, Sir Guy had leapt to his feet and shouted encouragement at his man, poking the seated sheriff all the while and saying, "I knew he could not be beaten. Yesterday

I laid a hundred mark wager at three-to-one odds! I should have had a wager with you on it as well! I'd have been a rich man! I couldn't lose!"

The sheriff looked sour and growled back, "Yes, Gisbourne, but now how are we to determine which one of these other bumpkins is the outlaw? Have I wasted my money on this silly tournament to get nothing in return?"

Sir Guy shrugged. "He must be here. My men are guarding all the roads out of Nottingham. They'll be stopping anyone who looks suspicious. I'm sure he'll not escape us this time."

"Ha. You're *sure*. You've been giving me the same assurances for a full year now. And what have we seen? You captured one of the villeins and couldn't even hang him. Spare me your boasts, until you've got something to show for them."

On the field, the herald was ready to begin the third round, though like everyone else in the vicinity he felt he was simply going through the motions for the sake of adhering to the letter of the law as far as the tournament rules were concerned. "Last round now. Jock o' Barlborough, take your shot!" Jock, determined to go out with dignity and show he was a worthy competitor, notched his arrow, took aim, elevated his bow, and loosed his arrow toward the target. He could see by the field judges' reaction that he'd made an excellent shot—though one not equal to Gill's mythic result. As for Gill, when his name was called he saw no point in trying to improve what could not be bettered. Instead, he decided to entertain the crowd with some clowning, and turned his back to the target and shot his arrow backward with his bow held over his head. The arrow fell a good hundred feet short of the target, and the spectators roared with laughter. By the time Robin stepped up for his last shot, almost no one was paying attention. But his name had been called, and he set to work. If Gill could pull off a shot like that, then clearly it could be done. And if it could be done, it could just as well be done by Robin as by the next man. He would focus all of his attention and all of his skill upon this shot, and if luck was on his side, there was still a chance for him.

He focused on notching his arrow perfectly on his bowstring. He concentrated on taking perfect aim at the red stake far down the shooting lane. He elevated his bow to what he now knew to be the perfect height for this distance. And as he began to draw the string back, he was conscious of every fluctuation in the moving air. Just as he had drawn the bowstring back to its utmost point, he felt the wind pick up. Instinctively, he adjusted his aim to account for that gust and loosed the arrow. It flew high into the breeze, sailing toward the left then hooking back to the right as the breeze carried it, plunging down and down toward the target until—Robin blinked a second to make sure he had seen what he thought he had seen—his arrow split the red stake at the clout's center in two.

After a moment's wonder a tremendous roar issued from those whose attention had still been on the contest. The field judges' mouths were wide open in disbelief, and those who had turned away from the competition in disgust or lack of further interest turned back, cursing themselves for having missed what might have been the greatest shot ever made in such a contest. And on the dais, Lady Maude was trying hard not to panic.

So astounded were his fellow archers at his miraculous feat, and so happy were most of them to see Gill o' the Red Cap get his comeuppance, that they surrounded Robin, and before he knew what was happening, Adam o' the Dell of Tamworth Town and Hall of the Mill had hoisted Robin onto their shoulders as he held up his bow in triumph, and they were bearing him toward the dais, where they expected to see him presented with the solid gold arrow by the sheriff's beautiful noble lady. The entire brace of archers trailed behind them, as well as some of the spectators from outside the roped barrier. Several of Gisbourne's guards were moving along that rope, trying to keep the crowd from overrunning the field in their enthusiasm.

The sheriff and Sir Guy were standing now, conferring with one another, and Maude could hear snatches of their conversation. "Is it the outlaw, do you think?"

"Who else could have made such a shot?"

"…clearly a disguise…"

"Call up my deputies…"

"…must be arrested on the spot. We'll see whether its Robin Hood in disguise or…"

Maude stood and smiled her sweet pasted-on beauty-queen smile and held out the golden arrow to present to the victor—who was carried toward her at the head of a crowd that threatened any second to deteriorate into an unruly mob. At the same time, from the corner of her eye she could see Gisbourne calling to four of his guards who were standing around the dais, and pointing toward the victorious Hodden of Barnesdale, who was most certainly moments from arrest.

Directly before Lady Maude on the dais, Hall and Adam put down the hero of the hour, who, grinning widely and showing the teeth she easily recognized as Robin Hood's, held out his hands to receive the arrow from her. And she, bending down to place the prize into his hands, took the opportunity to lean next to his ear and whisper, "Run like hell!"

CHAPTER SIX

After the space of an eye-blink, Robin took off without waiting for a further word. And in that instant, pandemonium erupted among the throng surrounding the dais. His fellow archers turned to each other quizzically, then loudly voiced their confusion, while Gisbourne rose to his feet, shouting to his guards, "After him! That man is Robin Hood! Put him in irons!"

And that cry brought even more of the spectators into the area around the dais, pushing and shoving and calling to one another, "Robin Hood! It's himself, there he is!"

"Where?"

"Just there, running off!"

"No, he's over there, the other direction!"

And some of this was simply confusion, and some of it was deliberate, with many in the crowd sympathetic to Robin and his men, knowing they had been charitable, or at least generous, to the poorest among them. Very few had any desire to see Robin caught. In the babble of tongues, none of Gisbourne's guards could hear any of the others, and none could see where amid the throng the one-eyed archer had vanished. Meanwhile, Little John and Will Scarlet, still in their disguises, lurked on the outside of the seething crowd, hoping to glimpse their leader and secret him away to where Much the miller's son was waiting to aid their escape.

But Robin was far from the outskirts of the crowd. Having made his initial spring for freedom straight away from the dais, he had snaked his way undetected back through the crowd to the city wall itself, and was making his way furtively along the wall, thinking to slide out unseen once he'd slipped past the mob. But he suddenly saw, over the heads of three or four people in his way, the helmet of a tall guard, standing against the wall himself and surveying the crowd from that vantage point. Robin halted, scratching his head as he pondered his next move, when suddenly a thin, shapely hand shot out from the alcove of a doorway he had just passed and, grabbing him by the wrist, pulled him insistently into that recess. Yielding to the beckoning hand, Robin slipped into the alcove to come face to face with the dark smoldering eyes of Lady Maude Peveril.

"In here, now, you simpleton, if you want to live!" she hissed at him, opening the door and dragging him behind her. Once inside, she locked the door and let out a sigh. Then her eyes caught him in a blistering gaze and she hissed again, "What did you think you were doing? You didn't realize from the beginning that this whole charade was my useless husband's trap to catch and hang you? Why would you give him the chance?"

Robin, pulling off his fake beard and scratching his irritated skin with great relief, shrugged and answered, "Well, that was the challenge, wasn't it? To tweak his nose and run off to play another day!" And he gave her that crooked smile she never could resist.

Maude rolled her eyes and looked to the ceiling. "Boys and their games!" she lamented to the unseen goddesses of the air. "Deliver me from their asinine games!"

"So what is this place?" Robin asked, hands on his hips as he turned about, examining the bare room with its staircase leading up to a platform high above, lit by windows cut in the stone.

"It's one of the guardhouses along the Nottingham city walls," Maude answered through clenched teeth. "Obviously." And as she began, for reasons Robin was not quite sure of, to remove her rich gown and strip herself down to her linen chemise she continued, "I claimed it for my personal tiring house this morning. So I was able to change here from my everyday gown into this rich item in privacy, and in a place close by the dais where they were going to park me for the duration of the contest. Now, get out of that silly costume."

Setting down his golden arrow and removing his eyepatch, Robin gave her a thin close-mouthed smile, not quite sure what the sheriff's wife was getting at.

"I made my fool of a husband pick clout shooting for the tournament because I knew you would come here and enter. I knew you couldn't stay away because you're…"

"Because I'm the best archer in all of England, you were going to say?" Robin grinned at her, tossing away his tunic.

"No. I was going to say because you're such a blithering arrogant ass!" Maude corrected him, pulling off the swaths of fabric wound around his midsection that had made him seem so rotund a bowman. "Anyway," she continued, "I thought you'd have less of a chance to win, and so put your head in the mouth of the lion, if you played at clouts, which you weren't used to."

"Oh ye of little faith," Robin quoted Friar Tuck. "You didn't know how eagerly my arrow seeks out the center of the target, no matter what the hindrances!" Now stripped of his disguise, Robin found himself standing naked but for his hosen, and it occurred to him to wonder just what Lady Maude had in mind.

"It's a very good thing you shaved your face smooth," she said, confusing him even more. Seeing his dumbfounded look, she continued, "With a beard, this disguise would scarcely work." And with that, she held her tasteful blue silk gown up to him to judge its fit. "An inch or two too short, I suppose, but no one's going to be looking at that. Now, off with your hosen."

Robin could now see that Maude intended to disguise him in her own gown to enable him to slip through the crowd, and Gisbourne's guards, undetected as a woman of some substance. He had to admit, it was an extremely clever scheme. But the removal of his hosen was having another effect on him, as he stood there in the small fortress with the lady Maude standing before him, still wearing the tiara in her hair but nothing else save for the thin chemise that left almost nothing to his imagination. I need not mention here what his first thought was. But his second thought, to give him his due, was of Lady Mary of Winchester, his Maid Marion—who, despite his own wishes to the contrary, was still completely deserving of that name, but who, with good reason he had to believe, might object to what had been his first thought.

Maude, on the other hand, had become excruciatingly aware of the physical manifestation of that First Thought, and her manner changed abruptly from businesslike to playful. Within seconds, she had doffed her chemise—thereby leaving nothing at all to his imagination—and reached out to take him in her hand. "Well!" she said softly into his ear. "I see you have one more powerful arrow to be loosed. Let's make sure it finds the center of its target, then, shall we?"

As he backed the lady Maude up against the wall, Robin stopped thinking of Maid Marion. Briefly.

*　*　*

Roughly five minutes later, much to Maude's disappointment, a newly disguised Robin Hood made his furtive exit from the guardhouse door, all passion spent. If any curious eyes were watching, they would have seen a fairly tall woman dressed in an expensive-looking blue silk dress and a chaperon—a cape and hood—of darker blue that covered her head, shoulders, and the upper part of her chest. Under her chin ran a barbette or chin-band, and a woman's coif like a white pillbox hat managed to cover her hair. The only thing those curious eyes might find noteworthy would be the leather boots protruding below the hem of the silk gown. Now, why do you suppose a woman so stylishly attired would make a fashion gaffe so egregious?

The honest answer to that, of course, was that none of the shoes made for Lady Maude's dainty feet could possibly have been persuaded to embrace those large stompers of Robin's. And he was in too much of a hurry to spend precious minutes trying to find a solution to that problem. Besides, Robin said, he'd be far more comfortable in his own boots, and if he were recognized by any of Gisbourne's guards, or the sheriff's deputies, he wanted to be able to break into an all-out run at a moment's notice, and for that he wanted his boots. "Besides," he reasoned, "is anybody really going to be looking at my feet?"

Lady Maude had murmured that every woman among the spectators on the green would very likely take in his feet as a part of his ensemble but chose not to argue, and barely had time to wish him luck as he darted out the door.

Feeling conspicuous, since he could feel that the gown was too tight in the chest and across his shoulders (a fault Maude had employed the chaperon in an attempt to conceal), Robin had to consciously remind himself not to skulk as he moved along the wall, since such a posture must inevitably draw attention to him. Nor did he want to invite notice by running or some other incongruous movement, even though he yearned to race through that crowd and leave all pursuers behind. And so he walked determinedly but without undue haste, standing tall and proud, like a noble woman making her way home in her own city. Whether Will Scarlet or Little John was standing outside the mob to look for him, he did not know. But he was fairly sure they would not recognize him in this garb, so he would have to find *them*, or, failing that, make his way to where Much the miller's son waited with his getaway horses just inside the wood outside of town. He had to admit, though, that a woman walking alone from the city into the woods was more than likely going to arouse suspicion. If he could come across a man—John or Will—to walk with him, he would look less conspicuous. And so he squinted his eyes, scanning the throng before and behind him for any recognizable face in the crowd.

And that's when he caught a glimpse of a familiar, gray-haired yeoman walking slightly stooped and wearing a gray tunic over green hosen. He had a yew longbow and a quiver of feathers slung over his left shoulder, and Robin slipped as smoothly as he could manage beside him on the right, taking his right arm in his own and murmuring in a breathy, high-pitched voice, "Just in from the country, father? Care to show a girl a good time?"

Jock o' Barlborough turned startled hazel eyes on Robin and, trying to dislodge his right arm from this strange woman's grasp, began to sputter, "What? Egad, you can't... I'm not... I think you need to bark up another tree, Missy!"

"Think again, Jock," Robin returned very quietly in his own voice. "I've got a golden arrow here that I might let you add to that quiver of yours if you just act natural and don't make a fuss." For Robin had indeed held on to his gold prize throughout his flight and his tiring house adventure, and had it hidden in the sleeve of Lady Maude's dress.

The startled Jock's head recoiled at the sound of Robin's voice and his eyes grew large and round as the great "O!" his lips were making. "Don't try to make a living as a traveling player," Robin continued *sotto voce*. "You'll starve to death. Now easy does it, just pretend like we're walking nonchalantly—calmly now, calmly…"

Jock was jerking his head this way and that, trying to locate anyone in the crowd who might be looking to capture his new companion. "Hodden of Barnesdale!"

"Indeed, it's me, old fellow, but please, don't say that too loudly. There are those here who seem to want to put an end to poor Hodden."

"So I noticed," Jock answered, finally settling into his role with a bit more ease and beginning a nonchalant walk toward the end of the city wall, from which Robin planned to stroll north of the city gate toward the outskirts of Sherwood, where Much waited and, he hoped, he'd also meet John and Will. "But that Gisbourne, he seemed to think you were somebody else. Which I'm starting to be convinced might very well be true, because this here disguise is a pretty good clue that maybe that whole Hodden of Barnesdale get-up was all a costume, too. So, tell me the truth now: Are you really this notorious outlaw, Robin Hood, like Gisbourne shouted out?"

Robin paused, holding his breath for a heartbeat or two. Jock had been friendly enough, and a great help to Robin, on the pitch of the archery field. But was it not possible that this helpful, guileless old man was in reality a plant, a spy placed among the competitors by Gisborne or the sheriff to try to ferret out archers who fit the general physical type of Robin Hood? Was he after all only a part of the sheriff's scheme?

But no, Robin told himself as they strolled arm in arm on the green and he looked deep into Jock's kind eyes. The old man was sincere. If he wasn't, Robin was a dunce. "Jock, I'm afraid that's just who I am. Now don't get excited and call out or anything like that. You help me get to my man waiting out there with my horses, and I'll give you the gold arrow you helped me to win, after working so hard to win it yourself!"

Jock, having regained his composure, walked on perfectly naturally, looking straight ahead as if nothing strange were going on. Here's a fellow who can keep his head when thrown unawares into the most unexpected situations, Robin was thinking. A good bloke to have around when others are losing their heads, perhaps. "I don't need to be bribed to help a friend," the old man cautioned. "Nor would I hesitate to turn you in if I thought you a menace to your fellow Englishmen. So tell me, Robin Hood of the Sherwood Outlaws, just why do you live as you do? The authorities seem to want to destroy you. To hang you in public view as a warning to any others who seek to live the same way. Tell me, why shouldn't I believe them and turn you over to them right now?"

Robin was beginning to doubt his own instincts now. Perhaps this Jock o' Barlborough was going to betray him after all? He swallowed hard, gripped Jock's arm more tightly, scanned the crowd still around them for any sign of Will or Little John, and then plunged into the best justification he could muster on such short notice. "The authorities who want to destroy us are men like Gisbourne, who only cares about his own position and his advancement in royal service. And like John of Oxenford, the venal Sheriff of Nottingham who uses his responsible position to skim more graft in taxes and tolls upon anyone coming through Nottingham every month than he can find ways to spend in a year. And I have that from the best of authorities—from one as close to him as his own wife."

"Or someone who actually *is* his own wife," Jock responded, "who gives you her own gown to aid you to escape." Still, he looked straight ahead and continued to walk slowly, having now reached the main gate into the city of Nottingham. So he's recognized the gown, Robin thought, steering Jock away from the gate and north along the road toward Sherwood.

"Yes, the lady Maude is truly my ally," Robin admitted. "If she trusts me above her husband, what does that tell you? And what about the citizens of Nottingham and the villages of Nottinghamshire? Honest yeomen, craftsmen, the people who work the land, widows, orphans, ask any of them what they think of the outlaws of Sherwood. We rob from no one who can't afford to give something back to the people they've squeezed their money out of to begin with. And we always give half of what we take to the poor people of the land or villages in need of help. That's usually our Friar Tuck's doing."

"Sounds like you play at being charitable to make yourself feel better about being a thief," Jock said drily. Robin was abashed.

"It makes confession easier, I'll admit," he answered. "But my men are all men who have been driven into poverty by the greed and cruelty of some of these same masters we steal from, or men who have been unable to succeed in their professions or who have seen their own livings taken from them. Or they are men who, because of things beyond their control—the size or shape or color or longings of their own bodies—have been cast out from their villages or families or farmsteads. They leave poverty, disgrace, and misery for the freedom and camaraderie of the forest life. And we do not starve."

"No, far from it," Jock allowed. "By all accounts, you dine quite well on the king's deer!"

Robin rolled his eyes at that. Indeed, he rolled his eyes from side to side, as the couple had now left the city walls behind them and were moving away from any stragglers left of the crowd that had now dispersed. And still no sign of John or Will Scarlet. Robin hoped they were not too conspicuous now that there was no crowd to hide them. But he answered Jock, "Poaching the king's deer? That charge is ludicrous. If there ever is a king anymore, where is he? The throne has been in limbo since the death of the old king whom I served for years. The breakdown of authority after Arthur's death is what caused local bullies like Gisbourne and the sheriff to seize what power they could, and that chaos is to blame for a lot of the sufferings that brought my men to me in the forest. As for the king's deer, the law that keeps anyone from shooting them keeps men starving. If the king wants his deer, let him come up here and shoot them! Otherwise, if we don't thin the herd, many of them will starve in the winter. So, no, I have no regrets about shooting the deer of Sherwood."

"I do admit that much of what you say makes sense to me," Jock confided. "I've been a soldier in my time, but cut loose by my old master several months ago. Too old to take the strain of the long marches with the same stamina as the twenty-year-olds. No great lords have seen fit to give me any position. I've been living from hand to mouth for some time now. But my archery skills are as sharp as they ever were. I thought if I won this contest, that golden arrow might be converted to enough money to see me through the foreseeable future. So yes, I can sympathize with the plights of you and your men. But I have to say, it's hard to take you seriously in that silk gown of yours."

Halfway between the city gate and the edge of the forest itself, they were just passing the path that led to the Blue Boar Inn, a favorite haunt of Robin's men when they had any business in Nottingham. And just as Jock made that last comment, Robin saw the disguised Will Scarlet and Little John coming out of the tavern door. Robin stopped and waited for them to approach, while Jock, confused by their sudden halt, whispered, "What are you doing? I thought you were in a hurry to reach the woods..."

"In a few moments, you'll have a chance to meet some of

my own loyal men," Robin said. "And then you can judge for yourself how seriously to take us."

Little John nodded to the couple that, for no apparent reason, seemed to be waiting for them at the intersection with the Great North Road. Will Scarlet, always ready with a courteous remark for the ladies, was just about to tell the tall lady in the blue silk gown how charming was her cape when he caught sight of the large leather hunting boots extending below the hem of her silk dress. Squinting into the face of the lady, he coughed and elbowed John in the ribs, until John took a closer look himself into Robin's face and guffawed.

"So," Robin accosted them. "This is how you watch over me and keep me safe? By guzzling tankards of Blue Boar's ale? I'd have been better off bringing a dog. At least he wouldn't have slunk off to a tavern." Robin, relieved at seeing his men, was only half in earnest, having feared for their capture while at the same time judging they hadn't feared much for his.

"Now, don't get your wimple in a bundle there, Lady Robin," Will Scarlet cried. "Our eyes were on you until you disappeared in that crowd. We'd lost all sign of you, and John suggested that you might make your way here, to the Blue Boar, thinking the Master might hide you."

Robin looked askance at John, winked at Jock, and encouraged Will to go on with a long "And…"

"And it turns out you weren't here, as you probably don't need me to tell you. We did, I'll admit, quaff a pint or so each of the good man's ale, but always with an eye to the road in case we saw you coming along. When we saw this old couple coming up the road, we figured the crowd was breaking apart and thought we'd come out and reconnoiter. And lo and behold, we've found you! So all is well."

"No thanks to you two," Robin chided. "I'm safe purely

through the aid of Lady Maude, who loaned me her gown to fool the guards, and this gentleman here, who kindly offered me his arm to lead me out of the lion's den."

"Well let's try to make sure he's not leading you out of a frying pan and into a fire," Little John said. "It's not going to take Gisbourne or the sheriff long to realize you're not in Nottingham itself or in what remains of the crowd outside the walls and to send a mounted troop this way. Much is waiting just a furlong way ahead, let's make some haste that way."

And with that he steered Will and Robin in the direction of the forest, waving his arms as if shooing sheep into a pen. Will Scarlet by now had recognized the man whose arm Robin clung to, and ventured, "You're Jock o' Barlborough, aren't you, old man? I have to say, you're one of the best archers I've seen— easily as good as any we've got in our band, wouldn't you say John?"

"So it is he, isn't it?" John answered, still shooing them all along at a quick pace. "Yes, I haven't seen anyone to match him, save Robin himself. And on occasion, yourself, Will."

But Scarlet knew his own worth better than anyone and was quick to gainsay John's diplomatic compliment. "Not I, I couldn't come near your skill, Jock. Robin, why haven't you talked this bloke into joining our fellowship?"

Robin gave a hearty and unladylike laugh, which may have drawn the attention of a few straggling folk who had now taken to the road behind them if their homes lay north of Nottingham. John started and made a sign with his hands to quiet down and keep a lower profile, and Jock smiled himself. Robin now spoke to him, "Jock, this is Will Scarlet and Little John, two of my closest companions among the Sherwood outlaws, and they seem intent on welcoming you to our little band of brothers of the forest. What do you say now?"

"I say I may as well give it a try," Jock said, rubbing his chin. "I've got little of my own except what I'm wearing on my back, and no one to miss me if I never go back to the hovel I've been living in. I'll join you, yes I will. Farewell to the grind of life!"

"And hello to you all!" said Much, the miller's son, as the group of four stepped into the shadow of the forest now two furlongs from the main gate of the city. He was mounted on a tall stallion and holding the reins of three other horses, including Robin's Daisy and Little John's Bishop. "I recognize two of the blokes I came here with." With that Much stared a long time into Robin's face until a broad smile cracked his own round, freckled visage. "And who knew our Robin could make such a beguilin' wench? But as for you, sir," he looked with laughing eyes at Jock, "I don't think I've had the pleasure."

"And you'll have to forego the pleasure for a few moments, we need to mount and be off right away. I'll take Daisy, and John needs to ride Bishop. Will, take the other horse and Jock, Much's horse should be able to bear your weight as well as his, if he'd be so good as to let you climb on behind him. Much, this is Jock o' Barlborough, our newest recruit. You can get acquainted while we ride."

"And did we win the storied Golden Arrow then, Robbie girl?" Much asked.

"We did indeed," Robin told him as he mounted, then placed the arrow in Much's hand once he settled into the saddle. "Put this in the pouch you've got hanging from your saddle. Oh, and find a place for this as well…" and with that Robin doffed the lady's coif that had adorned his head, and plucked from underneath it the rich tiara he'd lifted from Lady Maude's head, handing it to Much. "Nice gems in that. Ought to bring us a good return if we find a jeweler to take it." Much laughed while Will and John snickered, and Jock gave a nervous smile, wondering just what kind of scalawags he had thrown in with.

"And let's go cross country for a while," Robin said, kicking Daisy into a trot, "in case Gisbourne's guards had the foresight to block this road. And speaking of Gisbourne's guards—I have new information that they've been active up near Wallingwells. We need to talk about sending a party of our men after Thorvald and Friar Tuck!"

CHAPTER SEVEN

"**P**eace to this house," Friar Tuck pronounced as he crossed the threshold of the tidy lodging with the small garden a furlong way or two from the nunnery, where he'd been told the Widow Day lay with her fever.

"Oh, Master Friar, welcome ye certainly are," the old woman said from the couch on which she was lying. It was drawn close to the fire, which was burning cheerily.

"My good Mrs. Day," Tuck began in his friendliest voice. "I am visiting here in Wallingwells, and heard from the good Father Bernard here at the priory that you were laid up with an illness."

"Just a little indisposed, good friar. It doesn't promise to be mortal, so if you are here to beg some deathbed contribution for your house, you're wasting your time!" The widow was only half-joking.

Tuck was unfazed, having heard worse slanders against friars in his time. "No, no, my dear Mrs. Day, I'm not here to ask anything of you," the friar assured her as he shooed the cat away from the comfortable bench next to the woman's couch and settled himself in. "I'm here to give something to *you!*" And with that, he held up a large jar he had brought with him from Alison and Malyne's house, where he and Thorvald had again passed the previous night. "This is a broth from the midwife Alison, whom you may know? It's full of wholesome herbs that she believes will be nurturing for you in this illness."

At that, the old woman perked up. "Alison the midwife? I do not know her well, but her salves and potions are legendary in these villages for their healing properties. How very thoughtful of her to send it!"

"It should be heated up," Tuck said. "I see you have a pot over your fire. Is it empty? May I put the potion there to warm it?"

"Yes, yes," the widow urged him. "I have a girl who comes several times a day to help while I'm sick. She started the fire this morning and will come to give me dinner. But this will be better still."

And before she had finished speaking, Tuck had poured the contents of the jar into the brass pot. He sat again to wait for it to boil, and turned to the widow, nonchalantly introducing the subject he had actually come to discuss. "I suppose you have heard by now about the grisly events in the priory chapel yesterday," he began. "The gruesome head of this Willie of Worksop found hanging there near your usual place in the congregation? I imagine you felt your illness may have been a blessing when you heard, since you were spared that gory sight!"

"Well you may think so," the old woman said. "But I've seen a lot worse in my day. My husband was blacksmith here for the nuns for some thirty years, and he was called to help in a lot of situations. I remember one dead body he had to help with back in the day. Fellow was another blacksmith, over in Worksop. Bloodiest body I've ever seen. Anyway, as for this Willie character, let me tell you, he's not so much of a loss."

It was the same theme he'd heard from the priest and from the bailiff, Bryce. He thought he might get a different view from this woman, but it seemed she was even less sympathetic to the dead tinker than the men had been. "Do you say so, mother?" Tuck said. "Is it not a Christian soul we're talking about? Shouldn't we have some charity?"

"You're not here to try to get money out of me to pay for trentals for that man's soul, are you? You friars are always preaching about trentals."

Tuck closed his eyes, mentally telling himself he must be patient with this woman. "No," he answered as calmly as he could. "I don't actually belong to a particular house and do not engage in masses for the dead, so I am not interested in taking money to perform such rituals. I'm perfectly satisfied that the simple ceremony I assisted Father Bernard in performing laying this Willie to rest is sufficient for his soul. If he repented his sins and committed his soul to God before his death, it will suffice. If he did not, all the trentals in the world will do him no good. But that much is up to God. In this world, good mother, I am interested in seeing that his murderer is brought to justice. In that, I hope you can help me."

"You can hope all you want Master Friar, but I don't see what you think I can do. Isn't this the job of the magistrate, anyway? What do you care if a villein goes unavenged?"

Tuck sighed. "Master Crisp has… delegated the task to me for now. And I'm not talking about avenging Willie's death. I'm only seeking justice in what seems a brutal murder. If we don't know who killed him and why, how are we to know the same killer may not strike again, perhaps with someone you are more fond of than this Willie?"

"And why would anyone do that? No one close to me deserves anything of the sort."

"So you are saying that Willie deserved what happened to him?" Tuck said. "Why? Tell me why you think he was killed. Who had reason to dislike him so much?"

"All the women he wronged, of course. You know he was

nothing but a rogue who chased young women constantly, and the women called him 'Sweet Willie,' but he was never true to a one of them."

"No mother, I do not know anything about the man, but will respect what you tell me," Tuck responded. "Can you give me names? Which particular women was he most involved with?" And after a moment's thought, he added, "Are any of the women you're talking about women who would have regularly worshiped in that corner of the chapel with you, the corner where the head was found? Was that supposed to be a sign, do you think?"

"I know nothing about signs," the old woman replied. "But 'Sweet Willie' was certainly involved with several of the women there. That Kate and that Meggie both I shouldn't wonder. And if one or more of those young nuns weren't involved with him, I miss my guess. And that laundress, that Liptrot woman. She's the worst of the lot. She was all over him. It was sordid and revolting."

Tuck was taken aback. Elizabeth Liptrot had been almost as negative about Willie as old Mrs. Day was. "Sordid. . in what way?"

"Well, she lives in rooms in the convent, you know. He visited her there, I'm sure of it. But she didn't even have the decency to keep her shutters open when he was here so that I couldn't see what was going on. Why should an innocent woman do that, I ask you, hmm?"

Tuck sighed again. If this interview was any indication, this was going to be a long investigation.

* * *

Thorvald's job in this investigation spearheaded by the friar was to gather what information he could in the streets of Worksop and in the tiny village of Wallingwells. To do this he had adopted his one-time profession of merchant, bringing his cart into town and talking to local tradesmen about the possibility of taking their wares to other towns to see whether they might be marketable there. To convince locals that he was in fact involved in such a marketing scheme, he would need to purchase a sample item from a variety of local artisans to shop around in other towns, and for this, fortunately, he had several gold nobles in his purse, "though I didn't expect to be a-wastin' of 'em this way," he grumbled to himself.

On the main street of Worksop, Thorvald had parked his cart in front of the shop of a townsman who made leather goods out of material from a local tanner. Thorvald, inspecting some of the boots and gloves on display in the shop, was trying to move his conversation with the artisan leather worker Harold from his wares to anything the fellow might know about the murder victim. "Now most o' my goods I makes up custom fit as the orders come in," Harold was saying. "That way I takes the measurements and get a perfect fit, ya see. If you was gonna sell them in some other town, I'd have to just make up some in different sizes an' them that bought 'em would have to find whatever fits 'em closest. I'm not sayin' I'm not gonna do it, mind you, I'm just sayin' I'm not used to it is all."

"Well, 'ere's what we do, then," Thorvald said, the salesman in him taking over. "You let me 'ave this 'ere pair o' gloves and that there pair o' boots at cost, see, an' I'll shop 'em around some o' the towns round about, and I'll split what profit I make on 'em, an' if it works, I bring ya back some orders for more as well, see? An' everybody wins. You get profits from another source, I get a profit of me own, an' the villagers around get access to some well-made leather items they'd 'ave ta do without otherwise, see? What 'ave ya got ta lose?"

Harold nodded his head slowly, then more and more vigorously the more he thought about it, and he handed the gloves and boots over to Thorvald as a bit of money changed hands. And as they closed the deal, Thorvald mentioned, as if off-handedly, "That's perfect, that is. Now, if I could only find me a tinker around here to partner with, I think I'd 'ave found everything I'd been 'opin' for."

Harold raised his eyebrows. "A tinker, you say?"

"Right," Thorvald said, gathering up the gloves and boots to put them into his cart. "Not many villages 'ave got their own tinker, so if I found one 'ere we could probably make a small fortune shoppin' pots and pans and the like around the neighborin' villages."

"We did have a tinker here," Harold said helpfully. "Lived out o' town, he did. But he had the idea, same's you, to peddle his pots an' pans round about the shire. Traveled far an' wide, s'far as I could tell. He was hardly ever home. But I can't say he ever seemed a tinker's dam richer than when he *didn't* travel about. So I don't know as your plan is likely to work."

Thorvald grinned up at the craftsman. "Ah, but it's not just the travelin', my friend it's the *sellin'*, if ya know what I mean. So where is this fella? I'd still like to talk to 'im. Or, you said 'e *did* live 'ere. So 'e don't anymore?"

"Oh no, my friend. Willie the tinker is up and died, I'm afraid."

"Ah, well, I won't be lookin' 'im up any time soon then, will I?" Thorvald responded nonchalantly. "Old fella was 'e, then?"

"No sir," Harold said, apparently warming to his subject, much to Thorvald's delight. "No more than thirty-five, I'd say. When I say he died, I mean to say he were murdered. Murdered not more'n two weeks ago, I make it."

"Murdered!"

"Yes, and not just murdered, but his body cut to pieces, and his head taken. Nobody even knew who it was until they found the head a-hangin' in the nuns' chapel at mass yesterday morning."

Thorvald acted suitably disgusted, as in fact, he was even at the retelling of the horror he'd seen himself. "That's bloody awful. 'Oo coulda done such a thing?"

"No one knows," Harold answered, his voice taking on the timbre of one telling a ghost story. "They're saying it's some horrible ghoul that haunts the northern edge of Sherwood by night."

Thorvald scoffed. "Well, 'they' can say whatever they like, I'm sure, but what do *you* say? Did 'e 'ave a lot of enemies, this Willie the tinker?"

Harold puckered his lips in thought. "Oh, no more'n the next man, I should say," he answered. "Mind you, there was something about his past, though. Something he mentioned once when a few of the boys were teasing him after a few cups at the Loaves and Fishes." The glover's head tilted slightly, referencing an inn up the street that seemed to be the only place in Worksop where a cart driver might wash the road dust out of his throat.

"Ah. 'E was a regular there then, was 'e? And you?"

"And every other shopkeeper in town," Harold confided. "But a few of us was giving this Willie a jibe or two on account of his reputation, you know, as a hot lover, and saying as how he'd be getting himself caught by one of them women and made to settle down. And he got this weird look and muttered 'Never again.' I remember I asked him later, just between him and me, what he'd meant by that, and he told me he was married once, and it just wasn't for him. His wife died, as I gathered, and he said that was the best day of his life because it set him free. Now doesn't it make ya wonder why he'd be chasing women around here when he'd been so happy to get rid of the one he had?"

"Hmmph," Thorvald said thoughtfully. "Sounds like maybe 'e didn't like the woman 'e 'ad because, chained to that wife, 'e couldn't chase any o' the others 'e was lustin' after."

Harold laughed and put a hand on the dwarf's shoulder. "My friend," he replied between chuckles, "you've got old Willie figured out for sure."

* * *

Madame Veronica, the prioress of Wallingwells, had given Tuck this small room off the cloister in the priory, to conduct interviews with the various nuns in the convent. She had not been enthusiastic about the plan, but on Father Bernard's urging had finally relented. She was not happy about having her sisters' daily routines disturbed, and not at all sanguine about their being alone in a room with a man, even if that man was a member of the clergy. But Tuck assured her that the door to the room would remain open at all times, and Father Bernard that it would be good for the priory to have this matter of the bloody head at mass cleared up and put to rest, and so Prioress Veronica gave in and told Tuck he could have fifteen minutes with each of the sisters. Any more than that, she reasoned, might be an inducement to sin. Tuck himself considered that truly imaginative sinners could probably manage to sin in less than five, but made no argument.

It soon became quite clear to Tuck that his murder victim, Willie, was little known among the nuns. Several claimed to have no knowledge of him at all and, cloistered as they were, Tuck was not really surprised, since Willie had no official relationship with the nunnery. The cellarer, Sister Esther, did admit to a passing knowledge of the fellow, since he had repaired two of the priory's large kitchen vessels perhaps a year since. When asked if she'd seen any conversation between Willie and any of her sisters, Esther scowled at Tuck with her dark eyes and said she had not, though she had left him for a time in the kitchen with the cook, and she did not know whether he'd spoken with anyone there. The infirmarian, the young and lovely Sister Mary Barbara—the daughter Master Bryce had mentioned—said that she had occasionally seen her father, the convent's bailiff, speaking with Willie, she assumed regarding the purchase of pots and pans for the priory's kitchen. And oh yes, she admitted to running into the tinker on the street some few months past, when she had been out paying a visit to the Widow Day during one of her frequent illnesses, and, batting her long lashes at the friar, confessed that Willie had made a suggestive comment to her at the time.

"Suggestive?" Tuck had questioned, raising his eyebrows.

"'You shouldn't hide that beauty in a nun's habit,' he said, or words to that effect." Sister Mary Barbara pursed her lush lips and pouted. Tuck shrugged. Perhaps this was the kernel of truth in the Widow Day's wild charge that Willie had been the lover of some of the priory's nuns.

The beak-nosed nun he had noticed in the choir was called Sister Lucy. She was a local woman who had become a nun at seventeen and had never left the immediate environs of the priory since that time, except to go into the village of Wallingwells on occasion. She could not recall ever having seen Willie the tinker on any of those visits, but she did volunteer the interesting information that on the Sunday evening following the violation of the chapel by the bloody head, she'd heard violent weeping coming from one of the nearby cells. It might have had nothing to do with the murder, but she had thought she would mention it. The sisters closest to her own cell she named as Sister Anne, Sister Rebecca, and Sister Mary Eusebia.

Sister Anne turned out to be the older woman Friar Tuck had noticed in the chapel choir, the one with the prominent wrinkles about her mouth. On closer observation, Tuck realized that the woman's face was not at all as old as he had at first thought it was. She was perhaps in her mid-thirties, with deep hazel eyes that studied him intelligently and, he thought, coldly. But her face seemed care-worn, weathered by what Tuck felt sure had been a hard and bitter life.

"Sister Anne," Tuck began cautiously, holding her eyes in his for as long as he could. "One of your sisters whose cell is close to yours mentioned that she heard loud weeping coming from one of the cells in your wing of the convent on the night after Willie the tinker's head was found aloft in the chapel. As Mother Veronica may have told you, my purpose here is to look into Willie's death, the better to find his killer if we can, and so prevent any others perhaps from being slain." This last excuse had only recently occurred to Tuck—in his conversation with the Widow Day—and it sounded more convincing, he thought, than his less tangible motive of "seeking justice." In any case, it seemed to work better with the nuns.

Not, as it turned out, a motive that worked so well on Sister Anne, who simply laughed ironically. "Seriously, silly friar? You think whoever killed this Willie person—whom I have never met, let me add—is likely to kill anyone else? Don't you think the manner of his death argues something very, very personal, so personal as to come from a very private and passionate hatred of this particular person? It's hard for me to imagine that anyone could hate more than one person so much."

Tuck blinked and turned his eyes away from Sister Anne's steady stare. "Perhaps you're right," he muttered, sounding more conciliatory than convinced. In any case, he wouldn't pursue that line of inquiry with *this* nun, he decided. "Well, what about this crying? Can you tell me anything about that?"

"Well, it certainly wasn't *me*," Sister Anne asserted, and, looking at her sober, emotionless face, Tuck could well believe it. "As I said, I didn't know the victim, and I doubt if I'd have felt any sorrow at his demise in any case. Nor did *I* hear any weeping, whatever your other witness says. I pay little attention to noises at night. I hear the cock crow from the cook's house down the street, and that's what gets me up in the morning. But last night?" She thought a moment. "I *have* heard fairly loud cries from time to time coming from one of the cells in my neighborhood, though it sounded little like weeping to me. That night may have been one of the times. As I say, I've learned to ignore such noises if they don't concern me."

Tuck decided to drop that line of inquiry as well, and was about to dismiss Sister Anne when it occurred to him to ask, "Tell me, sister. How long have you been here at the Benedictine Priory at Wallingwells? I ask only because it seems most of the sisters I've talked to seem younger than yourself."

"Some of those youngsters have been here longer than I have," the woman answered. "It's only five years since I've taken the veil, and did so here at this convent, under the current prioress."

"You weren't a teenaged postulant here, then, like some of the others? You'd had a life in the world before coming here, had you?"

"And what has that to do with the murder of this tinker of yours?" Sister Anne said, fixing her stony eyes upon him.

"Well, all right. I won't detain you further, then, Sister Anne. It doesn't seem you have any information that will help us." And with that the woman rose to leave, until Tuck suddenly decided he couldn't let her leave without asking what he still thought was the most important question. "Oh, one more thing, sister," he began, as if it had just occurred to him. "One of the other women we've talked to suggested that it's possible at least one of your sisters may have had a… a gentleman friend, perhaps even this Willie. Have you observed any of your sisters behaving in a strange way that might suggest such a thing? Wandering where they shouldn't, perhaps, or keeping strange hours contrary to the Rule?"

Sister Anne gave another ironic laugh, as if such a suggestion was absurd. Then, recalling herself, she put on her serious face again, and glared at Tuck, saying, "Young Sister Rebecca is a flighty little thing. I've seen her carrying flowers on occasion, holding on to them as if they'd come from some lover, perhaps. Now I come to think of it, I think I've heard those loud cries from the direction of *her* cell. Worth looking into for you, I suppose, Master Friar." And with that Sister Anne left the room. Decisively, as if to say she was done with him.

Sister Rebecca, for her part, also had a distinctive laugh, but hers was more like the tinkle of broken glass. And she used it not when she was being derisive, but rather when she was unsure or nervous. Which was nearly all the time. She was the nun Tuck had noticed with the splash of freckles across her nose, and she had green almond-shaped eyes that squinted at him whenever he asked her anything. He was sure she must have a swirl of bright ginger hair under that wimple. But she vigorously denied ever having known anyone by the name of Willie, and never, *never* would she ever consider breaking her vow of chastity with some horrid man. Sister Rebecca, it seemed, had taken the veil here at the priory at the age of fourteen, and had done so specifically to avoid having to marry a man chosen for her by her father, a local brewer. The man had been considerably more than twice her age, and had breath that smelt of garlic to boot. The girl was now certainly no more than eighteen, and when Tuck asked her about the flowers Sister Anne had observed, Rebecca gave her tinkling laugh and said she liked flowers, and sometimes one of her sisters might give her a small bouquet just for the sake of friendship.

"Before you go, Sister Rebecca, let me ask you one last question," Tuck closed off his conversation with the young nun. "A couple of your sisters mentioned hearing loud cries, perhaps of weeping, coming from the vicinity of your cell on Sunday night, after the victim's head was found in the chapel. Is there anything you can tell me about that?"

Sister Rebecca's face glowed a fiery crimson as her nervous laugh tinkled from her abashed lips. "I'm sure I… heard no weeping that night. Certainly not. Loud cries? I've no idea what they were talking about, I'm sure." She failed to meet his eyes as she rose from her seat and made her way to the door. "Probably somebody praying, that's what it was." And with that she left.

"Well," said the friar to himself. "*That* was certainly convincing."

* * *

That evening at the Loaves and Fishes, the popular inn on the High Street in Worksop, Thorvald sat with his new best comrade Harold the glover, sampling a bit of the local brew and getting acquainted with a local carpenter called Paul. Paul was not so quick witted as Harold, but he was definitely a more enthusiastic drinker, and he was finishing his third cup of ale as Thorvald was trying to get him to understand his concept of the traveling salesman.

"It's got to be somethin' that'll fit in my cart, ya see," he was explaining for what seemed the fifth or sixth time. "A chair, let's say, or a small chest, or a stool."

"Or a table?" Paul asked, his lips protruding in a definite pout.

"Well, it'd 'ave to be a real small table, to fit in the cart, see?" Thorvald explained.

""People ain't that interested in tables, anyway," Harold put in. Like the others, he was lounging in the corner of the inn, elbows on the table and a foamy cup in front of him. "Except for small ones. If you've got a lot of people you're feedin' at one time, then you put up boards on trestles, don't ya?"

"Stools, innitt?" Paul commented, raising a finger as if he'd made a significant point.

"Stools, sure," Thorvald agreed, nodding sagely. "I could maybe sell dozens of those. But what I want to do, ya see, is just buy one o' each item at cost, and see what kind of interest there is in surroundin' towns, right?" Paul looked confused again. "'Ave another drink," Thorvald advised.

Paul's thinking face bore a serious scowl, and Harold stepped in again to try to clarify things. "Look, you know, it's kind of like old Willie the tinker used to do, see? Drive a wagon from town to town, fillin' orders as he went. Only Thorvald here'll be takin' orders from folks, and then giving them to us, and then taking them back out to them as ordered 'em."

"Ah, poor Willie!" Paul's mention of the tinker had struck a nerve in the carpenter and Thorvald was happy the conversation had got around to this without his even trying to steer it. Paul grew morose, though Thorvald saw no real difference between his sad face and his thinking face. Both bore the familiar scowl and the pout. "'He is gone, gone away, and we shall never see him more,'" the carpenter seemed to chant, lines, Thorvald assumed, from some old song.

"Good friend o' yours then, was 'e?" Thorvald asked, eager to follow up with a series of queries about the dead man's character and habits.

"Nah," Paul admitted. "Truth to say I hardly knew him. But

any man's death, especially one that gruesome, well it's gotta make you sit up and take notice, don't it?"

"It does at that," Harold replied, keeping up his end of the conversation, and he took a large swig of ale to keep Paul company.

"And what does it make *you* think of?" Thorvald asked Paul as the carpenter put down his cup and before he could lift it again.

"Makes me think as how I ought to get me a bit o' skirt like he done, before it gets too late for me!" Paul answered.

"I'll drink to that," Harold agreed, and both lifted their cups again.

"And just which piece o' skirt was this Willie chasin' before 'is untimely demise?" Thorvald asked. Then, thinking perhaps he'd shown too much interest for a casual conversation, he looked about the tavern to see if anyone else might be listening. He was surprised to see the bailiff John Bryce sitting by himself in a corner of the room, but Bryce seemed to be in his own world, not listening to his conversation. Resuming his mask of nonchalance, he laughed and added, "Maybe she's pinin' for 'er lost lover and needs some comfortin', eh?"

Harold and Paul and the ale found that comment particularly hilarious, and Paul put on his thoughtful face again, shifting the scowl ever so slightly. "He was visitin' that little dairy maid, Kate, with the parents who work the dairy for the canon's priory, but he ain't seen her in a while. I think he was hiking out more toward Wallingwells at night lately."

"So maybe you want to take a crack at young Kate, then, eh Paul?" suggested Harold. "Or maybe you'd like to be chasin' her yourself, eh Thorvald? Unless you're past them days, eh old man?"

Thorvald smiled wanly in the face of the guffaws that ensued from his two companions at that witticism. Then Harold leaned close and asked him in confidence. "Say, Thorvald old man, I got a question I'm wonderin' about. Little fella like you, when you have to do with the ladies… that fiddle stick o' your'n. Is it regular size, or is it like proportional to the rest of ya?"

Thorvald sighed. It was going to be a long night.

* * *

Sister Mary Eusebia was the last of the nuns Friar Tuck had determined to interview today, and she stepped boldly into the small room off the cloister, as if she were entering some sporting event or university debate. She was a hearty young woman, in her early twenties the friar guessed, and had dark eyes as deep as caverns, over which loomed a dark pair of eyebrows meeting above her nose. Tuck, sensing she saw him as an adversary, took care to frame his questions gently, in a non-confrontational manner.

"Mary Eusebia," Tuck began, good humoredly. "Is that a name you chose for yourself when you took the veil, then?"

"Indeed it was." She looked at him as if expecting more, but he simply waited, assuming she would explain. "The name is Greek, and it refers to an inner piety or spiritual maturity. A kind of godliness."

"And you chose the name as a quality you wished to aspire to, did you?"

"Oh no. I chose it because it's what people already called me." Tuck raised his eyebrows in surprise but again said nothing, waiting for the young nun to elaborate. "I have been associated with this priory since I was twelve years old, Master Friar. My father was a cloth merchant in Lincoln, and he knew the prioress here at the time, old Sister Catherine. He bundled me off here to keep me away from unwelcome suitors and to have me educated. Wanted me to be of some use in his trade, so I could read and write and figure."

"A kind father, then, concerned with your welfare and your future?"

Sister Mary Eusebia blew the air from her nostrils in a little fit of pique. "He was a brute," she declared. And under Tuck's questioning eyes, she elaborated, "just wanted to keep me for himself and figured I might as well be useful to him as long as he was going to keep me. But he'd already had his way with me before I ever had my monthly cycles."

Tuck turned pale as he felt his heart sink. And his mind flashed back to his own brutish father. "Oh my dear girl. Your own father?"

Her deep eyes looked back at him unmoved. Sister Mary Eusebia had long since transcended that shame and horror. "I was safe here." She waited. "He couldn't get at me here. My mother died my first year here, from shame and regret, I expect. My father waited patiently for me to come home, but I wouldn't. Not even for mother's funeral. And when I declared my desire to become a postulant here, there was nothing he could do. I had him checkmated. I never saw him again. And I hope he died screaming. In any case, he did die, the day I turned eighteen. And that was five years ago. And that's when I became a nun. So to answer the questions you're here to ask me: No I did not know this Willie the tinker whose head decorated our chapel on Sunday. No, he was no lover of mine. No, I haven't had any men paying me court here in the priory. And to answer one last question that you had no intention of asking me, no, I have never nor would I ever desire such a thing."

Tuck stared for a few moments into those deep brown eyes and then took a new tack: "Sister, it's clearly not a part of my investigation, but I am interested to know: You say it was others who gave you the name 'Eusebia.' Would you humor me by explaining why they gave you that name?"

She let a hint of a smile twist her mouth up at one corner. "It was because I learned so quickly. I could read Latin like a scholar by the age of thirteen. From that time I began to study the scriptures diligently. Every book, every line of the holy texts, and after that every commentary I could get my hands on from the library here, and some borrowed from other houses too. Jerome. Augustine. The Venerable Bede especially. The sisters took to calling me 'the Little Scholar' or 'Mistress Piety.' When I took my vows at eighteen, I chose 'Eusebia' to capture that idea of piety, of godliness."

Tuck thought about this for a moment and commented, "Your godliness seems of a singularly cerebral variety."

Sister Mary Eusebia gave Tuck a brief businesslike smile and then rose. "If you have no more questions, Master Friar, I want to get back to my cell. I have some reading set aside to finish this evening before compline."

As the young woman made her way toward the door, Tuck stopped her with another question: "Oh before you go, sister, I did have one more point I wanted to raise with you." At that, the nun turned for a moment, her heavy right eyebrow raised quizzically. "A few of your sisters have mentioned that on the evening after Willie's head was found, loud cries or weeping were heard from one of the cells in the neighborhood of yours and Sister Anne's and the others in that part of the convent. Did you happen to hear such crying? Can you help us in clarifying where it was coming from?"

Sister Mary Eusebia stood still for a few moments, now with both brows raised in surprise. Or was it alarm? Tuck could not tell. But what she did next was even more confusing. She turned toward the door again, and just as Tuck thought she was going to leave the room, she took hold of the door and swung it shut, turning the key in the lock. Befuddled, Tuck looked at the nun with blank eyes. She turned to him and said, "Brother Tuck, I want you to hear my confession."

Tuck's jaw dropped open, and in his startled state he babbled his first thoughts. "B-but I, I'm not prepared, er, this is not part of my responsibility here… shouldn't you be confessing to your own priest, Father… Father Bernard?"

"You're a friar. You're licensed to hear confessions. Friars regularly hear confessions of those who for one reason or another do not wish to confess to their parish priests. Your sacred duty is to hear my confession and I am requiring you to do so."

Tuck sighed. He was not prepared to argue with a scholar of Mary Eusebia's learning. "Very well," he conceded as she sat back down across from him with a look of triumph on her face. "How long has it been since your last confession, then?"

"Skip over the preliminaries, Master Friar. I'm familiar with the penitentials of Bede and of Theodore of Tarsus. There is one sin I want to confess to you that I have not felt at all comfortable confessing to anyone here. Let me just say that it concerns the loud cryings that have been heard of late coming from my cell."

"So it is *your* cell from which the cries are coming? It's you who are weeping?"

"Not me, Friar Tuck, and not weeping. Those are sounds coming from my special friend, Sister Rebecca."

"The little girl with the freckles?" Tuck said with surprise. "What is the meaning of these cries?"

Mary Eusebia lowered her head, raised her eyebrows, and looked at Tuck in disbelief. But it was clear she would need to spell things out with this friar. "Sister Rebecca and I. We sometimes lie together. We each need comforting and stroking sometimes. We stroke one another."

A slow look of realization dawned on Tuck's face. He searched his memory to those penitentials Sister Mary Eusebia had mentioned. A variety of sexual sins were listed, he recalled, but almost all he recalled involved sins by the male—varieties of adultery, of sodomy, in all of which women, if they were involved at all, were the passive participants, although they might have enticed the man into the sin. These were certainly sins a woman might confess. But it was difficult for him to even imagine sexual sins that might occur without a male present. But he did seem to recall a comment in Bede that specified "a woman fornicating with a woman," for which Bede prescribed three years of penance, or seven years if an "instrument" of some kind was used.

"So," Tuck cleared his throat. "You're confessing to fornication with another woman, then?"

"Am I?" The nun asked. Tuck was fairly certain she had thought about this a good deal. "Is simple stroking actually fornication? Had I been with a man would you call it fornication if he had only been stroking me?"

Tuck didn't know. "I... think not," was his only response.

"Doesn't fornication presuppose penetration? Isn't that why Bede suggests more serious penance for the use of instruments?"

"All right," Tuck agreed. "But then, in some way your relationship with your friend is at least an example of the sin of lust. Is it not forbidden in scripture? Might it be, shall we say, a version of the sin of Onan?"

"Not a word about it in scripture. I find nothing in Deuteronomy, or Exodus. Or Leviticus. But then, Moses was a man, wasn't he? As for the sin of Onan—but is it, though?" Mary Eusebia continued. "As I read the story in Genesis, Onan's act is sinful specifically because of the spilling of the seed. There's clearly no spilling of seed in my caressing and tickling my special friend."

"Perhaps not, but surely you are lusting in your heart," Tuck decided, feeling he was on surer ground here.

"Lusting? For what am I lusting, do you imagine?"

"For… for true fornication. I expect that as you fondle one another, you are thinking about true fornication, and that is what creates the excitement that leads to those cries you describe." Tuck really wasn't sure where he was going with this. How did he know what was in the minds of women? And how serious was this as a sin? Tuck regularly turned a blind eye toward Little John's relationship with Will Stutely, because he saw no harm in it—though the penitentials prescribed ten years of penance for that particular sin, and only three for this one. Didn't that make this more of a venial sin, if sin it was?

"Fornication? So you suggest that I am imagining being penetrated by a man while being stroked by my friend?" The young woman demanded.

"Indeed," Tuck nodded. "Of what else would you be thinking?"

Sister Mary Eusebia bowed her head to hide her smirk. "I assure you, brother Friar. Before God I swear to you: lying with a man is the furthest thing from my mind at such moments."

Tuck sighed again in frustration. "My dear," he said to the young nun. "Just what is it you want to confess to, then?"

"I want to confess to breaking the rule of silence during the prescribed periods in our cells. Obviously, our cries have disturbed our sisters, and in breaking that rule we have broken our vow of obedience."

Tuck's mouth hung open for several seconds as he digested that. He had more than an inkling that this young woman was not approaching this confession with the proper high seriousness. What he was more than a little sure of was that she was telling him these things under the seal of the confessional so that he could never betray her secret to Father Bernard, or anyone else. He, however, for his *own* part, would not debase the dignity of his office with regard to the confession. While it was clear to him he was not about to convince this young nun that her relationship with Sister Rebecca was a sin, he would at least take seriously the sin she *had* confessed.

"You must take your vows seriously," Friar Tuck told the penitent sister, who now sat with head bowed and determined to do penance. "To fail in obedience is a manifestation of the sin of pride, the chief of the Seven Deadly Sins." Of that much he was quite sure with this young woman. "In your cell this evening consider your sins, and say a hundred Our Fathers. Now go," he told the nun as she rose, adding "and sin no more."

Sister Mary Eusebia turned and gave him a half-smile before she turned the key and exited the room. Friar Tuck sighed for the third time in this encounter, and wondered whether there was anyone on God's earth who could understand women.

*　*　*

Thorvald's evening had been going downhill quickly. The conversation with Harold and Paul had degenerated from gathering some useful information about Willie and his habits to a candid evaluation of all of Willie's suspected girlfriends, followed by a further evaluation of every other woman in the greater Worksop area between the ages of fourteen and fifty. By now both Harold and Paul had degenerated into drunken stupors. A yawning Thorvald was feeling sleepy himself, and began to shift on his seat, preparing to get up and out to his cart and drive back to Alison and Malyne's cottage for the evening, when in the door of the Loaves and Fishes came a familiar face.

"Ralph!" Thorvald called as the burly cook shuffled into the inn. The head of the Wallingwells Priory kitchen swung his round, bald head about until he focused, scowling, on the dwarf at the table in the corner. He didn't smile when he saw Thorvald, but he did make his way over to the corner table and plopped himself down with a grunt next to the sleeping Harold, calling for some local ale. When he'd received a full cup, he took a deep swallow and at last turned to Thorvald.

"You're that dwarf from the church who cut down Willie's head."

Thorvald nodded. He was not surprised the cook recognized him, since he was fairly certain he was the only dwarf in town. But what he remembered about the cook was that Ralph had been more than a little negative about Willie the tinker. He might as well take this opportunity, Thorvald figured, to press the cook a little to see just what his objections were to the dead man. And since Willie's murder was the only thing he and the cook had in common, Thorvald could see no point in subtlety.

"And you're the guy 'oo 'ad nothin' good to say about the owner o' that 'ead," he responded to the cook.

For the first time the hint of a smile cracked Ralph's face after he reacted with a grimace to a large gulp of ale. "I couldn't stand the little wanker," he croaked out. To the unspoken question in Thorvald's eyes, he went on: "Thought every woman in the world was fair game for him. And they all liked him, 'Sweet Willie' with his fancy curled hair and his smooth shaved face. Blinked his baby blue eyes at 'em and they'd fall all over him."

Thorvald searched his memory. A wife and a daughter, he remembered, in Ralph's family. And as he recalled, Paul and Harold had ranked the daughter as a "10" and her mother as an "8" in their exhaustive catalogue of the Women of Worksop.

"So that's true o' the women in your own family then, too, is it?"

Ralph scoffed. "Well, my wife used to go on about what a handsome young man he was, with the nicest manners, and blah, blah, blah. I think she did it just to get me jealous."

"So you think 'e might 'ave been killed by some jealous 'usband somewhere?" Thorvald asked.

Ralph looked at him askance as he hunched over his ale. "You hintin' that maybe I was the one killed him, is that it?"

Thorvald shrugged. "Doesn't sound like you're gonna mourn 'im much, are ya?"

"I'm not saying I wouldn't have thought about it if he was ploughing my fields for me," the cook confided. "But I know he wasn't after *my* wife."

"And what about your daughter?" Thorvald asked innocently, looking down at his own empty ale cup.

"Nah!" Ralph responded, with a good deal more force this time. "Meggie wouldn't dare."

"Why d'ya say that?"

"She knows I'd wail on her, that's why," the cook said. Then when Thorvald seemed confused, he went on: "When that group of guards from Nottingham city were here two months ago, there was one of 'em kept coming around and I had to keep chasing him off with a meat hook. Then I found out she'd been encouraging the blighter, I let her have a whack or two, I can tell you. Even her mother didn't call me wrong that time. I swear she wouldn't do it again, let me tell you."

Thorvald paused over that information. Guards? From Nottingham? But before he had time to contemplate it, he noticed that familiar patron Master Bryce, the steward of the Priory who'd been sitting there for some time. Bryce now caught Thorvald's eye and nodded to him meaningfully from his table in the corner. Thorvald made a mental note to have a word with the steward later that evening, as the fellow seemed interested in talking to him, but perhaps not in the presence of the cook.

Suddenly, a cheer rose among the patrons of the Loaves and Fishes and Thorvald heard the heavy strum of a lute and a voice calling, "Drink up, my friends, and harken to me!"

A minstrel, Thorvald thought. Well, why not? He'd done enough snooping around for one day. He looked to the center of the room to where the performer stood on a chair—and tried to keep a straight face. It was Alan a Dale.

CHAPTER EIGHT

The Loaves and Fishes did have a few rooms to let for travelers coming through the area, but precious few travelers came through Worksop on any given day, and those rooms stood empty the majority of the time. James, the inn's proprietor, was a hospitable chap with a mouthful of teeth that had grown in well out of alignment and so was tagged with the surname Snaggletooth by all the townsfolk. His inn regularly did a far greater business as a watering place than as a lodging house, so he had been beside himself when two sets of visitors arrived on his doorstep the same day. Into the front room overlooking the street he put the first group of three, led by a certain Robert Fitz Ooth of Locksley, accompanied by a minstrel and an older yeoman calling himself Jock o' the Greenwood. The other pair of travelers, Reynold Greenleaf and his companion Will, James had put into the smaller back room on the inn's second floor. And while both parties were settling into their respective quarters for the night, Master Locksley's minstrel had come down into the public house to pass the hat and see whether he could pick up a few farthings or pence entertaining the customers. When Alan saw Thorvald, he breathed a sigh of relief, since it meant Robin's men would not have to waste time scouring the area to find their comrades.

Thorvald made no sign of recognition when he saw Alan, and

the minstrel barely glanced in the dwarf's direction. But by a squint, a blink, and a pair of shifting eyes, the two reached a tacit understanding that they would meet up later, after Alan's set, to fill each other in somewhere away from the prying eyes of the locals. And so when Alan had sung a version of "Bonnie Barbara Allen" and "The Cuckoo's Song," and followed it up with a Robin Hood ballad (why not?) about Robin's meeting with Little John, the minstrel had passed around his hat. And into it Thorvald had tossed a farthing of his own, just to prime the pump, and the minstrel had taken his lute and made his way up the stairs. Thorvald watched the direction Alan had taken, stalled for a few minutes so as not to seem too eager to follow, then bade good night to the comatose Ralph and Harold, and, yawning and stretching as if ready for bed, groped his own way up the stairs as if he, too—a stranger in this town—had a room on the second floor. Fortunately James the proprietor had not seen him, or he may have had some fast explaining to do.

When Thorvald knocked softly on the door of the larger room, it opened promptly and he was pulled in by several pairs of hands and, after the door had shut quietly and quickly the dwarf was pounded on the back in raucous welcome and greeted by a laughing Robin. "So!" the bandit leader cried. "Our resident curmudgeon is safe, I see! And what about our fat friar? He's not with you here? Where is he, then?"

"And what do you mean by worrying us all nearly to death?" Little John threw in, giving Thorvald no chance to speak. "You and the curtal friar promised to be home days ago!"

"I for one had terrible fears that you'd been captured by Gisbourne's troops," Will Stutely added. "I was that worried about what would happen to your poor horse after you were hanged..."

"They can't 'ang me, I'm too short to reach the noose," Thorvald said, then tried to answer the other questions he was being barraged with. "We 'ad no way to get a message to ya when we decided to stay longer. Tuck's fine. But 'e's got it in 'is 'ead that this murdered bloke deserves some kind o' justice, and 'e's bent on gettin' it for 'im. So we're staying at 'is old nurse's 'ouse outside o' town, an' 'e's probably there right now, beddin' down an' wonderin' where the devil I am. 'E spent 'is day at the nunnery, or that was 'is plan anyway. I been nosin' around in town, as you see."

"Nosing around for what? Is this what's kept you up here so long?"

"It is, John, now don't be gettin' excited. It's this body, ya see, Tuck was so insistent on givin' a proper Christian burial."

"Right, that's what you came up here for," Alan a Dale said.

"That and bringing money to a needy house," Robin added.

"Which is Tuck's old nurse, by the way. And none needier, I'd venture," Thorvald said. "But we found out 'oo the body belonged to, ya see, and the magistrate 'ere ain't worth the breath it'd take to damn 'im ta Hell. Tuck's got a bee in 'is bonnet, ya see, ta find the killer. Aw, it was bloody awful an' no mistake. Somebody 'ung the corpse's 'ead right there in the Priory chapel, can ya believe it?"

There was a loud gasp from the rear of the room and Thorvald looked up to see a complete stranger in the room with them. He was clean-shaven, stoop-shouldered from a good threescore winters of hard living, and dressed in a worn gray tunic. Thorvald stared into the stranger's steady hazel eyes that were staring back at him, and snapped, startled and wary, "An' 'oo's this 'oary-'eaded blighter when 'e's at 'ome, eh?"

"Name o' Jock o' Barlborough, at yer service, my friend," Jock spoke for himself, tugging his short forelock in a deference Thorvald was quite unused to. He looked questioningly at Robin, who completed the introduction.

"Jock's just joined our band, since you've been gone," Robin explained.

"Jock out-performed Robin at the Nottingham Archery tournament," Little John added, to Robin's annoyance. "Then Robin made a lucky last shot and took away the prize, but everybody knew who the better marksman was."

"Oh, now…" Jock demurred, but Robin laughed and went along.

"There's more truth in what John says than I like to admit," Robin said. "But Jock decided he'd join us, and I'm mighty glad to have his bow in our arsenal. But he's joined us here because his home town is close by, and we figured his knowledge of the area could help."

"Barlborough's just six miles or so up the road," Jock agreed. "I know the woods and villages up here quite well."

Thorvald shrugged. "Good ta 'ave ya 'ere, then, Jock o' Barlborough. Quite the powerful reaction ya 'ad there ta my story o' the murder, then, I noticed."

"Well, mutilation? Desecration of a church? These are pretty shocking sins, ain't they?"

"So they are," Thorvald agreed, looking down at his feet. "I been askin' folks around this town for a few days now just what this Willie the tinker was like, and what they all thought of 'im. Seems like 'e 'ad no real friends, far as I can make out. Not close to any of the men in town, and only had one use for the women. And I don't mean as cooks."

"So nobody's mourning for him especially hard?" Will Stutely said.

"Unless it's one of the women," Thorvald conceded. "The good friar 'as been talkin' to them—at least the nuns. There was some talk that this Willie's even had somethin' goin' on there. But Tuck 'adn't found any truth in that rumor, last I 'eard. 'E still 'asn't found time or opportunity to talk to any o' those other women that rumors 'ave connected with the dead man."

"I suppose we'll have to help out with that," Will Stutely said, "or we'll never get the two of you back where you belong. But can we really figure out who's the guilty party in this, if the local magistrate's not even looking?"

"Well somebody killed the bugger," Jock said. "And to mutilate the body like that? It was somebody who hated him, somebody in a rage. That could be one of these men that disliked him, angered and jealous over one of the women."

"Or one of the women in a rage," Robin added thoughtfully, "after being spurned by the rogue."

"Well, that narrows it down," Alan a Dale said. "It's either a man or a woman."

After the uneasy laughter that greeted that statement, Thorvald added, "Well, if you go by the gossip around 'ere, it ain't a man nor a woman, but some monstrous ghost, the Ghoul of Sherwood they're a-callin' it."

"Ghoul?" Robin's eyes lit up. "So… tell us more about that. That could be something we can use!"

"Use for what?" Jock asked, in some confusion.

"Don't ask." Little John said, shaking his head. "Believe me, you don't want to encourage him."

* * *

Sunday morning in the chapel at the Benedictine Priory at Wallingwells found Friar Tuck and Thorvald both standing in the back corner where Willie's bloody head had been on grim display the previous week. Friar Tuck stood by the Widow Day, who, feeling a good deal better after Granny Alison's healing broth, was glad to be out and at mass. Thorvald stood next to

his new best friend Ralph the cook, along with his family—
the fair Margaret, the even fairer Meggie, and the rather surly
looking son John, who stood several inches taller than his burly
father and whose dark eyes glared from their deep sockets like
a wolf's in the night. There was the wandering minstrel who'd
been entertaining at the Loaves and Fishes each evening since
Tuesday night, along with his boon companion, the young boy
Will Stutely. They were congregating with the regulars Tuck and
Thorvald had met the previous week—John Bryce the bailiff,
Oswald the baker and his wife Hulga, the laundress Elizabeth
Liptrot, and the one regular attendee they had not yet met: the
very lovely dairy woman Kate of Worksop. She had gold ringlets
and flashing blue eyes, and a dazzling smile that made the
friar suspect that, if any of these women would have been poor
Willie's downfall, Tuck's money would be on comely Kate.

But Tuck's musings were interrupted by the Benedictine
choir, as the nuns filed down the nave of the chapel singing the
Nunc, Sancte, traditionally associated with Terce:

> *Nunc, Sancte, nobis, Spiritus,*
> *Unum Patri cum Filio,*
> *Dignare promptus ingeri*
> *Nostro refusus pectori.*
>
> *(Come, Holy Ghost, who ever One*
> *Art with the Father and the Son,*
> *It is the hour, our souls possess*
> *With Thy full flood of holiness)*

Tuck knew the hymn well, and added his own voice to the
choir, but only loud enough for those standing directly near
him—the Widow Day and the dairy maid Kate—to hear. The

hymn, thought to be composed by Saint Ambrose of Milan himself, was considered particularly suitable for Terce, since it was at that third hour that the Holy Ghost had entered into the disciples at Pentecost. But Tuck, aware of what was soon planned for this service, could not help considering the irony of this petition for a visitation of that same Ghost.

> *Os, lingua, mens, sensus, vigor*
> *Confessionem personent.*
> *Flammescat igne caritas,*
> *Accéndat ardor proximos.*

> *(In will and deed, by heart and tongue,*
> *With all our powers. Thy praise be sung:*
> *And love light up our mortal frame,*
> *Till others catch the living flame.)*

The sisters moved slowly up the nave as they chanted these lines, Father Bernard coming behind them in an attitude of prayer. Tuck sighed apprehensively. Things were about to be lighted up in the chapel, all right, but it wasn't love that would do the lighting.

> *Præsta, Pater piissime,*
> *Patríque compar Unice,*
> *Cum Spiritu Paraclito*
> *Regnans per omne sæculum. Amen*

> *(Almighty Father, hear our cry*
> *Through Jesus Christ our Lord most high,*
> *Who with the Holy Ghost and Thee*
> *Doth live and reign eternally.)*

Oh yes, Tuck braced himself as Father Bernard stepped behind the altar to say the mass, a cry was about to be heard, but it was something quite different from what the sisters were singing of. Mentally, Tuck counted to three and then, as if right on cue:

"Horror! Horror! Pluck out these eyes, my God, that they shall never see such vile sights again!" The voice was loud and high, violent and unhinged. It continued to cry out in inarticulate screeches as the big man known as Reynold Greenleaf was supporting and dragging into the chapel the wailing, gesticulating form of the stranger known as Robert Fitz Ooth of Locksley. *And so it begins*, Friar Tuck thought to himself.

The processional had stopped, and the nuns in some disorder were murmuring among themselves, while Father Bernard had turned and rushed back to the chapel doorway to see what the disturbance was about. Robin was leaning dramatically against John's shoulder, as if he needed the big man's strength to hold himself up, and he had a dark grey cloak thrown over his shoulders.

"That face! That terrible face!" Robin was screaming, as if half mad with fright.

"What? My face?" the priest asked, taken aback.

"No, no," Little John said in a calming voice. "He's seen some horror in the woods. I cannot get any *sense* out of him as to what he saw!" And with his deliberate emphasis on the word *sense*, John shook Robin rather insistently with the hand that held him up.

"But that face," Robin continued, his hand on his forehead and his eyes closed. *Overdoing it a bit there, Robin*, Tuck said to himself, but the outlaw chief continued his histrionics: "It was a face without a face! No eyes, but great holes spurting blood. No nose, but a gaping hole in the middle of the face. Lips of rotting flesh peeled back to reveal hungry, devouring teeth!"

"And yet it could speak..." Little John whispered to him.

"And yet it could speak!" Robin echoed. "It flailed its razor-like claws in my direction—I have no doubt it could have dismembered me even as it looked at me…"

"With eyes it did not have…" John murmured out of the corner of his mouth.

"It had a spiritual sense!" Robin cried, hitting on an opportune thought. "Like any undead being, it sensed me without eyes or nose or ears!"

"And it spoke…" John coached.

"Aye, in great rasping echoes from its mangled maw it croaked out its commands to me: 'Find the one' it croaked to me!"

After a moment's silence Father Bernard encouraged Robin to continue. "Th… the one?" he stammered. "Wh… which one would that be?"

"'Find the one that Willie visited that night,' it cried out from those putrefied entrails…"

At that, the priest gagged, and even Tuck felt his gorge rise.

"'Find her and give her my message!' the foul fiend gurgled from its fleshless throat. 'Find her, and tell her…'"

Robin's pause here was, Tuck assumed, for dramatic effect, but it went on a bit longer than seemed optimal. Then Tuck realized that Robin really didn't know what the Ghoul of Sherwood was supposed to have said to him, since what he had expected to happen was that the woman, or girl, to whom Willie had been paying his court on the evening of his demise would become so frightened and panicked at Robin's description of the encounter that she would reveal herself by her screams or by fainting away. But as Tuck looked around the circle of female faces now surrounding this babbling Robert Fitz Ooth of Locksley, he saw concern and fear on their faces, but none revealed herself any more hysterical than any of the others, and Tuck feared the whole enterprise would sink.

Then Little John remembered his role and spoke up, "Tell her what? Tell her what? We're all waiting here on tenterhooks!"

Robin's eyes cast about anxiously as he sought to improvise. "'Tell her,' the Ghoul says to me, 'tell her I'm coming for her next! If she does not reveal herself in the congregation now, I shall be hunting for her from this time forth!'" At that unrehearsed bit of flummery, Little John's eyes grew large as the chapel's rose window. He cleared his throat and tried to lead Robin in a less frenetic direction. "But no one has seen this Ghoul of Sherwood in the daytime," he began. "How are we to know that you're speaking the truth, and not just trying to scare this congregation for your own secret purposes?"

"Does *this* look like I'm making all this up?" Robin cried, throwing off his dark cloak and revealing, as from a giant claw, four ragged slashes across his back, with gouts of blood surging from them. Even Tuck, who knew that these were painted in pig's blood provided by one of Alison and Malyne's neighbors, flinched at the horrifying sight—and now, at last, a few of the women screamed.

Robin fell into Little John's arms as if fainting, but kept his eyes squinting open to try to observe the faces and reactions of the chapel's occupants. Friar Tuck, more familiar with the faces than Robin, kept his eyes wide open and scanned the chapel. On his right the Widow Day seemed energized by the revelations, and was moving her head here and there in quick jerks like a little bird, trying to take in every nuance. Hulga, the baker's wife, looked dazed and was fanning herself with her apron, which she had kept on even to come to mass. The laundress Elizabeth looked stricken, and she wrapped her arms around herself tightly and leaned for support against the chapel's back wall.

A quick glance up the nave showed the nuns highly agitated,

chattering with one another and some appealing to the prioress once again to remove them from this place of horrors. Only two of them remained aloof from the general hub-bub: These Tuck recognized as Sister Anne, the middle-aged nun, who stared down at Robin and John with a stony face that implied a real anger at their antics; and Sister Mary Eusebia, whose dark eyes seemed to dance under her heavy brows as she smirked ironically at what she beheld in the rear of the chapel.

And when he looked to his left, Tuck saw first the young dairy girl Kate, who stood with her arms crossed and a thin-lipped, curious gaze aimed at Robin and John. Meggie, Ralph the cook's daughter, who had been most moved by the sight of Willie's severed head hanging in the church rafters, looked upset, but her attention was completely focused on her mother Margaret, who had actually fainted, and was leaning into the arms of her husband, while Meggie patted her mother's cheeks and fanned her with her bare hands. Meanwhile the son, John, stood staring down at this scene with his hands on his hips, looking angry and, Tuck was certain (though he could hear nothing above the din of voices in the chapel), shouting abuse at either his mother or his sister, or both.

As for the priory's bailiff, Bryce was halfway down the chapel's short nave, conversing with agitated gestures with Sister Mary Barbara, whose hand was on his arm in a soothing posture, as Father Bernard looked on.

Friar Tuck took in a deep breath and exhaled in a long, drawn-out sigh. It was time for the next part of the plan. As the best known and so most trusted visitors to the Worksop area, Tuck and Thorvald might look least suspicious if they circulated among the congregation taking in the locals' impressions of Robin's wild report. Alan a Dale had made himself known with his nightly entertainments in the Loaves and Fishes, so he was also tapped to do some assessment of the congregation's reactions, joined by the gregarious Will Stutely, who never felt like a stranger anywhere he went. Chiefly, they wanted to gauge the reactions of the women, since they still felt confident that if they could discover who it was Willie had been lately intimate with, it may go far in establishing a motive for the gruesome murder that Tuck was still eager to solve. Glancing around, Tuck noticed that Kate the dairy maid had no one else about her, and, with one more final sigh, he stepped toward her with an air of kindly commiseration, opened up a private chat with her.

* * *

"Kate of Worksop was duly appalled by Robin's story, though she freely volunteered that she didn't believe a word of it, nor in the existence of any Ghoul of Sherwood, until that final trick with the pig's blood. That did take her aback." Friar Tuck reached for another morsel of the roast goose that Jock had shot on the wing that morning while the rest of them were at mass. Or rather, at the chapel where mass was, once again, postponed. Now they sat around the small table in Alison's hovel eating another fine meal they'd supplied. Although tonight Alison herself was not present, having been called out for a consultation with a patient. "I was quick to ask Kate if she felt any qualms about, you know, being a love interest of this Willie. She just snorted at me. What made me think she was a love interest of Willie's, or any other clown from this backwater wasteland, she asked me. And I told her I'd heard that this Willie had been paying court to her up until a month or so ago. And besides, it had been duly reported that she had screamed and left the chapel upon seeing Willie's head when it was hung in the rafters."

"And what was her answer to that, then?" Robin asked. "She couldn't very well deny what everybody knows."

Tuck shot Robin a skeptical look. "Sometimes what everybody knows is just what somebody wants them to think. As for Kate, she just scoffed. She said sure, Willie'd been calling on her and trying to get her to come out with him, but she'd never been attracted to him, and thought he was just a slippery lecher and too shifty by half. Wouldn't trust him to muck out her stable, is how she put it. The only interest she'd have in him was if he'd put her in his tinker's cart and drive her out of town, because she'd do about anything to leave this place for good and go live somewhere finer. So no, she certainly wasn't the one he was with the night he was murdered. At least, not that she'd admit to. I asked her if she had to guess who it had been, and she told me if she had to guess, she'd say Elizabeth Liptrot was most likely."

"The old Widow Day said as much when you talked to 'er, right?" Thorvald said, quaffing a bit of ale to wash down his own morsel of goose before he continued: "And yet of all the women at the chapel, she was the one that 'ad the worst opinion of this 'ere Willie when we first met 'em all."

"You can ignore that kind of talk, I'd say," Malyne spoke up, not at all shy of giving her own opinions in this all-male examination of the women involved in the murder. "Of course, if he'd left her earlier for one of the other women, she'd do her best to prove that she didn't care. Unless, of course, she really didn't care. In that case, she wouldn't care."

Thorvald blinked at that logic, then forged ahead with his own report. "Well, I did talk up my good friend Ralph's family, and got close to the daughter Meggie, while she was a-fannin' 'er mum, who'd got light-'eaded and was 'uffin' and puffin' in 'er 'usband's arms. By the time I got there that son of theirs 'ad left off shoutin' at the two women, and neither one of 'em was about to share with me what all that excitement was about. Now that Meggie would 'ardly make a peep without 'er mother chimin' in to drown 'er out. But Meggie did say our Willie 'ad been after 'er same as 'e'd been your Kate, but then 'er mother says, breathin' 'ard the 'ole time of course, that Meggie'd 'ad nothin' to do with 'im, and says just what 'er father'd told me in the Loaves and Fishes: that since she'd been pursued as you might say by Notting'am guards a couple months past, Ralph and the mum 'ad been keepin' their little Meggie pretty well locked up, and wouldn't give that slimy Willie any encouragement at all. So naturally, it wasn't never Meggie as was Willie's companion that night 'e died."

"And so who did they think it was Willie was with?" Robin asked.

Thorvald glanced over at Friar Tuck, and then admitted, "Their money was on the laundress too, Elizabeth Liptrot."

"Well, I spent a pleasant hour or so with Miss Liptrot herself after the shock of our Robin's performance this morning," Will Stutely said, putting down his own drumstick and standing as if he were about to deliver an oration. "And let me tell you, she had much to say to me. I think she'd been bursting to talk to somebody, and wanted it to be somebody who was not a famous gossip in the town, and who wasn't about to judge her for what everyone suspected she'd been doing all along."

"Yes," Little John said. "I notice you were with her for quite a while. Took a walk with her around the lawn outside the chapel, even. She seemed quite taken with you, she did."

"Aye," Stutely winked at John. "I have a way with women. Always have."

"What a waste," John deadpanned.

"Well whatever the reason, my personal charm or just my good looks, this Elizabeth opened up to me. She didn't want to be overheard, which is why we went outside and walked. The women in town are too catty for her to confide in, she said, and anyway she's more comfortable with men. 'So you were comfortable with Willie then?' I asked her. And she blushed and admitted yes, he was her lover and confidante. Working for the nuns, of course, she didn't want a reputation for, you know, loose morals…"

"Fornication," Friar Tuck said in a low voice, shaking off his interview with Sister Mary Eusebia.

"Right," Will said. "And so she kept up a pretense of having nothing to do with him."

"As she insisted that mornin' when we found Willie's bloody 'ead," Thorvald said.

"But everybody in town knew about the affair anyway," Friar Tuck remarked. "All the women, anyway, knew she was seeing him, thought he'd even been with her that night he was killed."

"Well, she wasn't," Stutely told them. "Not according to her, anyway, and I believe her. Of all the women we've seen so far, Miss Liptrot is the only one who admits to a relationship with Willie. And she's the only one who's really expressed any true grief over his passing."

"Not that first morning she didn't," Tuck pointed out. "But I suppose that could be, as Malyne says, just her self-defense after he abandoned her."

"Count on it," Malyne said fixing one eye on Tuck's face while the other wandered disconcertingly off somewhere to the right. "She was saving face even in the midst of her sorrow. Don't ever let 'em catch you crying."

And Robin thought the girl spoke from experience. But he asked a general question: "But this Liptrot woman—a busty brunette, right? Someone in, what? Her mid-thirties? Why should this Willie take up with her if he was such a ladies' man as we've been led to believe? When there are young pretty things like the dairy maid and the cook's daughter to hand?"

"Well now," Will Stutely said. "Just because those girls were tempting doesn't mean they were tempted. Willie fancied himself a ladies' man, but did the women actually respond to him? Maybe they were flattered by his attentions, but that doesn't mean they fell for him—in spite of what your Widow Day says."

Tuck, remembering his interview with the infirmarian Sister Mary Barbara, the lovely young daughter of master Bryce, thought this very likely. "Still," he said, "why the middle-aged laundress?"

"She may have been the one woman in town that was actually interested in him," Alan a Dale suggested. "Maybe for her, unmarried and maybe lonely, he was what she was looking for."

"No doubt true," Will Stutely answered. "But she gave me another reason. According to her, Willie was first attracted to her because of her name. He loved the name Elizabeth, she said, because his dead wife's name was Elizabeth, and he still missed her. And she was around the same age as that wife would have been. She died something like ten years ago, according to Miss Liptrot. Drowned or something wherever they lived at the time—Barlborough of someplace like that she thought he'd said."

Jock suddenly drew erect from the post-dinner slouch he'd been in and cried out, "Barlborough? That's my home village. This Willie was from there, then?"

Robin looked thoughtfully at Jock. "Might be worth finding out about this wife, don't you think?"

Jock grunted and Thorvald suggested, "I been collectin' goods from local artisans as a cover for collectin' information. Maybe we could take a quick trip over there tomorrow or next day an' make like we're there ta sell some o' those items, 'ey? We might do some askin' around while we're there ta find out if anybody remembers this Willie bloke an' 'is wife Elizabeth."

"Worth doing for sure," Robin agreed. "But Will, you think this Liptrot woman might have been so angry over our Willie jilting her that she chopped him in pieces?"

Will frowned and shook his head. "I can't see it," he answered. "She doesn't seem the type."

"In my experience," Malyne said, standing up herself now and putting her hands on her hips, "anybody's capable of anything. Especially if this Willie was with another woman that night."

"Well maybe she'd be mad enough to attack him. But why not the woman he was with? Wouldn't she be the one she hated more? And anyway, I can't see her doing the chopping up. That's some real serious hating, that is. Anyway, she told me Willie had deserted her a month ago. Broke it off and she hadn't seen him since. Only she was sure he had a new girlfriend. She was sure that's why he left her. But she had her suspicions about Meggie, and Kate too."

"Ah, this just goes round in circles," Robin said. "One of these women is lying, you can be sure of that."

"At least one," Alan a Dale agreed. "Look, I don't know what it's worth now, but I did talk to the one other woman—at least the one other lay woman—nobody's mentioned yet." At that, the other men in the room looked puzzled, until Alan reminded them, "I'm talking about Hulga, the baker's wife. You know, the large woman with the round face and kind of vacant look?" Now the others showed some recognition. Hulga was not the kind of woman that men noticed, and they were all searching their memories to try to get a mental picture of the baker's silent companion.

"She can talk?" Thorvald quipped. "Never 'eard 'er open 'er mouth before this, I must say."

"Oh she can talk all right," Alan confirmed. "You might have noticed her fanning herself with her apron. Well, the fact is she was truly concerned about that threat about the Ghoul of Sherwood promising to hunt down the one that was with Willie that last night."

"What… you mean she…?" Robin burst out with a good deal of surprise. "If we thought the laundress was an unlikely lover, who'd have ever suspected the baker's wife!"

"No," Alan a Dale responded, shaking his head. "I don't mean that. She was concerned because of her best friend."

After a moment Friar Tuck exclaimed, "Margaret, the cook's wife! She'd have been Hulga's friend!"

"Correct!" Alan answered. "And Margaret was the one who was completely overcome at Robin's performance, wasn't she?"

"And here we thought she was upset on her daughter's behalf," Robin mused. "So what do you suppose was her relationship with her daughter?"

"You may well ask," came a voice from the door, where Alison was standing. Precisely when she'd returned from her visit no one had noticed, so they did not know how much she had heard of their ramblings. But what she said next threw a new light on everything. "I've just seen her daughter. The girl sent for me to see if I would perform an abortion."

"Meggie?" Robin said.

"Indeed," Alison responded. "The girl is at least two months pregnant."

CHAPTER NINE

Lady Mary of Winchester—"Maid Marion" to her closest associates—had dressed early and quickly in order to wait upon her lady, Countess Lydia Peveril of Chesterfield, who had sent a page to request her presence immediately. From a priest traveling from Nottingham the countess had just received an urgent message from her cousin, Lady Maude Peveril, the discontented wife of the Sheriff of Nottingham. It was marked for her eyes only, and contained news that Countess Lydia was sure would be of vital interest to her chief lady-in-waiting, and so spared no time in calling Marion to her private chamber to discuss the matter.

The countess's closet was a cozy room with a curtained four-poster bed on one wall and woven tapestries on the other three, depicting the hunt of a unicorn in bright red, blue and gold threads. As the countess and Lady Mary sat informally turned toward one another on the edge of the bed, Countess Lydia wasted no words, but merely handed Marion the folded piece of parchment, her earnest brown eyes looking deep into Marion's curious blue ones, and her brows drawn together with a worried crease between them. Shaking her blonde tresses back and forth in confusion, Marion took the parchment letter from the countess's proffering hand and began to read:

Dearest Cousin:

I do hope this finds you well. Please excuse the scrawl as this is written in some haste. I write with urgent news regarding the safety of our mutual friend, the outlaw captain of Sherwood. You are probably unaware of his recent triumph in the archery tournament hosted by my husband in Nottingham. In an impenetrable disguise, he absconded with the tournament prize—as well as a tiara of my own, but let that pass—and this so angered my husband and Sir Guy of Gisbourne that they joined forces and redoubled efforts to scour the forest until they find him. My husband has sent a dozen of his deputies alongside twenty of Gisbourne's armed guards northwards to flush out Robin and his men. It seems that a small company of Gisbourne's guards were bivouacking some two or three months ago near Worksop in the north of Sherwood, and were fairly certain the outlaws' camp was near there. They lacked the numbers to do a thorough search, but the Bishop of Hereford has recently given evidence to my husband that the outlaws' camp is in the north, and so the guards have convinced Gisbourne to let them start their search there. My dear coz, if you know how to get a message to Robin quickly, let him know of his imminent danger.

Your devoted servant,
Maude Peveril

Lady Mary felt like she'd swallowed her heart, and a prickly claw seemed to seize the back of her neck. All the strength left her limbs and a clammy sweat moistened her face. "W… we must get word to him! He must know!" she burst out, as Lady Lydia nodded vigorously.

"Of course, of course," the countess said. "I will send two of my castle guard immediately. But as you well know, even I am not privy to the location of Robin's secret camp. You, my dear, are the only one who's been there."

Indeed Marion had been a guest in Robin's winter camp at Creswell Crags—from which the outlaws had since, without her knowledge, moved south to their Old Oak clearing closer to Nottingham. Nor did she hesitate for a moment before volunteering, "Let me go!"

Lady Lydia looked at Marion from the corner of her eye. Naturally, she had expected Marion to volunteer. And naturally, Marion knew even as she said it that this was what Lydia had expected and counted on. But it was no less spontaneous for that. Lady Mary would never have entrusted such a message to anyone else. And Lydia knew she wouldn't.

"I will have Giles and one of the older guards, perhaps Sir Eustace, ride with you. That should be enough for your protection—you certainly have nothing to fear from outlaws on this mission, I should think."

"And if I run into Gisbourne's bullies?"

"If that happens, and they decide you look suspicious, then my whole garrison will not be enough to defend you."

Marion smiled grimly. "Then Giles and Eustace it is. How soon can we leave?"

"How soon can you be ready?"

"I'm ready now."

* * *

"Gill o' the Red Cap!" Robin cried in the silence following the revelation of Meggie's condition.

Jock o' Barlborough's ears pricked up and he looked questioningly at Robin. He was, of course, the only one in the house who knew who Robin was talking about, but he had no idea why Robin had brought him up. "Chief bowman of Sir Guy of Gisbourne's archers? What has he got to do with anything here?"

"You don't remember?" Robin prodded Jock. "What did he say about having a woman in Wallingwells?"

Jock's face fell as he remembered Gill's boast. "She had hair red as a fox," Jock remembered, "and a sprinkle of freckles across her nose. But surely this is just coincidence."

"How many young women have you seen here with red hair and a turned up, freckled nose?" Robin challenged him.

"But Gill was a loudmouth braggart," Jock argued. "What are the chances he was telling the truth and not just doing some wishful thinking?"

"Chances o' that are bloody good!" Thorvald broke in. "Every time I've talked to this Meggie's father, 'e's complained about 'ow 'e 'ad to fight off one o' them guards o' Gisbourne's that was after 'is daughter the 'ole time those troops was 'ere. It's got to be the guy you're talkin' about!"

"And if we can believe our laundress, Miss Liptrot, our victim Willie had nothing to do with Meggie—or at least she had nothing to do with him—until one short month ago," Friar Tuck said, adding "Willie could not be the father of this child. The likely candidate must be this red-hatted person. I should caution you though, Madam Alison, that the church frowns on abortions, though I know some of our theologians believe them permissible until the quickening..."

"And that is usually the fourth month, good friar, so in

Meggie's case we are well within the time," Alison answered, a blush of pique staining her cheeks.

"So…" Will Stutely began, drawing the vowel out thoughtfully, "where does that leave us with this murder inquiry?"

"It leaves us nowhere," Friar Tuck admitted, failing to note Alison's mood. "I avow, I'm beginning to despair of ever finding justice for our victim in this case."

"And are we quite sure that he deserves justice?" Alison returned, her fighting spirit now showing itself. "It seems that no one you've talked to is able to give you any clue as to what happened to him, no, nor does anyone seem to be grieving his loss overmuch."

Tuck stood up and shook his head vigorously, his jowls shaking in his fervor. "One at least is grieving—our laundress Elizabeth. Perhaps there are others. Willie was enough of a human being to deserve justice, if you believe as I do that God loves all those created in His image."

"Well what if this Willie deformed that image? Have you considered whether perhaps that Willie has *already* received his justice?" Alison now stood toe to toe with the friar, the former urchin she had befriended and protected in his youth and now had, perhaps, forgotten what he owed her.

Tuck sat back down and sighed, deflated. "Can such violence, such obvious blind hatred ever be called justice? According to the *lex taliones*, only someone who has killed deserves the punishment of death himself. Otherwise, what happens is not justice but vengeance, and that the Lord has reserved for himself."

"In my experience, He often needs a nudge. Or a hand," Alison muttered under her breath. Then she said aloud, "So you think that this Willie's killer deserves to die as well?"

Tuck shrugged. "It would be justice. It would be *lex taliones*."

"Well, I plan on takin' a new tack on this 'ere knotty problem," Thorvald said, changing direction before tempers grew too hot. "Tomorrow I an' our new friend Jock there will take my cart and my goods off to 'is 'ome town o' Barlborough to see whether anybody there can tell us anything about this tinker and 'is wife o' ten years past. Maybe that's where we learn somethin' of this bloke before 'e turned up 'ere."

"I'm with you there, Thorvald," Jock agreed.

"And it seems to me," Alan a Dale suggested, moving on from his own earlier observations, "that somebody ought to do a much more through questioning of this Margaret the cook's wife. Maybe, as you say, the laundress isn't the only one grieving the passing of our tinker. It's Margaret who had the biggest reaction to Robin's little interlude. I think we need to know why."

There was general agreement all around the room, but silence as they tried to decide who might be the best person to approach Meggie's mother. After a pause, Alison spoke up again. "Let me talk to her."

Friar Tuck, taken slightly aback, blurted out "You? But… I thought you were washing your hands of this quest."

Alison avoided meeting Tuck's eyes, and answered quietly, "I can't say I'm convinced that getting to the truth in this case is completely desirable. But if we *are* going to get at the truth, it seems obvious to me that Margaret will be far more likely to open up to another woman rather than one of you blokes. I have to visit the cook's home anyway to see how Meggie has reacted to the potion I mixed for her tonight. What could be more natural than talking to her mother about the daughter's health? It will be easy enough to bring the conversation around to our late misfortunes in the community. Rest assured, she will trust me and she will tell me far more than you could get her to tell you."

"That's decided then," Robin stepped in before Tuck could raise any objections. "And now, I think, it's time we started on our way back to the Loaves and Fishes for the night. Some of us have an early start in the morning. In fact, Jock, since you are heading out with Thorvald in the morning, why don't you stay here with the widow and her daughter tonight so that you can both leave in Thorvald's cart right away in the morning. Friar, if Jock stays here there will be no room for you, so take his horse and come with us into town. You can stay with Alan and me on Jock's pallet. Right? All right then. We'll meet back here tomorrow evening, and see what we've found out. Good night ladies, and a thousand thanks for your hospitality!" And with that Robin gave a gallant bow, and with a flourish exited the hovel, followed by his men. Tuck, on edge from his near altercation with his old benefactor Alison, was only too glad to put some distance between them for the night. Maybe he would feel better in the morning. But right now, his investigation seemed to be foundering in the mire.

* * *

The next morning, Friar Tuck rose early after a fitful night's sleep, and after breaking his fast told Robin he wanted to take Jock's horse for a ride. He was considering making another visit to the priory, he told his captain, perhaps to touch base with a few of the nuns again. In fact he was not sure what he wanted to do, but he believed if he gave himself some time to ride and think, he might find something he'd failed to see so far. In any case, he wasn't going to waste the day moping around the Loaves and Fishes.

As for the other outlaws, Robin wanted to lead them out into the forest surrounding Worksop and do a bit of hunting. If they could poach the king's deer here, that was fine with Robin. But a few rabbits or even waterfowl would be fine as well. Alison and Malyne lived from hand to mouth, and their putting up Tuck and Thorvald on a daily basis was a strain on their space and their resources, so Robin felt a responsibility to supply food for the two women as well as his own men as long as they were in town. He was a little disappointed that Jock was not with them, since the old man was so accurate with the bow that any hunting trek with him was almost certain to be quite successful.

But Robin also wanted to take the opportunity to speak with Little John about something he'd been concerned over for several days—indeed, since that revelation by Gill o' the Red Cap that Gisbourne's troops had been in this area but two months past.

He ambled slowly into the forest next to Little John, their bows hanging from their shoulders, letting Will and Alan get farther and farther ahead. When he was sure they couldn't be overheard, he broached the subject with his lieutenant: "John, I'm worrying a bit about something that's got nothing to do with this Willie business."

"And what's that, my lad?" Little John asked, bending down to pluck a blade of long grass and letting it hang lackadaisically from between his teeth. He, at least, had no worries.

"This Gill o' the Red Cap fellow, the one we suspect of being the father of this unborn child of Meggie's," Robin began. "You might remember him from the sheriff's archery tournament in Nottingham."

"Oh sure," John said. "Muscular bloke. Broad and stocky, Kind of a loudmouth."

"That's the chap," Robin agreed.

"He was the other one who should've won the contest instead of you," John drawled, chewing on his blade of grass and stretching nonchalantly.

Robin pursed his lips and closed his eyes with the mildest annoyance, which he knew was exactly what John was after, and so he went on without comment: "Well, you heard that he was in the area of Worksop and Wallingwells with a small band of Gisbourne's troops just two months ago. Two months ago when we were all encamped at Creswell Crags. And do you know how far we are from Creswell Crags at this very spot?"

Little John shrugged. "Day's ride?" he suggested.

"Five miles," Robin corrected him. "Five short miles. Now why would Gisbourne have his guardsmen up here anyway, unless it was to look for us? There's nothing going on in these small towns that could interest him. Other than perhaps getting a report from someone who's seen us in the area."

"Well, they've gone now and none the wiser, so we can breathe easy, I'd say."

"I'm not breathing easy. They were here for at least a week, as far as I can tell from what people've said. How could they have failed to notice a group our size but five miles away?"

"And if they did, what of it?" John returned. "How would they know who we were?"

"They had to have suspected. Who else would be camping in the forest with that many folks for an extended period of time?"

"Homeless folk, driven from the land or from their vanished villages? Times are hard, my lad. We've seen such folk ourselves."

"But not in such numbers. I tell you Gisbourne's men had to have suspected we were at Creswell Crags for the winter."

"But now it's getting on summer," Little John said, unconcerned. "And we've moved out of those caves. We're back at our summer quarters and no one the wiser. Even if we left scraps behind that they could identify as ours, they're too late. So what if Gisbourne thinks he's found our home? We'll find a different one next winter."

Robin scratched his head. "It still bothers me how close they were. What if the only reason they didn't try to arrest us two months ago is that they were too few in number at the time? Now that they've gone back to Nottingham, what's to stop them from convincing Gisbourne to send a much larger troop after us now?"

"Nothing, for sure," Little John agreed. "But that's also what they'll find at our old camp. Nothing."

"True," Robin said with a sigh. "Thank God everybody's out of there safe. They'll find nobody to connect the place to us now."

"Right," John ended. "Only trouble we'd have is if they decided to send a big force up here right now, and caught the seven of us here unprotected."

And with that John gave a big laugh, which caused Will and Alan to shush him exaggeratedly from the stand they'd made up in one of the trees just ahead. "You'll scare the game!" they whispered loudly from the fourth branch up. Robin, meanwhile, pursed his lips again, thinking of Little John's last comment. Now he was worried about *that, too.*

* * *

At the center of the village of Barlborough was a stone standing cross, erected, Jock explained to Thorvald, as a preaching cross. Mendicant friars or itinerant preachers might gather a crowd here on a Sunday or holy day, and entertain them with a sermon. There was no parish church within the small village itself, and the twelve or fifteen families of the village and the twenty-five or so who held small farmsteads surrounding it generally attended the church attached to Bolsover Castle. That castle had originally belonged to the Peveril family, but had passed to the Ferrers family on the death of Lady Lydia's great-grandfather, and so the village of Barlborough was now part of the manor of Lord Ferrers.

The village stood atop a steep bank of yellow sandstone from which, looking eastward, Jock and Thorvald could observe the flat farmland worked by most of the villagers as it sloped down toward Worksop and the River Ryton. The two of them had rolled into the sleepy village early that morning and had pulled their cart directly in front of the cross. Several villagers, going about their morning business, had looked on in interest, expecting the dwarf to break into a sermon on the virtues of whatever saint happened to be commemorated on this day, or, failing that, to do some cartwheels and put on a traveling show. But instead, Thorvald broke into a kind of sales pitch, extolling the quality of the carpentry and leather goods he had for sale in his cart. Accustomed to traveling eight or nine miles to Chesterfield for fairs in order to buy goods, a number of the villagers were immediately drawn to this odd little merchant. And after cautiously approaching the cart, several of them recognized Jock, whose presence made them comfortable about buying goods from this little man. In fact, within two hours Thorvald had actually sold most his stock, and had a substantial profit to share with his partners back in Worksop.

Of course, profit was not Thorvald's chief motive here, but it didn't hurt his mood. And the heavy traffic around his cart enticed a number of Jock's old acquaintances to stop by. And although Jock had not in fact lived in Barlborough for some twenty years, it was a small enough community for the people there to remember him, as they remembered everyone who had ever lived there. That, of course, was what Jock was counting on: Although Willie the tinker had apparently lived in Barlborough after Jock himself had left, no permanent resident of the town was likely to have forgotten him.

The third customer at Thorvald's cart was a villager by the name of Thaddeus, who ran the mill on the river at the edge of town. Jock remembered him as a talkative bloke who loved gossip, and if anybody could tell them about Willie the tinker, it would be Thaddeus the miller. "Thaddeus!" Jock began. "Are you still overcharging the farmers about for grinding their grain, then?"

"Whatever the market will bear!" the miller responded reflexively, in a gravelly voice that fitted his gruff exterior. Then studying his questioner's countenance, his grizzled face lit up in mild surprise, "Is it Jock? Jock, my boy, we haven't seen you here in a generation! I knew you'd left to follow the old lord Ferrers as an archer in the wars under the late king, but you never did come back. What have you been doing since?" he asked as he pumped Jock's hand, his dark eyes sparkling under their bushy white eyebrows.

"Oh, this and that," Jock replied evasively. "I got used to life as an archer. And you know, I had no family back here to lure me back. I wanted to see something of the world, you know?

And as Thaddeus finished his purchase of a new pair of boots from Thorvald, Jock thought back to an incident he remembered that might give him a chance to bring the conversation around to Willie. Thaddeus, after all, was about the same age as Jock, and so the outlaw knew they had some shared memories of the village, and he was pretty sure he knew one that Thaddeus could recall vividly.

"I do think about growing up here quite often, though," Jock continued. "You remember how we used to go fishing down in the Ryton there, eh? Pulling in pike and bream?"

"Ah, those were the days," Thaddeus agreed.

"And who was the fellow who used to come with us sometimes? What was his name again? Redheaded bloke? With the big ears?"

"Oh yeah, yeah," Thaddeus answered, shaking his finger at Jock and becoming more animated. "Piers! That was it. Piers the smith's son. Right. He was always a peppy little fellow. Shame what happened to him."

Jock just nodded in response, and Thorvald, left out of the conversation, was forced to ask, "What? What did happen to him?"

"Oh, drowned dead in the river not long after those days," Thaddeus answered, shaking his head ruefully.

"There's an undercurrent there that can surprise you if you're not expecting it," Jock told the dwarf. Then he continued, with a smoothness that made Thorvald hide a brief appreciative smile, "Did that current ever claim anybody since I've been gone? Seemed pretty dangerous to me."

"Well," Thaddeus answered, stroking his chin thoughtfully. "Seems to me the river's claimed a few folk over the years. I do remember a few years ago… well, maybe more like eight or nine… they said a young woman had drowned there. Never found her body, as I recall, but her husband seemed pretty torn up about it. Kept insisting they keep looking for her when they'd all given up. Left town for good right after that, I remember. Guess he couldn't stand the memories. But those folks only moved here a few years before. Funny thing, that. I never knew them very well. I remember he was something like your friend here, had a wagon and traveled around selling things or something like. So he was gone from home a lot. Then he was just gone."

After Thaddeus had left, Thorvald held Jock's gaze for some moments before chortling, "You, Jock, you're a natural born trickster, looks like. You're gonna be a big addition to our band. Silver tongue, that's you!"

Jock was less successful with most of the rest of Thorvald's customers as the afternoon wore on, but one of the last visitors to the cart was a woman Jock remembered well. He knew her as Ursula, wife of a yeoman farmer, but as a widow she now lived in town, and though nearly fourscore years of age she seemed as sharp as ever to Jock, and recognized him immediately as one of the boys her husband used to chase off for stealing eggs from his chickens.

The old woman shook a finger at Jock, her sagging, astonishingly wrinkled cheeks trembling as she spoke. "So, back are you? Become an itinerant merchant now, have you? Better than I would have thought you'd turn out, I must say."

"Madame Ursula, you don't look a day older than when I saw you last, and that was twenty years ago! Interested in any of our wares here? We have leather goods—shoes and gloves—and some nicely made furniture from our carpenter client…"

Dame Ursula looked over some of the stock in the cart, finally settling on a nicely polished rocking chair that Paul, the Worksop carpenter, had entrusted to Thorvald for his first sales trip. The elderly woman seemed to have been left well off by her husband, and didn't blink an eye at the fairly steep price Thorvald asked. "Let me help you carry that chair to your home, Ursula," Jock offered, but Thorvald said, "No, we'll just carry it there in the cart. I think we've made all the sales we're going to today, so we'll drop the chair off on our way out of town."

At that, Ursula's wrinkles rearranged themselves into a wizened smile. As Thorvald followed them in the cart, Jock walked with Ursula along the street toward her cottage. It was on the way there that Jock rather casually began his probing.

"You know, Madam Ursula, we've looked for a few other craftsmen who might have items we can market to the towns in this area. What other kind of goods do you think the folks here might like to see sold in the village? One thing we thought of was a tinker's goods…"

"A tinker we could use," she said, musing. "We did have a tinker here for a few years. It was after you'd gone, But the fella didn't stay very long. He never got on too well here."

"Oh? And why was that do you suppose? Not the most welcoming town in the Midlands, is it?" Jock said, with a teasing edge to his voice that Ursula picked up on… and, in fact, remembered from the days when Jock was a mouthy scamp.

"You watch your tone, young man," she answered the sexagenarian. "You're not so big I can't still put you over my knee!" Jock laughed heartily at the idea, and his old neighborhood scold laughed with him. "But no, Barlborough's not much different from most places, I suppose. Takes a generation before a stranger isn't thought of as an outsider so much anymore. But it wasn't just that. This Willie fella was always traveling around in his wagon, leaving his wife here by herself. And that's never a good idea."

"What… you mean she strayed did she?"

"Well, I don't know about that," the old woman answered noncommittally. "Though I'd a' been tempted if I was her. And who knows what *he* was doing on the road. But no, I mean to say they had their squabbles. And one day she was gone."

"Gone?" Jock echoed. This was not quite the same story they'd heard from Thaddeus. But he didn't press the issue—it wouldn't do to have Ursula think he was all that interested in the story.

"We never saw her again in town. Willie himself made a big fuss and claimed that he'd seen her in the river, and said we needed to save her or at least find her, but nobody ever found a body."

"Washed out to sea?" Jock pried casually.

"Or was never there to begin with. Who can say? She might a' just left him—that's what I'd a' done. And he may have made up the drowning story to save face. Or who knows? He may even have killed her, and tried to cover that up by claiming she'd drowned. They weren't close enough to anybody else in town for anybody to have really noticed when exactly she disappeared, and he disappeared himself not long after. Left town and never told anybody goodbye. Sakes alive, I'm lucky I even remember his name was Willie. Can't seem to remember hers at all. But it was a saint's name, I remember that. Eudoxia? Something beginning with an e. Edburga? Encratia? Ercongotha? Ethelburga? Oh..." and with that she stopped momentarily as if frozen in thought, then let out another hearty laugh. "No, it was Elizabeth!" And she and Jock shared another laugh as Thorvald stopped the cart in front of the lady's house and Jock carried the chair in for her, declining her offer of a mug of ale, and left the house in good spirits to join Thorvald at the cart. They were ready to make their way back to the Worksop vicinity, feeling they'd had a successful trip and learned a few things along the way.

But before he had even climbed into the cart beside the dwarf, Jock heard a booming voice behind him calling "Jock of Barlborough! I thought that was you!"

When he turned, Jock was startled to recognize, first, the bright red cap on the head of the burly man just climbing down from his horse. "Gill o' the Red Cap!" he answered in some disbelief. "What... what on earth are you doing in this place?" He blinked a few times, noting the column of men following Gisbourne's chief archer, and suddenly, with a sinking feeling in his stomach, was fairly certain he knew the answer to that question.

Thorvald, on seeing the line of armed guards and recognizing Guy of Gisbourne's coat of arms—the black lion on the field of gold—on their surcoats, immediately threw his cloak over his head and hunched down in his seat on the cart. He had no way of knowing whether any of these troops had ever seen him among Robin Hood's men, but he was quite sure that if anyone had seen someone of his description, they were not likely to forget him. "Keep a very low profile," he said to himself. And then he added, "No pun intended."

Hunched up and hidden beneath his heavy cloak, Thorvald kept listening closely to Jock's conversation with this loudmouthed newcomer, and tried to keep track of what was happening out of the corner of his eye.

"Quite a coincidence, seeing you here so soon after our archery meet! But then, come to think of it, why in the world *wouldn't* I expect to see Jock o' Barlborough *in* Barlborough! It's like, you see a red cap, you ought to expect to see good old Gill under it! Am I right?"

Jock laughed, more politely than humorously, glad that Jock did not actually realize how very *unlikely* he would be to see Jock here under normal conditions. But he did ask the one question of most concern to himself and to Thorvald: "True enough Gill. But where I *wouldn't* have expected to see you was here in Barlborough yourself. What on earth are you doing here? And with so large a following!" Jock looked back and counted fifteen pairs of guards, all mounted and all apparently under Gill's command, as they waited without a word for him to finish this apparently random conversation. Sneaking his eyes along the column, Thorvald could see, between the horses halfway down, a trio of figures on foot, who seemed to be forced to march alongside the troops.

"Well, it's a funny thing," Gill said, in answer to Jock's question. "You remember that Hodden of Barnesdale bloke the two of us were up against in the last round of that tournament? The one who got off the lucky shot and ended up beating me out of my rightful prize?"

"Well, I'm not likely to forget so soon. I'm not quite in my dotage yet."

Gill guffawed at that, throwing his head back so that Thorvald thought he might even fall off his horse. But he righted himself quickly and went on: "Well, turns out that was no Hodden of Barnesdale after all, but the outlaw Robin Hood himself, wearing a disguise, false beard and all!" Jock feigned astonishment, and Thorvald gritted his teeth, afraid of what was coming. "Well, the sheriff was pretty put out after that, and apparently this Robin even stole his wife's tiara on top of everything after she'd put it down somewheres. So Sir Guy, my commander, really put his foot down and said he wasn't gonna rest until he had this Robin and all his men in irons."

"Lord above," Jock began, and Thorvald thought it a pretty weak attempt at feigning surprise. "So you all think this Robin Hood character is here in Barlborough? I can assure you, he's not. It's not a big place to hide."

"Not necessarily here, but somewhere in this area. I was up around here with a few of my men a couple of months ago, and we were pretty certain we had those bandits' refuge located somewhere in the caves around Creswell Crags close by here."

At that, Thorvald nearly fell off his seat. To think they had been that close to detection by Gisbourne's men! What a narrow escape they had had, moving back south when they did. But Gill was continuing: "So after the sheriff's humiliation at the hands of the outlaw chief, Sir Guy has sent us up here in full force to roust them out. Trouble is, we've just come from Creswell Crags, and it looks like whoever was there has pretty much cleared out. We found evidence that a pretty good sized group had been staying there for a while, but they're not there now. We did find these three individuals poking around the area though. They claim not to know anything about Robin Hood, but then, they would, wouldn't they, if they were cohorts of his? Bring 'em up here, will you, Tom!" he roared back over his shoulder.

At that, one of the mounted soldiers left ranks and trotted up to the front of the line to where Gill was conversing with Jock, dragging behind him the three figures whose hands were tied and who were tied together. They stumbled, panting, sweaty and dirty, to stand before Jock, and as he looked at them with pity and sorrow, Gill asked him, "You're from these parts. You ever see any of these characters before? They're fancy dressed, you see. They from some rich house around here somewhere?"

Jock, eyeing them mournfully, shook his head. "No," he said. "I've never seen them before."

Thorvald, peeping out from under his cloak, was more violently moved. He had recognized the woman immediately. It was Robin's Maid Marion.

CHAPTER TEN

Like everybody else in the Worksop/Wallingwells vicinity, Margaret the cook's wife knew who Granny Alison was. And like most of the women in that same area, Margaret had found it necessary on occasion to make use of Granny Alison's services in one way or another. Seventeen years ago, it had been Alison whom Margaret had called upon as midwife to bring Meggie into the world. And just yesterday it had been Alison whom Margaret had called upon to ensure against Meggie's own child dropping uninvited into that same world.

So there was no great look of surprise on Margaret's face when Alison, leaning on her staff with her unrestrained white hair floating on the breeze, came out of the forest onto the road that led past Ralph the cook's small cottage a furlong way outside of the priory. Margaret simply opened the door to her visitor as the old woman crossed her threshold without breaking stride, and croaked out her greeting, "I'm here to see my patient. How is she? Has my potion had an effect?"

Margaret, perceiving that the midwife was speaking carefully on the chance that her husband or son may be in the house, quickly disabused her of that notion. "We can speak freely, Dame Alison, my husband and my son are at the priory preparing the midday meal for the sisters. I excused myself this morning to watch over Meggie."

"Those men, then, don't know about the pregnancy? Or do they not know about the termination?"

Margaret shrugged. "Ralph knows nothing. It would be months before he'd notice anything unusual in Meggie's girth. Her brother, though, has always been close with her. He and Ralph both were livid over the attentions that guard from Nottingham was paying to her when they were here two months ago. He… may suspect the girl is with child."

"And is she still with child? The potion has had no effect?"

"She certainly has pains in her belly," Margaret answered. "Nothing has happened yet."

"This Nottingham castle guard is the child's father then?" Alison asked, disinterestedly, as if it were simply a point of information.

After a short hesitation, Margaret nodded. "Yes. She's missed two of her monthly cycles since then. We truly need to keep her situation quiet."

"Yes, there is always hurtful gossip from the less charitable of our neighbors, isn't there?" Alison sympathized.

"Gossip is a small matter," Alison scoffed. "That's not the real problem. There's no telling what her father—or her brother, for that matter—would do if they suspected this was the state she's in." Meggie, who was lying in the cabin's other room, gave a low groan and Alison frowned.

The older woman tut-tutted and looked past Margaret into the room. "I should take a look at her," she suggested.

"Why not let her sleep for now? Sleep has to be good for her," Margaret argued.

"Sleep will be good for her after she miscarries. We ought to be sure the potion is working now."

Margaret deferred to the midwife's expertise and stood aside as Alison walked purposefully toward Meggie's bed.

* * *

That evening Robert Fitz Ooth of Locksley sat by himself at a table in the corner of James Snaggletooth's Loaves and Fishes, nursing a tall flagon of ale and pondering the perceived threat to his Sherwood enterprise by Gisbourne's newest tactics. Of course, it was possible that Little John was right, and that the outlaw band, having evacuated Creswell Crags for headquarters farther south, had come through a close call but was now safe as houses. But Robin couldn't afford to be cavalier about the security of his band, casual as he might be about most other aspects of life—including his personal safety. It was one thing to wind up the sheriff by carrying off the archery prize under his nose; it was quite another to put his men and their families at risk by casually failing to anticipate steps that Gisbourne or the sheriff might be designing.

If Gill o' the Red Cap was here with a unit of guards two short months ago, they were almost certainly seeking news of the Sherwood outlaws. It was in the north of Sherwood they had captured Will Stutely late last year. If they had been here and were searching, they could not have missed the camp at Creswell Crags. They had been simply too close to have plausibly failed to notice Robin's camp. The only reason they would have taken no action then must be that they were simply too few to take on Robin's entire band. But considering further, it had been obvious that the Bishop of Hereford, captured here in the north and entertained at the grounds of Peveril Castle, had been deliberately sent here to be apprehended and to draw Robin to Nottingham with his news of the archery tournament. That ruse having failed to bag Robin, what was the next logical step? Sending a force north that was large enough to capture— or kill—all of Robin's meinie. It was quite true, as Little John had said, that such a force could not succeed, since they'd be hunting miles and miles from the current encampment. But Robin and Little John, and Thorvald and Tuck, Will Stutely and Alan a Dale and Jock were all here now, in the very eye of that coming storm. Could the company survive losing that many limbs? And what of their friends here? Would Granny Alison and the deep-minded Malyne be arrested for helping them? The unfamiliar and unwanted weight of responsibility was making Robin uncharacteristically morose, and that was why he had begged off returning to Alison and Malyne's hovel tonight with the spoils of the hunt, and chosen to come back alone to the inn, to think things through by himself.

There was a group with three apprentices of Worksop craftsmen at one of the other tables, and a quiet man and woman at another. The only other person in the place—it was early yet—was slumped alone at a table across the room from Robin. Squinting through the dying light Robin thought he recognized the young man. A tall bloke he was, dressed in nondescript brown tunic and gray hose. He had sandy hair and deep, dark eyes, and Robin placed him immediately: it was John, the son of the cook, Ralph. Robin wondered: if the sister had been friendly with Gill o' the Red Cap—friendly enough to fall pregnant by him—then it may be that this cook's family was privy to some information about Gisbourne's guards and their activities during their recent visit to this area. Robin discreetly signaled Master Snaggletooth and asked him to serve the solitary young man another cup of ale and to put it on Robert Fitz Ooth's tab.

Robin watched as James brought the cup to the young man's table and pointed toward his own, and as the youth John peered toward him across the room. As James began to light lanterns and candelabra about the inn, John rose and carried his ale across the floor to Robin's table.

"I hear I've got you to thank for this," he said, scowling down at Robin, his dark eyes flashing from their deep sockets. "What is it you want of me?"

The corner of Robin 's mouth twisted upward at the young man's frankness. "No nonsense with you, eh? Get right to the point. I appreciate that. Sit down first, at least, will you?"

"No sir," John said. "You're that bloke that came into the church ranting about being attacked by some monstrous ghoul you said killed old Willie. Now you sit here buying drinks. What's your game then, eh?"

Robin shrugged. This boy was not an easy dupe, like some of the others in this town. "It's no game," he said. "Just trying to help."

"Help? Help who? What are you and your friends doing here, anyway? Whatever business you had should have been done by now. What are you staying around for, then?"

"Look," Robin said. "I want to find out what happened to Willie..."

"Well, you said it yourself. The ghoul of Sherwood killed him."

"Then tell me," Robin urged, figuring he had nothing to lose by asking a straight question. "Why did your mother faint when she heard the ghoul wanted to kill the woman Willie'd been with? And why did you..."

But Robin never got out the rest of his question. John took the cup of ale, stretched out his right arm and tilted it, pouring the ale over Robin's head.

* * *

Granny Alison had conceded to Margaret's opinion on her daughter's condition. The poor girl was worn out with pain and false labor, and the midwife had given her an herbal drink to help her get some sleep. Now Alison was sitting in the front room with the cook's wife sipping a cup of small beer and encouraging Margaret to share her troubles.

"So Margaret, why do you think the girl's father and brother don't realize what's going on in their own household?"

"Oh, Lord, they're men, ain't they?" Margaret said. "She's not showing yet at all, and they've got no idea. They knew that Gill fellow was sniffing around, but never knew what he did with her."

"Promised her marriage and all that, I suppose?"

"Didn't need to. Some of these honey-tongued blighters just tell the girls what they want to hear about how beautiful they are and how they're going to die if they can't get their spindle twisted. Talk to her like that and then tell her he'll take her away with him, away from a father that's keeping you under his thumb, you know how it goes."

"Yes," Alison said. "I've seen it all over the years. But this Gill left her right where she was, didn't he, and disappeared from here? And left her with a fatherless child on her hands."

"Which is why we came to you, of course," Margaret agreed.

"Of course," Alison said. And she let that thought hang in the air for a while. Then she quietly asked the question she'd been leading to. "You didn't come right away, though, did you? I mean, you did take a bit of time to come to me after all, I noticed. Did you think this Gill and his twisted spindle were coming back?"

Margaret scoffed. "That was never going to happen. I told Meggie that from the beginning. I warned her not to listen to his pleas. Did she pay attention to me? I tell you, Granny Alison, there's some as will never learn till it happens to *them*. I'll warrant Meggie is one of those."

"So why the delay? Why didn't you come to me right away?"

Margaret was biting her tongue. She badly wanted to open

up to this friendly ear, she had so little opportunity to talk to another woman who was not in fact a nun. But she had been frightened. She still was.

Alison shifted her eyes down and to the left as if deep in thought. "You know," she began coyly, "I've heard some talk about last Sunday in the chapel, how that Robert Fitz Ooth fellow came bursting in with that story of how the forest monster threatened to tear apart the woman who'd been with Willie the tinker the night he died. They told me that you fainted when the bloke said that. What was that about, then?"

Margaret looked at Alison with eyes big as ripe apples, then turned shyly away. "Where'd you hear that?" she asked quietly.

"It's all the gossips are saying right now," Alison shrugged.

"Hmmph. What *else* are they saying?" Margaret asked, almost listlessly.

"Well, some are suggesting it's because you were the woman this Willie was with that night. And I admit, it's not an implausible guess. I mean, you're still a fine looking woman, and who hasn't thought a younger man might be worth a tumble?"

Margaret scoffed, not deigning to dignify that with an answer.

"But me, I'm thinking there was something else scaring you. Something you thought might be your fault, even."

Now Margaret's head was in her hands and she was slowly moving it from side to side. "He was such a lecher, that 'Sweet' Willie. Always making indecent proposals to every woman in town. Elizabeth Liptrot was the only one to ever stay with him for more than one lark. But even when he was with her, he was trying to find some other woman to give him a tumble. I felt sorry for Elizabeth—she pretended she didn't care about his philandering because she didn't care about him and wanted everyone in town to think she was long over him, but she kept having him back, again and again. He did try approaching even me, you're right. He did it in the priory kitchen, when I was there helping my husband with the midday meal, and he came in delivering some pots or kettles he'd mended for the convent. He got me alone in the kitchen and started his sweet talk on me. Not as smooth a talker as that Gill, I'd venture, but he'd only had experience with country girls, not ones from big cities like Nottingham. Course his silly fawning didn't affect me at all, but it did make me think."

"And you thought," Alison encouraged her, "that he might just be Meggie's way out of her situation?"

Margaret gave a sigh of relief. It was some comfort to be relieved of the burden she'd been carrying so long. "Willie was a local lad. If he didn't want to marry her, we'd have ways of pressing him into it. The community would have forced him to do the right thing."

"So you offered Willie your daughter when you turned down his come on?"

Margaret laughed. "No, obviously, nothing that crass. I did chide him and say I was old enough to be his mother. Which wasn't true, of course—I mean, he was at least thirty-five. But I did tell him that my daughter was of marriageable age, and there were so few eligible young men in the area. Basically I implied that her father and I were looking for a suitable husband for her."

"And this Willie was fool enough to believe that you thought his being a lecher and propositioning her mother made him a good catch for your daughter?"

"It was better than waiting until her father found out about her condition. And it would get her out of that man's house. For heaven's sake, I've lived with him for twenty years, I know what he's like and I know what his fists are like when he's incensed, and she would be a lot better off out of this house. But when Willie died, the only choice was to come to you."

"So it was Meggie who was with Willie the night he was killed," Alison said.

"It was, I think, the third time. I'd arranged it on a night when the rest of us were all in the convent for some special evening meal they were having, and stayed overnight. She was by herself in the cottage. Meggie and I had planned to wait a few days after that, and then spring the baby on him. He'd either have to marry her or I'd send my son after him. I still wouldn't tell Ralph, for fear of what he'd do to the fellow."

"And your son knew of the meetings between Meggie and Willie?"

"No, no. I hadn't planned to tell him. But then, when I heard that Fitz Ooth fellow pronounce the ghoul's death sentence on Meggie, I broke down, I thought my scheme might be her death. And I did let it slip out that she'd been with Willie that night."

"And that's why your son was so angry with you that morning."

"Yes," Margaret said. Then, after a moment's pause. "But how did *you* know about that? You weren't there."

Alison gave her a tight lipped smile and a shrug. "Gossip," she said again.

* * *

Robin wiped the ale from his eyes and discreetly signaled James to bring him a napkin to wipe his face and hair. John the cook's son had stalked straight out the door after his demonstration, and Robin had lost his chance to speak with him, which at the moment he felt was totally fine. "Didn't want to talk to you either," he muttered under his breath, and when Snaggletooth brought him the napkin and broached the subject of paying for John's drink, Robin sighed, tossed tuppence on the table, and muttered, "*That* was money well spent."

But before he could get up from the table and head up to his room, Robin heard a loud voice from the street that he thought he recognized. It did not belong to a man he had any desire to see or be seen by.

"In here, lads, and set yourselves down for a spell. This here's my favorite watering hole in these parts, Jack and Claude can tell you! We spent many a rousing night in this dive back in February and March, and they've got the best ale in a day's ride, I swear to you. Master of the House!" Gill o' the Red Cap called. "Give 'em all a drink!" By the histrionic swing of his right arm, it was clear that Gill intended not only that the dozen men he'd come in with be served, but that he was buying the good will of the other six customers as well, and Robin certainly did not want to draw attention to himself by getting up to leave and by refusing the drink. Robin knew that his disguise at the Nottingham contest had been a good one, but he couldn't be sure that none of Gill's fellow guards had ever seen him in person. And the fact that he was dressed in the Lincoln green livery of the Sherwood bandits did not fill him with confidence in his anonymity. All he could do was keep his face down, pull his hood over his head, and blend as best he could into the woodwork.

Gill, by contrast, was definitely no shrinking violet. He shepherded all his men to the tables, and seemed to want to supervise James' serving all those cups of ale. Following the innkeeper from keg to tables, Gill was loudly pressing Snaggletooth to give him a room upstairs. The rest of his men were sleeping in tents outside of town, but he made it clear that as commander of the company, *he* at least ought to have the luxury of a room at the inn. "How'm I going to cuckold all the men in Worksop if I haven't got a room to bring their ladies to?" he bellowed, punctuating the question with a hearty laugh. Spreading his arms out and turning in a circle as if on display he continued, "They take one look at this and throw themselves at me. How can you blame them?" Whether he cared about, or even noticed, the dark looks he was receiving from the three apprentices and, for that matter, from James Snaggletooth himself, seemed unlikely. Robin couldn't help the brief smile that flashed across his face as he pictured Gill getting a few free ales poured over his own head.

"I'm sorry, sir," James replied with a stony face. "Our rooms are occupied. In fact, we have five men staying in the two rooms. We just don't have room for you, I'm sorry to say."

"Twaddle and balderdash," Gill exclaimed. "You can tell them to leave, right? Or put 'em all in one room and let me have the other one. Look, you know who I am, right? You know who I represent? I think I ought to have that room."

James pursed his lips, shaking his head. "Can't do it, sir. I've given my word."

"Your word!" Gill scoffed. "The word of an innkeeper? What's that worth? Just tell them I told you to do it. Or where are they? I'll talk to them."

After a quick glance toward Robin, James scrupulously avoided him, and looked apologetically at Gill. Robin felt for him. Gill's patronage must bring the Loaves and Fishes a nice profit when the man was in town. But Master Snaggletooth was not going to sacrifice his pride to this bully. "I regret to say, sir, that none of those men is in the house right now."

Robin blinked. He would have to remember James Snaggletooth in the future. Gill o' the Red Cap would remember him as well, but Jack, Gill's dark-bearded lieutenant, put a hand on his chief's shoulder and mollified the hot-tempered guard. "Let it go, Gill," Jack said. "Let's get drunk and shoot some dice!"

Like a magpie who's caught sight of something shiny, Gill's eyes lit up and he rubbed his hands together. "Right!" he bellowed. "Now who's anxious to lose their money? I'm about to show you how a winner plays at Hazard!"

The tension in the room eased, and there was a raucous buzz around the center table as Gill brought a pair of dice out from his pocket. Robin drained the cup of ale he'd been served at Gill's behest, as James walked over to him unobtrusively and, leaning down, whispered to Robin, "I've seen this before. He will be absorbed by this dice game the rest of the evening. He won't notice anything else around him." With that he picked up Robin's cup and walked off briskly, and Robin understood that he was being told now was the time for him to make his way up to his lodgings if he so desired. Slowly he rose, and furtively crept along the wall to the staircase that led upstairs to his room.

There was no torch or candlelight on the landing, but Robin noticed that he was not alone. Sitting against the wall, his legs stretched out in front of him, was John, the cook's son.

"So," the young man began. "I see that you are no friend of Gill o' the Red Cap either. Maybe we should talk."

* * *

"Meggie have any close girlfriends she might have confided in, about this pregnancy? Hard to believe just you and me and your son know about it."

"She doesn't really have any girlfriends. I mean, she talks to a couple of the nuns from time to time. That young one, Sister Rebecca, will giggle with her once in a while in the kitchen, and they'll have a little chat with those other young women on occasion, the little milkmaid from Worksop and the laundress Elizabeth, but she did fall out with Elizabeth when she got jealous over Willie. But he was never going to marry her, and everybody knew it *but* her."

"So, do you think it's possible that Elizabeth Liptrot might have killed Willie out of jealousy?"

Margret scowled and shook her head. "Hardly. She'd have done anything for Willie, and he treated her pretty badly. Just used her when he felt like it and then chased after other women. But she never batted an eye, never even thought of giving him up. Even after he broke off with her to start seeing my Meggie. No, she was jealous all right, but if she was going to kill anybody it would have been Meggie, not Willie."

"What about Willie? Might he have realized Meggie was pregnant? I mean, a man experienced in such things might have noticed changes in her body…" Alison didn't go on. It occurred to her that if, in fact, Willie had guessed Meggie's condition, and gone on to realize just what sort of trap was being prepared for him by the girl and her mother, he would have been a significant threat to Margaret and Meggie and their whole family—and Meggie's position in that family. Willie was not the sort of person to keep quiet about such a thing if there were any reason for him not to. Discretion was not his strong suit. All of which would have given Margaret, or Meggie herself, sufficient motive to have done away with him.

"Willie?" Margaret snorted. "He was hardly the sort to notice anything beyond the obvious. And he hadn't been with Meggie but a few times, all of them within a couple of weeks. He'd never have noticed anything."

Alison sighed. It seemed clear she wasn't going to get any closer to solving the mystery here. Maybe it *had* been some ghoul, or some avenging angel, who'd carried Willie off. It seemed to her there was a kind of justice in it, whatever Friar Tuck might say.

* * *

"So what have *you* got against that blowhard Gill?" John demanded of Robin. They had gone into Robin's room and lit a lantern the landlord had provided, to avoid being overheard by any of the raucous crowd below.

Just how much to trust this sudden ally Robin couldn't be sure, and so he answered vaguely, "Well, let's just say if he recognized me he might try to arrest me."

John nodded, pausing a moment before revealing he was not as easily fooled as some of his peers. "That Lincoln green does mean something hereabouts. You think that's what's brought 'em back here? Him and the army he's come with?"

"I think it's mainly a coincidence," Robin answered. "But I don't want to give him the chance to realize what a lucky coincidence it is for him!"

"Well I don't mind telling you *I* can't stand that puffed-up windbag. I mean, I hate him. Bragging in here to his cronies about being with my sister? Not caring about that getting all around the town, getting back to my father? My father gave Meggie a good belt when he heard it, and he would have killed that Gill if he hadn't been surrounded by his goons all the time. His bragging about that dairy maid Kate was one thing—she could take care of herself. She didn't put up with any gossip about her, and her parents don't have much of a reputation around here anyway. But my family's honor was at stake with this. His coming back here just brings it all back to all the gossips in the town. I swear, I'd cut his throat now if he didn't have his whole army around him. What do you think? Maybe together we can find a way? Maybe we can say that ghoul of Sherwood got him, eh? You seem to have a close connection with that beast."

Robin recognized that John had seen through his ruse. And his acting had been so convincing, too. But whatever was happening here, he knew he ought to talk John down from anything so bloody. "I think that ghoul has done enough damage in this area for now. Let's you and I bide our time. There are ways of getting back at the bloke without making a bloody mess of it. You stick by me and we'll both keep our eyes and ears open. If it's reputation you've been hurt in, that may be the best place to hit Gill. Like should be punished with like, my friend Friar Tuck would say. We'll fix this Gill forever in the sight of his men, so he can never live it down. How does that sound?"

John looked doubtful. But then he grinned. "That might be just the right thing for it," he finally agreed, and held out his hand. "If you can hatch the right plan, I'm with you on it!"

Robin shook the proffered hand. He'd just saved Gill o' the Red Cap's life. He doubted the guard captain would ever acknowledge the debt, though.

CHAPTER ELEVEN

Friar Tuck had ridden off that morning with only a vague notion of what he was going to do with his day. He knew he didn't want to waste it hunting—at least not for venison. He'd been on the hunt since arriving in Worksop for the person who had mutilated the body of Willie the tinker—a sinner like the rest of us, Tuck was the first to admit, but a child of God nevertheless. He was convinced of that, despite what Granny Alison had implied the night before. Who was she, or any of us, to say that the man's murder had been the working out of justice? If anything, it was revenge. And that could never be just, could it? And if this *was* vengeance, whose vengeance was it? And for what? He'd certainly made little progress in figuring any of this out yet, as, admittedly, Master Crisp, the local magistrate, could have predicted. As he rode, Tuck gently let his dapple gray horse amble down the road toward the priory.

Though he had not consciously admitted it to himself, Tuck was well aware that the only intelligent and completely honest responses he had had to his questions since he'd begun this investigation had come from the priory—specifically from the curiously frank and unvarnished admissions of Sister Mary Eusebia. Sure, it was just a hunch, but Tuck's experience with Sister Mary, and his subsequent musing on that meeting, convinced him that this nun was a woman of much discernment, and straight talk and honesty. If she knew anything helpful to his investigation, he felt confident she would not hold back. But would she talk to him again? Why should she? Perhaps through curiosity, he decided. She had a questioning mind, and if given the opportunity, he felt, she would want to see how this murder played out. *He* certainly would if he were she, so how could *she* not?

But first he was obliged to get past the prioress, Madame Veronica. And the prioress was not amused. She pursed her lips in agitation and frowned at the idea of this man taking private time *again* to speak with one of her nuns. Her florid complexion waxed redder than ever and her green eyes crackled in her broad face, but the persistent friar explained that he was sure Sister Mary Eusebia's knowledge was indispensable to the solving of the Willie the tinker murder case, and pleaded until Sister Veronica finally gave in. The second interview could take place, she agreed, but only on condition that it be held in plain sight of everyone else in the convent. That was fine with Friar Tuck, as long as the others could not hear what was being said. The friar suggested that he walk with Sister Mary in the cloister, and the Prioress found this to be an acceptable proposal—but only assuming Sister Mary Eusebia was willing to undergo more questioning (and Sister Veronica was not at all sure that was the case). Friar Tuck was invited to sit on a small bench in the cloister just outside the door into the convent's library.

It was the perfect place to wait because before long Tuck, who'd been lost in a reverie about the inhumanity of man, was startled when, emerging from the library, Sister Mary Eusebia appeared suddenly before him, an ironic smile of greeting on her fresh face, and her dark eyebrows raised quizzically.

"So, good friar," she greeted him with interest. "It seems you cannot get to the bottom of your deliberations without me, or so the Mother Superior informs me."

Tuck answered her in the same vein: "Well, sister, it's not so much that as that I was craving another humiliation on theological questions, so I'm counting on you to subject me to that. It's my version of a hair shirt."

Sister Mary Eusebia gave a hearty laugh in appreciation of the friar's wit, and motioned to him to get up and walk with her. "Come then, let's begin your discipline," she murmured, quietly enough so as not to be heard by a group of six nuns who were passing by together, their heads bowed in silent meditation as they walked the stone path of the cloister, with its delicately pillared balustrade that surrounded the large rectangular grove of pear trees in the midst of the priory. Tuck and Sister Mary walked in the opposite direction, keeping the library on their left, the better to speak without danger of being overheard.

"Sister Mary," Tuck said, uncertain of how to begin or even where he wanted to go with his questions. It had really been nothing more than a whim that had led him here. "The first time we met I was clumsy with my questioning. I truly did not know what I was looking for and was stumbling blind."

"Truly?" the nun answered. "I'd never have suspected."

Tuck by now knew when she was laughing at him. Indeed, when wasn't she? But now he simply tried a direct, honest approach. "Look," he began.

"I'm listening," she answered, smiling.

"I am a stranger here. I mean, I was born here, but have not returned to this neighborhood in thirty years. I know nothing about the various families and individuals that make up the community around this priory, other than what I and my friends have been able to observe in the few days we've been among you. Add to that the problem that so many of those involved with this Willie were women, and I, being but a celibate friar—and please don't make that face, I tell you I truly *am* a celibate friar—I have had so little experience with women that I find myself a poor judge of them, and perhaps you will see the difficulties I find myself in."

"I can see your difficulty," Sister Mary replied, her head down in a kind of mock seriousness. "It takes very little acquaintance with men to understand the few simple things that motivate them: power, violence, pride, food, and, of course, lust. Women are pretty complicated. And they're all different, so you can't just generalize."

Tuck sputtered for a moment, then shrugged. While he knew better than to accept the nun's brief enumeration of male obsessions, he knew that, like all stereotypes, there was some seed of truth there. "Sounds like a catalogue of most of the Seven Deadly Sins. I might have said drunkenness was another motivator, but like food that's just another form of gluttony. But it's certainly true that, since I've been here, I've heard much of men's violence and power over women—fathers, husbands, lovers—and I don't have to look any further than Willie himself to see what you mean about lust. So tell me, then: are any of the complex women surrounding this simple lust-driven Willie the tinker drawn toward violence themselves?"

By now they had come to the end of the first leg of the cloister rectangle, and turned to the right to pass the doorway to the convent's chapter house on their left. Sister Mary replied to the friar: "They don't come as naturally to it as men. But given the right provocation, I'm sure they could be."

At that point two of the other nuns (Tuck recognized Sister Esther and Sister Anne) passed them slowly, their heads bent in silent prayer over small breviaries in their hands. Tuck's companion waited till they had passed before continuing.

"Of course, in this case, the woman would also have to be strong enough to wield that axe in a way to cut up his whole body," Sister Mary Eusebia allowed. "I mean, I know *I'd* be able to do it. Don't look at me like that, of course I *didn't* do it—not that I'd be above it necessarily, but I barely knew the man. I could name a few other nuns here that would be strong enough. But I wouldn't inform on one of my sisters, even if I'd seen one dragging her bloody axe into her cell."

Tuck thought that an odd thing to say, and couldn't help blurting out, "And did you? See such a thing?"

Sister Mary Eusebia scoffed dismissively, then, with a teasing half smile, replied, 'I just said I wouldn't tell! But as for Meggie or her mother, they haven't got the strength. Now the laundress maybe—she'd got some strength in those arms from beating out sheets and the like. Maybe Kate the cowherd—she'd have had to use some brute strength to get those cows to do what she wanted. Though I don't think she's high on your list for Willie."

"She's not our killer?" Tuck responded thoughtfully as they came to the corner of the cloister and made to turn to circle around back to the library.

"No," the nun said decisively. "She didn't give two figs for *him*. Not that she and Meggie were on such good terms, though, frankly, but it wasn't Willie that came between them."

"No?" Tuck asked. "What was it then?"

"Oh, that guard from Sir Guy of Gisbourne's troops who was here back in February. Started up first with Kate, but switched over to Meggie before too long. Seems he found her a bit more willing to lift her skirts for him, or so the gossip went."

Tuck clicked his tongue. "And where does a cloistered nun like you hear all this gossip, then? You don't get it from studying the Church Fathers in the convent library, I'm pretty sure."

"Ah, now that truly is a scientific question," Sister Mary Eusebia began. "There are some philosophers who say that all truths must be traced to an authority. But our modern thinkers declare that there are three paths to truth: One is of course direct divine revelation. But there are few of us who get to experience that in this life. Another is through experience. And the other is by authority. For philosophical truths, we have the authority of Aristotle, or Augustine, or Bede to cite. For everyday truths, we have the gossip of women."

"Don't men gossip as well, in their pubs and such?" Tuck asked.

"They do, but they don't call it that. And if I'm going to find my Aristotle of gossip, I'm going to look to the women."

They'd come to another corner now, and turned again to the right to pass the convent refectory. Another group of nuns was approaching them now, and Tuck let them go by before continuing: "The first woman I talked to in this town, the Widow Day, was full of gossip. None of it true, as far as I've been able to determine."

"Ah, well, you went to the Baal priests instead of Elijah. My source, my Aristotle, is my own Sister Rebecca." Then with a conspiratorial air she bent towards Tuck and whispered "All the young ladies round and about the priory confide in her. She has that innocent air about her. And she never tells anyone their secrets. Except me, of course. We keep nothing from each other." And then, seeing the friar blush again, repeated in a whisper, "Absolutely nothing."

"But you seem to be implying," Tuck said, moving back into his comfort zone, "that none of these women had reason to kill Willie. What about the men? I mean, this guard you say was with Meggie…"

"Was long gone before Willie was killed," Sister Mary reminded him. "Maybe some protective father or brother would have killed him to assert their power over 'his' woman."

"So Ralph the cook, or his son John?" Tuck suggested.

"Do we know that Meggie was with Willie after she was with the guard? Did they? And would they have mutilated him that way? Why?"

"So if none of the women he lusted after killed him, and none of them had a man who killed him out of jealousy or possessiveness over their women, where does that leave us?"

Sister Mary Eusebia gave a short laugh. "You've been talking all along as if the only possible reason anybody might have to kill Willie was his sexual adventuring. Even *I* told you men are more complicated than that."

"Right. So you're saying maybe this murder has more to do with his pride, or his desire for power, or violence, or what... food?"

"Well, I'm pretty sure Ralph the cook did not kill Willie because he wanted to steal his recipe for blancmange," Sister Mary said. "But truly—what made you limit all of your questions to Willie's womanizing? Who first set you on that track?"

Tuck stopped, dazed for a moment. Had he been thinking about this all wrong? Who *was* it who had first talked about Willie the womanizer? It had been in the chapel on that Sunday morning they had first seen Willie's head hanging from the rafters. And it had been... who? The laundress, was she the first? He thought a moment. "No," he said aloud. "It was Bryce. The priory's bailiff, John Bryce, the fancy-dressed man. He complained about Willie being lazy and a womanizer. Said something about his not being able to pay his rent."

Now Mary had stopped as well. "If I were you," she said, "I'd look into John Bryce's relationship with Willie. It sounds as if he deliberately tried to lead people into thinking the murder must have had to do with a woman. Maybe that was to keep people from looking into anything else."

Tuck could have slapped himself on the forehead. Of course

she was right. He'd gotten himself stuck on an assumed motive, and this had colored everything else he'd been thinking about this murder. And when all you have is a hammer, everything looks like a nail. When the only motive you have is lust, he thought, everyone looks like a lecher.

"Now if I were you," Sister Mary Eusebia went on, "I'd strike while the iron's hot! There's Sister Mary Barbara in that group of nuns walking and meditating there," and she nodded at the group that they had recently passed, now across the pear grove on the other side of the cloister. Friar Tuck squinted and picked the stately beauty out from among her peers, among whom he also recognized sharp-nosed Sister Lucy and the sprightly Sister Rebecca. "You ought to approach that group and beg audience with Sister Mary Barbara. And then don't give her a chance to deny it: spring it on her and take her by surprise. Tell her you know all about her father's criminal activity with Willie the tinker, and you're giving her a chance to give you his side of the story."

Tuck looked askance at Mary Eusebia. There was a good chance she was setting him up, or using him just for a lark. He knew she had an irresistible urge to put people in uncomfortable situations. Or maybe that just applied to her relationship with him. But there was something in this new direction in his investigation, and he knew he should follow it up. "What?" he answered. "Just like that? But the trouble is I *don't* know everything about Bryce's relationship with Willie. In fact, I don't know *anything* about Bryce's relationship with Willie. What if she sees through my sham?"

"Whatever she says, it will tell you something. And I have found that the best way to get people to incriminate themselves is to catch them off guard. Go on, what have you got to lose?"

The uncertain friar shook his jowls for a moment and let out a few uncertain sputters, then set his jaw and with a determined stride took off resolutely to encounter the silent group of pacing nuns.

Sister Mary Eusebia smiled to herself. This friar was so easy to manipulate. She knew that Mother Veronica had set her pet Sister Mary Barbara to spy on her as she talked with Tuck here in the cloister walk. Setting Tuck on her like a herding dog gave her a warm feeling inside. She turned and started back toward the library. There was still time for her to finish studying Saint Augustine's argument against Jovinian, in defense of the celibate life. "That should be good for a laugh," she told herself.

* * *

Riding home on his dapple gray rouncy, Tuck breathed in the pleasant air of a fine late springtime twilight at the edge of Sherwood. He hoped to reach Alison and Malyne's hovel before it was very dark indeed, and he hoped there would be a bit of venison left, or whatever game Robin and Little John had managed to bag that day in the forest, while he shared with them the fruits of his own successful quest that day.

Sister Mary Eusebia had been right. And why did that not surprise him? After he had approached Sister Mary Barbara and separated her from her gaggle of trailing nuns, Tuck had simply and forcefully told her that he had been made aware of her father's dealings involving the murdered Willie the tinker, and demanded that she tell him all she knew, or he would be bringing charges of murder against Master Bryce before the local magistrate, George Crisp. Never mind that he hadn't a clue whether Bryce had anything to do with Willie, or even if he did whether or not it was illegal, or even if it *was* whether it could have led to murder: Sister Mary Barbara had cracked immediately. Her full lips had pouted prettily, and tears had sprung from those azure blue eyes and fallen from those long, luscious lashes, and she had immediately said, "It's true, it's true, they were involved in that scheme together. But I know my father—he's a gentle man. I've never known him to show any violence, to me, to my mother, to anyone. And he was always conscientious in his job with the priory as well. It was only after my mother died that he changed."

"Changed in what way?" Tuck had asked her. "Did he become violent then?"

"No, no," she'd said. "But he became bitter. He'd worked hard all his life, he said, and now he had reached the age when he and his beloved wife could have time for themselves, God had taken her from him."

"So he blamed God?" Tuck had asked with interest.

"God, and, by association, the priory, which he blamed, illogically, for making him work so much that he hadn't spent enough time with her when she was alive. So he wanted to make them pay."

"Putting Willie's head up there in the chapel might have been a good way of doing that!"

"No, no, not like that," Mary Barbara had said. "He wanted to get rich off of them. If he had to live without my mother, he wanted to do it as the richest man in the neighborhood. And since Willie was always late or short on the rent he owed the priory, my father forced him to help him by threatening to evict him if he didn't."

So, Tuck mused, Sister Mary Eusebia had forgotten one major sin in her catalogue of character traits of men: greed. That seems to have been Master Bryce's motivating quality. But then he had pressed Mary Barbara: "So how exactly did it work? What was Willie's part in all this?"

As bailiff, she explained, Master Bryce was in charge of all the priory's accounts, which were reviewed monthly by the prioress. The sisters might need supplies for the infirmary, for example—bandages, bed linen, herbs that could not be provided from the convent's own gardens. Master Bryce would order more than was needed, enter the actual cost in the account book, but provide the priory with only three quarters of what he had actually received. The remainder was passed on to Willie, who brought it along on the rounds he took for his tinker's trade, and sold what he could for whatever the market would bear. He returned the profits to Bryce, and the bailiff excused his rent. Bryce could do this with food and with supplies for the scriptorium and the chapel and anything else he oversaw at the priory. It was just that Mary Barbara naturally knew best the details of the infirmary, which was her own responsibility, and where she turned a blind eye to her father's thieving.

Tuck could see a number of ways such a nefarious partnership could go awry. Willie threatened to expose Bryce's chicanery to the prioress, for example, and Bryce killed him to silence him. Or Bryce discovered that Willie had been skimming more than his share of the profits before turning them in to Bryce—a scenario Tuck had no doubt was probably true in any case—and Bryce had put a stop to that. But it was shaky. Would Bryce really have killed the one man whose regular traveling made his scheme workable? Tuck didn't know. He had urged Sister Mary Barbara to confess her own sin of omission to Father Bernard, and to correct that omission by telling Sister Veronica what she knew, before he, Tuck, exposed Bryce himself. And that was how he had left things at the priory.

As the last crimson rays of the sun disappeared beneath the trees of Sherwood, Tuck and his gray rouncy pulled up to Mother Alison's hovel. Dismounting, Tuck smiled with anticipation of how his fellows would respond to this new information he was bringing. There was a bright firelight within, and he could hear the sound of many voices as he opened the door. But those voices hushed to silence when he came into the room. All eyes in the hut were staring at him, and finally Alan a Dale said, "Sorry, Tuck. We thought you might be Robin. He's not here yet."

"Oh?" Tuck said, unconcerned. "Why are you so anxious about his coming? … oh, any of that meat left?" He smelled the strong odor of roasted venison.

But Alan answered Tuck's first question only: "Gisbourne's troops are back in town, and back in force. And they've got a prisoner." Tuck looked up quizzically. Alan said, "It's Maid Marion."

CHAPTER TWELVE

A deep perpendicular line of worry separated the brows over Maid Marion's brilliant blue eyes as she sat alone, her hands and feet tied, in a large pavilion outside of Worksop. She'd been here, by her own estimate, at least three hours. She'd had no opportunity to fix her golden hair, or freshen up from her journey, or see to her gown, which was distressingly soiled and awry as a result of her arrest and rough handling by her captors. The head of the guard, this Gill of the Red Cap, had pretended to the status of gentleman, and had at least allowed her a stool on which to rest. Two guards stood outside the tent's entry, discouraging any fantasies she might have had of leaving her stool and hopping off on her bound feet into the surrounding forest. What exactly these men were going to do with her now, she could scarcely imagine. She had protested loudly and vigorously, when they'd taken her and her companions prisoners at Creswell Crags, that she was a gentlewoman in the service of the countess of Chesterfield, but her pleas fell on deaf ears. Only a titled *man*, it seemed, had any rank in the guards' esteem. Or at least in the esteem of Gill o' the Red Cap. Silly name, she thought to herself. What if she were to knock that cap from off his head and trample it in the mud? Who would he be then? Gill o' the Bare Head? Gill o' the Muddy Cap? Or maybe just Gill o' the Blasphemous Mouth.

Lady Mary was just losing herself in this reverie when the man himself burst into the tent. He stood before her huffing, as if he'd been exerting himself. His muscled arms hung down from his thick body like the limbs of a great oak, and he had very deliberately twisted his broad brown face into a smile. Marion thought at first he was trying to give himself a pleasant expression to make her more comfortable, but she soon realized this was the farthest thing from Gill's mind. It was a smile of evil he was wearing.

"Woman, I've just come from your bodyguard," he began. "I'm winded, as you see, from beating them so hard for such a long time. Stubborn bastards, those two." Marion's heart sank as she feared for young Giles and the venerable Sir Eustace. What would this beast do with them? But she was certain that to show weakness was to invite this bully's abuse, and so did not flinch.

"You will address me as 'Lady Mary,' churl," she bluffed. "And if you have indeed harmed my escort, I would not give much for your chances when Countess Lydia finds out. She will certainly take it up with your master, this Guy of Gisbourne, who will doubtlessly flog your own vile hide, if he is not a churl himself."

"Quiet, bitch," Gill responded. "That's the only title you'll get from me. You seem to have mistaken me for somebody that gives a good God damn. Now you listen to me: I'm going to ask you questions, and you're going to answer them. Truthfully. If not, you'll wish you had. My knuckles are pretty sore from the beatings I've just given your bodyguards. Your woefully unsuccessful bodyguards, I should say. So I don't really want to beat you as well if I don't have to." At that, he leered at her menacingly—a look that belied his feigned reluctance to use violence.

"But if I don't get the answers I want from you, I will do so, and my only regret will be that my sore knuckles will prevent me from beating you as hard as I'd really wish to. Now: shall we begin?"

* * *

In Alison's hovel, Robin's men set aside all thoughts of the murder of Willie the tinker to focus on the immediate problem. Maid Marion must be rescued, but first Robin Hood must be informed of her capture. It was Robin who must lead the effort, Little John insisted; they knew he would not trust her rescue to anyone else. But where was he?

"He said that he was worried about Gisbourne's men tracking us down. And I, like a hedge-born coxcomb, told him he was fretting over nothing. 'Oh, we've already moved south,' says I. 'What need we fear if Gisbourne sends his goons north?' Scramble-brained nit-wit!" And with that the big man smacked his own forehead. And not gently.

"Scrambling your brains further is not going to help any," Will Stutely advised him. "How do we find him? That's what we need to decide right now."

"When he parted from us after the hunt he said he needed time to think and went off by himself," Alan a Dale added. "So that means he's either on his way here now, or he's made his way back to the Loaves and Fishes. Seems to me we do what makes the most sense: Friar Tuck and Thorvald, you were staying here anyway, so why don't you wait here to see if he shows up? The rest of us were lodging at the inn. We'll head back and see if he turns up there."

"And if he doesn't show up at either place?" Jock o' Barlborough asked.

"Then Gisbourne's men have got him too," Little John said, putting all their fears into words. "But they won't do anything too vile to him here. Gisbourne and the sheriff will want him alive and whole when he gets to Nottingham, so they can hang him high before the entire town."

"Marion, on the other hand," Friar Tuck reminded them, "has no such guarantee. She has to be rescued here, and as soon as possible!"

"Agreed," Little John said, as he led the outlaws into the night.

* * *

"You were arrested at the place called Creswell Crags," Gill began, towering over Marion on her stool in a manner calculated to intimidate her. It was working. "What were you doing there?"

"We… I and my two companions had stopped there to have a mild repast and refresh ourselves on our journey. It's a pleasant place to picnic. We were on our way to visit our lady's ally, Sir Richard at the Lee, in his castle." Marion hoped if she dropped a few more nobles' names she might gain herself a little time, and a little respect from her interrogator. It wasn't working.

The blow was quick and unexpected. The back of his burly right hand whipped across her cheek quick as the flight of an arrow. It caught her unawares and rattled her thoughts. She blinked her eyes to steady her vision a moment before she felt the sting in her cheek and ringing in her right ear. He had actually struck her! Who did this bully think he was?

"How dare you…" she began, but got no further as the back of his left hand smacked her more solidly in the mouth and nose. Now she felt more than a sting and tasted blood on her lips. Perhaps it was not a good idea to remind the man of her social rank just now.

"You weren't listening," Gill growled in a subdued voice. "I said you must tell me the truth. I already know from what your two noble escorts told me that you were in that neighborhood looking for the notorious outlaw Robin Hood. You know, I am sure, that he and his gang of bandits are wanted for theft and for poaching the king's deer. They have also been guilty of the murder of some of my fellow guards."

In spite of herself, Marion had to scoff at that. "Completely innocent guards, I'm sure. Much like yourself, no doubt."

Quick as a bird of prey darting for a mouse, Gill's hand grabbed her flaxen locks and yanked her half off her stool as he bent his face close to hers and snarled with stale beer breath, "You speak when I say, girl, if you want a hair left on your pretty little head." Then he shoved her back onto the stool. "Now you're going to tell me *why* you were looking for this Robin Hood."

The full jeopardy of her situation was at last coming home to Lady Mary: She was alone, without the countess or her castle or any of her knights or servants in any position to help her. She had no idea where Robin or his men had gone, so she could not look for help from that quarter. She was completely at the mercy of this very large, very strong, and very brutal man who had, as he had made quite clear to her, absolutely no respect for her person or her position, and no one or nothing outside of his own conscience to rein in his violence. And there had been no sign that he had any conscience at all.

"I was sent by my lady, the countess Lydia of Chesterfield. This Robin Hood as you call him is pledged to her service—he is her designated forester on her estates. Perhaps these deer of which you speak are not the king's at all but deer hunted on the countess's own lands."

That, at least, did not enrage her questioner the way some of her earlier answers had. He looked at her askance and then laughed heartily. "And perhaps," he continued, "the rich prelates he has robbed were simply donating their funds to his outlaw gang's upkeep. Perhaps those guards he slew accidentally fell on their own arrows. And perhaps," now he grabbed her by the throat and hauled her roughly to be level with his twisted angry visage again. "Perhaps I won't throttle you after all. Perhaps after all I will simply turn you over this stool and rut you like any beast. And when I'm done, perhaps I'll let the rest of my men swive you in whatever ways they like. All two score of them. And perhaps, if you're still breathing after all that, we'll let you drag yourself back to your precious countess and tell her of your adventures, which might be hers as well if she really does protect this outlaw."

And with that he flung her back down onto her stool. "And then again, perhaps we won't. But you think about it for now, will you? I'm going to get myself well lubricated at this local bar right now. When I come back I'm going to be in a fierce mood. Maybe I'll be hoping you don't cooperate with my questions. But I'm going to want to know exactly where this Robin Hood is right now. And you're going to want to tell me. Believe me, you are." With that Gill o' the Red Cap stomped toward the exit, turning to her before he left and bowing with mock courtesy and murmuring, "Until we meet again, my dear lady."

* * *

When Little John, Will Stutely, Jock, and Alan a Dale had reached Worksop and stabled their horses, they paused momentarily outside the Loaves and Fishes, hearing the great buzz of activity from indoors. Will peaked furtively into a window that was open to the outside and saw within the large group of Gisbourne's guards gathered around a table in the center of the tavern playing at Hazard.

Will ducked quickly and whispered to the others, "It's

Gisbourne's thugs all right. I don't see Robin there. He may be upstairs, of course. Who wants to go up and see?"

The others all looked around to see who might volunteer. After a moment Will sighed, saying, "Some of them may know me from having imprisoned me and tried to hang me last year. So if I go in there and try to go up to our rooms, I could be recognized and give us all away. We could all be arrested."

"It's hard to disguise my bulk," Little John said. "A man in Lincoln green, and my size, couldn't be anyone but the notorious Little John himself. I'm probably not the best choice."

"They've already seen me once today," Jock o' Barlborough said. "Their captain, this Gill o' the Red Cap, knows who I am. But he doesn't associate me with Robin Hood and his band. I could go in, but I might be recognized immediately and waylaid, just because he'll want to stand me to a drink or some such thing. I know his type."

Alan scratched his head. "I could go in and start to sing and play. I've got my small gittern here in my gear, and no one there will be surprised or think it out of place, since I've been entertaining them here since we arrived. I could distract them all with a song, while Jock slips upstairs and talks to Robin."

"If he's even there," Jock said.

"Yes, if he's there," Little John agreed. "But if he is, tell him to open his window and drop down to us. We'll wait under the shutters."

And so it was agreed.

The bandits waited tensely outside the door to the inn, holding tight against the outer wall to avoid being seen from within, as Jock opened the door and began his nonchalant walk toward the stairway to the upper floor. Alan a Dale, readying himself to step through the door and act as Jock's distraction, gingerly peeked in at the corner of the window.

"He's walking slow, he's not looking left or right," Alan whispered. "Now he's maybe halfway to the stairs… the guards are engrossed in their dice… he's almost there now and… oh no!"

That last exclamation was spoken aloud, and Will and Little John were on tenterhooks to hear what had caused it. After two heartbeats that seemed like two months, Alan murmured, "Their chief, the big fellow, just recognized Jock. He called him over. Jock tried to shrug it off but the big fellow has his arm around Jock's shoulders. He wants him to have a drink with them. I'm going in."

"To do what?" Little John questioned.

Alan gave a tight-lipped smile and held up his gittern. "Born to sing!" he answered, and stepped in the door.

"Improvise! Improvise!" Alan said to himself as he stepped boldly onto one of Snaggletooth's chairs and from there onto the first empty table in the room. He saw Jock's eyes gazing forlornly at him, a few of the guards less interested in the dice game than the others raising their faces to give him an ear, and the folks at the other tables smiling toward him in anticipation of a song and a laugh. Alan struck a chord on his gittern and sang out at the top of his voice—he wanted to be sure that Robin could hear every word if he was indeed upstairs:

> *Now hearken folks, and hear my song*
> *I'll sing out loud and true,*
> *The tale of Locksley of the Wood*
> *And the chaste maid Mary too…*

He was fairly certain Robin would recognize his own alias Robert Fitz Ooth of Locksley, and unless he was dim-witted would know who was intended by the title "chaste maid Mary." He only hoped Gill o' the Red Cap wouldn't recognize them as well. But Gill seemed engrossed in his game, and Alan, groping for motifs and rhymes as he composed his song extempore, closed his eyes a moment to focus:

> *Now Locksley sat in his room above*
> *And did not hear his mate*
> *Calling below his shuttered window*
> *To tell him Mary's fate!*

So far so good, Alan said to himself. But how to describe Maid Marion's plight in front of her very captors without them knowing he was doing so? Well, he thought, let's try this:

> *"The bullies of the Baron Guy*
> *Have stol'n your maid so dear*
> *They hold her now against her will*
> *And fill her soul with fear."*

Now a few more of the guards were listening, but they had sympathetic looks on their faces. Nobody ever really believes that they are supposed to be the villains of the ballad. If he did his job as he should, Alan thought, each man of them would think he was Locksley. Including, he very much hoped, the "real" Locksley.

> *Now Locksley flung his shutters wide*
> *And leapt upon the ground*
> *To where he had a dozen men*
> *Awaiting all around.*

Okay, Alan told himself. Just a little exaggeration is all. A wee bit of poetic license. There were two outside. Two in here.

He took his men and fast they rode
To Mary in her need.
He killed the villains without remorse,
The lady, she was freed.

Most of his audience gave a little cheer at that. Let's see if they cheered when the lady was actually freed in that manner. Maybe that was wishful thinking. If they could free Marion without bloodshed, that would be Robin's preferred way. And his own as well. But the lady Mary would be rescued tonight, whatever it took. He knew Robin well enough to count on that as a surety. And now… how to end the song? He had to give it a conventional ending, or it would seem quite strange to the listening ears.

Now Locksley has his lady bright
And she's no more forlorn,
And all their strife is in the past
In her arms a bairn newborn!

Now Alan breathed a sigh of relief, and Jock gave a half-hearted cheer, looking around the room. Alan was a bit relieved when several of the other listeners took up the cheer and, to put the right face on his performance and avoid suspicion, he doffed his green cap and passed it around the room. Never miss an opportunity to pick up a few pence. Gill o' the Red Cap, he noticed, was so involved in his dice game he never looked up, so he certainly hadn't noticed anything amiss. With a wave of his cap Alan pocketed the coins and headed for the door where he was joined by Jock, who bade a quick farewell to Gill, who gave him a distracted wave. Snaggletooth and the regulars at the inn knew they were sharing a room, so it would be perfectly natural for the two of them to head out the door together.

"That was quick thinking," Jock whispered.

"I've composed better ballads," Alan said. "But none on such short notice. Let's hope Robin got the message."

* * *

Early in Alan a Dale's performance, Robin had shushed John the cook's son and focused on the words he was hearing. The name of Locksley convinced him the song was meant for him, and the reference to the maid Mary's capture made his blood boil. The leap from the open shutters told him just what to do, and before the song had ended he had thrown open the shutters in his room and dropped down into the tavern's yard, followed closely by the cook's son. To his anxious demands, Little John laid his hand on his mate's shoulder and told him as calmly as he could that the lady Mary of Winchester had been seen earlier that day bound with two members of her entourage and forced to struggle behind the horses of Gisbourne's crew.

"Who saw them?" Robin demanded. "Where is she now?"

"I saw her," Jock o' Barlborough said, now stepping toward the group with Alan a Dale. "Thorvald and I met this posse of theirs in Barlborough, on their way here. I'd never seen her before, of course, but Thorvald recognized her immediately. My understanding is they found this Maid Marion and her two escorts looking for you and your band at Creswell Crags, and arrested her immediately. Gill o' the Red Cap thinks she will be able to tell him how to find you."

"If he questions her… aggressively," Will Stutely mused, "he may get the idea of using her as bait for a trap to ensnare you. We really can't allow that to happen. She needs to be rescued right now!"

"And how do we accomplish that?" Alan asked. "We don't know where she is."

"The guards have all set up tents outside of town," said the cook's son, "in the forest clearing between here and Wallingwells. It's certain they are holding the prisoners there. They'll have them in one of the tents, or they'll have them tied up somewhere in the encampment."

"And when did this bloke join our crew?" Will asked, not unkindly.

"The minute he told me how much he hated Gill o' the Red Cap," Robin answered, then turned toward the local boy: "You can take us there?"

"Certainly," the cook's son replied. "But what do you plan to do? Take on the whole company of guards at once?"

Robin grinned at him. "Well, we do have surprise on our side. But listen, I've got an idea. But it involves you making your way to that camp, with Alan and Little John here. You're just on your way home, see? You can engage in friendly banter with the guards, while Alan and Little John surround the camp."

Little John scratched his beard. "Well... I know I'm big, but I'm not *that* big."

"No, now, I just want you to scout it out. See where the guards all are—the ones that aren't here, anyway—and see if you can figure out where they might be keeping prisoners."

"*That* I can do," Little John said. But what will the rest of you be doing while we're skulking in the bushes?"

Robin looked at Jock and Will. "I'm going to need these two for what I've got planned inside."

"Inside the inn again?" Jock asked.

"Absolutely," Robin said. "You're going to be my decoy. And Will? He's going to be my redeemer." To their puzzled looks, Robin merely murmured, "Follow my lead. John... and John... I mean Little John, you and Alan get going. I hope we'll join you before too long." And three went off to the forest, while three headed back into the tavern.

* * *

In contrast to the manner in which he'd left it, Robin entered the Loaves and Fishes bar room boldly and with purpose. He'd left off any idea of keeping a low profile in the urgency to deliver Maid Marion. If he was recognized, so be it. He was not going to lose Marion by being over-cautious.

Robin strode up to James Snaggletooth and in a booming voice demanded, "Master Snaggletooth! I understand some fellow has been in here insisting on having one of our rooms," and he nodded to Jock and Will on either hand.

The confused master of the house gave Robin a befuddled look, then glanced over toward Gill o' the Red Cap, who had heard the challenge and looked up from his dice, the eyebrows raised quizzically on his broad face. Then he bounded up and approached Robin, matching bravado with bravado.

"Yes, I need a room of my own to stay in, and I'm sure you'll be glad to yield it up to the commander of the king's guards. Why not go up and get your things out of the room and I'll be moving into it right now."

Robin put his head back and looked down his nose at the captain of the guard. "King's guards?" Robin echoed mockingly, looking over at the table where Gill's cronies were looking up from their dice. "I thought you were from Nottingham."

Gill bristled and sputtered, "From Sir Guy, castellan of the king's fortress in Nottingham." Then with a scowl, he added, "You don't want to get on the wrong side of me, fellow. I'm not an enemy you want to have."

Ignoring the threatening implications of Gill's bluster, Robin hadn't taken his eyes off the Hazard table. Jock and Will exchanged nervous glances, neither understanding just what Robin had in mind.

"You're playing at Hazard here?" Robin asked, as Gill's color rose to match his famous cap.

"Yes, we're playing Hazard," Gill growled. "What are *you* playing at? Are you going to vacate that room for me or not?"

Robin feigned great interest in the dice game, finally responding to the guard's demand in an offhand way: "Well, why would I do that? What would there be in it for me?"

"What's in it for you?" Gill o' the Red Cap roared. "How about I don't break your arrogant neck, you uppity little villein?'"

"Yeoman," Robin corrected. "Say, can anybody get into this game?" The question was directed at Jack, the guards' lieutenant who had organized the game. Jack knew better than to answer for himself, and raised his eyebrows toward his captain.

Gill, sensing an opportunity to win this confrontation without resorting to an all-out brawl, now changed his tactics and made a proposal. "You seem like a sporting man," he said, now placing a ham-sized fist on Robin's shoulder. "Are you willing to risk your room on a throw at Hazard? Or are you too craven a coward to chance it?"

Now Robin finally turned slowly toward the fuming Gill and smiled, pleased that the guard had finally taken the bait. "So, you win the throw, you get to have my room," Robin itemized to Gill, making sure they were agreed on details. "I win the throw, I get to keep my room?"

"Right," Gill agreed. "Will you do it or are you a coward?"

Robin twisted his face into a puzzled mask. "That's not really the question, is it?" he responded. "It's more like 'Will I decline, or am I stupid.' Why would I risk my room for nothing when I can simply keep it without playing?"

The fuming Gill snorted and stomped a few steps back and forth before exploding, "Well what do you want, then? What do you want me to put up against this room?"

Robin looked thoughtful for a moment, then looked toward Jock o' Barlborough. "Jock, didn't you tell me you'd seen these guards earlier today, dragging some strumpet behind their horses?"

Jock, taken aback slightly, answered, "Well, they had a lady in tow. I don't think I ever used the word 'strumpet' with regard to her…"

"Don't put too fine a point on it, Jock," Robin interrupted. "If these fine gentlemen had arrested her, what can she be but a slut? Now here, then, is my proposal, mister Captain of the Guard." Now Robin finally met and held Gill's eyes for the first time. "I will risk my comfortable room in this inn for a free hour's time with this strumpet of yours. I haven't had a woman in a good long time, and I understand this one was a pretty classy one—blonde, blue eyes, fancy dressed. You put up a roll with her wherever you've got her stashed right now, and I'll put up my room, and *I'll* take the dice as caster and roll for it."

Gill scowled again. He wanted that room. He did not want to stretch out in a tent out there on the rough ground with a chance of rain tonight. What was the woman to him? An opportunity to get some information about this outlaw he was chasing, nothing more. Not only did he have no reason to protect her from unwanted sexual encounters like this one, it was actually to his advantage to let this fellow have her. Perhaps it would loosen her tongue if she realized he wasn't bluffing about having every man in his command use her. So for Gill, it seemed obvious that he had nothing to lose. If he won, he'd get the private room. If he lost, he was a step closer to pressuring the woman into offering up the information he wanted. It took him only a few moments to make up his mind to accept Robin's challenge. "All right," he said. "We'll play it your way."

"Right!" Robin agreed. Then he turned to Will Stutely. "Will!" he said. "My dice, please!"

Will blinked twice, gave an involuntary half grin, and reached into his pocket where he always kept his special dice. He handed them to Robin, who snatched them up and declared, "Gentlemen, the main is seven."

CHAPTER THIRTEEN

In the wake of Little John's departure with Will, Jock, and Alan, Tuck and Thorvald tried to explain the significance of Marion's capture to Alison and Malyne.

"The lady Marion is Robin's… well, perhaps you might call her his inspiration," the friar explained.

"What, she inspires him to rob people?" Malyne asked.

Tuck closed his eyes, praying for patience, and wondering where to start. "He doesn't rob *people*. He robs rich prelates. Anyway, I mean she inspires the good in him. She's his beloved, she ennobles him."

Malyne scoffed. "This is like that love-from-afar, she's-too-chaste-for-me kind of thing some of your minstrels will sing about, then? He's got to earn her love by valiant deeds? Which include what? His robbing people?"

"Prelates, not people," Tuck repeated. "Anyway, it's not like that…"

"'E loves 'er, an' 'e wants to bed 'er. That's what it is," Thorvald clarified, helpfully. "But she might be too 'igh class for 'im. 'E's not sure. So neither is she."

"He would like, indeed, to marry her," Tuck clarified in his own way. "But he is of yeoman stock, while she is noble. An impoverished noblewoman, to be sure, but noble nonetheless."

"And so they love but love chastely," Alison interpreted.

"And so she is still known as 'Maid' Marion."

"She is," Tuck agreed. "But to be clear, Marion is not only important to the band because of her relationship with Robin. She has helped us in some of our difficulties in the past. She is a favorite of the men."

"Well, I hope there shall be a good outcome for this problem. I hope your Robin can find a way to rescue your Maid Marion from her imprisonment," Malyne shrugged.

"And I hope that we can find a way to talk him down and keep him from doing anything too rash without considering the consequences if it's here that he shows up after his wandering today," Tuck added.

"I wonder," Malyne said, a thought striking her, "what he's going to do with this Maid Marion if he *does* rescue her. Where can he keep her without these Nottingham guards finding her again?"

"You're not really wondering are you?" Alison asked. "You know as well as I do that they'll bring her here."

Malyne laughed. So did Alison. Tuck looked embarrassed, but couldn't deny that this was probably correct. Where else could they possibly hide an escaped prisoner? Meanwhile Thorvald was brooding over Marion. He had known and admired her younger sister a great deal—the lady Elizabeth of Winchester. It was she whose honest chiding had turned his life around when he had been making his living by carrying out the lawful sentences, often involving the inflicting of cruel punishment, on convicted prisoners. When she died a martyr he'd wept like a child. Now her sister was a prisoner, and his insides were in turmoil as he thought of the ways she could be tormented.

Tuck saw this and tried to think how he might keep the dwarf—and himself—from dwelling too anxiously on Marion's predicament, when there was nothing they could do. This might be the chance to talk to Thorvald and the women about what he'd learned that day at the priory.

"Well, while we're waiting," Tuck began, "I did want to tell you what I found out today. I didn't just waste the day, you know, I was still looking into our Willie's murder, and thinking about it brought me back to the priory."

"Ah, those people," Alison scoffed. "They're all really just more interested in keeping the reputation of their precious priory unbesmirched than they are in solving the murder brought home to them in their very chapel."

"Not all of them, I think," Tuck said. "I've got some straight and true answers from at least one of the nuns. Sister Mary Eusebia I mean."

"Oh, *that* one," Alison laughed. "Young Lynette as was. Always a precocious child. But that father of hers! What a brute."

"Oh… Lynette was her name before she entered the nunnery?" Friar Tuck asked thoughtfully. "I hadn't realized that. I suppose all the nuns changed their names when they took their vows."

Alison shrugged. "They become the Brides of Christ, as they see it. So they take on new names to mark their changed lives. Dame Veronica now, she used to be Sarah when I knew her many years ago. Her cellarer was called Rachel before she became Sister Esther."

"And Sister Lucy was called Anne originally," Malyne continued, "and sister Anne was called Elizabeth. Young Sister Rebecca was called Deborah as a child. As for Sister Mary Barbara…"

"She is the only one of the sisters I know who actually kept her given name," Alison mused, "since she liked the fact that it was already the name of a Christian saint, but combined it with 'Mary' to become a new person."

"Well, maybe not so completely new a person. She still seems pretty entrenched with her father, the bailiff," Tuck suggested.

"That would not be unusual, given the circumstances, the position he holds at the priory," Alison said. "But why is this of significance for this murder? You don't think that she, or her father, could be guilty of this heinous act, do you?"

"I can't say anything certain," Tuck answered. "But I did find out, and from Sister Mary Barbara's own lips, that John Bryce the bailiff is not the priory's most trustworthy servant."

"No?" Malyne said, her eyes showing a vivid curiosity, although Tuck could not tell exactly where she was looking. "Do tell!"

And so the friar related in as much detail as he could what he had learned about Master Bryce's activities with the coerced Willie in marketing goods appropriated from the priory and funneling the profits into his own purse. His listeners were stunned at the revelation, the disbelieving Alison shaking her head and murmuring, "And he always made such an effort to appear so completely respectable…"

"Of course," Tuck responded. "The better to hide his crimes. But this sheds a new light on Willie's murder, perhaps, wouldn't you say?"

"Not so sure," Thorvald reflected. "Bryce 'ad a prosperous business goin' on with our friend Willie. Why would 'e go an' mess all that up by murderin' the travelin' tinker?"

"Well, there are a lot of reasons why a couple of blokes engaged in nefarious activities might fall out," Tuck speculated. "Maybe Willie starts to feeling a bit too put upon, and demands a bigger share of the loot—maybe he even threatens to turn Bryce in to the prioress, or to the magistrate. Maybe Bryce decides it's better business to shut Willie up for good than to keep taking his chances with him."

"Could be," Thorvald conceded. "But if 'e kills Willie 'e's also killin' 'is business. Now I'm gonna tell you somethin' you don't know."

Tuck looked up quizzically, as both women turned suddenly curious eyes toward him. Or in Malyne's case, in his direction.

"This John Bryce approached me himself, one evenin' when I was at the Loaves an' Fishes. Says 'e 'eard I was plannin' on peddlin' the wares of some of the local craftsmen to several of the other villages round about, and 'e says e's got lots o' goods 'imself 'e'd like to market that way if I'm willin' to take it on. Says 'e 'ad a system, but unforeseen difficulties 'ave made 'im abandon 'is old arrangement. Says 'e can really make it worth my while."

"Those unforeseen difficulties being his murder of his partner?" Tuck suggested.

"*Somebody's* murder of 'is partner, that's for sure," Thorvald said. "But 'e seemed kinda desperate to me, like 'e didn't know where to turn. Bryce is a pretty calculatin' bloke. I can't see 'im killin' Willie without a plan o' what to do afterwards."

"Unless Willie made him really angry, and he killed him in a fit of passion," Tuck suggested.

Thorvald shrugged. "Maybe. But 'e don't seem all that passionate a fella."

"And don't forget, whoever killed this Willie dismembered him with an axe. Why would Bryce be that vindictive? If it was a sudden fit of passion, why did he happen to be carrying an axe at the time?"

As Tuck was trying to come up with a reasonable answer to that question, the four of them were startled by a sudden pounding on Alison's door. They froze and looked at one another, and Thorvald exclaimed, "It's Robin! I'll let 'im in. Now remember we need to break the news to 'im gently about Maid Marion—can't 'ave 'im takin' an axe to somebody in a fit o' passion."

Thorvald had reached the door by the end of his warning and yanked it open with a greeting, "Robin, me lad, ya must...," but the words died on his lips and his head jerked back in surprise.

The others quickly crowded about the door to see what had so silenced Thorvald, and were met by the imposing form of George Crisp, the crown's official local magistrate. Huffing with the effort of having ridden to this out-of-the-way shack, the magistrate shook his canine jowls and gazed with dewy, sympathetic eyes at the object of his search.

"Dame Alison?" Crisp began. "I'm sorry, but I am here to take you into custody. You're under arrest for the murder of Meggie, the cook's daughter. Please come quietly, without a fuss. I really don't enjoy this, any more than you."

* * *

Alison simply looked puzzled, as if she could not possibly have heard the magistrate correctly. "Meggie?" she responded in disbelief. She glanced bewildered at Friar Tuck, as if he might have a clue to understand this conundrum. "But… but I just saw her yesterday. She was quite alive when I left her, you can be sure. And I haven't left this house since—I call on my companions to witness."

"How did she die?" Tuck asked pragmatically.

"Poison," George Crisp said languidly. "She'd been abed, as you know if you saw her yesterday, with pains in the belly. Her mum found her this afternoon when she came back after helping with the midday meal at the priory. She had died sometime this morning. When the girl's father came home he asked some questions and then sent for me."

"So it's Ralph, the cook, that's accusin' 'er then?" Thorvald asked. You know 'ow quick-tempered 'e is. 'Ave you considered all the possibilities 'ere?'

Crisp sighed as if considering all the possibilities would be a Herculean task, and then explained: "Ralph tells me that he knows, that his wife told him, that this Alison the local witch…"

"Midwife!" Malyne corrected, not without an edge of rancor.

"That this Alison gave their Meggie a potion 'tother day, and that she's been having these pains ever since, and that now she's up and died from it. There's no marks on the body, I checked for that!" The magistrate said this with a kind of swagger, as if no one could say he had not investigated this matter fully. "Ergo, it must be poison. And Alison is known to have been the one give her the potion. Ergo, I'm arresting her."

"What possible motive would my mother have to murder her patient?" Malyne asked, a note of panic making her voice quaver.

"Motive?" the magistrate echoed, as if the word were unfamiliar to him. Then he scoffed, "I never heard that witches had to have any particular motive for their wicked deeds. The devil gets into 'em and poof! There goes another victim."

"But surely it's just as possible that someone else came to the house while Meggie was alone and ill," Tuck proposed. "They might have easily given her some sort of poison under the guise of trying to help her."

George Crisp shook his bulky head. "Nah, now you're not being logical. Alison's the only witch we know around these parts—her and her daughter," he now looked menacingly at Malyne, "So nobody else could have come by with a poison potion."

Tuck glared at him for a moment, trying to follow the convoluted logic of that statement. Failing that, he shook it off and took a different tack. "But Master Crisp, you have to consider the connection between this murder and the murder of Willie the tinker."

"Don't have to do anything of the kind," George Crisp shrugged. "The two've got nothing to do with each other."

"But of course they do! Listen, you remember you gave me the task of looking into Willie's murder."

Crisp looked doubtful, scratching his head. "I remember you asked me if you could ask around and I said I didn't care. That's not exactly…"

"Well, I *have* been looking at it, and there's a lot of things that make this murder of Meggie suspicious," Tuck insisted, talking while sorting out his thoughts on this new development. "Look, Willie died on a night after he'd been with Meggie—we know that much to be true."

The information was definitely news to the magistrate. His eye widened and he leaned his round head forward slightly. For him, it was a huge reaction. "That so?" he asked Tuck.

"Yes! Whoever killed Willie might have done it out of jealousy, and killed Meggie for the same reason," Tuck suggested.

"But Willie was killed by something supernatural, the ghoul of Sherwood!" Crisp argued.

"And how do we know that same ghoul didn't kill Meggie? Didn't we have a warning that this was going to happen, from… from that Locksley fellow who ran into the ghoul in the woods?" Tuck was a little bit embarrassed to use as a part of his argument a story that he knew to be completely fictitious—and one that nearly everyone seemed to have dismissed—but he was trying what he could to shift suspicion from Alison, and as his thoughts caught up to his words, it occurred to him that these two murders may very well be connected. It made sense that two such murders, so close together in this isolated village, were almost certainly linked. Someone, probably the same someone, had had it in for both Willie and Meggie and the most likely motive had to be their secret liaison.

George Crisp, though he had come to it slowly, had decided against Tuck's argument. "The killings are nothing alike," the magistrate said. "In Willie's case, you had a body hacked apart in ghoulish fashion. Violent death. Bestial. Obviously a ghoul. This murder? Subtle. Poison, almost surely a woman, I'd say. They do always say poison is a woman's weapon."

"Just because people say it, don't make it the truth in this 'ere case!" Thorvald broke in, exasperated.

"And just because a killer killed one way the first time, doesn't mean he won't kill another way the second time," Tuck added. "This killer takes the opportunity to bring whatever works to his new crimes…"

"I'm not buying it," the magistrate said, turning to Alison, who during all this exchange was slumped over and speechless in grief, as her daughter held her in her arms weeping. "Come, Miss Alison, I must take you in now." There was a gentleness in his arrest of her—he took her almost sympathetically by the arm and led her out the door, turning back to Malyne to say, "As there's no jail in town, I'll be holding your mother at Worksop Manor until we arrange to have her trial, and that should be within a few days. Sorry ma'am. I'll be taking her now." Malyne could not stop crying, and Tuck stepped to her to comfort her as she wept on his shoulder.

As the magistrate placed the deflated Alison on his tall horse to ride before him toward Worksop, Tuck called out to him. "Master Crisp! As I continue my investigation of Willie's death, let me look into Meggie's as well, to see if I can, in fact, prove a connection!"

The magistrate shrugged. "Do what you like, gentle friar. If you can prove her innocent at her trial, so be it. If not, she'll probably hang. Good evening to you all." And he mounted his horse and trotted off. Tuck, Malyne and Thorvald stood looking at one another with collapsed faces.

CHAPTER FOURTEEN

In the dim light cast by the prison tent's candelabra, Marion's tongue was lodged in the corner of her mouth and her brows were lowered in concentration as she twisted her hands this way and that behind her on her stool, rubbing them incessantly against the back of her seat, determined to set her hands free if it were humanly possible. Having been at this for hours, she was almost ready to concede that, in fact, it was *not* humanly possible. All the time she was dreading the return of that beast Gill o' the Red Cap—an adversary who had shown he had no respect for courtesy or for rank, and certainly no regard for common decency, and whose threats of physical violence and even ravishment she had no reason to doubt. Her throbbing jaw and the bruise on her cheek were ample warrant that the brute Gill would stop at nothing to break her resistance—and maybe her neck as well.

But what could she do? The captain of the guard wanted particularly to discover the whereabouts of Robin and his outlaw band at this precise moment. But the truth was that Marion did not know where the bandits were hiding. She had first encountered them in their quarters at Creswell Crags, and knew only that they had recently abandoned that site. She was certain they had moved south somewhere in Sherwood, but even if she was willing to reveal their new lair—a willingness to which Gill's threats and violence were bringing her closer by the minute—she was no closer to knowing the precise spot than Gill was himself. But why would he believe that?

Now, despairing of her attempt to loosen her bonds, and unsure what she could possibly do even if she *were* able to free her arms and feet, considering the two goons guarding the tent, she worried about her escorts. The unfortunate youth Giles and the faithful old Sir Eustace, whose only involvement in this mess had been their accompanying herself, had been overwhelmed by the twenty guards who had surrounded them at Creswell Crags. They barely knew Robin Hood or his men, and certainly knew nothing of his history or his current whereabouts. She supposed they had been subject to even more brutal displays of Captain Gill's methods of interrogation, and prayed they were not badly hurt. Indeed, the thought of them actually lifted Marion's spirits for an instant, as she considered the possibility that they might not be as closely guarded as she, and that if they were able to escape, they might be her only hope for delivery from the clutches of her ruthless captor. But that thought gave her only a momentary solace, as just then she heard the brazen, booming voice of Gill o' the Red Cap accosting the two guards who secured the entrance to her tent prison.

"Right, men, at ease!" his raucous voice thundered just outside the tent. Marion stiffened in anticipation of his entrance. "I'm taking this fellow in there to give our virginal Lady Mary a green gown straight off—the first of many..."

"Why him?" one of the burly guards objected.

"He won her in a dice game," Gill answered honestly. "But don't let it bother you. You'll get your turn. Everybody will get their turn with this one, I promise. Now stand aside!" There was a bit of grumbling but Gill shoved his way into the tent as Marion began to gasp for breath and feared she would swoon before the threatened event, and so lose her ability to resist with all her strength, as she had determined. But breathing deeply, she raised her head again and glared in the direction of the tent's entrance, giving an unintended screech when the burly figure of Gill—looking huge and monstrous in the dim shadows of the candelabra—stalked into the tent, and then, when she saw who it was that was following close behind the captain of the guards, she had to stifle a shout of surprise and delight.

The tears of relief and joy that burst from her eyes at the sight of her own gallant Robin were, fortunately for them both, interpreted by Gill o' the Red Cap as evidence of her despair, and he joyed in goading Marion's anguish with threats of an irresistible torrent of further violations to come. "That's right, bitch, I sold you to this fellow in a tavern. But don't worry. When he's done with you, I'll let my two guards out front have at you. After that you've got another dozen of my men to entertain before morning. By then you'd better be ready to tell me where your precious Robin Hood is, or you'll get worse treatment tomorrow."

"That's fine," Robin told him, averting his eyes from Marion's so as not to give anything away. "But I won *my* time with her, and I didn't invite an audience. So, if you don't mind, I'll want the tent to myself for the duration!"

"All right," Gill said, throwing a wicked leer in Marion's direction. "But don't be too long. I've got a couple of randy bucks outside who'd like to get their spindles twisted before the night's over." And as Gill left the tent, he could be heard ordering his guards, "Give our prize winner half an hour with the slut. Then you can have your turns. I'm heading back to the Loaves and Fishes. I'm not spending the night out here."

As soon as Gill had left the tent, Robin was upon her, lifting her from the stool and holding her in his arms. "Oh Robin," she sobbed, "I dared not hope for this. But how are you here?"

"Shh," he whispered in her ear. "Not now. We haven't a moment to lose." And with that he had unsheathed his knife and was cutting the bonds on her hands and feet. "NO WENCH, STRUGGLING WILL AVAIL YOU NOTHING! YOU'RE AT MY MERCY, AND TRUST ME WHEN I SAY I HAVE NONE!" He boomed in his loudest voice, for the benefit of the guards he knew must be listening outside, and then whispered to Marion, "Are you hurt? Can you move quickly once we are out of here?"

"NO! I BEG YOU SIR, HAVE PITY! I AM A GENTLEWOMAN BORN, AND A VIRGIN!" Marion screamed in her best panicked lady-in-distress voice. "Get me out of here and I'll run like hell," she whispered to Robin.

He grinned at her whispering, "That's my girl," and stepping toward the back of the tent, raised his knife and slashed a gaping hole in the tent's wall, at the same time shouting, "NOW, WENCH, YOU'LL FEEL MY FURY AND LUST!" After which he kicked over the candelabra to shroud the tent in darkness.

Marion gave a last impassioned screech at the top of her lungs, followed by "NO! DON'T! IT'S TOO MUCH!" as, with another drawn-out scream that faded gradually into the night, she grasped Robin's hand and the two of them rushed headlong into the forest without looking back.

* * *

The two guards at the pavilion's door waited for a few minutes and then looked at one another curiously. "They sure got quiet all of a sudden," Claude, the taller of the two guards, observed, picking his teeth.

"Yeah," replied Burt, the younger and bawdier of the two, with a grin. "I guess she stopped struggling, then, eh? Must be enjoying it then!"

"Maybe," Claude agreed. "Or maybe just stopped fighting." He listened again, and then frowned suspiciously. "Or… has something happened to' em? It shouldn't be *that* quiet."

"Perhaps they're dead," the voice of Will Stutely came to them, approaching from the dark.

The slower guard Claude looked up with a questioning face as the two figures of Will and Jock emerged from the darkness of the trees. "Stand where you are!" he ordered them, raising his spear to brandish in their direction.

"What are you two doing here? Who are you?"

"Oh, we're just a couple of local boys," Will said easily.

"On our way home," Jock joined in. "Just taking a short cut."

"Didn't really know you had all these tents out here," Will added.

"Well, we do," said the more aggressive Burt, "and we don't want you bumpkins snooping around here, so why don't you clowns just move along now."

"Got no reason to stay," Jock said, holding out his hands in a gesture of deference.

"Just wondering about what you were listening to there in that tent…" Will began.

"We weren't listening to nothing!" Burt insisted.

"No, I suppose not," Will agreed, "since the last thing we heard you say was that it was too quiet."

"So it's quiet? So what?" Burt challenged him.

"So like I said when we came up," Will continued. "Maybe they're dead."

"What are you talking about?" Claude wanted to know. "Why should they be dead?"

"You mean you haven't heard?" Will asked, looking with disbelief at Jock, who had no idea where Will was going with this but was perfectly willing to play along.

"I guess they haven' heard," Jock said, keeping up his end of the conversation.

"Heard what?" Burt goaded them, only half believing these two unwelcome guests.

Will looked meaningfully into Burt's eyes for a moment before he said quietly, "The ghoul of Sherwood."

Burt and Claude looked at one another solemnly before Burt scoffed and blurted, "Pull the other one."

"No, seriously," Jock picked up the thread. "Haven't you heard anything about Willie the tinker since you've been in town? Fellow that was killed in the woods—not far from this spot, now that I think of it. Killed here and dismembered. Bloodiest murder ever seen in these parts."

"And you talk about gruesome?" Will continued. "Stuck his head right up there in the chapel at the priory. Horrifying."

Claude looked a bit ill at the thought, though Burt still seemed a bit skeptical. "Yes… I guess I heard something about that. But why should this ghoul want to have anything to do with us?"

"Oh, this is his lair," Will insisted. "You're camping right in the place he likes to lurk. Sure, I'm telling you, this is the place he loves to hunt. I wouldn't give you two farthings for the lives of whoever was in that tent."

Claude and Burt looked at one another again, this time with a bit more concern on their faces. Not that they cared at all what happened to the stranger their captain had brought in to violate their captive, but they knew that if anything had happened to the young woman, it was they who would be blamed. And so Claude said, "Maybe we'd better go in there and check on them."

Burt shrugged. "Captain said not to."

"But then," Claude said, "Gill didn't count on no ghoul of Sherwood."

Burt shrugged again. "Well, I don't care if we bust in on the old dance. Let's go see what's goin' on in there."

Leading with their lances, the two guards turned to step into the pavilion, moving gingerly when they realized the tent was in total darkness. Meanwhile Will and Jock followed close behind, each of them holding a large stone. "Just a tap behind the ear," Will whispered to Jock as they followed the guards into the dark tent.

After Claude and Burt had slumped to the floor of the darkened tent, Will relighted the candelabra and he and Jock trussed the two guards up back to back with the bonds left from Marion's wrists and ankles and, grabbing the dormant lances just in case, the two bandits slipped out of the tent through the newly sliced back door and took off through the woods toward Alison and Malyne's tiny shack.

* * *

When Robin and Marion reached Alison's hovel after an hour or so of skulking through the shadowy forest, they were welcomed with great joy by Friar Tuck and Thorwald, while Malyne shyly made Lady Mary's acquaintance and offered her some small beer after her ordeal. Everyone was solicitous of her and made her sit in one of the few chairs in the house until she breathed more freely and felt like sleeping.

Unfortunately nobody else was in the mood to get any rest, because they were now trying to bring Robin up to date on the arrest of poor Alison. Robin gave a long-suffering sigh, with one more crisis to deal with, and closed his eyes. After a few deep breaths, he opened them again and charged ahead. "All right," he began. "We know that Alison herself cannot be guilty of poisoning the girl. Then we need to ask what motive anybody might have had to kill her, and whether this has any connection with Willie's murder."

"My thoughts exactly," Tuck agreed, continuing, "for now we need to suspend our worries about Willie and focus on Meggie's death. What we do now can't change anything about Willie's murder, but if we don't act quickly it's Alison who may be in trouble. Master George Crisp has declared her trial must take place in a few days, and before then we've got to be ready to prove her innocence. So… why should anyone want to kill this child?"

"She was pregnant." Malyne made the matter-of-fact announcement baldly and without emotion, moving her eyes in an eerie sweep of the room that left all the men awkwardly looking down and shifting their feet as if they themselves were guilty and were being examined by some supernatural being. Marion, lounging in her chair, opened one eye and muttered, "Ah. Well there's a motive for somebody."

"Meggie had known for a few weeks, and so had her mother, but I'm sure it was not generally known," Malyne continued. "And they'd just engaged my mother to see about ending the pregnancy—didn't want Meggie unwed with a child."

"So they're claiming whatever your mother gave the girl to bring it off, actually poisoned her," Marion concluded.

"But I know my mother could not have done so," Malyne cried. "She knew the properties of all the herbs she used. Some midwives will prescribe a dose of pennyroyal to end a pregnancy, but Alison knew that to be poisonous, and to sometimes cause the death of the mother. She would not have used that. She would have given Meggie a dose of soapwort mixed with sage. That would often do the trick without too much damage to the girl herself. I cannot believe that my mother's potion would have done anything to hurt Meggie."

"And we are certain that this poisoning of Meggie was not done in order to cast blame on Alison? To frame her for murder and get her hanged? Meggie being collateral damage?" Robin suggested.

"Everyone in this county loves my mother!" Malyne countered, glaring about as if daring anyone to challenge her. "She has delivered most of the children born here for the past thirty years, and helped many a woman in sickness or in need!"

"No one could be more innocent than Alison," agreed Tuck. "I'd swear to it. No, the target here is Meggie. It's Alison that's collateral damage."

"And the girl's pregnancy the motive," Robin continued. "So what would cause someone to want to kill a woman simply because she's pregnant?"

"Could be the family's honor, for one," Thorvald suggested. "I know from talkin' to 'er father Ralph, the cook, 'ow much 'e was bent on keepin' 'er from doin's with the likes o' that Willie feller. Finds 'er bearin' a bastard kid, flies into a temper, and bam!"

"But Meggie was poisoned," Malyne argued. "Her father wouldn't have poisoned her in a sudden rage."

"More a woman's weapon," Marion suggested, opening her eyes for a moment. "We have it on the magistrate's authority. So could the mother have done it?"

"Margaret, the mother, is the one who came to Alison to ask for her services," Malyne informed them. "She's not about to ensure that they go so terribly wrong. She'd be implicating herself as well as Alison."

"All right," Tuck said. "If honor's not the motive, then what about jealousy? Was there somebody who'd have been jealous that Meggie was having Willie's child?"

"Didn't we go over this ground once already?" Thorvald said. "And didn't we agree that nobody would 'a been jealous of Meggie and Willie, 'cause nobody really liked Willie, except that laundress, woman, Liptrot. And we didn't think 'er capable of killin' Willie. Would she 'a been more capable o' the poison?"

Robin had frozen in place at the suggestion of Meggie's baby having been Willie's. Now he burst out with the new evidence he'd taken in that night, stunning the rest of the people in the hovel. "Willie wasn't the baby's father," he said with authority. "I heard it from her own brother tonight. Willie was just a poor sap that Meggie and her mother were hoping to get to marry Meggie and make the child legitimate. The father was the captain of the guard, Gill o' the Red Cap."

There was a stunned silence for a moment, until Marion burst out with disgust. "That brute sired a child on this murdered girl? Somebody should have killed *him*, not her!"

"Her brother was very keen to try," Robin told her. "Till I talked him out of it."

"Why on earth would you do that?" Marion spat bitterly.

Robin, looking slightly cowed, shrugged impotently. "I... I was worried for the lad. Gill did have two dozen guards around him. I rather thought young John would have been dead himself long before he'd got close to Gill."

"But if the brute raped his sister..."

"No, no," Robin stopped her. "Even John did not claim that's what happened. I gathered that the girl had given herself to your brute willingly. What her brother was incensed about was that he'd left her alone afterwards, without another thought."

Marion made a face as if she were about to be sick. "Why on earth would a young girl lie down willingly with a swine?" she asked.

"Now, consider," Malyne said. "How many young women do you suppose there are between Wallingwells and Worksop and all the land in between? And how many marriageable men? If even a wanker like Willie the tinker can have women thinking about him as a possible mate, what do you think the girls are going to do when they see a manly stranger, a captain of the king's guard no less…"

"Captain o' Sir Guy o' Gisborne's guard," Thorvald corrected *sotto voce*.

"Whatever," Malyne brushed him off irritably. "Captain of any guard, come swaggering in here throwing his authority around. Here's a man who outshone anybody around here. Here's somebody that might take you away from here altogether and set you up in Nottingham or York, or London even, can snatch you from obscure poverty and set you up in style somewhere luxurious—who do you think wasn't setting her cap for him? Why, if I was younger and not a cock-eyed hag I'd have been after him myself!"

Marion just rolled her eyes, but Robin took up the thread. "All right then. Who might have been so jealous that she'd kill the cook's daughter?"

"What do you mean, kill the cook's daughter?" Came a shocked and anxious voice from the cottage door. It was young John, Ralph's son, who'd just arrived at the house.

* * *

John sat like a stone on the only bench in the room, morose in the corner of Alison's twenty-five by twenty-five-foot shack into which Alan a Dale and Little John now also squeezed along with Marion's escort, the young squire Giles and the knight Sir Eustace. Even before that group had settled, Will Stutely came knocking along with Jock, with two new lances in their hands and the tale of their cashiering Marion's two guards fresh on their lips. That made twelve people in that cramped space, enough that Malyne remarked it was a good thing her mother was not at home, since she could not have fit in the house. And now while young John's sister's murder had of necessity been revealed to him without much ceremony, leaving him stunned in the corner, there were a few other things that needed to be dealt with promptly.

The freeing of Marion's escort had been fairly simple, according to Little John. The cook's son had steered them undetected to the guards' camp, where they quickly found a tent with only a single sleepy guard at the door, whom they had gagged and tied almost before he had realized he was being assailed. And the boy John had also led them to where, on a hunch, he believed the guards' horses were tethered: The five escapees had made off with a like number of the guards' mounts.

"Then here's what we do," Robin said. "You, Giles and Sir Eustace, take two of those new horses and ride straightaway to the countess's castle, to tell her what's happened here to her emissary. I have a feeling she may have something to say about this."

"Shouldn't we be taking Lady Mary with us, to get her out of harm's way?" Sir Eustace suggested.

"I'm not going anywhere as long as Robin is in danger here," Marion pronounced, and crossed her arms. And so without further ceremony, the two guards set off, wanting to put many miles between themselves and Gisbourne's guards while those troops slept.

"As for you, Little John and Alan, I want you to take Will and Jock south—take the other three horses and the one outside that Tuck borrowed earlier. Don't go back to the Loaves and Fishes but leave straight from here. I want you far from this place before those soldiers wake up and remember what you looked like. Head into Sherwood and back to the camp at the Old Oak."

"And leave you here to face Gill and his men alone?" Little John objected.

"What are we, the 'ired 'elp?" Thorvald said, looking over at Friar Tuck.

"Tuck and Thorvald weren't part of the escapades tonight, so they'll be the ones to see things to the end here. And we've got to stay to keep Marion hidden and guarded as long as Gill is loose. Malyne, she can stay here, I hope?"

"Why not?" Malyne shrugged. "Everybody else does."

Little John was adamant about staying with Robin, still believing his bad advice had been instrumental in putting Robin in danger that night, but Robin convinced him it would be better if he left. "You think someone your size would be able to hide in this county without being recognized?" the bandit leader told his lieutenant. "It's dangerous for all of us if you stay here. But do this: if you don't get word from me in two days that we've solved these two murders, bring our men in force with bows at the ready."

Little John raised his eyebrows; Robin had never before been so ready to take on seasoned soldiers like Gisbourne's guards so openly and directly. The capture of Maid Marion, if it accomplished nothing else, had succeeded in arousing Robin's fighting spirit and he was ready to take on the mysteries of Worksop and Wallingwells and the ghoul of Sherwood, even if Gill o' the Red Cap, Sir Guy of Gisbourne, the Sheriff of Nottingham, and the king himself and all their armies came in to drag him away. But he hoped they wouldn't.

There was a lot more breathing room in Alison's shack, now that it was only Malyne and he, with Marion, Tuck, and Thorvald—and poor John still silent in his corner. "Now," Robin said, "just what are we going to do about Alison and the murder of Meggie?"

"Should've killed that Gill o' the Red Cap tonight, and not let him get away with all this," the cook's lad was muttering.

"Now, boy, you know Gill can't have been behind Meggie's murder," Robin cautioned. "She was poisoned earlier today, and Gill was still on his way here with his men, and after that drinking at the Loaves and Fishes."

"He's the one put that bastard in her," John insisted. "Everything that happened since is his fault."

Tuck was willing to accept that there was some truth in the boy's assertion, but didn't feel up to engaging in a theological discussion of necessary vs. sufficient or proximate causes, and merely answered, "Well somebody else was the one that gave Meggie the poison, and if we accept that it was not Alison herself, then we need to get a look at the scene of the crime."

"The what?" Malyne asked.

"The place where we know the murder happened. John, are you willing to take us to your home, to see where your sister was killed and who might have had access to it before Meggie was found poisoned?"

John looked at Tuck through red-rimmed brown eyes staring out from behind doleful scowling brows. Sobbing, he nodded affirmation, then hung his head and wept. Malyne patted the boy's broad shoulders and offered to make him a soothing draft that would help him sleep. But wary of any potions just now, John begged off. The lady of the house did, however, give him a blanket, and told him he was welcome to sleep there in any case that night.

"And tomorrow morning, at first light," Friar Tuck told him, "we'll give Meggie's room a thorough going over. There's got to be something there to give us a clue to the murderer."

Robin sighed. He was far less sanguine about their prospects. And what would Tuck do if his old neighbor and godmother was found guilty of murder? And could any answer ever be found as to who killed Willie, the mystery that had brought Tuck and Thorvald to this place? Oh well, Robin thought as he stretched out to sleep on a straw mat on the floor of the hovel, with his five other companions in that tiny shack. At least Marion was safe. For now.

CHAPTER FIFTEEN

As it turned out, Gill o' the Red Cap did not remain "loose," to use Robin's phrase, for long. Gill was still passed out drunk at one of the tables in the Loaves and Fishes—he'd been forced to sleep there, having failed to win one of the upper rooms at Hazard (even though, as it turned out, none of the occupants of those rooms spent the night in them either). Quite early the next morning Claude and Burt, both with raging headaches, found their way into the tavern. They were accompanied by Gill's black-bearded lieutenant Jack, leading a dozen other members of Gisbourne's guard, including Edward, the sleeping guard who'd been tied up by Little John and Alan a Dale before they rescued Marion's escorts.

Jack, scowling with annoyance and egged on by Claude and Burt, who were annoyed in their own right, gave Gill's inert body a not altogether gentle kick in the side where he sprawled across the table, flanked by two of his gambling mates in similar states of unconscious stupor.

"Eh? Wazzat?" Gill growled hoarsely, blinking his eyes the better to unblur them, and smacking his lips to try to free his tongue from the great reem of flannel he seemed to have swallowed during the night. "Oh... Jack, zatchoo?" Now Gill rubbed his right hand over his face and shook his head to see if somewhere underneath that thick dull ache a brain might be lodged, waiting for someone to use it for a change. "So, lieutenant," he finally managed to say, shaking himself into a kind of military bearing. "Reporting for your morning orders?" Then first noticing Claude and Burt, he had a vague recollection that he had last given them some pleasant duty to perform… had it been last night?

Then suddenly it came to him in sharp definition, the vision of the battered and bedraggled Lady Mary of Winchester, tied hand and foot on that stool in the prison tent, and a slow leer came over his newly animated face. "And you two—come from breaking in that wench are you? Been at it all night then? Well go on, make your report. Who's guarding her now?"

Burt, gingerly feeling the great lump behind his left ear, answered with a barely articulated whine, "I suppose the bloke you let into her tent before you left has probably been guarding her, ever since he cut a hole in the back of the prison tent and made off with her."

Gill frowned deeply, not yet quite realizing the full extent of the calamity. "Well then, what are you doing here? Why aren't you out chasing them? I want that bitch brought back here and I want her here this morning, and that shifty dice-cheating bastard with her! What are you waiting for?"

Now Claude came forth and broke the news of the other part of their evening fiasco to their commander. "We can't chase them because they've been gone for hours. We've no idea where. We've only just woken up ourselves." And in response to the bewildered jerk of Gill's head and hands Claude added, "The dice-cheating bastard's two accomplices knocked us out with some heavy rocks before we could get any kind of sense of where he'd taken the lady."

Gill sputtered like a boiling kettle before exploding with, "They can't get away! We'll get those two bodyguards of the girl's to reveal where they've gone. I'll roast them alive to have the truth out of them. Then I'll string those fugitives up like a marionette show before I'm done with them!"

And with that the short, unassuming guard named Edward stepped forward to deliver the final straw to Gill's load of bad news: "Captain, I'm sorry to report that as I was guarding the two male prisoners last night, I was overpowered by three large men—one of them *exceedingly* large—and left bound and gagged in their tent while the three of them untied the prisoners and made off with them."

To his credit, Gill o' the Red Cap was not deflated by this news, nor did he let his men see him show frustration or panic. "Right!" he exclaimed, standing up and taking command of the situation. "These clownish yokels are about to learn a hard lesson about interfering with the business of the king's guard. I want every man in this company mounted and ready in a quarter of an hour to scour the countryside for the fugitives. We'll make this entire shire bleed if we have to until they give up these villains if they're harboring them!" Then an idea struck him. "We'll go first to that countess or whatever she was that the wench kept throwing at me... the countess of Chesterfield, she said. I don't care how precious or noble she is, she's going to learn that the king's guard has power over anyone in this county, by God!"

"You'll find it's going to be quite impossible for our entire company to mount up," the lieutenant Jack remarked. He did not say "Sir," nor did he stand at attention. He merely made the statement in a matter-of-fact way in a flat-toned voice. "For you see, five of our mounts were stolen during the night."

Gill wheeled, now beginning to lose his composure, mainly at Jack's failure to jump to attention to obey his orders. "Then let all but five of the company mount up, and let the five without mounts begin a house to house search of this village, and damn it, let them burn down any house they suspect one of these renegades might be hiding in! Starting with this one!!" He looked around at the Loaves and Fishes, and saw James Snaggletooth's eyes suddenly bulge from his chagrined face. "Deny me a room when I demand it, will you?" Gill muttered, then shouted at Jack: "Now jump to it! I won't have your insolence on top of everything else!"

Jack, however, did not move. He only allowed a barely visible flicker of a smile to dart across his bland face before he added one more bit of information, "Let me point out one more thing, *Captain*." That last word was spoken with an unconcealed irony. "Men, tell us what color all of your ruffians were wearing?"

At that, Claude, Burt, and Edward all spoke up in unison with one loud voice: "Lincoln Green."

At the word, a look of cold recognition swept over Gill o' the Red Cap's visage, and he sat down again looking deflated and stunned.

"Yes," Jack now went on, mercilessly. "Your blind obsession with imprisoning, questioning, and, may I say, tormenting a group of completely innocent travelers entirely blinded you to the fact that the actual target of your mission, the outlaw Robin Hood and his band of Sherwood outlaws, was here under your nose, and your churlish obsession with your gambling and your drunkenness allowed your prisoners to escape with the aid of the very men you were seeking to capture. And now all have vanished into the forest without a trace. And with five of Sir Guy of Gisbourne's horses."

"Well," Gill began to rally, trying to brazen it out, "We've had some bad luck. We'll do what we can to mend it and I'll explain to Sir Guy…"

"Nothing. You'll explain nothing to Sir Guy, because as of this moment I am relieving you of command."

Gill's head jerked back as if he'd been punched in the face. "You… you're *what*?" he said. Then, as the words sank in, he leaned forward belligerently and bellowed back, "You and what army?"

Jack blinked, then answered calmly, "Well, to be precise, the army that is standing behind me now," and by this time the full complement of Sir Guy of Gisbourne's assigned company was standing supportively behind Jack, now the acknowledged leader of the troops. "I may as well tell you at this point," Jack continued calmly and confidently, "that Sir Guy took me aside before we started up here on this mission, and confided to me that he was not entirely confident in your ability to lead troops, but that he felt compelled to put you in charge of this mission because of your rank. He did say, however, that I was to keep close watch on your actions, and that if at any time I seriously questioned your judgment or your decision-making ability I was to relieve you of command and return the company—and you with it—to Nottingham for a reassessment as soon as possible."

As the full impact of his subordinate's words registered, a deflated Gill slumped over and looked less aggressively and more pathetically into his former lieutenant's face. "And you… you're saying that you… question my judgment in this mission? My conduct as commander?" he said, still with some disbelief.

"Drunkenness, gambling, flagrant arrests and torture of the king's innocent subjects, the deliberate threats of further abuse of local citizens, and, oh yes, humiliation by the very outlaws you were charged with arresting—I'd say those things amount to a significant pattern of bad judgment. Gentlemen?"

With that five of the guards stepped forward and tied Gill's hands with some of the very bonds he'd used to imprison his guests of the previous night, and proceeded to lead him out of the tavern toward the guards' camp. It was a matter of a mere two hours before all the tents in the camp were broken down and stowed, and the guards all mounted and ready to move out—all except five of them, who were reduced to marching behind the mounted soldiers because there were not enough horses for the entire company. At least they had been promised a chance to ride later, when another group of five would be required to march. And soon the company of Sir Guy of Gisbourne's guards could be seen exiting the vicinity, riding two by two, with the single figure of Gill o' the Red Cap, bound upon a horse in the center of the file, head down as a prisoner moving toward judgment.

Word had spread quickly, and most of the town of Worksop turned out to see that very public exit, and some of them actually cheered the departure of that company that had come claiming to represent the king but had succeeded, instead, only in arousing public resentment. In all the excitement, no one realty noticed the pretty young dairy maiden standing at the edge of town, her arms crossed, watching the troops leave with a deep frown on her pensive face.

*　*　*

The home of Ralph the priory cook was another cruck wattle-and-daub construction with a thatched roof like Alison and Malyne's hovel, but in a different category altogether. This structure was a good forty feet by thirty, and had two central wooden trusses that divided the house into three bays. From the outside, Tuck could see and admire the several windows on the ground floor, and two on an upper floor on the east side, all of which were lined with glass. It was clear that the cook's family, doubtless as a result of their secure employment at the convent, were people with a dependable income.

Ralph's son John, still shaking with rage and shock at the

report of his sister's death, opened the door to find that neither of his parents was at home. "It's likely they'd be with Father Bernard now," Tuck told him, "seeking spiritual comfort and planning the funeral rites for poor young Meggie."

"Meggie…" John's voice trailed off and tears glistened in his eyes as he leaned on the door handle while Tuck and Thorvald entered, followed by Robin, who was glancing down the street at an even larger house built of stone.

"Who's your rich neighbor?" he asked, oblivious to John's sorrow, or deliberately ignoring it in the hope of conducting this inspection of the girl's deathbed without the distraction of her brother's unspent grief.

"I believe that would be the new home of Master Bryce," Malyne answered for the subdued John, her green eye looking off somewhere in the direction of the stone manor.

"Ah," Robin mused. "A fair bit of profit to be made from skimming off your employers' chattels, then, eh?" he surmised from what he had learned of Bryce's doings from Tuck over the past several hours.

The interior of the cook's house opened first into a roomy hall, the largest room, with a central hearth around which were a few chairs where members of the family might have sat to eat or to warm themselves. The floor, like Alison's, was covered with straw. To the left of the large room was a smaller service area with a stone oven, around which were arrayed several earthenware pots with lids, as well as brass pots and pans. Tuck could not help but think that Willie the tinker had probably made a few sales to this house, and perhaps had met Meggie as a result. To the right of the hall was a storage area, above which were the second floor sleeping rooms reached by a wooden ladder.

"Anything look unusual to you down here?" Tuck gently asked young John, who looked about the rooms without enthusiasm, vaguely shaking his head. "No," he answered. "Nothing disturbed. Pretty much as I left it yesterday."

"Then let's see what there is to find upstairs," Tuck said. "Can you show us where your sister would have slept?"

"She was in her bed when I left her," John said, climbing the ladder to the loft. "She hadn't left it for the past few days, she was that sick."

One by one his four guests climbed after him, into the loft where it was not possible to stand erect under the slanting eaves. The loft was divided by curtains into three distinct sleeping rooms, each with its own straw mattress. "My bed is in the front of the house," John told them. "My parents' in the center. That one furthest to the rear is… was… my sister's. It's where she must have died." The young man's voice cracked on the last word. Robin, determined to push through, answered, "Right then," and, stooping, turned left from the ladder and poked his way into the girl's room. There was really space for no more than one of the visitors to enter the room at the same time, and so one by one the four guests took in the contents of Meggie's chamber.

Robin noted the straw mattress and a heavy blanket—in her illness Meggie must have had chills despite the warm late spring weather. The room smelled of sickness, a condition in no way lessened by the chamber pot in the corner of the room. Next to the bed was a low table on which sat an unlighted candle and an empty earthenware cup. Robin saw nothing that might be considered a clue to the girl's murder, and with a sigh ducked out of the room and made way for the friar.

Friar Tuck noticed nothing more significant than Robin had, unless it was the window in the girl's room. Looking through the distorting glass, Tuck could see a few chickens and a colorful rooster in a small pen in the yard behind the house. He could also see the Widow Day's small home across the way, and wondered whether that proximity could be of any significance. Tuck also was particularly drawn to the cup on the table. He wondered if it was there simply to quench Meggie's thirst in her illness. If so, why was it empty? After a few moments, though, Tuck had to admit that he had learned much less than he'd hoped at the scene of the crime.

When he backed out, it was Malyne's turn to scan the room. The four men looked at one another while Malyne stooped under the eaves, and Robin sighed. Tuck, however, was optimistic. "I'm glad we've brought Malyne, I have to say," he began with a kind of forced cheerfulness. "She's a skilled midwife, like her mother. If anything in that room looks out of joint, incompatible with the way her mother would have left it, then Malyne ought to be able to recognize it right off. She's much more likely to find some clue in there that we men wouldn't recognize. I mean, really, what do *we* know?"

"Well, I can tell you what *I* know," John said with some vehemence. "I know what that room looked like when I left, and what it looks like now, and I don't see any difference at all."

"Even this cup?" Malyne said as she came out of the room, holding the clay mug and sniffing it in the process.

"The cup?" John said, then shrugged. "It's ours, from downstairs. I suppose she was thirsty. Mother must have given her a drink before she left for the priory yesterday."

"No," Malyne shook her head. "Your mother didn't give her this. This cup contained pennyroyal, and plenty of it. I'd know that minty smell anywhere. This I what killed your sister."

Thorvald sniffed at that revelation, then took his turn examining Meggie's sleeping area. Unlike the others, the dwarf did not have to crouch to go into the room, and could look about more comfortably, and from a closer perspective. He did so while Malyne continued her own analysis of the room.

"I'm also assuming that none of you bothered to actually look into the chamber pot in the corner," she said. The men looked at her blankly, each of them wondering why on earth they might have done such a thing, but Malyne rolled her mismatched eyes, which in her case made quite a sight. "You know that physicians will examine their patients' urine and nightsoil to get a full picture of their health. Well I learned two things from my examination. First, Meggie had been vomiting recently, likely as a result of this poisoning and not my mother's potion administered a couple of days ago. Secondly, there is a profusion of blood in the bottom of the bucket—a sure sign that mother's potion did finally achieve its objective and the pregnancy was ended before Meggie's murder."

Thorvald, still having his look around the girl's room, glanced at the chamber pot in the corner and decided very quickly that he would take Malyne's word for it as to what the bucket contained. But as he looked toward that corner of the room, he noticed something amid the straw that covered the floor. It was nearly the same color as the straw, and was very easy to miss, though Thorvald could see it clearly now, as he bent close to the floor. "Ha," he thought to himself. "If this isn't a clue, what is?"

"'Ere!" he called, bursting out of the room and waving his find in the air. "It was on the floor, 'idden amongst all that straw! Look at this now! Somebody was 'ere, an' it sure as goodness wasn't anybody from this family!"

Friar Tuck grabbed the item Thorvald was waving around. It was a glove. And not a simple cloth one, but rather one made of a soft pale-yellow leather, likely from a calf or kid. It was a glove for someone with expensive tastes and an ample budget. "Well this is something new," Tuck said thoughtfully.

And while Tuck and Robin contemplated that, Thorvald turned to Malyne, asking, "An' by the way, you sure about that cup you found? I mean, 'ow do you know that cup ain't the one your mum give Meggie to bring it off?"

"I know," Malyne said definitively, "because my mother never mixed any of her potions in milk. And there's still a few drops of milk in the bottom of that cup."

* * *

What followed these events passed in whirlwind fashion for Friar Tuck as he tried to put a case together to defend his mother's old friend and protector against what he was now convinced was a completely baseless charge of murder.

The first major event of the day, following their examination of the crime scene, was deeply satisfying for Robin and his companions, most notably for the cook's son John: They were able to stand on the street and watch as two dozen of Sir Guy of Gisbourne's finest warriors rode off without ceremony, out of Worksop and out of the neighborhood, With Gill o' the Red Cap bound in subjection amid the mounted column—and with Robin crouching well hidden behind John, Malyne, and the friar. But the evacuation of the troops meant Robin would need to hide no more as he helped bring this mystery to a close.

Nor, for that matter, would Maid Marion. Robin, Tuck, and Thorvald decided after they watched the Nottingham guards disappear over the horizon that they would move that night back to the rooms at the Loaves and Fishes in order to give Malyne some relief from her unwonted company of the past several days. They hoped, though, that Marion would be able to stay with Malyne—so that neither one of them would be alone in this time of stress. Malyne was quite willing to comply, and after that was decided she bade them farewell for the time being in order to return home and tell Marion the news.

John was obliged to head into the priory to find his parents and Father Bernard, to see what had been decided about his sister's final rites, and Robin and his men accompanied the young man, waiting for him outside the priest's vestry, where he was meeting with the grieving parents. When John came back out, he told the three outlaws that his sister was to be interred the following morning.

They did return to Malyne's briefly that afternoon, to let her know about Meggie's funeral, and were surprised to learn that the women had had a visit earlier from the magistrate, George Crisp. Crisp had determined that he would set Dame Alison's trial the following day as well. For Tuck, this was unwelcome news. How, he reasoned, could he provide any defense at all for Alison if everyone he might wish to call as a witness would be at the victim's funeral on the same day?

But for Robin, the news seemed to provide an opportunity, not a problem.

"Look, Tuck, here is what we do: We appeal to Master Crisp and tell him about this difficulty, and we get him to change the venue of the trial from wherever in Worksop he planned to hold it to the chapel at the priory, where the funeral takes place."

"You actually think that lazy magistrate would do anything so reasonable as that?" Tuck spat.

"Of course," Robin said. "Think what he's like: He'll be happy not to worry about finding a place himself to use as a courtroom. He'll feel good about looking like he's giving Alison a fair trial, which he probably never really thought of doing himself. And he'll show everybody in town what an important fellow he is."

"And how will he do that?" Tuck asked.

"By telling everybody at the funeral that they are not allowed to leave afterwards," Robin said. "In case any of them are needed as witnesses."

Tuck allowed a brief smile to curl his lips as he considered Robin's plan. Then the three of them, Robin, Tuck, and Thorvald, started off toward Worksop, first to meet with George Crisp and settle the venue of tomorrow's trial, and then to sit around a table in the Loaves and Fishes and plan the case for Alison's defense. Robin smacked his lips at the thought of consuming a good amount of James Snaggletooth's ale. Whatever happened, this did not promise to be a night when any of them would get much sleep.

CHAPTER SIXTEEN

The by now familiar chapel at the priory was fuller than Tuck had ever seen it. Since Meggie had been the daughter of the nuns' cook Ralph, she was thought of as a part of the priory family, and Father Bernard and Madame Veronica had endeavored to give Meggie a full requiem mass, complete with the priory's fine choir. Tuck was reminded of his first glimpse of the sisters, and looked again for Sister Lucy with her beak-like nose, pecking away at the notes of the chant; and for the wrinkled lips of Sister Anne, those dark eyebrows of Sister Mary Eusebia, and the freckled nose of Sister Rebecca. He also recognized the wide mouth of the cellarer Sister Esther and the blue eyes and long lashes of the infirmarian, Sister Mary Barbara, who were lending their own sweet voices to the chants. But when he yielded himself to the music and drew back from the individuality of the sisters, he saw them once again in their Benedictine habits as a flock of blackbirds, sweetly trilling woosell thrushes that he loved to watch as they gathered by the dozen in the branches of Sherwood. He closed his eyes as they began the notes of the *Dies Irae*:

> *Dies irae, dies illa*
> *Solvet saeclum in favilla*
> *Teste David cum Sybilla.*

*[Day of wrath, day that
will dissolve the world into burning coals,
as David bore witness with the Sibyl.]*

Tuck shook his head and opened his eyes. He could never understand why this hymn of the Last Judgment was sung at every requiem mass. He knew the idea was to remind the mourners that their own deaths were imminent, and that they should be preparing their own souls for judgment. A *memento mori*. But weren't we all gathered here at this time to remember and to grieve for the loss of the poor young girl Meggie? And not to think of ourselves? Tuck sighed. It didn't much matter what he thought after all. He wasn't going to change centuries of Church tradition. He did quietly resolve that, should he be called upon to say a requiem mass for the soul of one of the Sherwood outlaws fallen in the service of Robin, Lord of Misrule, he'd accidentally leave out the reminder of the Day of Wrath. None of his own flock would miss it.

Now Tuck let his eyes flit about the chapel to take in what attendees he recognized. Given the courtesy of chairs directly before the altar in the front of the nave were Meggie's family: her father Ralph, mother Margaret, and brother John, all looking devastated by the sudden unlooked-for death of their healthy, vigorous young daughter and sister. They were overwhelmed and, more, wanted somebody to pay for this loss. Master Bryce was there near the front, dressed in an expensive-looking blue tunic and leather shoes with the toes curled upwards in the new fashion. And there stood the laundress Elizabeth Liptrot, along with the baker Oswald and his round wife Hulga. Widow Day was there as well, along with, as far as Tuck could determine, anyone and everyone who lived in tiny Wallingwells or the country roundabout, including, of course, Malyne, who'd come with Robin, Marion, Thorvald and himself to be present at the girl's memorial.

A good portion of Worksop was present as well, including several of Thorvald's contacts from the town's artisans, most of whom he'd met at the Loaves and Fishes. The inn's proprietor James Snaggletooth was here too—Tuck wondered who was watching the tavern—and the dairy maid Kate of Worksop. The magistrate George Crisp was also here, of course, standing at the back of the chapel at the door to ensure—per his bargain with Friar Tuck—that no one would be leaving this chapel before he opened court here to try Dame Alison for Meggie's murder. And, of course, Alison herself was present, dressed in a simple understated gray cloak of homespun wool and sitting (for Master Crisp had procured a small stool for his prisoner) as unobtrusively as possible right next to the magistrate's stout form, in direct sight of his droopy hound-like eyes. It was a curious twist, certainly, to have the deceased's alleged killer so visibly present at the victim's requiem mass.

> *Quantus tremor est futurus,*
> *Quando judex est venturus*
> *Cuncta stricte discussurus!*
>
> *[How great a tremor is to be,*
> *when the judge is to come*
> *briskly shattering every grave!]*

Friar Tuck's mouth tightened into a thin line at the grim irony of the hymn's words. Looking at Master Crisp, Tuck nodded with the certainty that the judge had indeed come, not to shatter every grave but at least to guard this one. Was there anyone in that crowded church now who might be trembling at the thought of the coming trial?

> *Tuba, mirum spargens sonum*
> *Per sepulchra regionum,*
> *Coget omnes ante thronum.*

> *[A trumpet sounding an astonishing sound*
> *through the tombs of the region*
> *drives all men before the throne.]*

All men, and all women, the ones who mattered in this case of Alison's, were indeed here in the chapel, and Tuck wondered, when Master Crisp announced that they must all stay for the trial, if there would be some grousing. Would some of them actually have to be forced to stay, "driven before the throne" as the song put it?

> *Mors stupebit, et natura,*
> *Cum resurget creatura,*
> *Judicanti responsura.*

> *[Death will be stunned and so will Nature,*
> *when arises the creature*
> *responding to the One judging.]*

Tuck reviewed in his mind the strategy he had worked out with Robin and Thorvald the previous night. They had gone over every bit of evidence they had collected, and he for one was confident that he knew whom to blame in Meggie's murder. Whether death and nature would be stunned he didn't know, but he was fairly certain several of those present would be stunned at the person who would be forced to respond to the one judging, Master Crisp.

Judex ergo cum sedebit
Quidquid latet, apparebit:
Nil inultum remanebit.

[Therefore when the Judge shall sit,
whatever lay hidden will appear;
Nothing unavenged will remain.]

Tuck's grim smile broadened. "Nothing unavenged will remain." That was definitely the intention. Because if things worked out the way they had planned, they would not only have revealed the killer of poor Meggie, but would have solved the mystery of Willie's mutilated body as well.

* * *

The requiem mass was coming to a close as the choir chanted the *In Paradisum*, and Friar Tuck was growing eager with anticipation of the interment of Meggie's body, which would be in the floor of the chapel itself, after which he knew Alison's trial would begin. He looked over to where he thought Robin would be standing next to him and found instead Maid Marion, who shrugged her shoulders and whispered to him conspiratorially, "He said he heard something outside and went out the door to see what it was."

"Hmmph," Tuck responded, looking back toward the door where George Crisp still stood, his arms crossed like a general surveying his troops. He wasn't sure he could carry this off with as much confidence if Robin were not in the congregation when he presented his defense, and his mind quickly began a frantic calculation, planning what scheme he might fall back on if Robin failed to return. The friar continued to sweat through the end of the mass and on into the brief interment ritual, toward the end of which he breathed a sigh of relief as Robin slipped quietly back to his side.

"You nearly had me cringing on the floor," Tuck hissed to Robin as he slipped back into place. "Don't do that to a poor begging friar unless you want to see me interred with little Meggie as long as they've got the tomb open!"

"Quit your squawking you fat friar," Robin whispered back, smiling good-naturedly. "You'd be a lot less flustered right now if you knew what's waiting for us outside."

Tuck scowled quizzically at the outlaw chief, but Robin had no more to say, and the two of them now waited quietly—though in Tuck's case not especially patiently—for the ritual to end.

When the end had come and Father Bernard had closed his final prayer with a chanted "Amen," the crowd within the chapel began to stir, with Meggie's family rising slowly and tearfully from their seats near the altar. But at the rear of the nave George Crisp was speaking, far more energetically than he was accustomed to.

"Stay where you are, gentles all, please stay where you are!"

From the front of the church, Father Bernard also tried to calm the congregation. "Friends," he called in his preaching voice. "As many of you know, our local magistrate, Master Crisp, has requested the use of this venue today in order to conduct the trial of Mistress Alison, who is accused, as you must have heard, of the murder of this young lady whom we have just committed to her Maker."

"That's right!" called some of the folk among the crowd, and "Hang the witch!" was heard from a few others.

"Now I must insist that you all stay where you are for this trial. I understand that a number of you may be called upon as witnesses in this case," Master Crisp informed them from the door, where he still stood with crossed arms, though now he was crossing them like a petulant teenager who might not be getting his way.

Because he might not. A significant number of the congregation were making their way toward the door, grumbling, "I don't need to be here," and "I'm not a witness to anything," and began to push their way past the magistrate.

"Hard to be a one-man law enforcement program," Robin mused, seemingly unconcerned as a dozen people shoved their way out the door, Master Crisp being unable to stop them all by himself.

"Well we can't let this happen!" Tuck blustered. "Look—some of those people heading out the door are witnesses I'm going to want to talk to—there's Elizabeth Liptrot, and a whole group from Worksop—Snaggletooth and the dairymaid and lord knows who."

"They're not going anywhere," Robin said calmly, and steered the friar toward the chapel door to show him why this was so. Tuck reached the door to stand next to the goggle-eyed Master Crisp, who was just as astonished as Tuck was. Surrounding the west side of the chapel facing the door was an armed force of close to fifty men. At its center, on horseback, sat Lady Lydia Peveril, the countess of Chesterfield. She was flanked by her senior guard Sir Eustace next to the young squire Giles on her right, and on her left by the Moor Sir Palomides, in full armor astride his great warhorse, the destrier Zulfiqar, next to Little John, his great bow at the ready. Ranged around to the left were more than a dozen additional Sherwood outlaws, and to the right most of the rest of the knights of Lady Lydia's guard, plus more than a score of sturdy peasants brandishing staffs, bows, or even farm implements.

"You see?" Robin said over Tuck's right shoulder. "She conscripted the men of her estate for a temporary feudal service to come to our rescue when she heard how Marion's escort had been treated by Gisbourne's guard. And our men got to our camp quicker than we figured, and quick-marched up here. The two forces met up on the way, and came into town together. I explained the situation to them just now, and they're going to guard this place until we've proven Alison's innocence." Tuck turned his head in time to see Robin's grin, then he, and the group that had shoved its way out the door, heard the commanding voice of the countess from atop her steed.

"People of Wallingwells and Worksop," she called at the top of her voice. "You are a royal preserve, as part of Sherwood. But the king has not exercised his prerogative to police this corner of the realm. As Countess of Chesterfield, I cannot sit by when there is lawlessness on my borders, and I am here with these men to ensure the public tranquility in this part of the realm. These forces will continue here until your local magistrate, Master Crisp, has finished his legal business today. All of you are to return to the chapel as he has instructed you and obey his orders for the rest of this trial."

There was no hesitation on the part of the deserters after that speech, and the frightening sight of the armed knight at her left hand, both of which convinced them that it would be in their best interests to turn around and file back through the chapel door. Which they quickly did. George Crisp, his authority unexpectedly bolstered by this unlooked-for military support, threw out his chest and marched back into the chapel to assume the role of judge and jury in the case against Mistress Alison.

CHAPTER SEVENTEEN

"For my first witness, I'd like to question Mistress Alison herself, Your Honor," Friar Tuck began his defense. He looked to the rear of the chapel where Alison stood next to Robin, Little John, and the countess Lydia, who had all come in to stand guard at the door and ensure a peaceful courtroom. The old woman made her way slowly through the standing congregation, most of whom were present only in protest, and grumbled audibly as she came forward. Master Crisp was seated in the priest's chair on the side of the altar, and a single chair for witnesses was placed before the altar facing outward, toward Friar Tuck where he would be asking the questions. The sisters were seated in the choir behind the altar and the witness's chair, while the congregation stood behind Tuck. Father Bernard, standing to the side, held a manuscript of the Vulgate with a gilded cover, and he proffered it to Alison, asking her to take an oath on the Bible that her testimony would be the unvarnished truth. At this a kind of awed silence fell over the room, and Alison took her seat.

"My dear," the friar began, addressing his old godmother in gentle tones. "As you are well aware, you stand here accused of murdering the young woman Meggie, daughter of Ralph the cook. Are you guilty of this crime?"

"By no means," the old woman responded clearly and boldly.

"I swear it before almighty God."

"Then why is it, do you think, that you were accused and arrested?" Tuck asked.

"It was known that I had given the girl a potion a few days before her death. Those who knew of it speculated that she died of the potion I gave her."

"And why do you believe these people to be wrong?"

"Because what I gave Meggie to drink was only soapwort mixed with sage. It's a fairly mild potion, and has never been known to harm any patient, and I have used it on quite a number of patients over the years. That's why." Alison looked at him as if that should be enough.

"And let me ask you one more question," Tuck continued. "How exactly did you administer this potion to the girl?"

Alison looked askance at her questioner, wondering what was the point of such a question, but shrugged and answered anyway. "The way I always do: I mixed the potion at home and brought it to the girl in one of the small bottles I keep for such things."

"And brought the bottle away with you?"

"Of course," Alison said. "I need them for my work. I brought it home."

"All right. Thank you, then, Alison, those are all the questions I have for you," Tuck dismissed her.

Master Crisp pursed his lips and commented. "Well, is that your case, then, Friar? I've already heard all this. We only have her word for these things, no one else can verify them, ergo…"

"Your Honor, I've only begun," Tuck replied. "And let me assure you, everything she has said can be verified by others. Let me begin by calling my next witness. I call Margaret, the victim's mother."

From directly in front of the witness chair, from which the family had not moved since the funeral, Margaret the cook's wife rose and seated herself in the chair, after first taking her oath. Tuck, aware he was speaking to the mother of the murdered girl, took pains to make his questions as sympathetic as possible. But it was, of course, crucial that the truth come out in his questioning.

"Now, Margaret, let me tell you first how sorry I am for your loss. I can think of nothing so painful as the loss of a child."

Tears were forming in Margaret's eyes and she nodded her head. "It's very hard," she agreed. "Especially a girl Meggie's age. She was just getting to the age when she might be married and give us grandchildren, you know?"

Tuck nodded, turning away from the woman as he gently inserted his next question: "So why precisely had you gone to the midwife to request a potion for your daughter?"

Margaret, considering her previous answer, was somewhat tongue-tied at this. "I… well, she… I mean to say…"

Master Crisp, apparently thinking this was his cue, barked out, "You did take an oath before God, madame. Surely you can answer truthfully."

"Meggie was with child," Margaret announced stony faced, glancing around at the congregation with a challenge in her eyes as a ripple of surprise ran through them—at least through the ones who were not already privy to that information.

"And so you went to see Alison to ask her for a potion that would terminate…" the friar coaxed.

"That would end her pregnancy, yes." Margaret finished. "And she agreed to do so. That is what the potion was meant to do."

"All right, we've clarified that," Friar Tuck continued. "Now I have one more question for you: Can you tell me who was the father of this unborn child?"

Again Margaret balked, looking with pleading eyes at the magistrate, who simply made a rolling motion with his hand, as if to say, "Get on with it."

Tuck again decided to coax her. "There were a number of people in town who were of the belief that Meggie was seeing Willie the tinker regularly. If there was a child, most would assume that Willie was the likely father."

Now Master Crisp sat up with some energy. "Willie the father? Blimey then, you mean these two murders might be connected?"

"Willie was not the father," Margaret admitted. "The father was the cock-of-the-walk captain of that bunch of Nottingham guards that just left town."

Another ripple of sensation rolled through the congregation as Tuck clarified, for Master Crisp's sake: "You're saying that the father was Gill o' the Red Cap?"

"He and none other." Margaret stated decisively.

"And isn't it true that you encouraged your daughter to become the leman of the tinker in order to trick him into marrying your daughter?" Tuck sprung this on the lady without warning.

"I… she… it would have worked. He was taken with her. If he hadn't died, she'd have been fine." Now the mother melted again into tears. "We'd have had our grandchild, and she'd have been safely married. And still alive."

That final comment did not do Tuck's case much good, but he'd got what he'd wanted from this witness, and let her go back to her seat.

The time had come for what the friar knew was going to seem a step off course, and he furrowed his brow as he contemplated it, looking to the back at Robin, who knew where this was going and nodded. Tuck took the soft pale glove from the inside pocket of his habit, and called Thorvald to the stand.

In response to Tuck's questioning, the dwarf testified that he had found the fashionable glove nearly hidden amid the straw that formed the floor of the cook's house, indeed that he had found it in the straw in Meggie's own bedchamber. "It was 'ard to see, as it was 'idden in the straw and was about the same color," he confirmed, adding, "I only saw it because I was a good deal closer to the floor than what anybody else was"—a statement that netted him a sympathetic chuckle from the congregation, as, of course, was intended. Tuck and Robin had gone over this with Thorvald closely. They could not bring Malyne to the stand to testify to what they had found in Meggie's room, since people were likely to believe she would say anything to help her mother's case. John would be considered too close to the case of his sister's murder to give unbiased testimony, and Robin himself—well, let's just say after his "ghoul of Sherwood" tale many people were likely to associate him with tall stories. It had to be Thorvald, and the more sympathetic he could be, the better for their case. And so when as a sort of "oh by the way" moment Tuck lifted up the cup they had found in the cook's house, and Thorvald readily affirmed that, yes, this was definitely found at the side of Meggie's bed, the friar had gotten just what he'd wanted from his mate. When Thorvald left the chair Tuck surprised everyone in the courtroom by calling as a witness Harold, the artisan leather worker from Worksop.

"Uh… my good friar, I've found it easy to follow you so far, but what is this silliness? I'll not have you wasting the court's time on frivolous things when we've got a murder case to try here…"

"Very quickly, Master Crisp, this won't take but a minute, and it will be quite clear how relevant this is to Alison's case, I promise you!"

"Well," George Crisp sniffed. "Hurry up about it, then. I don't want this to take all day."

Harold took his seat nervously and swore his oath, but his posture as he sprawled on the chair was a clear indication that he was far from comfortable. Tuck tried to put him at his ease.

"Now then, my good fellow, Harold is your name and, as my friend Thorvald tells me, you are a glover, is that not the case?"

At the mention of Thorvald's name, Harold raised up his head and, finding the dwarf where he had sat back down in the congregation, grinned at him with the four or five teeth he had left in his mouth, no doubt remembering some of the ales they had downed together in the Loaves and Fishes. "That's right," Harold answered. "A glover and sometime cobbler. Ol' Thorvald there has taken some of my goods and peddled 'em round some of the villages in the neighborhood."

"Right," Tuck said, trying to get beyond the small talk before Master Crisp lost his patience. "Well, what I want to talk to you about today is just one glove. This one, as it happens," and with that Tuck placed the fine leather glove Thorvald had just identified into Harold's hands.

"Ah!" the glover said, examining the glove closely. "That there is a kid glove, that is. Made o' the softest goatskin leather. And a finer made one you'll never find. Just look at the workmanship on that glove," and with that he held the glove up for Tuck and Master Crisp to see, pointing along the stitching on the fingers. "Not many in these parts can afford a glove o' that fine quality, I can tell you!"

"So you'd say only someone with means, and with an expensive, even a fastidious, taste in clothes could afford such a glove?"

"Oh, absolutely," Harold answered, and then added, to Tuck's delighted surprise, "I made that glove on special order for Master Bryce. He's the only one around here dresses *that* high and mighty!"

There was a minor uproar among the spectators as that revelation was made. Friar Tuck had known that the glove had to be John Bryce's if it belonged to anyone he'd met in either

Worksop or Wallingwells, but hadn't anticipated Harold would be the tradesman who had made the glove and would recall precisely whom he had made it for. That was a break in their favor. As Harold left the witness chair, the friar called John Bryce to testify.

Master Bryce, sighing and harrumphing his displeasure at being called to the stand in such a case, swept showily into the witness chair. He wore a dark green outer cloak that was lined at the collar with what looked like rabbit fur. Over his simple linen tunic he was wearing a velvet blue surcoat from Italy, embroidered with flowers, and his green hosen ended in fine leather shoes whose pointed tips curled upward in the current courtly style. His hat, of the same blue velvet material as his surcoat, was in his hand, brandished in showy deference to the court, for which he felt no deference at all.

"Master Bryce," Tuck began politely. "You are the bailiff or, perhaps one might say, the reeve of the priory in whose chapel we now sit, are you not?"

"You know that I am, friar, and so does everyone here," the bailiff responded testily. "Please don't waste my time with superfluous questions."

Tuck raised his eyes at the tone, but continued unintimidated, "Then let me ask you straight off: Master Harold the glover testified that this glove, found at the scene of the girl Meggie's murder, is yours. Do you admit the truth of this?" And with that he handed Bryce the glove.

The bailiff, scoffing, took the glove and barely looked at it. "I have several pairs of gloves. I can't be expected to remember where I obtained all of them. Perhaps this Harold imagines he made this for me, I cannot verify whether he did or not…"

"Then perhaps you'd be interested to know that the glove you have in your hands now is not the glove from Meggie's room at all, but was obtained by a certain friend of mine early this morning when you were out, from your very own rooms here in the priory?" With that Tuck looked back at Robin—a friend whose light-fingered tendencies did occasionally tempt him to pilfer things from rooms that were not his own.

But this information had rattled Bryce. "You... what? You were in my room?" He blustered.

"Not I, no," Friar Tuck replied piously. "As I say, my friend, who only took this glove, which by the way had no mate. That's because *this* glove," and here Tuck held up the actual glove found in Meggie's room, "is the true mate to that one. And it was found yesterday in the dead girl's room. Can you explain this? Did you perhaps loan a single glove to a one-handed killer who was going to visit the girl? Or had you given it to the girl earlier, as a token of your love before she threw you over for Willie the tinker because she was impressed by his poverty?"

"Enough of your drollery, Friar, you're not entertaining people here," Master Crisp cautioned him, though if Tuck had liked, he could have contradicted the magistrate by pointing to several smiling faces in the congregation, particularly among his friends in the back. Master Crisp added, "And you, bailiff, answer the question."

Tuck could see the wheels turning behind Bryce's steel gray eyes as he ran over scenarios in his head that might exonerate him from what he was about to be forced to admit. "All right, it's true then. I suppose it was indeed my glove."

"And you dropped it there in Meggie's room when you visited her in her sickbed, yes?" Tuck testified for him.

"I must have done so, yes," Bryce admitted. "But it does not follow that I am the one who killed her! She was quite alive when I saw her, and when I left her!"

"You say," Tuck responded. "I put it to you: Meggie knew,

through her intercourse with Willie—and I mean that in the most innocent sense possible—that you were using him to peddle goods that you were pilfering from the priory in your role as overseer, and now he was dead she was threatening to denounce you! Isn't that why you were there?"

A shriek came from the chorus as Sister Mary Barbara covered her face in shock and shame, and when Tuck looked to the right of Bryce's daughter, he saw the dark thundercloud that had lowered on Madame Veronica's visage. But Bryce was shouting, "No! No! What put such an idea into your head? It's… it's pure slander, that's what it is!"

"Is it indeed?" Tuck replied. "I remind you that you swore an oath upon taking that seat. Is this what your oath before almighty God means to you? Shall I invite your daughter and accomplice, the priory's infirmarian, down to testify as well and see if as a religious she will take such an oath seriously?"

Bryce looked behind him into the choir and saw what effect Tuck's accusations were having on his daughter, and relented. "All right, then," he sagged in his seat, the starch apparently drained from his backbone. "It's true that I had an… arrangement with the tinker to accept certain… articles I had obtained and to market them while he was making his rounds. But the girl never threatened me, and I certainly *did not* kill her! I had no reason to!"

"Then why," Tuck pressed, "did you visit her sick room when her family were all out? Just doing your Christian duty—your Corporal Works of Mercy—were you? Visiting the sick?"

Bryce, recovering a bit of his bravado, responded in the affirmative. "I was. That's just what I was doing. Oh, I don't mean that I make a practice of visiting the sick throughout the parish, but I did want to see her and see that she was likely to recover. I was… concerned for her."

"Just what exactly concerned you about her?" Tuck pressed. "Why her particularly? Something about your relationship with her lover?"

Bryce scoffed. "Willie was a low-life maggot. He had no more business being with a girl as lovely as Meggie as he had with… well with that countess standing back there." From the door, Lady Lydia gave the bailiff a friendly nod. "What I actually was going to see her about—laugh if you will—was to see whether she might be willing to consider a suit from a man of my age."

This time the shriek from Sister Mary Barbara was one of shock and disbelief. But Bryce went on. "Willie was dead. And no, I didn't kill him either, though I must say I saw his demise as an opportunity. Look, you know I've been a widower for six years. It's difficult, when you are used to a woman in your life, to be wifeless so long. I'm a deal older than Meggie was, but such marriages are common, and I had money that she would inherit when I was gone. My own daughter is a nun—I could scarcely leave the money to her."

"Particularly since you'd stolen it from her own priory," called a voice from the congregation that sounded suspiciously like Robin's.

But Bryce ignored that and continued: "It was a fine match for her—the best she was like to get in these parts. Of course, at the time I did not realize she was with child."

"And, in case Willie had shared the secret of your partnership with her, you would get the added benefit of having under your control the one person, besides your daughter, who knew about your criminal activity."

Bryce looked at the friar with hatred burning in his coal-gray eyes, but he did not answer. Tuck asked his follow-up question: "And so what was Meggie's response to your proposal?"

Bryce shrugged. "She told me to talk to her parents. If they were in favor of the situation, she said she would raise no objection. Sadly, news of her death followed so hard upon that, I never got the chance to broach the topic with the cook or his wife."

Tuck looked over at where Meggie's family sat dumbfounded at this information, the mother Margaret weeping copiously into her hands. The irony of the situation did not escape Friar Tuck: If Bryce had only made his declaration a bit earlier, perhaps Meggie would never have taken up with Willie. Perhaps Willie would still be alive. Perhaps Meggie would. Who knew how differently things might have turned out?

But the court must now deal with the reality of what had in fact happened, not the fantasy of what might have done. "I have," Tuck continued, "one more question." He held up the cup he had earlier asked Thorvald about. "When you talked to Meggie, did you notice whether this cup was sitting on the low stand next to her bed?"

Bryce, taken aback by this unexpected question, shrugged. "I can't say I was looking around the room much. Not to really notice what was there and what wasn't…"

"There was almost nothing there," Tuck pushed him. "The mat she was lying on. The straw on the floor. The chamber pot in the corner. The low table on which was a candle and…"

"A candle and nothing else," Bryce said, nodding as if he did now in fact remember. "I did look at the candle. But there was no cup there at that time."

"You're sure?" Tuck pressed him.

"Absolutely," was Bryce's decisive answer.

"Then I have no more questions for this witness," the friar concluded. "And next I want to call…" and with that he squinted up at the assembled nuns in the choir, his eyes seeking out the bench on which Madame Veronica sat with her officers. Tuck's eyes passed right over the Mother and her cellarer Sister Esther, much to her relief, and lighted on the nuns' infirmarian: Sister Mary Barbara.

When he spoke her name, George Crisp growled at him: "Why is this necessary, friar? The girl's father has just admitted everything, so why put his daughter through more shame? Haven't you got what you need from them?"

"I'm calling the priory's infirmarian for an entirely different reason, Master Crisp. You'll see."

"I'd better," the magistrate growled. "I don't want to see the nuns manhandled by some ruffian friar."

"I'll handle her with… with kid gloves," Tuck said, his tongue planted firmly in his cheek.

When Sister Mary Barbara had taken her oath and her seat, Tuck approached her in friendly fashion and said, "Sister, I've called you to testify because, as you are the infirmarian of this priory, you are the one person available, besides Alison herself and her daughter, who has some experience with drugs and potions. Since I can't call either of them to testify, because the court would assume a bias on their part, I want to ask you some questions about medicinal potions; I am sure you will be honest and completely objective. Is that a reasonable expectation, would you say?"

Mary Barbara lowered her long lashes demurely and said with becoming modesty, "I'm sure I can't claim to an expertise equal to Mistress Alison, who has decades of experience with herbal medicines, but I do have a basic knowledge of maladies and the kinds of potions that will heal them, yes. And I've taken an oath before the Almighty to speak only the truth, so you may have no qualms that anything I say will deviate a jot or tittle from the unvarnished facts."

"Well," Tuck reacted, looking at the floor. "That's all we can really ask of you, isn't it? Now Sister," and with that he lifted up the cup they had found in Meggie's room. "I'm going to ask you to examine this cup and say whether you can tell us anything of what its contents might have been when it was last used?"

Sister Mary Barbara gracefully reached to take the cup from the friar's hand and looked into it. She shook it around a bit and then brought it to her nose. An instant later she jerked her head away from the contents and quickly handed it back to Tuck, nodding her head with some vigor.

"You can identify the potion, then?" Tuck prompted her.

"Pennyroyal," Mary Barbara declared. "A very strong potion of it. The minty smell is the giveaway."

"And can you tell us, in your experience, what is pennyroyal used for?"

"Most often it's used for the grippe and other diseases of the lungs," the infirmarian told the court. "It's also used for stomach problems, such as constipation."

"Anything else?" Tuck pressed.

The nun cleared her throat and then added, "It is also a popular remedy for pregnancy."

"A… remedy you say?" Tuck responded. "You mean to say it is used to cause miscarriages in pregnant women, yes?"

"It is used in abortions, yes," Mary Barbara clarified.

"Interesting that you call it a 'remedy,' then," Tuck continued thoughtfully. "Although I would suppose that in a nunnery, pregnancy would be a condition that one would want to remedy, is that not so?"

Sister Mary Barbara reddened visibly but did not answer.

"Tell me, Sister," Tuck went on. "Is this pennyroyal a drug that you would prescribe in order to 'remedy' a pregnancy?" After a pause, Tuck added. "Hypothetically speaking, of course."

The infirmarian cleared her throat again and stammered a

bit. "I… uh… well if I… well, hypothetically speaking, I would avoid using pennyroyal for that purpose unless it were all I had to hand at the time."

"And why is that?" Tuck asked innocently.

"Because pennyroyal is a dangerous drug. One must be very, very careful with the dosage. It has been known to kill not only the unborn child, but the mother as well. No, it is a potentially deadly drug in the wrong hands." And with that Sister Mary Barbara let her eyes scan the members of the congregation as if she were searching for someone in the crowd. Tuck tried to follow her eyes, but could see nothing or no one in that press of bodies.

Tuck now asked a question that had just occurred to him, and to which he had not suspected an answer: "And in your present position as infirmarian of this priory, have you ever had occasion to prescribe this remedy for anyone in your charge?"

Sister Mary Barbara glanced quickly over her shoulder to where her prioress Madame Veronica sat, watching her with an icy stare under scowling brows, then turned about and, remembering her oath, which she took quite seriously, murmured "I have," and then quickly clarified: "You must remember, though, that not only my sisters in Christ are in my care, but often laypersons who work in the priory or are our neighbors in Wallingwells come to me for… ailments."

Tuck smiled grimly, then followed up with the obvious question, although he was already certain of the answer. "And was Meggie one of these neighbors, Sister Mary Barbara? Did you give her this cup?"

The infirmarian had seen the question coming, but still bristled at it. "I did not, Master Friar! I swear it by almighty God and in this holy place."

"Truly, truly, my dear, rest assured I did not think you had,"

Tuck assuaged her. "But the question had to be posed. Now one last question: Is there anything else you noticed about the cup that I gave you to examine? Anything further your senses told you?"

The nun looked puzzled for an instant, then a light came into her deep blue eyes and her lush lips broadened into a close-mouthed smile. "Yes indeed," she stated firmly. "It was not only the mint flavor of pennyroyal I smelled, but also the unmistakable scent of sour milk. Whoever gave that cup to Meggie had diluted the pennyroyal draft in a cup of milk."

Now Tuck had gathered all he needed from the testimony of the lovely infirmarian, he allowed her to go back to her seat in the choir, though he did not envy her her place next to her unhappy prioress, not after the testimony she had just given, not to mention her father's before her. He next called his penultimate witness in this case, surprising most of the congregation by summoning to the stand the town's old gossip, the Widow Day.

After she had made her way among the murmuring of the crowd, and with a good deal of grousing about the discomfort it gave her to traverse the length of the chapel to this seat in the front of the room, the Widow Day took her oath and was seated, with a loud sigh and grunt of relief. Friar Tuck welcomed her with extreme courtesy.

"My dear Mrs. Day," he began. "How pleasant to see you again. Please, madame, tell me how is your health today? No lingering effects from that fever you were dealing with some days back?"

"Fair to middlin', good Friar, fair to middlin'," the old woman answered. "I must say, that good broth you brought me from our Mistress Alison worked wonders on that score, I can tell you. Didn't do anything for my rheumatism, I'm afraid, though. I wonder does she have any nice herbal remedy for that do y'think?" And then her head went up with a start and she added, "Oh… I mean, if they don't hang her for murder and all."

"Well, as a matter of fact," Tuck replied, "you can help us keep that from happening if you just answer a few small questions for us today. Would that be all right?"

"Sure it would, sonny," the Widow Day answered. "And it'll go better if you stop condescending to me like I'm some simple old lady. I may be an old lady, but I ain't simple. Now ask your questions."

Tuck, feeling chastised, continued with a trifle less enthusiasm: "Mrs. Day, you do spend a good deal of time, when you are not under the weather, keeping track of what goes on in the neighborhood of the priory, is that not so?"

"I keep an eye on what goes on, if that's what you mean, yes," the widow replied, and then added, as if she were being accused, "Why? There ain't no harm in it."

"No, no, surely not," Friar Tuck agreed. "No, what I mean to say is, your house actually is situated directly across the way from the cook's house, isn't it? That would have given you an excellent view of the comings and goings at the murder scene just two nights ago, wouldn't it?"

The old woman thought back, and then nodded her head in agreement. "Sure it did," she said. "I reckon I probably saw as much as anybody else in the neighborhood might have seen."

"Good, excellent," Tuck was salivating now, thinking he'd got to the heart of the matter. "Can you tell us, please, whether you saw any visitors coming to Meggie's house while her family were out?"

"Visitors?" the widow mused. "Well, I saw him, as has already testified," and here she pointed directly to where John Bryce had retreated, as he hoped unobtrusively, into the midst of the congregation. There were a few snickers, and the Widow Day added, "All dressed like one o' the Nine Worthies he was, with scarlet hosen and fur-lined cloak like some great lord or bishop.

Anyway, he went in not long after the rest of 'em had gone to work…"

"Yes, yes, Mrs. Day," Tuck broke in, a bit irritated. "We do know about Master Bryce, he's already testified. But were there no other visitors that day?"

"Well," the old woman paused to think. "No… no…. not any as you'd call visitors…"

"So…" Tuck coaxed her. "Do you mean that you did see someone else around the house?"

"Well, yes," the Widow Day agreed. "I mean, I saw that dairy maid Kate come by with her basket. She'd been about making deliveries at the priory, you know."

Friar Tuck gave an exasperated sigh of relief. "So Kate of Worksop was there then. Why didn't you count her as a visitor?"

"*That's* no visitor," the old woman snorted. "That's the neighborhood slut!"

There was a good deal more that the Widow Day could have said on that score, but she would get no opportunity, since that was all the information Tuck needed on that question. He dismissed the old lady, but with the caveat that he might ask to recall her again later if her testimony was needed. The puzzled Master Crisp, assuming the friar's defense was over, couldn't see why he'd made that request, but nodded his assent.

Friar Tuck then called Kate of Worksop to the witness seat.

The dairy maiden, wearing an ankle-length brown tunic with a clean white sleeveless surcoat and a thin leather belt, her golden curls covered by a white barbette and chin band, made no delay in striding determinedly toward the front of the chapel. There was a fiery glint in her eye and Tuck could not help thinking, "Oh dear, she's going to try to brazen it out, isn't she?"

But he could not have been more wrong. When she took her oath and sat in the chair, Tuck thought to confront her without preamble with the question, and began, "Kate of Worksop, did you…"

"Yes, I killed her," the milk maid said, boldly and clearly. "I'm only sorry I couldn't have killed her little bastard's father as well, but that was not in my power."

As Tuck looked toward the back of the chapel to see Alison collapse into the arms of her weeping daughter Malyne while Marion embraced both of them, the chapel erupted into astonished shouts and raucous conversation until Master Crisp, now firmly in charge of the situation, called for quiet, and took over the questioning of the confessed murderer himself.

"Young lady," the magistrate began, "you realize that what you are admitting to here is a crime that carries the penalty of death? Do you still want to confess?"

Kate turned her brilliant blue eyes on the judge. "What? You think everybody here doesn't know I must have done it with all that clever evidence the friar has put before them? So what if I denied it? You'd put me on the rack or some such thing and I'd end up confessing anyway."

"Yes," Master Crisp agreed. "I'm afraid I'd have to insist on it."

"Then why should I bother to deny it?" the young woman persisted. "That baby of hers was put in her by that rake and scoundrel Gill o' the Red Cap, the captain of the king's guard."

"Sir Guy of Gisbourne's guard…" Tuck said under his breath.

"Well he had chosen me first!" Kate went on. "He was the only means I had of getting out of this provincial, deadly dull place. Of getting out of this wretched tedious life and the monotony of dealing with those great bovine imbecilic cows day after day until I'm the age of that nosy old woman you just had up here. And nothing to do then but look out the window and gossip about what I see. No thank you."

"So this Gill was your way out?" Tuck encouraged her.

"The only way out! And he said he loved me and would take me with him to Nottingham. So yes, I let him have his way with me. And a week later he drops me for this bitch of a cook's daughter. So she's going to go to Nottingham instead of me? I don't think so!" And with that the dairymaid flashed one of her brilliant smiles, but there was a good deal of malice in it.

"After another month or so I find I'm pregnant myself. Oh yes, Friar, don't look so surprised. Who do you think that nun was talking about when she said she'd helped someone else with an abortion lately? And I have to thank her, not only for helping me get rid of the burden of that lying rotter's child, but for introducing me to the marvelous properties of pennyroyal. Oh, it wasn't hard for me to get some myself—just had to bat my eyes a little at the infirmarian at the Augustinian monastery in Worksop. They use it for colds there, can you imagine?"

"Then you killed this Meggie, you say, out of jealousy over this man, this Captain Gill?" George Crisp was trying to follow it all, and fortunately was not too far behind.

"Oh, I didn't care so much about the man," Kate clarified. "But she'd stolen him from me, and with him my chance for another life. She was going to get that chance, and that's what I couldn't forgive."

"But he'd abandoned Meggie as well," Tuck said. "He used her just as he'd used you…"

"Well I didn't know that at the time, did I?" Kate said. "I mean, I'd heard some rumors that it was Meggie's love'd been killed by the so-called 'Ghoul of Sherwood,' and when I stopped in that Sunday and saw that bloody head hanging over there, I actually thought at first it was Gill himself— which is why I screamed and ran off. But even when I knew he'd left her too, I couldn't forgive her for stealing him from me. Maybe if I hadn't seen that head—felt the satisfaction of thinking Gill was dead—I wouldn't have dreamed about getting rid of her the same way. But I saw it. And then I did it. And that is the whole story. Let's say I'm throwing myself on your mercy, Your Honor." And with that she fixed him with her startling blue eyes.

"Yes, well, I suppose people do that," George Crisp said distractedly. Then he sat up straight and pronounced in his most official voice, "Kate of Worksop, dairy woman, I find you guilty of murder in the death of Meggie the cook's daughter of Wallingwells. Ergo, I sentence you to death by hanging, the sentence to be carried out once I receive royal approval."

Tuck started a bit. The magistrate had not mentioned anything about obtaining the king's approval before executing Alison. Perhaps the blue eyes or the appeal to his mercy had wrought some effect on him. Or perhaps he had developed some qualms about the finality of taking a human life after hearing Kate's confession of having taken Meggie's so cavalierly.

Whichever it was, Tuck had no objections. All he really wanted to hear was the magistrate's next order:

"The woman, Mistress Alison, is hereby pronounced innocent of this crime, and is to be released forthwith."

*   *   *

Tuck had seen the next question coming, and he knew his work was not yet over for the day. There was one more murder to be solved.

Robin had called in Little John and Sir Palomides from the men waiting outside, and the sight of those two intimidating presences coming down the church's center aisle effectively punctured any remaining arrogance Kate may have been feeling.

It was when they held Kate gently but firmly by each elbow that George Crisp raised the question.

"So!" he began. "Are we to assume that this woman was also the first killer, the one that beheaded Willie the tinker?"

Tuck fought down the resentment and frustration the question provoked. "Your Honor, you heard the woman testify that she was not even aware of the identity of the first victim."

"Well, she could have been lying about that," the magistrate said. And, upon seeing the skeptical look on Friar Tuck's face, added, "That's easier to believe than that we actually suddenly have two *different* murderers in our small community."

"That's ridiculous!" Kate exclaimed from between her formidable jailers.

"Your Honor," Tuck continued patiently. "Why on earth would the girl Kate confess to one murder and not the other? She can only hang once."

That fact finally sank in, and the magistrate, looking a bit deflated asked, "Well, who then? Who killed Willie?" Then, with a glimmer in his eye, he suggested, "The Ghoul of Sherwood?"

Tuck sighed and looked down at his feet. He did not want the magistrate seeing the look on his face. Then he replied, "Your Honor, there is no Ghoul of Sherwood."

Master Crisp, looking puzzled, gestured back to the door where Robin still stood guard. "But didn't your colleague back there say he'd been accosted by the…"

"It was a ruse, sir," Tuck explained with strained patience. "In order to try to unearth evidence that was not forthcoming." There was an audible gasp among the more gullible in the congregation, and Tuck continued: "However, if Your Honor will indulge me a few more moments, I think I can shed some light on this question if you let me recall my last witness, the Widow Day."

Over the buzz among the crowd George Crisp rolled his right hand saying, "Well, get on with it. Proceed, proceed. And remember, Mrs. Day, you're still under oath!" And once again, the old woman dithered her way out of the congregation and into the witness seat, where she heaved her body into the chair with a voluminous flop.

Friar Tuck welcomed the widow back with a pleasant smile and told her he was glad to be able to speak to her again, and the old woman, conscious of her own importance in the day's proceedings, brushed off the friar's niceties and urged him to get on with it: "Well," she said, "what can I tell you this time?"

"Mrs. Day," Tuck began. "You spend a good deal of time looking out your windows, as I think you showed us a few minutes ago. When I first talked to you in your house a while back, you mentioned to me that there were nuns in the priory who you suspected were carrying on with Willie the tinker. Tell the court: Did you say that because you actually *saw* one of the sisters with him?"

"Well," the Widow Day looking thoughtful. "If I remember right, it wasn't with him so much. It was one I saw following him early that morning."

"Early... which morning?" Tuck asked, then snatching at the new information said excitedly, "Was it the morning he was killed?"

The old woman shrugged. "I don't know when he was killed. I know it wasn't long after that I heard they'd found a body in the woods. I don't know that it was that day. I do know I'd heard the rooster crowing from the cook's house, and I thought it was really early, much earlier than usual. It was still quite dark. But it woke me up, and so I looked out the windows."

"So this is when you saw the nun?" Tuck pressed.

"Well first I saw the young womanizer."

"Willie the tinker?" Tuck tried to clarify.

"Himself," the old woman agreed. "He came out of that Meggie's house, where she was alone that night. And he headed toward the woods."

"And the nun?" Tuck encouraged her.

"It was a few more seconds, and then she came out from the shadows on the other side of the house, and she followed him."

"And did you see which of the sisters it was who followed him that night?"

"No, no, it was too dark. All I could make out was her habit."

"Well," Tuck said. "You've been very helpful, Mrs. Day. Is there anything more, anything at all, you could tell us that you noticed about this nun?"

"No, no," the old woman said, rubbing her chin thoughtfully. Then she shrugged and added, "Well, now that I think of it, there *was* that axe she was dragging."

Tuck scanned the choir, looking into the faces of the various nuns of the Benedictine Priory of Wallingwells. His eyes went straight to Sister Mary Barbara, her bright eyes pleading with him not to call her as a witness again. They flitted over Sister Lucy's birdlike face and Sister Esther's ample lips. His gaze moved over Sister Rebecca's sprinkle of freckles and lit on Mary Eusebia's dark brows and curious eyes, which were looking back at him with some amusement and curiosity. Tuck had the impression she knew exactly what he was going to do. Finally his gaze rested on the strained pale face of Sister Anne.

"Your Honor," Friar Tuck said. "I'd like to call Sister Anne as a witness."

The gaunt nun looked startled at first, as if awakened suddenly from a dream. Then, with her sisters patting her and cooing solicitously, Sister Anne made her way out of the choir and into the witness chair, where she agreed to take her oath before God almighty that she would tell the truth.

"Sister Anne," Tuck began. "When I first spoke with you, you told me that you had never met the victim, Willie the tinker."

Sister Anne scoffed and muttered under her breath, "Victim," and gave a short laugh.

"Well," Tuck continued. "I'm asking you again, and this time you are under oath. Were you acquainted with this Willie?"

He stared at Sister Anne, who stared impassively back at him with her cold hazel eyes. After a few moments, George Crisp said to her, "Does the witness need to have the question repeated?"

"No Your Honor," the nun said, never taking her eyes from Friar Tuck's. But still she said nothing.

"All right, let me go this way," Tuck said. "You told me also that you had only joined the convent about five years ago. Can you tell us what you were doing before that time?"

"I was living in another town near here. I was drawn to a vocation later in life."

"But what had you been doing?" Tuck pressed. "Did you live with parents? A husband? Did you work the fields?"

Again, the nun made no further comment, but merely stared with icy coldness into the friar's eyes. "Let's try this," Tuck said, changing tactics once more. "I won't call them as witnesses, but Elizabeth Liptrot, the laundress, has told us of her own relationship with Willie." He glanced to where he had seen the laundress among the crowd earlier, and noted her shrinking with embarrassment at her own personal life being brought up. "And she had said that Willie told her himself that he was drawn to her because of her name—his wife, he had said, was named Elizabeth."

Still only the cold stare.

"And I have it on the authority of Malyne, daughter of the lately accused Mother Alison, that you assumed the name Anne when you took your vows. According to her, your name *had* been Elizabeth. Is that the truth?"

Sister Anne finally blinked. She sighed, and said, "It's a common enough name."

"Now, Willie told everyone that his wife had drowned," Tuck continued. "My colleague Thorvald informs me that on one of his peddling trips to the village of Barlborough he heard of a woman drowning there in the River Ryton eight or nine years ago. This woman's husband was quite upset that they never found the body."

"That's a sad story," Sister Anne responded. "Why tell it to me?"

Tuck was beginning to lose his patience. "When I first talked to you," he started again, "you told me there was no chance that the ghoul who'd killed Willie would murder again, because the way he died showed that his killer was enraged, that the killer must have felt a bitter and uncontrollable hatred toward Willie himself. A very personal kind of hate." He paused a moment before plunging on. "The kind of hate a wife might feel for a husband who had beat her and abused her and had tried to murder her by drowning her in a river."

"And who wouldn't?" Sister Anne exploded. "Who wouldn't hate such a beast? The welts I had from his beatings! I can still show you the marks of his cruelty on my back and ribs and neck." She paused, taking a deep breath in preparation for a continued onslaught. Now that the ice had broken, the words gushed from her like water released from a dam. The breath she let out came quavering forth like a sigh suppressed, and she went on:

"You think his womanizing was notorious here? He's *always* been that way. Even when we were married. It was my shame that he would be out every night drinking and whoring, and I'd hide all the knives in the house before he came home, he was so mean when he was drunk. And when he'd come home, if I said anything to him, he'd beat me bloody for my 'insolence' as he called it. I spent five years under his tyranny there in

Barlborough, until he met another pretty young thing he thought it might be more fun to be with and decided he'd get rid of me for good. He was far gone with drink and he had that black look in his eye, and I still have his finger marks on my neck where he tried to throttle me. I got out of that with a knee to his groin, but he came up grasping one of his great metal pots and swung it at my head, knocking the life out of me for a time. When I came to, he was throwing me into the Ryton there in the middle of the night. I tried to scream but he'd gagged me and tied my feet and hands together. He never said a word, just stood on shore and waited to see my head go under the water."

"I think," Tuck responded when she finally paused, "that we can agree you had sufficient motive to kill him."

"I had my senses back by then, and the cold water helped bring me into full consciousness. I knew enough about the water to stay calm and float on my back, and I was washed ashore perhaps half a mile downstream. I was able to free my hands by slicing the bonds on a sharp stone, and so freed my legs and removed the gag. By then it was morning. I knew better than to go back to Barlborough and besides, if he thought I was dead, I was free of him forever. So I continued to walk downstream. Worksop was the first village I came to."

"So you've been in this area the entire time?" Tuck asked. "Wasn't Willie aware of you?"

Sister Anne sighed. "I got work on a farm outside of Worksop and kept very much to myself. I didn't even realize he had moved to the neighborhood until about five years ago. His fling with his new love back in Barlborough had fizzled out pretty quickly—I wonder if she was too smart to let him abuse her, or if he tried to murder her as well? Well, once I knew he was in the area, that's when I decided to take the veil. For one thing, he could never find me here. For another, I thought devoting myself to the Church and the Benedictine order would take some of the hate and rage from my heart. Bah. Little chance of that when you've been treated as I had been. It was when I knew he had taken up with Meggie, that sweet young girl of the cook's I'd watch grow up around the priory, that's when I vowed I would do something about it. I didn't want him to do to her what he'd done to me—and who knows how many others."

"And so you followed him from Meggie's house..." Tuck prompted.

"I knew her parents and her brother were staying overnight in the priory because of the feast day coming up, and so I figured he'd be with her that night. I stopped by their chicken coop and roused the rooster so he'd crow early, and Willie would get up and have to make his way home through the woods when it was still black night. The axe I'd actually found near the chickens—Margaret must use it to cut off her chickens' heads. But it was an inspiration to me. Nothing has ever felt better than bringing it down on that monster's head."

"But why hang the head in the chapel?" George Crisp interrupted.

Sister Anne looked up at the magistrate and smiled wanly. "I wanted people to know who it was. I wanted to make sure he received a proper burial. I was, after all, his wife in the eyes of the Church. He was a monster who didn't deserve to be alive on this earth. But five years as a Benedictine has convinced me that God is the ultimate judge, and my own revenge won't last beyond the grave. So like you, good Friar," and now she resumed her cold icy stare into Tuck's eyes, "I wanted to see that he received a Christian burial."

The magistrate sat up again and adopted once more his official tone of voice, saying, "Sister Anne of Wallingwells Priory, this court..."

"Has no jurisdiction!" came a cry from the choir. Tuck closed his eyes. He knew that voice. He looked up to see Sister Mary Eusebia coming down from the choir to stand before the magistrate. She was being followed by Madame Veronica, looking quite out of sorts.

Mary Eusebia addressed Master Crisp as soon as she'd reached the side of Sister Anne. "Your Honor, I think you will find that, according to the Compromise of Avranches, Sister Anne as a Benedictine is entitled to *priveligium clericale*, that is, the benefit of clergy. You know that in English law the clergy—both secular and regular clergy—are outside the jurisdiction of the secular courts and are to be tried, instead, in an ecclesiastical court under canon law."

Madame Veronica, not so nimble as her younger sister, was following Mary Eusebia down from the choir as quickly as she could, and arrived in time to follow up: "This means, Master Crisp, we thank you for your attention to this matter, and will take our sister into custody now and keep her in her cell until the ecclesiastical court can be assembled to try her for her crime."

The magistrate, recognizing the truth of Sister Mary Eusebia's point of law, nodded with a checkmated chagrin on his face, and waved them all away. Sister Esther the cellarer, who had followed her superior down, took Sister Anne not ungently by the arm, while Mother Veronica took her by the other, and the two sisters led her out of the chapel, followed by the entire choir in single file—all but Sister Mary Eusebia, who lingered a moment looking at Friar Tuck with a smirk.

Tuck couldn't suppress a tight-lipped smile of his own, looking at her expression, and sighed. "I suppose you knew it all along?" he probed.

At that, the scholarly sister actually gave a light laugh. "I'd only reveal that to you in the confessional," she answered. Tuck couldn't help but laugh himself.

CHAPTER EIGHTEEN

As they might have expected from a liege of her munificence, the countess Lydia Peveril of Chesterfield invited Robin Hood and his companions to stop at her castle before heading back south to their encampment for a feast and a celebration after closing this matter of the Wallingwells murders successfully. Robin had readily agreed, and he and Maid Marion had ridden off together with the countess, who was escorted by Sir Palomides on his most courteous behavior astride his magnificent warhorse Zulfiqar. They were followed by the countess's knights, squires, and the men of her household and lands who had taken arms for this service, and Robin's men brought up the rear, led by Little John and Will Stutely. John, brother of the murdered Meggie, had taken it into his head, after spending the evening undermining Gill o' the Red Cap with his new friend Robin Hood, to leave his parents to their roles in the kitchen of the Benedictine Priory of Wallingwells and join the meinie following the outlaw life in the forest of Sherwood, and was marching with his new comrades Alan a Dale and Jock o' Barlborough.

Thorvald and Friar Tuck, having come to Wallingwells initially on their errand of mercy, felt that their journey would be best rounded off by returning with Alison and Malyne to their hovel and bidding adieu to them there. Tuck borrowed one of the company's new horses for the nonce, and Thorvald naturally drove his cart, wherein he gave Malyne a ride home while Alison rode before Tuck in his saddle. The short ride gave Tuck a chance to engage his old godmother in private conversation before taking his leave of her.

But it was Alison who opened up the exchange. "So, that nun who interrupted Master Crisp with her legal challenge, you knew her? I saw you talking with her afterwards."

Tuck gave a half-amused snort and said, "We talked a few times during my investigation into the tinker's murder. I found her… interesting. Maddening. Amusing. Provoking. She's incredibly learned and clever, as I think she showed today. She confessed to me… well, things that disturbed me. Of course I can't reveal what was told me in the confessional. But I have difficulty understanding her. She's not like anyone else I've met."

"Not necessarily a bad thing," Alison suggested.

"No, not at all," Tuck admitted, then went on, "I do wonder if Sister Anne will receive just punishment from an ecclesiastical court—though obviously as a member of the clergy myself, I support the case being tried there."

"You came here to see the unknown corpse given all necessary rites, and you achieved that. When you knew who the dead man was, you sought to obtain justice for him. Are you afraid that Sister Anne the murderer will escape that just punishment by the ecclesiastical court?"

"Well," Tuck began. He had been considering the matter ever since Sister Mary Eusebia had stopped the court proceedings. "The Church had always forbidden clergy to shed human blood. That means they will condemn what Sister Anne has done, but they will not take her life when she is found guilty. They are forbidden to shed her blood by the same token. Doesn't Christ say in his Sermon on the Mount, 'You have heard it hath been said, An eye for an eye, and a tooth for a tooth. But I say to you do not resist evil: but if one strike thee on the right cheek, turn to him also the other'? So the court will not punish Sister Anne with like for like. She will be assigned hard penance, but she will perform it and she will remain in her priory."

"And this will satisfy justice for you?"

Tuck considered the question and sighed. "Who am I," he answered thoughtfully, "to say what is just? God is the ultimate judge of the universe, and the Church is his conscience on earth. I have found out the killer. Whatever the Church decides is just, I will consider justice to have been served."

"And what about the dairy maid, Kate?" Alison continued. "If she hangs, will that be just?"

Tuck was feeling less merciful in Kate's situation. "The king may decide to be merciful in her case. Perhaps she will only lose an eye or a hand, and be spared the hanging. But between the two of them, I must say I would rather see Sister Anne spared. She was driven by her own sufferings at the hand of the tinker, and her concern for the girl Meggie."

"I can't say her method was less heinous. An axe murder? Quite barbarous I'd say."

"Yes, but an act of passion. Kate killed Meggie with poison prepared deliberately ahead of time, and her motive was only jealousy. Meggie had not harmed her," Tuck argued.

"And yet the outcome was the same," Alison mused. "Both victims lost their lives."

"But one of the victims was a rather wicked young man. The other a—more or less—innocent young girl," Tuck suggested.

"Well, come to that," Alison added, "it was a rather wicked young man who was the cause of Kate's jealousy, and it was her anger at him that led to Meggie's murder."

Tuck shook his head with some chagrin. "It's true. You know, everywhere I've looked in this case I've run across men behaving badly to women. Willie obviously with Sister Anne—beating her, cheating on her, even trying to murder her. Gill o' the Red Cap seducing young women and then deserting them once he'd got them pregnant. And some of those nuns in the priory—they fled there because their fathers beat them or raped them and they went there for refuge. It's enough to make me ashamed of being a man myself when I see how badly men treat their women in the secular world. Worse than they treat dogs or horses, many of them."

Alison smiled indulgently on Tuck. "It's seldom a man has enough self-awareness to see it," she said. "But don't sink too far into self-hatred yet. It is still only a minority of men who do so. Look at yourself and Robin and the men of his outlaw band. You may be outlaws, but it seems none of you treat your women thus. Nor have we seen that Ralph the cook…"

"Ralph beat his wife and his daughter, and Margaret was hoping to get Meggie away from him by setting her up with Willie. So even your short list is faulty."

Alison closed her eyes and bent her head down. "I stand corrected. But we saw no evidence that his son John would follow in his footsteps. Nor does the baker seem to be such a man, or the priest, or Master Crisp…"

"He's married?" Tuck responded with some surprise.

Alison shrugged. "Many women would see him as the embodiment of security in a place like ours. Even Master Bryce. Though a swindler and thief himself, his daughter seems fond enough of him, and he probably would have been a solid husband for Meggie. Though I'm certain he won't be working for the priory any more after today. Even Sir Guy's guards had a lieutenant who saw fit to cut short Gill's rampage when he saw it was twisted and wrong. So no, you cannot say that *all* men abuse their women. But the fact is, they definitely all *could*, and the law squints at such behaviors. Ah, Tuck we women are born with the dice loaded against us in the Hazard of life. It's almost unheard of for a woman to gain the upper hand in a relationship with a man."

"I see that," Tuck nodded. "I have *seen* that. And yet, is it their place to kill the men who have mistreated them? Does the Almighty not say, 'Vengeance is mine, I will repay?' How can it be right to take justice into their hands this way? Some sort of justice must be exacted against such women, for the sake of peace in our commonwealth."

"*Lex talionis*, I know, you've said it before," Alison said. "But when such an abused woman snaps, might that not be seen as this very justice against the man who has misused her?"

"God's justice is not the same as man's justice," Tuck insisted. "But as for the abuse of women by men, it explains to me, at least in part, a phenomenon I found within the convent walls that has puzzled me. You know there are women who… for lack of a better term… will fornicate with other women?" And suddenly, ashamed of his words, he turned red and apologized to his godmother. "I… I'm sorry Mother Alison, I grow too broad of tongue."

Alison bit her lips for a moment. She hadn't foreseen this turn of the conversation. But after some thought she answered, "My son, I am quite aware of such things. One does not treat women's ailments for as long as I have without seeing everything there is to see. So you ran across such a situation in the nunnery?"

"Indeed," Tuck picked up the thread eagerly. Since he spoke only in the abstract, he did not feel he was betraying the seal of the confessional. "I realize now that women may be driven into such relationships by the abuse of men!"

Alison answered now, deliberately and thoughtfully, "I think it may be so in some cases." And after a long pause she added,

"I'm pretty sure it was the case with your mother."

That was a blow that fell from nowhere on Friar Tuck's mind. "My… my mother… you're saying my mother was…"

"I'm saying your mother was a woman of the sort you are referring to. She was a woman who enjoyed the company of other women. And one who was driven to that gentle companionship by the brutality of your father. You know what a beast your own father was. You came to me to escape him when he had beaten your mother to death like a disobedient cur."

"But how do you know that my mother was drawn to such women?" Tuck wanted to know, still shaking his head in disbelief. "Would she not have been discreet about such a thing? Would she not have kept it…"

"Between herself and her lover, yes," Alison agreed. "And so she did. But you see, my son, I know because it was me she came to."

"Ah," Tuck let out an enormous sigh of recognition, while raising his brows in stunned surprise. "So you and my mother…"

"Were lovers, yes. For many years. For as many years as your father brutalized her, she had me to come to for comfort. For her sake I protected you when you ran from home. For her sake I took your sisters in after he died, may the Lord bless their souls."

Tuck had stopped his horse before Alison's hovel and felt he could not move. Alison slipped down from the saddle and stood on the earth facing him, looking him in the eyes. Thorvald's cart was still a few furlongs behind them, so no other human ear could hear what Alison told him next. "And it was for her sake that I killed him."

"My father? You…"

"I brought him a venison stew shortly after we buried your mother. Made as if it were an act of charity, him having lost his wife and having no woman to cook for him. He was too stupid to even see the irony in that. There was talk in the village that he was to be brought up on charges for having beaten his wife excessively, but I knew better than to trust the law—the law of men—to bring justice to such a man. I loaded that venison stew with wolfsbane. He never knew what hit him. And I brought the stew and the dish I'd delivered it in back to my house with me. No one ever suspected."

"I see," Tuck answered, reviewing everything they had just been saying on their ride here.

"What do you think, then, Tuck?" Alison looked into his face to read any expression she may have kindled there. "Should I then be brought before the court? Do you want to bring your father justice?"

Tuck swallowed and put up his hands in a helpless gesture. "Whatever my father's sins," he sighed after a long pause, "I'm sure he has paid for them now. And whatever your sins," he made a sign of the cross over Alison's head, "may God absolve you of them. That is, if you truly repent."

"God knows the state of my soul, and of my repentance," Alison answered gravely. Then she smiled and bowed her head slightly to Friar Tuck. "Thank you, good friar, for your charity and for your visit. You are welcome any time at my door." And after a moment she added, "For her sake." And with that she disappeared into her house.

Lady Lydia's banquet was a scrumptious feast. She sat with Robin Hood at her right hand, seated next to the lady Mary of Winchester, and the courteous Moorish knight Sir Palomides on her left. The knight, well-known as a gourmet of the most discerning tastes, had waxed poetic in his praise of the starter course of walnuts, pears, and root vegetables pickled in salt and vinegar and then soaked in honey and white wine, and topped with a bit of fennel seed. This had been followed by pike floating in galantine sauce, made of brown bread crumbs, vinegar and wine, powdered cinnamon and ginger. And the countess's cook had outdone himself with the main course, a roast swan with chaudon sauce, after which Sir Palomides began to tease the countess that he would leave the table and head for the kitchen, where he intended to convince her chief cook Oswald to leave her employ and join the outlaws in their forest abode, so he could always be at Palomides' beck and call. But when the dessert came out in the form of red wine peach tarts and almond cakes, Palomides became speechless and simply moaned as he filled his mouth with tarts.

The countess took advantage of the lull in the Moor's conversation to turn to Robin, interrupting his flirtatious banter with Marion, to tell him of the letter she had recently received from her cousin, Lady Maude, wife of the Sheriff of Nottingham. The letter had taken just two days to arrive, since Lady Maude had put it in the hands of a priest who happened to be on his way from Nottingham to Chesterfield and the countess had received it not long before she had left with her troops on the way to Wallingwells.

"Master Robin, my cousin writes that her birthday celebration in Nottingham was a great success, and that the archery tournament proved to be most exciting. Apparently an otherwise unknown bumpkin by the name of Hodden of Barnesdale won the golden arrow, much to the surprise of everyone involved. She says she was so thrilled at the outcome that she was in ecstasy for some time afterward. She does add, however, that if I see you I am to mention to you that immediately after the tournament concluded, she missed her gem-studded tiara that had been her husband's birthday gift to her—and she wondered if by chance it had turned up somewhere in Sherwood?"

Robin maintained a perfectly straight face, though Lady

Marion could not hide a smirk, knowing what Maude's letter had *really* said. But Robin brazened it out, saying, "A gem-studded tiara? No…" he pretended to search his memory. "I can truthfully say I have not seen such a thing anywhere in this neighborhood. But you may tell your cousin that I will keep my eyes peeled in case anyone is carrying such a thing along the Great North Road through Sherwood."

Little John, sitting with Will Stutely, Alan a Dale, and Friar Tuck at a long board to the right of the countess's head table, could not stifle a laugh as he was drinking his wine, and as a result a gulp of wine shot up into his nose and he yelped with pain and irritation. Stutely pounded his back to help him get his breath back and Little John choked out a curse. "Devil take that Robin! He can say that with a straight face. What did Much end up getting for that tiara?"

Will thought a moment and said, "I think he broke it up and sold the gems separately. Pretty sure he ended up with a few hundred nobles after that."

"Well," John said, clearing his throat and blinking, "since Much broke up the tiara, Robin can truthfully say he hasn't seen it."

"Hasn't seen it recently, anyway," Alan said.

The outlaws' new recruits, Jock o' Barlborough and John of Wallingwells, who were seated at the same table, listening much and saying little, looked at one another curiously, and Jock turned to Little John and observed, "So you really do engage in theft as a group? It isn't simply poaching game in the king's forest?"

Stutely gave the two neophytes a wry smile. "We only steal from those who have plenty of wealth, which they've amassed standing on the backs of the poor. Prosperous prelates. Affluent aristocrats."

"Dishonest officials whose riches come from graft," Alan a Dale added, "like the Sheriff of Nottingham."

John of Wallingwells shrugged, a silent acceptance of the justice of this strategy. Then Friar Tuck added, "We also give half of what we've taken in to the poor. That's where the money came from that I gave Mistress Alison and her daughter Malyne, to see them through the next months. It had to come from somewhere."

Jock nodded at that, falling in with the Sherwood outlaws' world view. And as he did so, Robin Hood, wishing to turn the conversation from the topic of tiaras, stood up and called for attention.

"I want to make a toast!" Robin said, raising his silver cup of wine. "To our brother Friar Tuck!" Tuck looked up and reddened. "He solved two murders and saw justice done where no one else had the knowledge or the desire to do it! To Friar Tuck!"

"To Friar Tuck!" Everyone at his table echoed loudly, and quaffed some more wine.

"And now," Robin continued, "I understand that our minstrel Alan a Dale has composed a new ballad to tell the story of Willie the tinker!"

With that, Alan stood up and brought his small gittern out from under the table. He walked to the center of the countess's great hall, bowed to the head table, plucked his strings, and began this song:

> *Sweet Willie he has gone to his love's door,*
> *And gently tried the pin:*
> *"O sleep ye or wake ye, my bonny Meggie?*
> *Rise up, let your true love in."*
>
> *The lass got up and ran to the door,*
> *And gently she lifted the pin,*

Then into her arms so wide and so long
She embraced her bonny love in.

"Oh will ye go to the cards or the dice,
Or to a table of wine?
Or will ye go to a well-made bed,
Well covered with blankets fine?"

"Oh I will not go to the cards nor the dice,
Nor yet to a table of wine;
But I'll rather go to a well-made bed,
Well covered with blankets fine."

"My fine little cock sitting on the house top,
You shall crow not till it be day!
And your comb shall be of the good red gold,
And your wings a silver grey."

The cock being false, untrue he was,
And he crew an hour too soon;
They thought it was the good day-light,
But it was but the light of the moon.

"Oh no, alas!" says Meggie then,
"This night we've slept over long!"
"Oh what is the matter?" then Willie replied,
"The faster then I must be gone!"

Then Sweet Willie rose, and put on his clothes,
And snatched up his stockings and shoes,
And took by his side his berry-brown sword,
And into the forest he goes.

As he went into the deep, deep trees
And down yon dreary den,
Great and grievous was the ghost he saw,
Would fear ten thousand men.

"Oft have ye travelled this road, Willie,
Oft have ye travelled in sin;
And ye never said so much for your soul
As 'Dear Maker bring me home again!'

"Oft have ye travelled this road, Willie,
Your bonny love to see;
But ye'll never travel this road again
Till ye leave a token with me."

Then she has taken Sweet Willie,
And riven him from ear to ear,
And on every seat of Mary's church
She flung Sweet Willie's gore;
And right above his love Meggie's place,
Hung his head and yellow hair.

Her father made moan, her mother made moan,
But Meggie made much more;
Her father made moan, her mother made moan,
But Meggie tore her yellow hair.

When Alan finished, the great hall erupted into enthusiastic applause, and Friar Tuck looked down at his feet with an ironic smile. This is the way the whole murder saga of Willie and Meggie would be remembered, with the sensational bloody details of the gory head in the church foregrounded. It was just as well, he thought. Let Sister Anne's part in it and Meggie's own subsequent murder fade from memory. Why focus on the guilt of the nun and the milkmaid? If justice could not be achieved in the murder of his own father, how could he really expect it in the case of Willie or Meggie? What was justice, when men were all sinners? Yes, and women too it seemed. All we can do is love one another. Wasn't that Christ's commandment anyway? And, Tuck was beginning to believe, thinking of Robin and Marion, of Little John and Will Stutely, of Alison and of Sister Mary Eusebia, that any love was good love after all.

CAST OF CHARACTERS

Alan a Dale: A member of Robin Hood's band, Alan a Dale is best known as a jongleur or minstrel who entertains the men with ballads of his own composition, or that he has learned from others. He is also one of Robin's younger followers, and one of his better archers. He is one of the married outlaws, living with his wife Ellen in Sherwood after being married by Friar Tuck.

Alison: A midwife and herbalist living with her daughter Malyne in a poor hovel between Wallingwells and Worksop. Alison was a close friend of Friar Tuck's mother when he was growing up in the area, and shielded him from his father's anger after his mother's death. Tuck refers to her as his "godmother."

Alan of Winchester: Formerly a corporal under Robin Kempe in the king's guard, Alan followed his old commander into a life in the forest after Camelot fell, and now is one of the outlaw band of Sherwood. As a former well-trained soldier, Alan is one of the most skilled archers in Robin's band.

Arthur Bland: A very large and muscular man who had formerly made his living as a tanner. Upon meeting Little John, the huge tanner wanted to test his mettle against the equally large woodsman, and when Little John bested him, he decided he'd rather join Robin's band than keep his former profession, and joined the Sherwood bandits, a few teeth lighter after his skirmish with John.

Bishop of Hereford: The bishop is one of the wealthiest prelates in England, and proves an easy mark for Robin Hood and his men when he makes his way along the Great North Road through Sherwood. In the previous novel, the bandits relieved him of a thousand gold marks when they entertained him for dinner. In this novel, he knows better than to carry such large sums through Sherwood.

David of Doncaster: The youngest of Robin's band, and recently turned sixteen during the course of the previous novel. An orphan, David has found a home with the outlaws of Sherwood. Tradition says that David of Doncaster was a yeoman wrestler.

Elizabeth Liptrot: Laundress at the Benedictine Priory of Wallingwells. Elizabeth is a middle-aged woman who was intimate with Willie the Tinker and resents the other women he was involved with.

Ellen: The wife of Alan a Dale, and lives with him among Robin's outlaws in Sherwood. She is one of the youngest and most outspoken of the women who live with Robin's men, and is very knowledgeable in herbal lore.

Father Bernard: The resident priest at the Benedictine Priory of Wallingwells. Responsible for holy services and confessions, he is at the same time administratively subject to the Prioress.

Friar Tuck: A Franciscan, though he belongs to no house and lives with Robin and his men in the forest. He sees to the outlaws' spiritual needs, and is licensed to hear confessions, though he does fight at their sides if need be. He is in charge of most of the outlaws' charitable ventures, taking a half of all they take from their rich marks to give it to the poor. Here, his sense of justice will not let him rest until he can solve the mystery of Willie's murder.

George Crisp: The magistrate of the Worksop-Wallingwells area, and so is the representative of the king's justice in the region. He is, however, unimaginative and somewhat lazy, and inclined to take things at face value. The idea of actually investigating a crime is foreign to him, and while he doesn't welcome Friar Tuck's interest in the crime of Willie's murder, he doesn't stop his investigations either.

Gill o' the Red Cap: Chief archer in Guy of Gisbourne's guards. He is one of the chief competitors in the sheriff's archery contest, and later leads Gisbourne's guards in their search for Robin's men in and around Worksop—where he has been involved with more than one of the local ladies.

Guy of Gisbourne: The commander of the royal fortress of Nottingham Castle. Determined to enforce royal authority in Nottinghamshire, he vows to track down the outlaws of Sherwood and hang them. His guards have been investigating the possibility of Robin's men hiding out in the north of Sherwood.

Haakon: "Skipper" Haakon is a Norseman and former Viking who, having given up the sea, still manages to keep his hand in the robbing and looting trade as a member of Robin's outlaw band. His seaman skills occasionally come in handy, if any of the outlaws need a boat.

Hulga: The wife of Oswald, who is employed as baker for the Benedictine Priory of Wallingwells. She is a large, phlegmatic woman, and some two inches taller than her diminutive husband.

Jack: Second in command of Sir Guy of Gisbourne's troops, Jack acts as lieutenant to Gill o' the Red Cap. But he has also been secretly assigned by Sir Guy to keep an eye on the unpredictable Gill.

James Snaggletooth: So nicknamed because of his jumble of teeth, Snaggletooth runs The Loaves and Fishes, the local inn and tavern in Worksop where Robin and his men find rooms.

Jock of Barlborough: One of Robin's chief opponents in the Nottingham Archery contest, the impoverished former soldier decides to join Robin's band of outlaws after the tournament. A native of Barlborough, a town close to Wallingwells and Worksop, Jock proves an invaluable aid in solving the mystery of Willie's murder.

John, cook's son: Brother of Meggie and son of Ralph and Margaret, the cooks of the Benedictine Priory at Wallingwells, John hates Gill o' the Red Cap and wants vengeance upon him because of his treatment of John's sister. In the end, he makes a decision to join Robin's band of outlaws.

John Bryce: The bailiff, essentially the business manager, for the Priory of Wallingwells. He seems to have profited from his position: He dresses fashionably and looks down on the likes of Willie the tinker. He has been a widower for some six years, and has one daughter, Mary Barbara, who has taken the veil at the priory.

John Naylor: See "Little John."

John of Oxenford: See "Sheriff of Nottingham."

Kate of Worksop: A dairy maid who supplies the Benedictine Abbey of Wallingwells with milk, butter, and eggs. She is an attractive young woman who is unmarried and lives with her parents in Worksop. She is, however, the object of at least two bachelors' attentions. She is discontent with life in Worksop and wishes she could leave the place.

Little John: Robin Hood's right hand man. Born a villein on a manor belonging to a monastery, John fled his servitude and became an outlaw in Sherwood. He is tall, strong and imposing, and is in a committed relationship with Will Stutely. When necessary, John goes by the pseudonym "Reynold Greenleaf."

Lydia Peveril, Countess of Chesterfield: Lady Lydia is the unmarried countess of Chesterfield and castellan of Peveril Castle on the northern edge of Sherwood. Because of their invaluable assistance in rescuing her from kidnappers and supporting her claim to her inheritance, she has adopted Robin and his men as her own "foresters" and thus, officially, her servants.

Maid Marion: Robin's nickname for Lady Mary of Winchester. Former lady-in-waiting to the old queen (i.e., Guinevere), Marion is now chief lady in the entourage of Lady Lydia Peveril, Countess of Chesterfield. Still unmarried at twenty-one and without prospects, she is romantically entangled with the yeoman Robin Hood, though marriage seems unlikely due to their different classes.

Mary of Winchester: See Maid Marion.

Maude Peveril: Lady Maude Peveril is the wife of the Sheriff of Nottingham. She is a cousin of the countess Lydia of Chesterfield. She is a love interest, or at least an occasional bedfellow, of Robin Hood.

Meggie: The young daughter of Ralph, cook at the Benedictine Priory at Wallingwells, and his wife Margaret. Meggie is an attractive young girl who is the target of the amorous ambitions of at least two men in the area.

Madame Veronica: Also called Mother Veronica, she is the prioress of the Benedictine Priory of Wallingwells, and thus Mother Superior to all the nuns of that community.

Margaret: The beautiful Margaret is married to Ralph, the cook at the Benedictine Priory at Wallingwells, and is the mother of the girl Meggie as well as her mercurial brother John.

Oswald: The baker for the Benedictine Priory of Wallingwells. He is a small, thin man, with a large wife named Hulga.

Palomides: Sir Palomides was a knight in the court of the old king (Arthur) before his kingdom's demise. A Moor born in the Middle East, Palomides became a Christian when he joined the Round Table, mainly because of his love for the lady Isolde, who preferred Sir Tristram. When Arthur's kingdom fell, Sir Palomides could find no other lord in Britain who would take him on as a knight, and chose to join his old friend Robin in his outlaw band. Palomides is known for his culinary skills, as well as his skill in music and poetry.

Ralph: A large, good humored fellow, Ralph is the cook who runs the kitchens at the Benedictine Priory of Wallingwells. He is married to Margaret, who assists him in the kitchen, and the couple have two children: John and Meggie.

Robin Hood: Leader of a band of outlaws in Sherwood Forest. Of yeoman status, Robin's real name is Robin Kempe, and he is the former captain of the guard under the old king (King Arthur). Now he poaches the king's deer and robs rich nobles and prelates on the Great North Road through Sherwood. When necessary, he goes by the alias "Robert fitz Ooth of Locksley."

Robin Kempe: See "Robin Hood."

Sheriff of Nottingham: Robin Hood's oldest and most persistent enemy, the sheriff, John of Oxenford, is a corrupt royal official who rakes in a good deal of money through bribery and the illegal seizure and taxation of goods that come through Nottingham. He is married to the far from pliable Lady Maude Peveril, and tends to give her a good deal of freedom.

Sister Anne: One of the nuns of the Priory of Wallingwells. She is a middle-aged sister who lived a hard life before taking the veil about five years since. She has a practical manner and an ironic outlook.

Sister Esther: Essentially second in command administratively at the Benedictine Priory of Wallingwells, Sister Esther acts as Mother Veronica's cellarer, in charge of the community's supplies of food and drink.

Sister Lucy: Lucy is a local girl who joined the Priory of

Wallingwells at seventeen and has never been beyond its environs. She has a beaklike nose and a birdlike manner.

Sister Mary Barbara: The daughter of the bailiff John Bryce, Sister Mary Barbara is a beautiful young nun who acts as Infirmarian for the Benedictine Priory of Wallingwells.

Sister Mary Eusebia: A member of the Wallingwells Priory since the age of twelve (mainly to escape her abusive father), she took the name "Eusebia" because of her great piety and learning. She exudes a great deal of self-confidence with her scholarly knowledge, and she has a special friend in Sister Rebecca.

Sister Rebecca: Rebecca is a bright young girl who took the veil at fourteen to avoid an unwanted marriage. She has red hair, green almond-shaped eyes and a sprinkle of freckles across her pretty face. She has a special friend in Sister Mary Eusebia, in contrast to whom she is perpetually nervous and skittish.

Thorvald: An old dwarf with a white beard, who formerly drove a cart in which he carried prisoners to execution or other punishment. Later he gave up that trade to become a merchant under the old king, but since the king's fall he has taken to the forest with his old acquaintance, Robin.

Wat o' the Crabstaff: Wat is a part of Robin's outlaw band who was once a tinker, but was convinced by Robin to give up that trade and join the outlaws of Sherwood. A crabstaff is a quarterstaff, which is Wat's favorite weapon.

Widow Day: The Widow Day is an elderly (but sharp) widow who lives in Wallingwells near the priory, and who is well-informed about the goings on in the neighborhood, having little to do but look out her windows.

Will Scarlet: Everyone knows that one of the most popular figures in Robin's band is Will. However, the early ballads do not seem to agree on his last name. Thus if you read the early ballads, there seem to be three different Wills in Robin's band: Will Scarlet, Will Scathelock, and Will Stutely, unless of course, they are all referring to the same character. I've made them all different. Will Scarlet is Robin's nephew, one of his younger followers. He wears a scarlet hood over his Lincoln green livery, and has blond hair and blue eyes. He's one of Robin's most loyal men, and one of his best archers.

Will Scathelock: Scathelock, the un-Scarlet, is a tall, lanky, middle-aged member of Robin's crew, known as a reliable and experienced woodsman. Because of his stalwart trustworthiness, he is often left in charge of the outlaw camp when Robin and Little John are away,

Will Stutely: Stutely, even younger than Will Scarlet, is generally considered the handsomest of Robin's crew. He is a slight young man with a freckled and tanned face and sparkling brown eyes. He is deferential to Robin and courteous to ladies and others, but has a particularly caustic wit. He also likes to use doctored dice to win at Hazard. Stutely is Little John's particular friend, and the two share a tent together.

Willie the Tinker (also known as Willie of Worksop or Sweet Willie): First murder victim of the "Ghoul of Sherwood," his body is found mutilated in the forest. Willie was a tinker and had formerly been married but lost his wife. He has recently been paying court to Meggie, the cook's daughter.

ABOUT THE AUTHOR

JAY RUUD is a retired professor of English at the University of Central Arkansas, now devoting much of his time to fiction writing. He has retold the traditional legend of King Arthur for modern readers as a series of Merlin Mysteries, the final volume of which, *To the Great Deep*, was published by Encircle in the fall of 2020. *Ghoul of Sherwood* is book two of the Robin Hood Mysteries after *Sleuth of Sherwood* (Encircle Publications, June 2022). He's also written scholarly books, including an *Encyclopedia of Medieval Literature* (2006), *A Critical Companion to Dante* (2008), and *A Critical Companion to Tolkien* (2011), as well as the first full-length study of Chaucer's short poems, *"Many a Song and Many a Lecherous Lay": Tradition and Individuality in Chaucer Lyric Poetry* (1992), a book that was reissued by Routledge in October 2019 after 27 years.

He taught at UCA and chaired the English department for 13 years, prior to which he was Dean of the College of Arts and Sciences at Northern State University in Aberdeen, South Dakota. He has a Ph.D. in Medieval Literature from the University of Wisconsin-Milwaukee, and is married to the thoroughly awesome poet and novelist Stacey Margaret Jones. He has two more or less adult children, and as many spectacular dogs as grandchildren (four). He has been to all seven continents, is a lifetime Chicago Cubs fan, and dabbles in community theater, where he once played his own daughter's mother. Follow Jay Ruud on Facebook and @GildasOfCornwall on Instagram.